# VETERAN

# VETERAN

Gavin G. Smith

GOLLANCZ
LONDON

First published in Great Britain in 2010 by Gollancz
An imprint of the Orion Publishing Group
Orion House, 5 Upper St Martin's Lane,
London WC2H 9EA
An Hachette UK Company

A CIP catalogue record for this book
is available from the British Library

ISBN 978 0 575 09409 3 (Cased)
ISBN 978 0 575 09410 9 (Trade Paperback)

1 3 5 7 9 10 8 6 4 2

Typeset by Deltatype Ltd, Birkenhead, Merseyside

Printed in Great Britain by Clays Ltd, St Ives plc

The Orion Publishing Group's policy is to use papers that are natural, renewable and recyclable products and made from wood grown in sustainable forests. The logging and manufacturing processes are expected to conform to the environmental regulations of the country of origin.

www.orionbooks.co.uk

To Ruth & James Nicoll.
Two members of an extraordinary generation.

# Prologue
# Dog 4

The soldier's environment is mud. It doesn't matter where they go. Tundra, woods, jungle, even paved colonial suburbs, by the time a few thousand tanks, walkers and armoured personnel carriers have tramped through it, once the defoliants have been sprayed, all that's left is mud.

What we terraform we can still destroy. It's why all the colonies look the same to me. It's also how I knew I was dreaming; I couldn't taste the mud, couldn't smell it. This was more like watching a viz. My dreams were becoming less real than my time in the sense booths, but what was another loss?

*It had been a forest once. You could still see the rotted stumps of alien trees pushing up through the plain of mud. Defensive trenches ran across the plain in a way that was probably supposed to be planned but looked utterly random to me. The harsh burning brightness of Sirius A was sinking beneath the horizon; even from the fourth planet it looked huge and too near for a sun to someone who'd grown up on Earth. Behind us the much smaller Sirius B was rising, casting its pale twilight light.*

*I watched our shadows shrinking and distorting in the changing light. The strangeness of it added to my feeling of being comatose with my eyes open. Four days, no sleep, kept awake by Slaughter and amphetamines. None of this seemed real and it hadn't at the time. Which was a good thing because what we were doing was thought of as difficult and dangerous, driving through an enemy armoured push.*

*Off to my left I saw Mudge pop out of a trench as he gunned the armoured one-man scout hover. He was on point. He wasn't even military, certainly shouldn't have been out with us. He was a journalist; sense, viz and even old-fashioned print if the heroin made him nostalgic. Howard Mudgie, Mudge to his friends, a crusader when he started, then a war junkie, now a burn out and as good a soldier as any. That was why he was on point. His scout hover sank out of sight again.*

*Nobody was talking. Our encrypted comms lines were silent; everyone was too tired. All around us They advanced. Their heavy tanks made out of what looked like chitin and reactive liquid. Their honeycombed ground-effects drives glowing pale blue like Sirius B. They were in a staggered line as far as the eye could see in either direction.*

*According to the orbital data I had received, this new front was over two hundred miles long. They were just rolling up the joint British, French and Congolese task force as they went. Their troops were still in the tanks; they were big enough to act as APCs as well. Their Walkers policed the gaps between the tanks. Organic mechs with tendrils and rotary shard guns that fired bone-like razor munitions. It was the Walkers that were making the Wild Boys' life difficult, that and trying not to dump the Land Rovers in a trench. That would've been crap as well.*

*We were covered in mud. It was everywhere, except on the weapons, which had been treated with a stayclean finish. Spinks slewed the Land Rover round a tank. They were ignoring us if we ignored them. Close behind us Ash sent up a similar wall of mud as she followed us in the second Land Rover.*

*I saw the trench coming but didn't need to mention it. Spinks was jacked into the jeep. In the weasel-faced Essex wide boy's head was a 3D topographical rendering of the surrounding terrain. It was as up to date as our orbital support, Mudge's sparse scout data and the vehicle's own sensors would allow.*

*Spinks found the high ground and gunned the Land Rover over the trench. This used to be exciting. In the air, I saw Mudge shoot by beneath us in the trench. We showered him in mud, once this would've caused comment. I barely registered the jarring impact as the Land Rover sank into the earth, the independently driven smart tyres biting into the mud for traction.*

*'Walker,' I said quietly as we skidded round another tank. Spinks didn't show a sign of paying the slightest bit of attention but the Land Rover was suddenly going in another direction. Straight at one of their tanks.*

*'There's not enough ground clearance,' I muttered, mainly to myself. Spinks was already committed. Shards started coming our way. Something hit my helmet. At first I thought I'd been shot but it was Gregor folding the heavy plasma gun down and lying on the bed of the Land Rover.*

*'Get your head down,' he told me. If he hadn't, I doubt I'd have had the presence of mind to do so. Under the tank their ground-effects drives pushed us and the Land Rover down. It was like a warm wind. I heard something get torn off the wagon and we were out the other side. I barely noticed when we hit the second Walker.*

*Spinks wrapped the front of the Land Rover round the Walker's legs. We stopped and it had its legs knocked out from beneath it. I was vaguely aware of Gregor bailing out of the Land Rover. I looked next to me to find an alien war machine lying on the wagon, tendrils flailing. It looked like parts of the alien machine were bathing in what used to be Spinks. Flailing tendrils flung bits of him around. I tried to feel something for my friend and squad mate but there was nothing there any more.*

*I could hear shouting from the rest of the squad. I climbed out of the Land Rover, and then stopped. I'd forgotten my SAW. I turned and went back for the weapon. More shouting. The Walker was trying to right itself. By rights one of its tendrils should've torn my head off by now. Then I had the SAW in my hand. The smartlink connected to the palm receiver, and the weapon's crosshair appeared on my internal visual display. It sounded to me like I started screaming. There was an orange blossom, flickering but permanent at the front of the SAW, it seemed to go on for an age. The Walker's carapace looked as if it was rapidly distorting as I played the SAW across it.*

*Things went quiet as my audio dampeners kicked in. Gregor was at my side, his railgun held high on its gyroscopic mount as he fired it down into the Walker. The SAW muzzle flash stopped. At some level I knew that meant I'd fired off the entire cassette. I'd put two hundred rounds into the Walker. I felt a hand on my arm, strong, boosted cybernetic strength pulling me back. It was Gregor. How did he have the strength, always there getting me out of trouble?*

*Mudge was in front of me. I was pushed pillion onto the bouncing hover scout. I heard the sound of superheated air exploding behind me. Hydrogen pellets heated to a plasma state impacted again and again into the Walker as Bibs fired the heavy plasma cannon on the other Land Rover. I was vaguely aware of the sensation of moving as we began to bob across the mud.*

*'Where the fuck's our artillery! Where the fuck's our air support!' Mudge screamed with more anger than I could muster, but he always had better drugs. He knew the answer, like I did. We were finished here. Dog 4 and the rest of the Sirius system was Theirs now. I just hoped They'd let us get to an evac site.*

# 1
# Dundee

I awoke from the dream with a start. My knuckles ached from where I'd tried to extend my blades; I ran my fingers over the domed locks, a compromise to let someone with my capabilities walk free after he'd served his country and his species. A right that had been won in blood and vacuum.

The bruises from last night's pit fight were now tender memories, thanks to my body's implanted internal repair systems. As ever I wondered why the same systems couldn't help me with the white-hot throbbing lance of pain that was a dehydration headache. The pain seemed to live just behind the black polarised lenses that replaced my eyes. Why was it that man could create millions of tons of complex engineering capable of travelling across space but could still not find a cure for a hangover? One of the many skewed priorities of our society.

Too much good whisky, the real stuff made in the distilleries out in the National Park, had caused my hangover. I sat up on the cot in the porta-cube, massaging my throbbing temple with my left arm, the one that was still flesh. The matt-black prosthetic right arm reached for my cigarettes. Like the whisky, the cigarettes were the good stuff, hand-made somewhere in the Islamic Protectorate.

I lit the cigarette with my antique trench lighter, a family heirloom, apparently. Family. What were my parents thinking when they had me? The war was already thirty years old then. Why was anyone having children? Mind you, they'd been patriotic, probably thought it was their duty to breed so their offspring could grow up, get recruited, indoctrinated, chopped, augmented, mangled, chewed up and spat out to be a burden on society. I wasn't on active duty so I liked to consider myself a burden. I inhaled the first pointless lungful of smoke of the day. My internal filters and scrubbers removed all the toxins and anything interesting from the cigarette, turning my expensive vice into little more than an unpleasant affectation. It's these little luxuries, I thought, that separate me from the rest of the refuse. When it came down to it, the hustling, the leg breaking, scheme racing and pit fighting was just to make enough euros to augment my paltry veteran's pension. After all, what're a few bruises and contusions if it means good whisky, cigarettes, drugs, old movies and music, and of course the booths.

I considered starting drinking again as I had little on that day. A quick scan of the cramped plastic cube that I existed in told me that I had drank more than I thought I had last night. Which would explain the constant pain in my skull.

'Shit,' I muttered to the morning. I thought about checking my credit rating but decided that would just upset me further. A search of my jeans turned up some good old-fashioned black-economy paper euros. I'd won them for second place at the pit fight in Fintry. I'd been better than the kid who beat me but the kid had been dangerously wired, dangerously boosted and hungrier than me. I reckoned he had maybe another six months before his central nervous system was fried. He'd probably been fighting with the cheap enhancements to feed his family.

I'd just wanted to get drunk. I counted the money, stubbing the cigarette out in the already-full ashtray. I had enough to spend a day in the booths. Almost mustering a smile at this good luck I dragged on my jeans, strapped on my boots and shrugged on the least dirty T-shirt I could find with a cursory search. Finally I pulled on my heavy tan armoured raincoat. I ran a finger through my sandy-coloured shoulder-length hair; it was getting too long. I tied it back into a short ponytail. Sunglasses over the black lenses that used to be my eyes and ready to face another day. Ready to face it because I was going to the booths.

The Rigs were so poor that we didn't even have advertising. It had started before the last Final Human Conflict over two hundred and fifty years ago. Apparently there had once been fields of fossil fuels in the North Sea and these huge rusting metal skeletons had been platforms designed to harvest the fuel. When their day was done they had been towed into the harbour to be dismantled at the Dundee docks. When they had stopped dismantling them the Tay had just become a dumping ground. More and more had come until they filled the river and you could walk from Dundee to Fife on them. Provided you knew how to look after yourself.

Quickly they had become a squatters' heaven for people largely considered surplus by the great and the good. This of course included veterans – vets. I stepped out onto the planks of the makeshift scaffolding that ran between the stacked, windowless, hard plastic cubes that signified my middle-class status in the Rigs. Off to my right Dundee was a bright glow in comparison to the sparse lighting on the Rigs.

Lying on the ground by the door to the cube was a young boy, no older than thirteen. He was unconscious. A victim of the intrusion countermeasures that I'd added to the cube to stop myself from getting ripped off any more than was strictly necessary. I sighed and pulled a stim patch out of my coat pocket and placed it on the kid's arm. Scarring over the boy's chest told me that he'd already fallen victim to Harvesters once.

'Wake up,' I said, shaking the boy. 'You want to get harvested again?' I asked him. Startled eyes shot open and the kid backed away from me so quickly he almost went off the scaffolding and into the liquid pollution that passed for the Tay these days. I watched him as he got up and ran off.

'And don't try and rip me off again!' I shouted redundantly, before wasting some more money and lighting up another cigarette.

It was a hot night. Quickly sweat began to stick my clothes to my flesh. I cursed the malfunctioning coolant system in my armoured coat. I could've done without the coat but that was an invitation to get rolled. My dermal armour was good but not a patch on the coat. It covered me from neck to ankle with slits in the appropriate places to allow me access to weapons, had they not all been locked down. I could get the coolant system fixed but I only had just enough money for a day in the booth.

I kept my head down as I ran the gauntlet of begging vets. I tried to ignore the staring infected empty eye sockets, the scarred bodies and missing limbs of the decommissioned cyborg vets who did not have the cash to pay for civilian replacements for the enhancements that had been removed. Head down, collar up, I considered turning on my audio dampeners to filter their pleas out.

'Not today, brothers,' I muttered to myself as I strode by. It could just as easily have been me there had I not made special forces. The augmentations and the training I'd been given were just too expensive and bespoke to throw away on a human scrap heap like the other vets. I'd been canny enough to arrange a military contract that had not rendered me a lifelong slave, but even after my term was up they still had the right to call me back as a reserve. Despite the dishonourable discharge I was still on the books (though no one ever really came off) as part of the wild-goose-chasing XI units, but they were largely a joke.

There had once been a disastrous attempt at dumping ex-special forces types into space. This was cheaper than paying our paltry pensions and it meant we couldn't go home and become really well trained and dangerous burdens on society. However, a change in policy meant we were still considered valuable enough to remain whole, even if that whole was mostly plastic and alloy. Of course all the most lethal stuff was locked down until they needed it.

I glanced down at the locks just behind the knuckles on each of my hands. There was another lock on the shoulder of my prosthetic right arm and I could always feel the inhibitor in one of my plugs at the base of my skull that dampened my wired reactions. In many ways the dampener was the worst. Reactions like I'd had when I'd been in the SAS made you feel like you were on a different plane of existence to the rest of pedestrian humanity. Giving that up had been hard. I still felt like I was walking through syrup sometimes.

Hamish looked after the booths. Hamish was revolting. He had a thick curly beard and a mass of naturally grown, curly, dirty, matted hair. He was naked, filthy and fat; eating some kind of greasy processed confectionery in the armoured cage from where he overlooked the sense booths. I tried hard to suppress my disgust at the man, whose foul odour I was managing to smell through armoured mesh. Nobody ever saw Hamish leave or sleep. He always seemed to be here. His bulk was such that he probably couldn't leave if he wanted to.

'Jake!' Hamish cried enthusiastically. Instantly annoying me. I didn't like the contraction of my name. 'How long?' he asked, wiping bits of the pastry on his bloated hairy torso. I held up the dirty paper euros.

'A day please. My usual,' I said with as much pleasantness as I could muster.

'You sure? No nice virtual snuff orgy? Maybe you want to have sex with the pres? No? Usual it is. Let's see the readies.' I pushed the paper notes into the secure box. Hamish scanned them for authenticity, liquid explosives, contact poisons, surveillance and various other things before they slid through to his side. The sense pusher counted the notes, his greedy smile faltering as he did so. I felt panic rising within.

'Uh Jakob ...' Hamish began.

'What? What!' I demanded. 'There's enough there!' I shouted.

'Guess you didn't hear I'm putting my prices up. Not to worry. There's enough here for half a day and some credit for your next trip.'

'No!' I said, unable to believe, or at least cope with what I was hearing. In my mind I ran through the numerous ways in which I could kill or cause pain to Hamish. Of course some of them meant I would have to touch him. I lifted my prosthetic arm to punch the armoured cage that protected him. I felt rather than saw the cage's protective systems activate, weapons unfolding from the walls and ceiling to cover me.

'Now, now, calm down,' the still-smiling Hamish said in a conciliatory and patronising tone. 'I was just joking; a day it is.'

'Really fucking funny, Hamish,' I muttered, lighting another cigarette. There was an ever-so-slight shake in my left hand, the one that was still flesh. 'You do know what I used to do for a living, right?' I snapped.

'You and everyone else round here, pal. Booth twelve's free.' I turned and stalked into the sense arcade.

Inside was a long corridor lit with dim red lights, many of which were broken. On either side of the corridor were reinforced steel doors. I found booth number twelve and looked up at the lens before the door and gave Hamish the finger, so of course he made me wait another minute. Finally the steel door shot up. Inside, a vet minus both his arms, one of his legs a jury-rigged and botched-looking home prosthetic, was sitting on the foam mattress of the bunk. He was still plugged in though obviously not receiving. He ignored me.

'C'mon, man. That was never two hours. My daughter sent me the money for this. It's her combat pay! She fights to keep you safe... I fought to keep you safe from Them, you bastard!' he screamed into the air. Hamish was as ever deaf to this.

'You and me both, pal,' I said and grabbed the vet with my prosthetic arm, my left arm removing the plug. Augmented muscle slung him out the door and across the corridor into the other wall. I tried to ignore the sound of a homemade prosthetic snapping. The metal door rapidly slid down, cutting off the sobbing. The booth was red plastic. It smelled strongly of semen; some users had no imagination. I lay down in the niche that formed the bunk, sinking into the cheap foam mattress. I reached behind my head and inserted the jack into one of my plugs.

I was gone, immersed in the usual, the program that Vicar had written for me. Subtle, beautiful, other-worldly (though not in a way that would induce horrors) music played as one by one my senses were deprived, as I divorced from the self. I faded away. I stopped existing.

Everything that was me, the pain of wounds inflicted and received, the terror inflicted and received, all that I'd seen and done drifted away in a sense of profound dislocation. The things that I didn't think the human mind was supposed to deal with, acts committed in the war against Them, the genocidal alien other locked in perpetual conflict with humanity, were gone. All that was left was an unfeeling abstract floating in nothing.

And just like that I was yanked back. As ever it was too short but this time something was not right. I checked my internal clock, a mere two hours. Enough was enough. I was going to find a way to kill Hamish; he was taking the piss now. I pulled the jack out from the back of my neck and slid off the bunk towards the door, but it did not slide open. I hit the manual door switch but nothing happened. I was getting concerned. This was beginning to feel like some kind of burn.

'Hamish, you're just making things worse for yourself,' I said evenly. Just the slightest hint of threat in my tone, assuming that Hamish was listening.

On my internal visual display the integral communications link was flashing. Opening it up formed a small split screen in the corner of my vision. I recognised the man on the video comms link, short dark hair neatly trimmed, suave features, a degree of refinement to an underlying feeling of malice and violence. A warm smile belied by the absence of feeling in two very pale blue eyes.

I tried my best to remain passive in the face of the comms icon of a man I hated, a man who'd tried very hard to kill me.

'Sergeant Douglas,' the man said. He sounded genuinely pleased to see me. His tones educated and cultured, pure upper class of a vintage old enough to remember a time when breeding actually mattered.

'Go and fuck yourself. I'm not in the army any more. You and I have nothing to say to each other.'

'Nonsense, Jakob, mutineer or not you're still a reservist.' Major George Rolleston said, smiling again. 'We have a code eleven, you've been reactivated.' I barely gave this a second's thought. A code eleven. XI. Xenomorphic Infiltration.

'A bullshit wild goose chase. Get someone else. Turn my program back on.'

'Don't be like that, Jakob. I recruited you especially. After all, who more than I knows your efficiency?'

'Even if I agreed to be reactivated—'

'Nobody's giving you the choice, Sergeant,' Rolleston interrupted smoothly, breaking the unwritten rule of special forces etiquette again and using my rank.

'Even if I decide to be reactivated,' I reiterated through the sub-vocalised equivalent of gritted teeth. 'I won't work with you, you piece of shit.' Rolleston merely smiled.

'But Jakob, both Josephine and I are looking forward to working with you again,' Rolleston said, and there was the threat, I thought. Josephine Bran, Rolleston's pet killer, Royal Marine sniper, SBS with Rolleston and then seconded to Special Operations Command, someone that the other operators feared. A pale, quiet, unassuming girl, a shy girl who enjoyed and excelled at killing far too much, they called her the Grey Lady. She was the perfect servant for men such as Rolleston.

'You turned on your own men. You tried to dump them; they served you and then you tried to space them.'

'Perfectly legal and as per my orders,' Rolleston said and it was true: a vagary of interstellar and colonial law had meant that there was a loophole covering the wholesale murder of a government's own troops. A loophole that had since been removed in the outcry that followed the British government's attempt to alleviate the social problems caused by special forces vets.

'You tried to kill me, you bastard!' I spat at him, losing my temper. Suddenly the smile disappeared from the Major's face.

'And you led a mutiny, a court-martial offence for which you and that journalist should have been executed.' Then the smile returned to Rolleston's cold face. 'That reminds me. Have you heard from Howard recently?' Suddenly I was even more suspicious. My co-conspirator in the troopship mutiny that had saved our lives and the lives of other special forces and intelligence operators had disappeared shortly after Earth fall. All attempts to find the whereabouts of Mudge had turned up nothing. The last I'd heard from him he said he was trying to find Gregor MacDonald, another disappearance that Rolleston had been involved in.

'What do you know?' I demanded. Because Rolleston knew all right: he'd have done something to Mudge. He'd know what happened to Gregor, he knew it all, and he knew I knew. He'd string me along on hope to get me to do what he needed. His smile disappeared.

'Let's stop messing around, Sergeant.' The door to the sense booth opened. 'You have been reactivated. You are back on full pay, and if you track the XI and bring this matter to a successful conclusion I will award you a bonus sufficient to fund your addiction for a week.' I stepped out of the booth and looked up and down the corridor, almost expecting to see Private Josephine Bran waiting for me, but the corridor was empty.

'I though all this XI was bullshit,' I said. 'I didn't think They stood a chance against our system defences let alone Earth's.'

'Can you see why we would want people to think that?' Rolleston asked somewhat patronisingly. I found the idea that They could infiltrate Earth side somewhat disturbing. I really didn't want to find myself fighting the same war again, except this time unpaid and in the streets of Dundee. A text/picture file appeared on my internal visual display. 'This is what we know so far. Keep me up to date. Oh, and one other thing,' the Major said, smiling. I did not respond. 'We'll unlock you, but keep the locks; you'll need them again when this is over. Collect your weapons from your strongbox.' With this Rolleston's face disappeared.

There was a faintly audible clicking noise from my knuckles and shoulder. Smiling I looked down and picked the locks off like they were scabs. From thin slits just behind each knuckle four razor-sharp, nine-inch ceramic blades extended slowly, and then suddenly disappeared again at my mental command.

Next I reached up and opened the Velcro-secured concealed panel on the shoulder of my armoured raincoat. On silent servos the shoulder-mounted independent laser slid out and ran through its field of fire. A small screen appearing on my visual display showed what the weapon saw, superimposing a crosshair on where it would hit if it fired.

I lit a cigarette. I'd been putting off the best until last, afraid that they were not going to give me this, let me be this free. Taking a deep breath of smoke, I held it, reaching behind me for the restraining plug wired to my central nervous system inhibiting my boosted reactions. It came away in my hand and suddenly I was alive again. The world slowed down as I sped up, feeling like a razor cutting through a slow-moving and turgid reality.

I passed Hamish's cage; Hamish was not in it. I walked out onto the rough planks of the jury-rigged catwalks that ran through the Rigs. I finished the cigarette and flicked it into the superstructure. My shoulder laser spun up, tracking it. There was the bang of exploding superheated air as a ruby-red light momentarily illuminated the corroded orange metal of the ancient oil rig. The cigarette butt ceased to exist.

# 2
# Dundee

I made my way through the tangle of metal and shanty town back to the stacked plastic cubes where I lived. I clambered up the stairs sending the code to open the door to the porta-cube. Entering, I looked around trying to remember where I'd left the army-issue strongbox. Finally, in a pile of dirty washing and antique, actual paper books I found the supposedly unbreakable composite super-dense plastic box. Touching the lock button it clicked open.

The two matt-black guns lay in their moulded foam surround. I picked up the Tyler Optics 5 first. I slid a battery into the handgrip, checking it manually and then running a diagnostic on the laser pistol. I placed the compact weapon into a moulded holster and attaching the holster just behind my right hip. I clipped a battery holder to my belt, and placed a flat recharging cell into a slimline compartment in the raincoat.

Next I took the Sterling .454 Mastodon revolver out of the box. The enormous, solid, old-fashioned revolver felt like a toy in my prosthetic right arm. It was this trusty large-calibre weapon which I'd rely on to put one of Them down, if one of Them had made it Earth side. I stripped the revolver down and cleaned the already-clean weapon. Then I checked the revolver's action. Satisfied, the Mastodon became a familiar and welcome weight beneath my left arm in its shoulder holster. I clipped speed loaders with different loads to various easy-to-reach places.

I practised drawing both weapons through the conveniently placed slits in the armoured raincoat, checking the smartgun link, ensuring it was calibrated properly; the crosshairs appeared in my line of sight – in theory, where the bullet or beam would hit. First with one gun, then the other, then both, and finally with both weapons and the independently targeting shoulder-mounted laser. Eventually I was satisfied that all was as it should be.

Holstering the weapons I headed for the secure storage cube I rented to get my bike. After all, the government was going to be paying for fuel for the duration so there was no sense in walking. On my way down to the storage cube I split-screened my visual display and began to read through the information that that piece of shit Rolleston had sent me.

I rattled down the scaffolding steps past various plastic sheeting and cardboard lean-tos. Grubby, scrawny, suspicious faces, illuminated by the flickering flames of foul-smelling trash burners, glared at me. To them I looked well fed and wealthy. I ignored them as I enjoyed the buzz of having wired reactions again. I read through the Major's report, it was like an old-style UFO sighting. It was full of ifs and speculation.

The crux of it was one of the strategic orbital platforms, part of Earth's supposedly unbeatable ring of defences, had detected a faint echo in some rarely used spectrum. The echo was regular enough and moving towards the Earth with sufficient speed for the commander to order speculative firing on this ghost. The result of this firing may or may not have been a hit on something that may or may not have been space junk. The sensor system that had cost the taxpayer millions of euros was inconclusive. AI analysis of the ghost's trajectory suggested that if it had been something and indeed had been shot down it might have landed on the outskirts of Dundee. Orbital imaging of the area had again proved to be inconclusive but had found what it termed a 'disturbance' and a 'possible trench'.

I shot down the Kingsway, my enhanced central nervous system and reactions jacked into the control system of my Triumph Argo. No longer sure where I ended and the bike began. I wished I'd had access to my boosted nerves when I raced in the schemes. It would have saved me from a number of nasty wipeouts. I raced past row after row of identical fenced-in corporate wage-slave habitations. The guards at the gate watched me go by. I was travelling fast enough that all they would see was just a fractal line of light as I shot past.

By the time I'd finished reading what amounted to one of the vaguest briefings I'd ever been given, in a lifetime of vague briefings, I was pretty sure it was just another wild goose chase, an overzealous air force officer shooting at dust. I was overjoyed at the idea of investigating a possible trench. I checked the coordinates of said trench. It was outside the city in the National Park that made up the vast majority of Scotland and some of northern England.

Only a few people had access to the park, to the rest of us it was off limits. Those people who did have access were either key to the running of the park in some way, like my father had been, or very rich and powerful. The park was off limits supposedly for the countryside to recover from the nuclear exchange two hundred and fifty years ago and the pollution that had gone on before and after. I, on the other hand, had always thought that they wanted all the troublesome people in the cities where they could keep an eye on them.

I passed Camperdown, the maintained parkland for the mid-level salary types who lived on the Kingsway and were not quite wealthy enough for entrance to the National Park proper. In a lay-by at the side of the road I saw the salary men and women's offspring. They were middle-class street tribes standing by alcohol-burning custom cars older than them. Wearing designer clothes, doing designer drugs and toting designer handguns. They studiously ignored me as I roared by. I wasn't enough of a victim to get their attention.

Ahead of me was the checkpoint that would take me out into the National Park, away from the grime, closeness and proximity of the city. I'd spent the first thirteen years of my life in the park. My father, retired from the military, had worked as a hunting guide; my mother ran a business repairing fishing boats. Dad had taught me all about the country, how to survive, how to track, navigate, what the different fauna and flora were.

After a disgruntled client had killed him my mother didn't have the money to stay in the park and we had to move to the Fintry Schemes in Dundee. She couldn't quite scrape together enough money doing odd mechanical and electrical repair jobs to pay the rent and keep us fed. That was when I'd first gone to the pits. I was thirteen at the time. My mum had been a hand-to-hand combat instructor in the Paras and part of her family was Thai. Using the Muay Thai skills she'd taught me growing up, two hours a day every day, I was pretty good. I began putting more food on the table, paying my way competing in the clean unaugmented fights. Eventually I'd actually volunteered for the army, 5 Para Pathfinders like my dad. I thought the money I could send back would improve things for my mum but it was to no avail. She died shortly afterwards from a tainted dose of her favourite drug. Thinking back I don't think I've ever known anyone who's died a natural death.

The air was already beginning to smell better, more like air. I approached the checkpoint. Dundee was just a glow in the distance behind me. The barriers were up and police officers had already taken aim at me with their electromagnetic pulse rifles. I didn't slow down. Instead I transmitted the priority security clearance that had been part of the information that the Major had sent me. There was frantic activity as the barriers sank into the ground and the police moved out of the way and I raced past their wheeled APC.

I was out. I sucked in the cool night air, free of the city. The Triumph screamed down narrow roads, fields on either side, ahead of me in the distance the dark outlines of hills. It may as well have been another world. Dundee could have been a bad dream.

The 'possible trench' was about three miles off the Coupar Angus road, across a ploughed field. I put the Triumph into stealth mode, quietening the engine as much as possible. Using dirt and farm tracks, I approached as close as I could get to the coordinates I'd been given. Eventually I had to park up. I secured the bike and stood for a while acclimatising myself to the noise of the countryside before I set off on foot. I considered drawing one of my pistols but decided it would be a little melodramatic. The stillness of the night was calming.

I moved carefully but not as stealthily as I was capable. I enhanced my hearing and sight, regularly sweeping the area with thermographics. The rest of the time my cybernetic eyes were on low light, amplifying the ambient light of the moon and stars. Occasionally I would just stop and wait, let the nightlife become used to me before moving off again.

The coordinates of the possible trench were just off the summit of a low hill. As I approached the hill I stopped and had a look around. My father had taught me to track and 5 Para had improved on what I'd been taught. Even at night I could see the tracks of what looked to be a four-wheel drive. The tracks were fresh, someone had been there not that long ago.

Thermographics showed cooling chunks of heat surrounded the top of the hill. It was about this time that I wished I'd brought a motion detector. I drew the TO5 secure in the knowledge that there was nobody around to ridicule my possibly overcautious action. If there was anyone around, they would probably be who I needed to shoot anyway. Tactically the situation was not great as it was all open ground up to the heat signatures. Just because I couldn't see anyone around didn't mean there wasn't anyone there.

They used various castes of soldier. Each one appeared, according to the scant intelligence we had ever managed to get on Them, to be genetically created for a specific purpose. Their front-line soldiers, nicknamed Berserks, were bad enough. They were capable of going toe to toe with the most cybernetically enhanced trooper and even light power-armoured troops.

The Berserks weren't the worst. The worst were Their much rarer silent killers. The ones that I'd lost the most friends to, the ones that had been predictably nicknamed Ninjas. Though I'd always thought of them as pieces of night that killed. They were genetically created or modified bioborgs, full of internal weapons and designed for stealth. They could control their body temperature and if They were going to send an infiltrator it would make sense to send a Ninja or an iteration thereof. It was fear of these things that kept me standing stock still in a field just outside Dundee.

'Oh, this is bullshit,' I muttered to myself. Keeping low, I held my laser pistol in a two-handed grip, the weapon extended in front of me as I headed up the hill.

I confirmed that the possible trench was in fact an actual trench, a deep one. Parts of the earth glittered, reflecting moonlight where it had turned to glass. Scattered around the site were bits of some kind of dark composite material difficult to focus on. I wouldn't have found them had it not been for how much heat they gave off – though they were rapidly cooling. The material was the contradiction of a solid liquid that I had hoped to never see on Earth.

At the end of the trench was a needle-shaped craft roughly the size of a very large coffin. I'd seen them before. My shoulder-mounted laser pushed its way through the break-open panel of my coat and began to pan around behind me. I was more than a little nervous now. This was one of Their infiltration craft. An unpowered craft that was shot from a mass driver, designed to penetrate planetary defences and glide in. This one showed blast scoring, presumably from the orbital lasers, a result of the speculative fire. It looked like it had come in pretty hard but it was open and empty.

Suddenly I was aware of just how sensitive my boosted senses were and just how much noise there was out on that field. I mentally dialled the contact line that the Major had given me. I swung around behind me, bringing the laser up as I heard a sound, then again to my right at another rustle in the undergrowth. You're rattled, I told myself. Calm down.

'Yes, Sergeant?' Major Rolleston was smiling as his representation appeared in a small corner of my internal visual display. The familiar surge of anger was muted by my current fear.

'You have a problem,' I said. 'You've got a Needle here. It's been damaged and come in hard but it's empty.'

'Assessment?' Annoyingly, the Major was playing army. I swung around again at another sound.

'You have a Ninja down here. Possibly injured, but their self-repair systems will have it up to full capacity in no time.'

'A Ninja? Are you sure?' Rolleston asked.

'No, I'm not sure; maybe they've sent one of their caterers. What else would they send!'

'Can you handle the situation?' I was a little taken aback by this question. Could I handle it? What was he talking about?

'Of course I can't fucking handle it; it's a Ninja. One of these things killed two of my squad, did God knows what to MacDonald and nearly took the rest of us out before we managed to get it, and that was with mil-spec gear.'

'Calm down, Sergeant. Are there any signs of where it is?'

'Can you actually hear me?' I asked as I spun around again. 'It's a Ninja, would you like me to spell it? They don't leave tracks. Oh!' On the ground by the trench there were tracks. I put my paranoia aside for a moment and crouched down to examine them.

'Sergeant?'

'Shut up.' Rolleston seemed to ignore the insubordination. The tracks showed hiking boots going up the hill, possibly from the four-by-four I had seen the tracks from earlier. They left the hill dragging something, something with two legs and two arms. I relayed what I had found to Rolleston.

'It would seem that your Ninja was more badly damaged than you thought,' Rolleston said.

'They heal quickly.'

'Well then, you had best find it quickly and destroy it, yes?'

'What are we dealing with here?' I asked, but the Major had gone.

I tried to figure this. Who had taken the Ninja and why? Had Rolleston already sent XIs up here? Collaborators? Was there a fifth column on Earth? That didn't make sense.

There were xenophile individuals and cults on Earth and in the colonies. Many of them were just the young rejecting everything about the total war that gripped humanity. Most of these cults were pure fantasy and few of them were about Them; after all, all They wanted to do was kill and destroy every human they found.

Humanity had first come across Them in the Sirius system, though that was not where They came from. Initially called Sirians until the Syrians in the Islamic Protectorate had complained. Then they were called Doggies for a while, after the Dog Star, but that did not seem to do Them justice. It was still squaddie parlance for Them however. Nothing was known about Them. They had just come across humans in the Sirius system and started killing and never stopped. Their goal seemed to be to annihilate humanity and They had done so right across the four colonial systems. Collaboration with Them was species suicide so a fifth column made no sense.

# 3
# Dundee

I followed the tracks to the road, sending out data requests as I walked back to the bike. I straddled the bike, sitting low between the two huge wheels, and pressed the ignition. The bike growled into life. I received an answer to one of my info requests. The checkpoint on the Coupar Angus road had processed a park ranger pickup truck about half an hour before I'd gone through it. The truck had been heading into Dundee.

It may have been nothing, a different four-by-four to the one whose tracks I'd found, but so far it was all I had to go on. Also the pickup, according to the vehicle's profile, had the correct tyres to make the tracks that I'd found. I received the ranger's address. It was inside the city limits, some mid-level habitation block. Private but with reasonable security, probably full of police, civil servants and retired officers, as well as park personnel too poor to live in the park.

The gate was opened for me as I approached the habitat. I had sent my clearance ahead of me. The habitation block was a series of four-storey identical flats with a walkway connecting them all, just off the Broughty Ferry Road. You could look down the hill to the skeletal metal city that was the Rigs. A darkened city illuminated only by flickering electric lights and the trash-can fires here and there. I nodded at the security guard with the assault rifle at the gate.

Parking was at a premium and probably something that the inhabitants liked to argue about. I considered parking behind the muddy park service pickup but decided against it. I looked over the vehicle; in the flatbed I found telltale traces of a black fluid. It was definite now: the park ranger had transported it. I was left wondering why some people were storing a dangerous alien killing machine in their apartment. I guess they couldn't afford a dog. Who could?

Heading up the stairs, I decided that the Mastodon would have the best psychological impact on the ranger and ballistic impact on the Ninja. According to the park service personnel files I'd received, the ranger was one Morton Rayment. He lived in the apartment with his girlfriend Joy Sverdlof. Thermographics told me that there were two human-sized heat sources in there. It seemed unlikely that either of the heat sources was the Ninja. This did not mean that the Ninja wasn't in the apartment, just that I couldn't see it. Though both Rayment and Sverdlof still seemed to be alive, which was promising.

Moving quietly along the walkway I made it up to their apartment and palmed my very illegal lock burner. Boosting my hearing, I stopped to listen, amplifying the muffled voices through the paper-thin walls and filtering them until I could understand their conversation.

'... what if the authorities trace it to me?' This was the male voice, local but well educated, presumably Rayment.

'Bit late for that now, should've thought about that before you loaded it up.' This was presumably Sverdlof, probably second generation but you could still hear traces of her eastern European accent. 'Look at all this money, just think what we can do.'

'How? It's all black, we can't declare it.' Rayment said. His voice was becoming a panicky whine. I was wondering how this guy had had the balls to load a potentially dangerous alien life form into the back of his pickup. I wasn't sure I'd have the balls. I'd have been more likely to turn it into a puddle. I slipped the lock burner into the apartment's card slot.

'There are lots of things you can do with black money – you can get stuff you can't get with real money,' The woman said. I slipped into their apartment. It was a tiny box. They were stood over their mock-pine table in the dining/living/kitchen area. On the table were piles of dirty paper cash. Rayment, still wearing his ranger's uniform, was stood looking nervously at the piles. Next to him, greed lighting her eyes, was Sverdlof. Neither of them had heard me enter though they were standing opposite the door. This was good. This meant I wasn't completely useless.

Rayment looked up as I said,'Isn't that the truth?' and lost control of his bladder as he found himself looking down the barrel of the huge revolver. His hand not going anywhere near the automatic holstered at his side.

Sverdlof was made of sterner stuff. She made a dive for the apartment's personal defence weapon in its rack on the wall. My left fist caught her on the chin, picking her up off her feet and sending her flying onto the small two-seater sofa, which broke under her weight. She sat up glaring at me, looking feral and angry. Clearly I had pointed the gun at the wrong person. I brought the Mastodon to bear on her.

'This,' I said, nodding at the revolver, 'is more than capable of shooting through walls, and I can see through them, do you understand?' The girl nodded, Rayment just shook a bit. I moved into their small bedroom and as soon as I was out of sight the girl began to move towards the PDW. I poked my head back out of the bedroom. The girl froze.

'Do I have to shoot you? For fuck's sake, darling, sit down,' I told her. She just glared at me.

'Do as he says!' Rayment pleaded. Sverdlof gave him a look of contempt before sitting down. Clearly she was poorer than him and the money meant more to her. I searched every place that they could hide one of Them. It was not in the apartment. I had assumed as much when I'd seen the cash but I had to check.

I came out of their tiny bathroom, having ensured it wasn't in there showering. I headed back into the living area just as the apartment's rapid response unit turned up. In this case the rapid response unit was a fat guy called Larry with a pump-action shotgun.

'I have already given you my clearance, now go away,' I said. Larry looked me up and down, sizing up his chances and not really liking them.

'I'm sorry sir,' Larry wheezed, trying to recover his breath from the run to the apartment, 'but we are contractually obligated to protect the inhabitants. I'm going to have to ask you—' Then I was holding Larry's shotgun.

'You did the best you could, Larry, now fuck off,' I said, beginning to lose patience. Larry turned and left with one final apologetic look at Rayment and Sverdlof. I turned to the pair of them.

'Where is it?' I asked, my eyes drifting to the large bundles of cash on the table.

'Where's what?' Sverdlof replied. I sighed.

'Look, I am going to find out what I want to know anyway. The only real question for you guys is how hurt or dead you get in the process.'

'Maybe, but what if whoever took it from us is a bigger bastard than you?' she asked.

'Is he a more immediate problem?' I said. 'Look, you've got your money; you can do a bunk. Though chances are whoever has the thing is not going to be a problem for much longer.'

'For fuck's sake tell him,' Rayment whimpered.

'Why don't you tell me, Morton?' I asked.

'What's it worth?' Sverdlof asked.

'Why don't I beat it out of your boyfriend?' I said.

'Ex-boyfriend.'

'You're leaving me!' Rayment said and burst into tears.

'Hard to see why,' I said, looking at the park ranger with mild bemusement. Sverdlof nodded. She seemed to be weighing up her options, and like Larry she did not like the conclusions she was coming to.

'We sold it to Cassidy MacFarlane,' she finally said. This confused me.

'The pimp? Why?' Sverdlof shrugged. 'What sort of state was it in?' I demanded.

'Pretty messed up, leaking, not moving much, not making any noise. Difficult to tell with those things. It didn't seem very threatening.'

'How long ago?'

Sverdlof shrugged again. 'Maybe an hour.'

'Know where he was taking it?'

'No,' she said. I was pretty sure she'd told me as much as she could. So I nipped back into their bedroom and came back with a small sports holdall and began filling it with their black money, the Mastodon still levelled at Sverdlof.

'What are you doing?' Sverdlof shouted.

'Taking your money,' I told her, feeling like a total bastard. I was secure in the knowledge that official business or not there was nothing they could really do. Reporting it meant incriminating themselves. Not that I really cared one way or another. Let the Major sort it out.

'What am I going to use if I have to run from MacFarlane?' Sverdlof demanded. I ignored the question. Finally with all the money packed I backed out of the tiny apartment, Sverdlof glaring after me.

'Come after me and I will have to kill you, you know that,' I told her. Sverdlof just continued to glare at me with undiluted hatred in her eyes.

I left the apartment, closing the door behind me. As the door clicked shut Sverdlof started screaming, berating Rayment for cowardice. Not that there was much he could have done, except maybe not wet himself or burst into tears. I smiled and then spun round bringing the revolver up.

Leaning against the wall a few feet away from me was Josephine. She looked as drab and nondescript as normal. Rumour was that she had had herself surgically altered to look as uninteresting as possible. She was difficult to describe because nothing stuck out about her appearance. Even her clothes were drab.

'Losing your touch?' she asked, not looking me in the eyes. She always avoided eye contact. I lowered the gun and then holstered it.

'Oh, hi, Josey,' I said sarcastically, trying to mask my fear. The Grey Lady had always unnerved me. She was right though. Josephine was good but she should not have snuck up on me that easily. She shook her head.

'The Major wants you to do it,' she said. I knew exactly what she meant.

'And if I don't?' I asked.

'Oh, you know,' she said awkwardly, examining her nails. 'He'll just make making you miserable his hobby.'

'He's not doing that already?' I asked.

'Give me the money, Jakob,' she said shyly. I sighed.

'This is fucking petty even by his standards. You turn up to rob me?' I asked. She shook her head.

'Give me the money and go and kill them.' She sounded quiet and meek. I dropped the bag of notes at her feet and tried to walk past her. She held a hand out. It just touched my chest but I stopped.

'I'll cover for you just once,' she said and looked me in the eyes. My mouth went very dry and I swallowed involuntarily. She dropped her hand, letting me past. As I went down the steps the muzzle flashes from inside the apartment illuminated the car park briefly.

I rode through the superstructure of the Rigs. Moving just a little faster than was safe for the rickety wooden boards and metal sheets that passed for roads. I wanted to stop, return to the cube, start drinking and maybe listen to some music. Try not to think about the two poor fuckers I'd just got killed for doing what we all have to do to survive. I knew, however, that if I did that Rolleston would keep on hounding me.

Now I'd seen the Grey Lady I had a sense of urgency. I wanted this wrapped up and forgotten. I also needed the promised week in the sense booths, being fed by a drip, getting bedsores, my muscles atrophying and most importantly achieving a total loss of self, to forget about all this.

Although I'd never been a special forces operator who enjoyed his work particularly, I also had to admit that the feeling that came from my enhancements, the feeling of moving like lightning when everyone else was mired down, was something I never grew tired of. So I was going to kill some stupid people and take out one more of Them. Big deal, another tiny step in a conflict that seemed to consume everything.

They were the only other life that we'd ever encountered in space and we were at war with Them. This had to be a tiny drop in the ocean to the universe. Yet sometimes, when space was filled with bright beams burning across the night. When I was waiting in an assault shuttle for a drop, my life in someone else's hands. When I was watching other shuttles tumbling towards planets to burn on entry. Sometimes it looked and felt like the entire universe was at war.

# 4
# Dundee

The Forbidden Pleasure was neither all that forbidden nor pleasurable. It had once been a container ship. Most of the containers had been scavenged long ago to create what I liked to think of as the upper-class neighbourhood on the Rigs. The remaining containers of the horribly corroded three-hundred-year-old craft had been sectioned off with cardboard walls and turned into a production-line-style knocking shop. This was the place where the inhabitants of the Rigs came to experience the meat.

The bridge had been stripped out long ago, non-supporting bulkheads cut through and the whole deck converted into some impoverished idea of what a lounge bar was supposed to be. It was a sick joke. A taunt to the people forced to live on the Rigs. I climbed up the metal stairs to the bridge deck. I dampened my enhanced hearing to drown out the grunts, sighs, the faked orgasms and the screams of pain. I was trying not to think about how working here or in one of the other flesh parlours in the Rigs was one of the few chances to make a living the young on the Rigs had. Though they were used up quickly.

I tried to slip into the bar on the bridge deck as inconspicuously as possible, but my long coat and the way you move with reflexes as wired as mine gave me away. I eased into one of the high chairs at the bar, aware of eyes burning into my back. The bridge bar was for the high-rollers, by the standards of the Rigs. The rest just took their turn at the turnstiles in the lottery-like system on the foredeck. The security was violent young men and women with cheap ware and assault rifles.

The boys and girls in the bar were the youngest and freshest, the least damaged. The badly chalked menu above the bar suggested that you could pretty much do to them what you wanted as long as you had the money. I couldn't see Cassidy but there was a lot of his muscle in the bar. Young crazies with too much cheap ware, bad drugs and weapons they did not know how to use. Most of them would be draft dodgers. Too dangerous to recruit by the time their number came up or, rather, more trouble than they were worth. The rest were clients, mainly the entrepreneurial class of the Rigs. Dealers of whatever they could find to deal – drugs, booze, smokes, medicines, weapons, space and life.

At one table sat a corporate salary man, quite a high-ranking one judging by his retinue of guards. He was slumming. He was probably here to snuff someone. His katana, the badge of office for corporate swordsmen, lay sheathed on the table in front of him. I wondered how many people he had slain with that sword in promotion and tender duels to get where he was today. I had a pretty good idea about how this was going to go down and I resented that I would become anecdote fodder for the slumming salary man. There was the sound of automatic weapons fire from the foredeck. I had my hand on the butt of my laser pistol before I thought about it. I hadn't been wired this high in a while. Nobody else flinched. Nothing new, just another example being made.

'Drink?' I looked up at the barman. He was a vet. One arm missing where they had removed a prosthetic when he had been discharged, the other hugely muscled from illegal boosters, stimulants and overcompensation. His eyes were cheap Coventry-made implants. Probably replacements for the military-grade ones he'd had removed. The angry red scar tissue around the eyes pointed to a botched job. The implants were probably painful with low resolution.

'Have you got anything nice to drink?' I asked optimistically. The barman smiled ironically and shook his head. 'Anything that's safe to drink?'

'Not so much,' the barman answered, his accent broad Dundonian. I put some dirty paper euros on the bar.

'Have a drink yourself and I'll have one of whatever you dare to drink.' The barman gave a snort of amusement and came back a minute or so later with two dirty glasses containing a murky liquid. I raised my glass to him.

'To slipping standards,' I said, and tipped the contents down my throat trying desperately not to taste it. I think it was supposed to have been whisky, though the aftertaste of turpentine gave it away a bit. I grimaced and looked at the glass.

'Takes the edge off, doesn't it?' the barman said.

'It's an acquired taste,' I said as politely as I could manage.

'I know you?' the barman asked, and he would do. As an unspoken rule when you moved onto the Rigs you had to prove that you were more trouble than it was worth to mess with. If you didn't you were going to end up spending all your time fending off chop merchants wanting to sell you for second-hand mil-spec ware. So when I moved in there had been a few strategic deaths and acts of violence on my part to ensure I got left in peace. I shrugged off the barman's question.

'Cassidy about?' I asked. The barman started to answer.

'Who wants to know about Mr MacFarlane?' a voice that was all street bravado asked from behind me. I glanced round and saw what I guessed would be the first abject example of the night. He was young and had something to prove. I bit back my initial sarcastic retort. The over-revved street muscle was stripped to the waist to display the operation scars for lots of new muscle. He was also high on some kind of combat drug, judging by his jitters, and of course his watching peers were implicitly egging him on. In the waistband of his combat trousers was an automatic of a calibre too large to be of any practical use except to intimidate or hunt big game.

'My name is Jakob Douglas and I have a very important proposition for MacFarlane.'

'Doesn't everyone?' the young muscle asked.

I shrugged but said nothing.

'Well?' the muscle said, slightly confusing me.

'Sorry, I thought the question was rhetorical. I don't know, is the answer.' The muscle was not quite sure how to take this. I cursed myself. I'd made this guy feel stupid, which would in turn lead to anger, which would in turn lead to me having to kill him.

'Look, son, I know your story and I know your life. I know what you're doing and I don't want to hurt you. I just want to see MacFarlane and make my offer.' The muscle looked amused. He turned to his audience of fellow toughs.

'He's worried about hurting me,' he said, laughing. None of his friends laughed. I tried again, desperately trying to keep this boy alive for no good reason I could think of.

'Let me guess, you've got some scary-sounding street name like Razors, Deathboy or Heed-the-Ball.'

'Cordite.'

'I don't want to know what it is. I'm just telling you about your life in an attempt to lengthen it and save myself some trouble.'

'Listen to him, boy,' the barman said. 'He's special forces, or was.' I said nothing, just watching, hating the inevitability of this.

'So what? You vets are all piss and wind ...' Cordite found himself looking down the barrel of the Mastodon.

'Mine's bigger than yours,' I said. 'Now what you're feeling is peer-group pressure. You can't back down because you're being watched by the people you're trying to impress, and it will be humiliating if you don't do anything.'

Though I knew it would be worse than humiliating. This boy's career was over. He was going from predator to prey in the Rigs' food chain after this. Somewhere in Cordite's drug-addled mind he realised this too. I read the movement in body language almost before it happened. I felt the world of the bridge bar slowing down until it was like everyone else was moving through thick mud as my reflexes kicked in. I let everyone see that Cordite was going for his gun. I even let him touch the weapon before I pulled the trigger, already shaking my head sadly as I did. The two feet of muzzle flash scorched Cordite's dermal chest armour. My audio dampening kicked in, compensating for the deafening roar of the oversized revolver. In what seemed like slow motion to me, I watched the bullet pierce the boy's armour, enter the chest cavity, pick him up off his feet, and then the explosive charge in the bullet detonated, sending liquefied and scorched parts of his internal organs squirting out of the entry wound.

I lowered the enormous smoking pistol as Cordite hit the ground. Many of the other muscle had their hands on their weapons, including the salary man's guard. The salary man was just watching me with casual interest. Anecdote fodder. I looked down sadly at the corpse I'd just made. Ignoring the threat of the rest of MacFarlane's security in the bar, I opened the chamber of my revolver, took out the spent round, pocketed the smoking cartridge and replaced it with a new, loose round from my pocket before holstering the pistol.

I looked around the bar. Changing to low light, I saw the table at the back. The fat-looking guy, ostentatiously sporting his wealth, smoking a cigar, decadent make-up, and wearing fashion ware, the two prettiest girls in the bar with him and guards who did not look like they had their heads stuck up their arses.

'You have your sacrifice,' I said angrily. 'You going to listen to me now?' MacFarlane took a drag of his cigar. The cherry flaring up illuminated the white-painted skin of his fleshy, bearded face, his red-gloss lips and dark eyes.

'Natural selection,' he said, nodding towards Cordite's body. 'Thank you for culling my herd.'

'I don't have to stop there,' I said and then cursed myself for such an obvious response.

'You do in a room full of my men. You may get a few but you're still a dead man.' MacFarlane was smiling, pulling one of the girls in closer to himself, presumably to use as a shield if it came to that.

I began calculating my plan of attack. The order the muscle in this room would die.

'I don't think you're right, but it'll mean fuck all to you because you go first,' I said evenly. I was beginning to find this macho bullshit tiring. MacFarlane gave this some thought.

'So you don't want to speak to me?' he asked sardonically, apparently enjoying himself. I just sighed, deciding to be quiet until somebody said something worthwhile or I had to start shooting people.

'What do you want?' MacFarlane asked, apparently growing bored.

'You bought something from a park rang—' I managed to get out.

'Kill him,' MacFarlane said. Oh for fuck's sake, I thought as the world around me slowed down again. The Mastodon was in my right hand, the laser in my left. A ruby-red beam joined the muzzle of the laser pistol to one of MacFarlane's bodyguards as he tried to stand up. There was the sharp bang of exploding superheated air molecules and a scream from the guard as some of his flesh became red steam.

I swung the Mastodon under my extended left arm and pulled the trigger. The huge revolver round caught one of MacFarlane's men as he tried to bring a sub-machine gun to bear. The bullet hitting him with such force it blew him through the bridge window and sent him tumbling to the deck below. My shoulder-mounted laser pushed itself through the break-open panel on my long coat. The split-screen targeting system appeared on my internal visual display, imposing crosshairs on the two gunmen diving for cover behind the bar. The laser hit one of them in mid-air; the second gunman managed to get behind the bar. The shoulder laser tracking him took an informed guess as to where he was and fired again, the ruby beam stabbing through the bar. There was a howl of pain.

Guided by the smartgun link, I fired the Tyler twice more at MacFarlane's two remaining guards, catching one in the temple, turning the back of his head into a steaming mess on the wall. MacFarlane was screaming, trying to use the two terrified girls as cover. The other guard tumbled out of the way. I'd underestimated him, or his ware anyway.

I swung to the left. The two gunmen at the table by the broken window were trying to bring their weapons to bear. The Mastodon fired again, catching one of them in the chest, and three bright red beams fired in quick succession took the other one down.

Then things became interesting for me as low-calibre, high-velocity, rapidly fired rounds began impacting on my long coat. Most of their kinetic energy was absorbed but a few of them were making their way through to my dermal plating. I started running and dived behind the bar. Trying to work out where the fire was coming from. I landed hard behind the bar. Bottles exploded, showering me in cheap unpleasant booze.

Looking up I found the gunman who had dived over the bar previously, whimpering. He was clutching a wounded leg where half of his thigh had been seared off by my shoulder-mounted laser's blind fire. Moving more on instinct and boosted reflexes than anything else, I let the Mastodon drop to the floor and reached forward, my right metallic hand a clenched fist. The four nine-inch knuckle blades extended from their housing. They pierced the top of the wounded gunman's skull and drove down with such force that his facial features contorted. I retracted the blades in a spray of blood, bones and grey matter and picked up my revolver again.

Moving through the visual spectrum to thermographics, I looked through the bar to see who was shooting at me. I saw an orange blossom of muzzle flash from the table where the salary man had been sitting. The bodyguards had decided that I was a threat to their employer. The red beam of my laser seared my thermographic vision momentarily as I burned through the bar and into the salary man's head. There was a cessation in the gunfire.

'Your client's safe now!' I shouted angrily. 'Mind your own fucking business!' There was no return fire. The heat outlines of the salary man's bodyguards told me they were staying in cover, their guns cooling.

I stood up. Further down the bar the barman was watching me. He inclined his head toward the port stairway to the bridge. Filtering through the noise I heard boots ringing off metal stairs. I was still worried about the whereabouts of MacFarlane's remaining bodyguard. I'd somehow managed to lose track of him.

I ignored the wild shot from MacFarlane's underpowered but still very fashionable, last year, automatic pistol. Walking to the doorway, still using my thermographics, I was suddenly treated to the silhouetted spectacle of mass, impoverished rutting. The containers were giving off a lot of heat into the summer night air. However, I had more pressing matters as reinforcements came pounding up the stairs. I reached the top of the stairs and began firing down with both the revolver and the laser. Firing rapidly but accurately thanks to the smartgun links. Shooting through one gunman to get the one behind him. My shoulder laser stabbed out repeatedly into the containers at those guards who thought sniping would be a safer option. Glass exploded around me and a few bullets hit my coat, penetrating but being stopped painfully by my dermal armour.

The firing stopped and I swung back behind part of the bulkhead, both my weapons hot and empty. The speed and strength of the wired and boosted enhanced kick that caught me in the side of the face had sufficient force to spin me round. It was rank amateurishness on my part that the kick had caught me out. Then the other guy made a mistake. He did not press his advantage.

I tried to shake off the ringing in my head and looked up at my opponent. MacFarlane's final guard wore a knock-off expensive suit that was big enough to allow him to move. He had no hair at all anywhere on his gleaming skull. A few tattoos crept up past his collar line. His movements suggested that his ware was top-notch and he actually had skill. He was bouncing easily on the balls of his feet, his hands in a lazy guard. This was MacFarlane's showpiece fighter, his fashionable martial artist, the best reactions, muscle and skills that the street economy could provide.

'Square go?' MacFarlane's pet martial artist asked. Tradition, see? It didn't matter that we both had high-end skills developed initially in the Far East, this was still Dundee. I should have shot him, but I looked around at the carnage I had wrought on my own, just me, nobody else. I felt the buzz. I holstered my guns. The combat high stupidly making me feel invincible. My shoulder laser tucked itself away.

The fighter smiled and threw something at me as I began moving, but he was wired almost as well as I was. The lighter hit me and I went up in flames from all the cheap booze I had been covered in. Was this supposed to stop me? It wouldn't even hurt until I slowed down. Red warning symbols had come up on my visual display as I moved towards my opponent. MacFarlane's martial artist swung out with his fist at me. I spun out of its way.

One of the first things I'd been taught in the SAS is that you never use a kick in a serious fight. They're too slow and anyone who knew what they were doing would take you down before your foot got anywhere near them. However my mother had brought me up to use Muay Thai, and I was wired, and I was angry and I was on fire.

The spinning roundhouse kick hooked into the back of the boosted martial artist's skull. Staggering him, the flames forcing him to move out of the way. A side kick to the torso knocking him further back. I slapped his counter-attack out of the way, vaguely aware that my hair was on fire now. I leapt into the air, my burning knee catching the martial artist hard under the chin. He flew back, and while still in mid-air I extended my leg out and kicked him in the chest.

Landing, I closed the distance and elbowed him on either side of his head. He tried to recover, kicking me, but I raised my leg to block him and then kicked him in the knee. The knee broke and he hit the ground. As he tried to get up I kicked him in the sternum, flipping him over. My claws went through his chest and into the metal floor beneath him.

I stood up. Despite dampened nerves and internal painkillers, the flames were becoming too much. The chemical retardant of the fire extinguisher came as a welcome release. The barman put the extinguisher back beneath the bar. On the bar was a dirty glass of the same muck we'd drunk earlier. I picked it up, knocked it back and made a disgusted noise.

The coat was a little blackened but would be fine. My jeans were mostly destroyed and my skin was burnt down to the dermal armour on the bottom part of my legs. My left hand and much of my face had been burnt. My hair was a burnt brittle mess coming away in clumps. This burnt visage was what MacFarlane saw as I made my way towards him, slowly reloading my guns. The remaining patrons and hookers in the bar just lay low as I passed. Some of them whimpered, but most were used to scenes like this.

I stood over MacFarlane, still smoking gently. One of the girls had managed to escape but the other one MacFarlane was using as a shield, the pretty gun in his other hand. The pimp was lying between the table and the couch he had been sat on. Not for the first time I wondered how people like this managed to control all the psychopaths they had working for them. I pulled a chair out and sat down, lighting a cigarette, the flickering flames illuminating my ruined face. MacFarlane was desperately trying to think of a way out.

'That's illegal ware. You're boosted way to high. They'll kill you for that, you know, take you down. CSWAT will be on their way.'

'I'm working. Let her go,' I said, meaning the terrified sixteen-year-old girl. MacFarlane seized on this. He put the little gun to her head.

'Yeah, yeah. Walk out of here or I'll kill her.'

'Chivalry is alive and well in Dundee,' I said sarcastically. MacFarlane did not seem to understand. I sighed and fixed him with a stare. I'd been told that black lenses had the effect of making their owners look like soulless monsters. An effect probably further heightened by my burnt appearance. I pointed the Mastodon at the pair on the floor. 'Come to terms with your death because you have sent a lot better men before you,' I said to him. 'I don't care about some stranger's death. It just seems to be a waste to me, so decide if she's going with you.' The girl started crying, racking sobs shaking her body. MacFarlane considered my words. He let her go and she scrambled away. It was probably the single best act he had ever done in his life.

'Where is it?' I asked MacFarlane.

'In the stateroom,' MacFarlane said, overcome with hopelessness.

'The what?' I asked.

'The captain's cabin. Two decks down, you can't miss it. It's the nicest cabin, the fucking captain's cabin.' I got up and then stopped.

'What did you want it for?' I asked, still assuming that there was some kind of suicidal Them fifth-column cult on Earth. MacFarlane seemed confused at the question.

'Well, I was going to pimp it,' he said, as if that was obvious. I let this sink in and started to laugh. MacFarlane looked pissed off that I was laughing at his grand business plan.

'I could have charged a fortune to let people come here and fuck one of those things, just like they fucked us,' he said defiantly.

'You idiot,' I managed between the laughter. 'It's a biological machine designed for killing.'

'We could have cut holes in it,' MacFarlane said defensively. This only made me laugh harder. Small men, small ideas, I thought.

'You mean you are confronted with something from another planet, a completely alien species, and all you can think to do with it is fuck it?' I asked. MacFarlane obviously did not like being laughed at and was becoming angry despite the danger.

'What's so funny? People will pay to fuck anything ...' The report of the Mastodon was very loud in the bridge. MacFarlane slumped to the ground. I exhaled smoke, all trace of amusement gone. I looked at the corpse of the pimp for a moment and then stood up.

'Mister?' a timid voice said. I turned to look at the frightened girl MacFarlane had used as a shield. I didn't answer her. Instead I reached down and searched MacFarlane until I found the pimp's money roll. 'You're wrong, you know,' the girl said. I peeled off some of the dirty euros and offered them to her. She snatched them out of my hand and I pocketed the rest.

'Yeah? About what?' I asked.

'About it being a killer.' I turned to look at her. 'It's not a killer, it's beautiful,' she said. I had no idea what she was talking about but something about her earnestness bothered me. I headed towards the internal stairs that would take me down to see one of the monsters that had killed so many of my friends. Was it psychologically healthier to want to have sex with an alien or just kill it? I wondered. You'd hope it depended on the circumstances.

# 5
# Dundee

Despite the ruin of my face I was feeling no pain as I edged my way down the stairway deeper into the ship. The subdued lighting and peeling red paint were a long-forgotten attempt at ambience, but now, to my drug-addled brain, they gave the place an other-worldly feel.

I reached the bottom of the stairs and stopped. My hearing could pick up the sound of heavy breathing around the corner, the sound of nervous people shifting. I looked through thermographics but warm pipes and a multitude of people in surrounding rooms confused the images. I peeked around the corner and brought my head straight back as two nervous gunmen let rip with SMGs loaded with slugs too high a velocity for the weapons. The bullets ripped through the bulkhead where I'd been standing and continued on their path. I heard a scream. One of the stray bullets had caught a working boy somewhere deeper in the ship. I had retreated part the way back up the stairs.

'It's all over,' I shouted. 'Everyone's dead. MacFarlane's dead, you're not working for anyone any more. Just walk away.' There was a discussion between them as to the merits of my offer.

'Bullshit, man!' One of them shouted. 'You're government, you're going to kill everyone who came into contact with it.'

'Then why haven't I?' I asked, wondering why people made it so hard for me not to kill them. 'Look it's up to you, either you die here now or you take your chances and walk away.' There was another discussion followed by the sounds of feet pounding metal. I glanced around the corner; both the gunmen had gone.

Leaning against the bulkhead, I replaced the shells in the Mastodon with disrupter rounds. They were specifically designed to inflict the most damage on the liquid flesh technology of Their bioborg killers. My hand was shaking. I was afraid. I had spent so much time Earth side, where nothing was frightening compared to the war. I'd forgotten what the fear was like.

The last time I'd faced a Ninja I had been armed to the teeth, pumped on combat drugs, aided by my squad, and many of them still ended up dead, not to mention the weirdness that happened to Gregor. If this was one of their Ninjas then it had better be very injured or I was screwed. It was then I heard movement from the next corridor.

Looking around the corner, I saw about twenty of the more upmarket (by rig standards) hookers heading into what I assumed was the captain's cabin. Angry johns were following some of them. I pinched the bridge of my nose, crushing burnt skin; vague signals of pain pushed their way through the drugs and the nerve dampening. Unsure what to do, I made my way down the corridor, straight-arming one of the johns, who was trying to drag a teenage boy back to a cabin by the hair. I pushed my way through the hookers, a task made easier by my frightening burnt appearance, to the door of the stateroom.

It was definitely one of Them lying on the cabin bed. Manacles that presumably had been shackling him lay on the floor now. It was the most human-looking one I had ever seen. It was like a human-shaped and proportioned pool of oil, its head a smooth featureless black dome. There were no visible weapon appendages apparent but I knew that Their Ninjas were morphic. In terms of apparent physiology the only real difference was it had seven long fingers on both hands and it looked slightly smaller than the average human. The light formed rainbow-like reflections in its flesh and I could make out a distorted view of myself – for the first time I could see the burn damage.

I watched my reflection extend the revolver towards the alien. The hookers rushed to the creature and surrounded it, forming a shield between it and me. As they touched it some of its reactive liquid flesh solidified. Their touch also caused ripples all over it, like pebbles dropped in a dark stream. I'd seen this before. The black liquid on the floor and the cot meant it was injured. Good, I thought. The thing was moving, trying to push its human shield away.

'Get out the way,' I ordered tersely. The hookers did not move though they looked terrified. 'Now!' I roared. Many of them jumped, a couple of them started crying softly. The tears made me feel like shit. These people were among the lowest on the food chain. The exploited's exploited and they had nowhere to go but down as they became more and more used up. It was why I'd always preferred the artifice of the sense booths. This didn't stop me from pulling back the hammer on the revolver, largely an affectation but it was intimidating. More were crying but they did not move; they seemed ready to die for this thing. I wondered if this was some kind of phermonic effect, a form of psychological warfare or mind control that the wounded alien had used to influence the prostitutes.

'What are you doing?' I asked softly, though the revolver did not waver. I wanted this bad day over with.

'Please don't kill him,' said one of the prostitutes, a boy whose age I did not want to guess.

'Why?' I asked.

'It's not a bad thing,' replied one of the other hookers, a slightly older girl. She was not crying, though she looked scared, but her life had probably used up all her tears. She was pretty. The kind of pretty that wouldn't make her pimp want to put her under a laser to turn her into a sleazier version of whoever that week's face was and then have her work off her debt for the surgery. She had a bob of black hair, freckles and pretty brown eyes. I looked at her, though the revolver's smartlink enabled me to keep aiming at the Ninja on the cot.

'You don't know what you're talking about. I don't know what you think you know, but I've seen these things before and they just want to kill humans. It's doing something to you. I'm not sure what, but whatever it is, it's not real. I can give you some money but you need to get out of the way.'

'Have you ever spoken to one before?' the girl asked. I groaned inwardly. My initial interest was giving way to irritation. To make matters worse, the comms icon on my visual display started winking. The Major was trying to get through.

'They don't communicate with humans; all they want to do is kill. Do you understand?' I told the girl.

'This one talks,' the girl said. I was lost for words. I'd never heard of this happening before. Not to the air force's Space Command first contact team that was initially murdered by the genocidal aliens, nor at any point during the war. I took Rolleston's call while deciding what to do next. An image of the Major appeared in a small box at one side of my visual display.

'You've found it.' It was more of a statement than a question.

'Yes,' I sub-vocalised.

'Neutralised it?' the Major asked.

'Not yet.' The digital representation of the Major looked troubled momentarily.

'Problems?' he asked.

'Of a sort.'

'Of what sort?' the Major asked, becoming impatient.

'Collateral,' I answered. I knew the lack of information would infuriate the Major.

'Neutralise them as well,' he ordered.

'I'm not shooting a sixteen-year-old girl,' I answered. The prostitutes surrounding the wounded alien were aware that I was having a sub-vocal conversation but their protective encirclement remained firm.

'You'll do as you're told,' the Major growled.

'If you didn't want me to do this my way, why bother getting me to do it in the first place? After all, Bran's here on the ground.' The Major looked like he was about to issue more orders, probably backed with threats that I would have had to take seriously. Working on the principle that it was easier to ask forgiveness than permission, I thanked the angry-looking Major for his call and broke the link.

I switched my attention back to the girl.

'What's your name?' I asked.

'My real name or what we tell the customers?' she asked, trying to use bravado to overcome her fear and failing.

'Whichever.'

'Morag, Morag McGrath.' I assumed it was her real name and briefly wondered who would call their child Morag in this day and age.

'Okay, Morag, let's hear what it has to say,' I said.

'You can't hear it,' she said. 'You don't have enough flesh.' Nice, I thought. If the girl was to be believed, a member of an alien race that wanted to wipe out humanity was questioning my humanity. On the other hand, very few of the hookers had any form of cybernetics. They couldn't afford it, and most of their customers wanted smooth flesh, not hard metal and plastic. I smiled.

'That's convenient, Morag. How's it talking to you and your friends?' I asked.

'It's like a tickle.' It would seem that Morag was now the spokesperson for both the alien and the rest of the prostitutes. Morag seemed to be thinking about what she was going to say next. 'Back here,' she said after some consideration, touching the back of her head.

What the fuck was going on? It was almost like a cult. It had to be exerting control over them. Perhaps they were more susceptible because of their youth. The problem was at any moment Bran was going to turn up and kill everyone.

'Okay, Morag, you've seen the vizzis, yes? Them, the aliens who attack us and are trying to wipe us out, the war we've been fighting for the last sixty years, a war for survival, yes?' She nodded.

'Well that,' I said, nodding towards the alien, 'is one of them. An infiltrator, what we call a Ninja, and it is here to kill someone, and I have to stop it. What it's doing is called mind control. I'm afraid I'm going to have to move you and get on with it. If you can leave the room, you should. I'll try not to hurt any of you.' As one they all wrapped themselves around the wounded alien, causing ripples in its wounded physiology. All except Morag.

'No,' Morag said, suddenly sounding more confident. I looked at the human shield and then Morag. Wonderful, I thought to myself.

'So you've been in this thing's presence for a couple of hours and you're ready to die for it?' I asked.

'It's hope.' The girl turned to the alien. 'No,' she said, tears beginning to well in her eyes for the first time since I'd entered the room. The young prostitutes began disentangling themselves from the alien lying on the cot. Now all of them were crying. Morag turned to me. 'It doesn't understand why you could hurt a member of your own race. It doesn't understand why we're treated like this. It doesn't understand why everyone does not have as much food and safety as everyone else,' she said through the tears. I didn't really have an answer. My childhood had been bliss compared to hers and her only way off the Rigs was the draft lottery.

Now I had a clear shot at the alien, I aimed. Once more I caught sight of my distorted burnt features reflected in the black pool of its body. We both looked like monsters. It did not matter if it was talking to the kids, controlling them, I had to kill it, like so many others, to get the Major off my back and return to normality. The fights, the races, the booze and the sense booths, my normality. I lowered my gun.

'Okay,' I said through gritted teeth. 'Ask it why They fight us.' Morag seemed to think for a while.

'Defence,' she said finally.

'Bollocks.' I raised the revolver and started to squeeze the trigger. Then I relaxed and gently pushed the hammer down and lowered the gun. I'm still not sure I could tell you why. I just wasn't in the presence of malevolence, and it was my instinct telling me this. The instinct that had come with the original meat, not the metal and plastic I had become. There was audible relief from the prostitutes.

'Thank you,' Morag said.

'Great, just great,' I said. What the fuck was I doing? This was treason. I was siding with an enemy I hated and who wanted to destroy me and everyone who looked like me. And why was I doing this? I was doing this because of the say-so of a few cheap rig whores.

I was sure I was being mind-controlled or this was part of some new psychological strategy of Theirs. But the people telling me not to kill the alien were people I had no reason to distrust. The man telling me to kill the alien I neither liked nor trusted. The scale of it was terrifying: it was too big and I couldn't possibly take responsibility for this.

The touch of the thing on my burnt skin was disgusting. It was like some kind of abrasive vinyl substance just beneath the surface of black water. It was not that it was an unpleasant sensation I was receiving from tactile feedback sensors and the few remaining nerves that hadn't been burnt, it was just what the thing rippling in my arms represented what I'd seen its brethren do. Colonial township after colonial township, their civilian populations completely butchered regardless of age, nobody spared, their remains displayed in warning. Villages that seemed to be painted in human flesh, fences made of human skin.

I couldn't explain what I was doing, why I was carrying this thing to the Forbidden Pleasure's helicopter pad, where MacFarlane's aircar was parked. I was still assuming it was mind control. Nor did I have the slightest idea of what I was intending to do with it. Morag walked with me.

'What are you doing?' I growled.

'I'm coming with you, Mister.' I really didn't have time for this. I turned round to the girl, and she looked up at me, brown eyes wide and wet.

'A lot of bad people are going to be coming for me—'

'But they'll come here first,' she said. She had a point.

'I'll drop you somewhere,' I said and continued towards the aircar. She had to jog to keep up. The lock burner opened the car and I placed the alien across the back seat. Morag climbed into the passenger seat. The Saab smelt damp and faintly of shit and blood. People had been hurt in it. I overrode its security before starting it up and jacking into the car's system. I didn't like some of the diagnostics I was seeing on my internal visual display but the pimp's car would have to suffice. With a whine the car took roughly to the air. We climbed out above the jumbled superstructure of the Rigs. The sparse and intermittent lights and trash fires winked at us through ancient, corroded and tangled metal.

'Morag,' I said to the prostitute who was cradling one of humanity's enemies on the back seat. She wriggled free and leaned towards me. 'I need you to reach into the big pocket on my jeans and remove what you find there.' She looked at me sceptically. 'Just do it,' I ordered her brusquely. She did as I asked and pulled out a smooth black rectangle of expensive tech. 'Jack me in,' I told her. She pulled on the jack, reeling out the cord and pushing it into one of the four plugs in the back of my neck. I felt it click into place beneath my skin, once a deeply unpleasant sensation, now commonplace.

'What is it?' she asked, her voice showing curiosity despite her underlying fear. The nose of the aircar sank as I powered it forward and headed towards the neon of central Dundee.

'Most soldiers and all special ops people have transponders implanted in them so they can be tracked on the battlefield.' I nodded towards the black block she'd just jacked me into. 'That is an electronic countermeasures block. I'm going to jam my signal.' I left out that the transponders were also of use for when the amount of plastic and metal outweighed your soul and turned you into a machine deep in the grip of psychosis. I also left out that while on active service most special ops types could switch their transponders on and off. For those times when it was important nobody knew where you were or what you were doing.

Everything went white, bright white. My flash compensators tried with little success to damp down the brightness. My audio filters shut down so I felt rather than heard the explosion. They were still letting in the frequencies that allowed me to hear Morag's terrified scream and the sound of metal being punctured. The aircar was hurled forward as I desperately tried to control the machine. Through the drugs I was dimly aware of the heat and the signals that would normally be pain coming from my leg. I was also dimly aware of wetness on my trouser leg and wetness of a different consistency coating me. I realised I was tasting alien.

As the bright light subsided I managed to piece together what had happened while brutally bringing the car's backup system online. Morag was sobbing silently; I think she was too scared to make a noise. Foul-smelling steam surrounded the aircar. Debris floated or fell past us, some of it raining down on the car. I could see the outside through a hole in the floor of the car. There was a matching one in the ceiling and in my badly bleeding leg.

Behind us there was a steaming crater where the Forbidden Pleasure used to be. The crater was rapidly being filled with the polluted river water of the Tay. Even after everything I had seen I was still appalled that Rolleston, or his masters, would use an orbital weapon on an Earth-side city. The alien had also been hit, shot through the car. Much of its liquid flesh coated the inside of the car, though there was still a semi-solid, faintly humanoid mass on the terrified Morag's lap.

It was Bran, it had to be, somewhere on one of the rigs. Probably perilously close to where she'd called in the orbital strike. She had us in the crosshairs of her smartlinked sniper railgun. She'd killed the alien, tidied up the witnesses and given me a warning shot because there was no way she would have missed unless she chose to. Blood was pissing out of my leg, pooling in the footwell and even leaking out of the hole made by Bran's railgun.

I managed to keep the Saab in the air as I reached into one of the many pockets of my long coat and removed a stim patch and attached it to my neck. It would keep me awake but I needed to do something about the bleeding; my self-repair systems were good but I was losing way too much blood. I cursed myself for not having brought my first-aid kit. The split screen on my internal visual display showed me what was going on around the aircar. I was controlling the vehicle through my interface; this left my hands free to search for an in-car medical kit. I found one but most of its contents were long gone.

Morag was still sobbing quietly. Her world, regardless of how bad it had been, had just disappeared in a moment of light and heat.

'Morag?' I said. She ignored me. I could see her fading into shock. 'Morag!' Her head jerked around to face me. 'Can you fly this?' I asked her. I already knew the answer but I wanted her mind on something else. She shook her head, her lips tight and bloodless, face pale under her make-up. I cracked a smile on the burnt visage of my ruined face. 'That's unfortunate.' She gaped at me before my completely inappropriate humour made her smile and shake her head. I held the wound on my leg closed and headed for the city.

# 6
# Dundee

I broke into the car's autopilot systems and gave it illegal instructions. I sent out a heavily coded text, cycling it through the cryptography sub-routines of my ECM block and screaming it to emphasise the urgency. The Rigs were no longer beneath us; we were over dry land now. Beneath us were the huddled makeshift stalls, rafts and junks of the harbour markets. Many of the people were making their way to the riverside to see the aftermath of the explosion. I suspected that many of them thought that They had come and were attacking Earth. After all, They would obviously start with Dundee, I thought, smiling to myself.

The bright commercial lights of Dundee's Ginza were up ahead of us. Flashing neon hologramatic signs simultaneously offering us all the happiness that material goods could offer while warning us of the sacrifices that we all had to make because of the war. There was also news from the front, the duelling strobes of light from yet another space battle above Dog 1, cut with ground action, armoured vehicles, mechs and tired infantry wading through mud in one direction and air ambulances going in the other.

We were on the outskirts of the true Ginza. Scum like us were kept out by heavy police and store security presence. Outside the true Ginza were the knock-off shops and cheap food stalls that the rest of us could afford. All of it hidden beneath the raised toll roads that salary men and women used to get to work and to go shopping. The true Ginza looked like a bright fairy-tale world compared to what the salary men and women called Underside and the rest of us called Dundee.

I nosed the aircar down one of the off ramps into Commercial Street. People eyed the wealth of an aircar suspiciously as we landed. Most of them were just people trying to make a living in Dundee's non-corporate grey economy, but I could see the usual spatter of ultra-violents and conscientious-objecting gangsters. Some of the more proactive ones made their way towards the car as the door slid open. I turned back to the rear seat.

'Can you carry it?' I asked Morag urgently. She nodded, her face a tear-stained mess of cheap make-up. 'Find something to wrap it in. Nobody can see it, do you understand me?' She didn't seem to be listening. 'Morag!' I said. She looked up at me.

'They'll be tracking us?' she asked.

'Maybe, maybe not.'

The bonnet of the car slid back accordion-style at my command and I removed the car interface jack from my plug and began tampering with the aircar's fuel cell. A little trick insurgency training had taught us.

'You all right, pal?' I heard a voice behind me ask. 'Your leg sore?' I turned around to find myself looking at an ugly young man with bad cybernetics and even worse skin. He was wearing this year's iteration of what the street scum around town wore. He took one look at my burnt features and general poor mood and backed off, his hand coming out of his armoured tracksuit top. 'No problem, pal,' he said, having decided against robbing us.

I turned back to the car and finished what I was doing as Morag got out. She had wrapped it in the tartan car blanket that seems to come free with every car in Scotland. The blanket was dripping with its ichor. I gave the ECM block its last instruction then removed the jack and dropped it into the footwell of the aircar, praying that Vicar had done what I'd asked.

'C'mon,' I said, and we headed towards the corner of Commercial and High Street. There stood an ancient pre-Final Human Conflict stone church. Moving light from within the building backlit the stained-glass windows covered in hundreds of years of city grime. Behind us the aircar took off. Morag watched it head down the High Street beneath the raised roadways. It wouldn't defeat satellite surveillance but hopefully it would slow Rolleston down enough to buy us some time. The only problem was I had lost my ECM block. I would need another or they would get my transponder.

'Isn't that really illegal?' she asked.

'Treason, associating with prostitutes.' I turned to look at her. 'I think you're a bad influence on me.' She managed a weak smile again but I think it may have been for my benefit. Hand inside my long coat, I approached the thick armoured double doors. The fact that they opened as I pushed gave me hope.

*

'… the white light was not Them! No! It was not one of their infernal weapons! The white light was from the sky, from heaven, it was judgement! The spear of God, a warning to those who would indulge in unholy couplings!' To give Vicar his credit he could adapt and improvise to make his sermons topical.

Inside was bare undressed stone. The stained-glass windows had holograms projected onto them. The stylised hellish vistas gave the inside of the church a reddish glow that seemed somehow warm, belying the horrific imagery. There were a number of plastic pews, where the truly wretched and miserable sat being lambasted by Vicar's sermons. Behind the altar and off to one side I could see Vicar's work area, various tools and banks of equipment, much of it jury-rigged or built from scratch by himself.

Vicar stood in the pulpit. Presumably it had once been made of wood but that had probably been traded, or burnt for fuel a long time ago. Now it was just a metal and plastic frame.

Vicar himself looked the same, maybe a little older, a little wilder around his already wild eyes. He wore a black vest and dog collar, his powerful frame just beginning to go to seed. He had a long unkempt salt-and-pepper beard, and still-human eyes if you ignored the look in them.

Half his head was covered in long, matted curly hair, the same salt and pepper as his beard. The other half was ugly military tech, a built-in, fast and powerful computer, but as with most military tech it made absolutely no concession to design aesthetics. I could see more elegant add-ons that had presumably been done by Vicar himself in order to keep up with technology and improve his shelf life as a hacker. In his day he'd been one of the best, and as such was drafted into the Signals Corps, and from there he became Green Slime, Military so-called Intelligence. Vicar was still no slouch today, though presumably he had been superseded, like all of us, by the younger, faster and hungrier.

'Out!' I barked at Vicar's ragged congregation as I limped into the church, holding the wound in my leg together.

'This is a house of God!' Vicar screamed at me, drool dangling off his beard. The congregation tried to decide who they were most afraid of. My Mastodon being pulled free of its holster gave me the edge, and the desperate-looking congregation scrambled out the door past Morag and me.

'Lock us down, Vicar,' I said. 'Now!' Vicar ran an appraising glance over the state I was in. His eyes lingered on Morag, still in her worn basque, before finally looking at the car blanket dripping black ichor onto the floor.

'What kind of party are we having, Jakob?' he asked.

'Lock it down,' I said again, this time more forcefully. Behind me I heard numerous heavy-sounding locks clank into place on the armoured door, now that the last of the congregation had gone. Vicar smiled his mad, wild smile as concertinaed salvaged armour plate unfolded around the walls and roof of the old church.

'There used to be a castle on this land as far back as AD 80,' Vicar said.

'Fascinating. Did you do it?' I asked. Vicar was staring at Morag, undisguised lust in his eyes as they travelled up her body. He moved closer to her as I grimaced and tried to hold the wound in my leg closed. Morag flinched slightly but held her ground as Vicar reached out and touched her.

'And the woman was arrayed in purple and scarlet colour, and decked with gold and precious stones and pearls, having a golden cup in her hand full of abominations and filthiness of her fornication,' he said quietly, as he used his soft fleshy fingers to move her head from one side to the other, his voice low, breathy and excited.

Suddenly he yanked the travel blanket from her, and its contents fell to the ground with a wet thump. Vicar looked furious. I wasn't sure if it was for show or not. His voice rose until he was shouting furiously into the frightened young girl's face.

'And there appeared another wonder in heaven: and behold a great red dragon, having seven heads and ten horns and seven crowns upon his heads.' I really didn't have time for this. This was why I hated dealing with hackers.

'This is important, Vicar,' I said harshly. His head twitched round to look at me. 'Did you do it?'

'You owe me,' he said, smiling and then casting another glance at Morag.

'Did you do it?' I asked again. I was beginning to feel angry despite the fact that ostensibly I was trying to get Vicar to do me a favour.

'Do you know where we are now?' he further irritated me by asking rhetorically. 'I mean humans as a people?'

'Did you do it!' I was looking around, trying to think of a contingency. Had Vicar hacked into Dundee's traffic control and sent misleading information about our landing? Was he using ECM to block my transponder?

'We have opened the second seal; war is on the land,' he said, quieter now, the glint of mania still present in his eyes. I opened my mouth to angrily demand an answer to my question again. 'Of course I fucking did it!' he snapped. 'You owe me.' His gaze went to Morag again and then to the alien bleeding black ichor onto the stone floor of the church.

'They're not aliens, you know,' he said. I gritted my teeth as the painkillers I had taken for the burns were either beginning to wear off or just weren't up to the task. I limped over to one of the pews.

'Have you still got the med suite?' I asked. My question seemed to shake him out of his thoughts. He looked up from the wounded alien and then down at my leg. He nodded.

'You're wounded,' he said.

'Not for me,' I replied, and then pointed at the alien. 'For that.' Vicar looked down at it, seemed to give some consideration to the matter and then shrugged. He picked its light form up and walked down past the altar and into the nave. I stood up and followed at a limp, Morag with me.

There were various banks of electronic equipment here. Most of it was for net running or building and maintaining electronic equipment, but there was some ancient jury-rigged medical diagnostic and treatment equipment. I was being generous when I described it as a suite.

'This is unlikely to do any good,' Vicar said. 'Doubtless Their physiology is as incompatible as their psychology.' He began hooking up the alien to his equipment. I searched around on top of one of his other dirty workbenches until I managed to find some accelerant and a knitter and went to work on my leg. Moments later Morag handed me some salve to clean and soothe my burns.

'This is weird,' Vicar muttered as he began firing up the equipment.

'Oh, you think?' I asked sarcastically.

'Your background notwithstanding,' he said, meaning my time in the SAS. 'I was seconded to Military Intelligence during my active service and we knew nothing about Them. We knew no more than the average squaddie and we could never get hold of one of Them or any of Their tech. It was always destroyed before it got to us. All we knew was They wanted to kill us, that They hated us.' He frowned, presumably as he received some information on his internal visual display.

'You said they weren't aliens?' Morag asked nervously. Vicar turned to look at her. Once he had had an eyeful he started talking again, though still staring at her.

'There is no apparent purpose to Them. They appear to exist only to inflict suffering on humanity. They are here to test us.' Morag seemed to be drinking in his words.

'So what are They?' she asked falteringly. I knew what was coming. I'd heard variations of this spiel before.

'Demons,' Vicar said, as dramatically as he could manage. Morag looked up at me and I shrugged.

'He's not a demon,' she muttered quietly and then looked down at her hands. Vicar either didn't hear her or chose not to respond. He got the Ninja settled into the cradle of the ad hoc medical suite and turned to look at me.

'What's going on? What are you doing with this?' he asked, nodding at the creature. I realised I didn't really have an answer, at least not one that made sense. What was I doing? I was taking the word of a group of rig hookers over my chain of command and committing treason against my entire species at the same time.

'I want to talk to it,' I said. Vicar's head jerked around to look at me, his businesslike manner gone.

'Who're you running from?' he demanded.

'Rolleston,' I said. Vicar nodded.

'Understand this,' he said, pointing at the creature. 'Those are the servants of the adversary. If They speak They will only offer lies and we have no business communing with Them.' He turned back to look at the creature.

'That sounds like Rolleston,' I said, though I didn't really mean it. Vicar was busy examining his machines, a look of concentration on his face.

'Repent,' he said, though clearly his mind was on other things as he searched through an old filing cabinet. 'Or else I will come unto thee quickly, and will fight against them with the sword of my mouth.' He found what he was looking for, pulling out a solid-state memory cube, something that could hold an unimaginable amount of information. He placed a couple of jacks into two of the plugs in the back of his skull, plugging the other end of one into the medical suite and the other into the memory block. I stood up.

'What are you doing?' I asked. Vicar ignored me. His eyes rolled back up into their sockets, an affectation that signalled he was in the net. I took this opportunity to search around Vicar's workspace until I found what I was looking for. There were a number of different ECM blocks. I picked what I thought was the best one and ran a diagnostic on it. It wasn't working right so I chose another and another until I found one that was still functioning properly.

'That'll cost you,' a disembodied voice said. Morag jumped, but it was Vicar, in the net but presumably still linked up to the internal surveillance systems of the church. The voice came from a speaker on the pulpit.

'How are you intending on paying for all this, by the way?' Vicar's tinny disembodied voice asked.

'I'm sure we can work something—' I began, not really having a good answer. Fortunately the alien lost all cohesion at that moment, distracting us from the topic of money. One second it was solid, the next there was black liquid raining down on the stone floor of the church and soaking through the patched fabric cradle of the medical suite. I looked at it in astonishment, though I don't know why. I'd seen this happen to the aliens all through the Sirius system, but for some reason here, in my hometown, it still seemed to come as a surprise. Morag let out a little whimpering noise.

'Vicar, what's going on?' I demanded.

'It's all right,' came the tinny voice from the pulpit's speaker. 'It was pretty much dead when it got here,' said Vicar coming out of his net-running trance. 'But I managed to save some of it.' He looked thoughtful and surprisingly sane.

'What are you talking about?' I asked. I was beginning to think that I had risked my life for even less than usual.

'It's like I said, we never got our hands on one before. Their dissolution was always too perfect, all that was left was genetic junk.' He then lapsed into apparent deep thought again.

'So?' I demanded. This seemed to break him from some kind of reverie.

'Hmm? Oh, yes, well, according to the diagnostics I've run it appears They are some kind of bio-technological construct. Though it is just possible that They have occurred naturally, or rather They have much more control over how They evolve. That would explain the different castes, the Ninjas and the Berserks.' This was old news, it had been posited for some time. I couldn't really see how it would help. 'The technology is almost like naturally-occurring nanites, only it's liquid. It's difficult to say what these aliens are. The race itself could be the individual cells and each bioform may be a colony or even an entire civilisation of Them.'

'Well that's very interesting, Vicar, but what does it mean?' I asked. There was only so long we could stay in the church before Rolleston worked out where we were.

'I'm not sure,' he mused. 'What it does mean is that our intelligence should have had this info years ago.'

'Shoot to kill?' I said, meaning the policy of utter eradication whenever we encountered them. Vicar shrugged. Then something occurred to me. 'With technology like that, why not go viral? They could wipe us out in moments.'

'I don't know, perhaps some kind of societal taboo? Perhaps they see it as a form of suicide, but with this information we could certainly do it to them.'

'If we hand this over then we can end the war?' I asked.

'If we hand this over then we provide our masters with the means to end the war,' he said. He sounded doubtful. But this was a weapon; our masters liked weapons and they also liked victory. 'And when he had opened the second seal, I heard the second beast say, come and see. And there went out another horse that was red: and power was given to him that sat thereon to take peace from the Earth, and that they should kill one another: and there was given unto him a great sword,' Vicar said as he straightened up to face me.

'I don't understand any of that,' I said.

'War is loosed upon the land, the second seal is open,' he replied, talking to me as though I were a particularly dense child. 'Perhaps the war is the important thing. It's the taking part that matters after all.'

'What are you talking about? You mean they wouldn't use this information?'

Vicar just shrugged.

'I don't think we should give them the info,' Morag burst out. Both of us turned to look at her. She looked frightened, as if she wished she hadn't spoken. 'I mean, would it be that easy? To reprogram their bionanites to attack them?' She seemed to have a much better grasp of what was going on than I did.

'It depends on how cooperative They're being,' said Vicar. 'I hacked the creature, or rather it gave me entry, and with technology that sophisticated it should have taken me a lot longer. I should have needed to build a whole new set of equipment to translate the alien data and I should have had a tremendous fight on my hands against alien intrusion countermeasures.' I still wasn't following and it must have been obvious by the look on my face. There were rumours that certain technology would allow meat hacks through interface plugs, but if it existed then it was blacker than black. 'All DNA is information, but before it died it made certain information compatible with my systems.' This still wasn't making any sense to me. I hated information technology.

'You downloaded it,' Morag said, surprising me again. Vicar nodded.

'That was what the solid-state memory block was for,' I said, pleased I could finally make a contribution to the conversation. Vicar nodded again.

'It's isolated in there. I've set up a routine that's building it an environment.'

'I want to speak with it,' I said.

'Then you talk with the adversary ...' Vicar began.

'And hear only lies,' I finished for him.

'He's not like that,' Morag said.

'You are just a whore, one of his already, and you have been seduced,' Vicar said, getting back into character. I couldn't understand why Morag looked so upset. Surely she'd heard crap like this before, and probably worse.

'Why do you talk like that?' she asked. Vicar ignored her.

'Religious mania,' I answered for him. 'A lot of hackers get it. They say they see things in the net, the face of God, shit like that. It's the dislocation of net running, I think. It's like isolation and they start to hallucinate. Something about it triggers the parts of our brain to do with religion; they all end up like this or madder.' I left out that Vicar had been on Operation Spiral, an attempt by the UK and US governments to hack Their communications infrastructure.

'There are things in the net,' Vicar said quietly and then looked me straight in the eyes, his madness reflected in my black lenses. 'And I do not believe in God.' Suddenly his madness looked really sane in a way I could not explain, and this wasn't the first time either. I remembered the coldness of space and the blood of humans on my hands. Despite the fact that Vicar was just looking into inhuman black lenses I broke eye contact first.

'So what are you doing here?' I asked.

'Preparation,' he said. I decided it was a waste of time trying to get a straight answer from him.

'I want to speak to it,' I repeated. Vicar shrugged. He walked over to the workbench and held up a plug connected to the memory cube. I pulled a rusty folding chair over to the bench and sat down.

'Take your time,' Vicar said. 'Your whore can work off some of your debt to me.'

'I don't think so,' I said, my voice sounding cold even to myself.

'I don't mind,' Morag said timidly. I looked over at the frightened young girl and then back to Vicar's leer.

'I do. Vicar,' I said. He ignored me. 'Vicar,' I said loudly and reached for his arm with my cybernetic right hand, exerting just a little too much pressure. His head snapped round to look at me. Why was I doing this? She was a hooker; what difference did it make to me if she went with Vicar? 'I appreciate what you've done for us, I really do, but if you lay one finger on her I'll take the laser to your groin. Do you understand me?' I asked. He glared at me and then turned to Morag.

'And I gave her space to repent of her fornication; and she repented not. Behold I will cast her into a bed, and them that commit adultery with her into great tribulation, except they repent of their deeds. And I will kill her children with death.' He spat at her. Morag looked like she was about to cry.

'Pack it in!' I told him. I looked at Morag stood in the chapel, wearing her working gear. Vicar was still staring at her, intimidating her. Presumably made easier by the fact that she was only wearing a basque, torn fishnets and panties.

'Have you got any other clothes that Morag could wear?' I asked him. He turned to look at me, an unpleasant grin on his face.

'You want her for yourself, don't you?' he said. 'Play the protective routine so you don't have to pay? Is that it? Cheap bastard.' I was tempted to hit him but we needed him. I leant in close to him, close enough to smell the gum disease.

'Clothes,' I said. Vicar directed Morag to some donated clothes he kept to hand out to his congregation and then plugged me in.

I felt the familiar sense of floating and dislocation, loss of the sense of a physical self. The software he was using was the same as they used for the sense booths, sending information to my brain via my interface plugs to make the virtual environment feel real. It wasn't like running the net – normally it would be completely safe, there were feedback safeguards in place – but the alien was an unknown. If it was as sophisticated as Vicar said, then perhaps I was in actual danger.

The environment rushed up around me in a pixelated haze, the resolution slowly improving. It wasn't the high-definition neon animation VR of the net but rather the more naturalistic realism of sense software. I felt familiar boots sink into familiar mud. I was on a plain surrounded by the sawn-off stumps of dead alien trees. I was wearing full battle gear, my Heckler & Koch Squad automatic weapon strapped horizontally across my chest.

What the fuck was Vicar playing at? I was back on Dog 4. In the distance the horizon lit up in an artillery duel. Above me the bright lances of light strobed across the azure night sky, as our fleet and Theirs went at it in high orbit. A figure was making its way towards me through the dead forest. I tried magnifying my optics, unsure if it would work under the rules of this environment. It did and I was less than pleased to see Gregor making his way towards me. He was also in full battle gear, the hardened ceramic breastplate with kinetic padding and a suit of reactive inertial armour beneath it. His railgun was slung up on his right side on its gyroscopic mount. The entire right side of his body was a smoking mess, all but gone; he was practically walking on bone. I reached up to touch my face, expecting to find it also burnt but instead found the smooth hard flesh of skin and sub-dermal armour. It was just like Dog 4, just like my dream.

I considered firing a burst into the visage of my old friend, just to see what would happen, but found that I couldn't quite bring myself to shoot at something that looked so much like him. It approached me and stopped. Its eyes were black pools with stars in them. I waited. Nothing.

'Do you have to look like that?' I asked. It looked too much like a failure, a mistake, a betrayal of mine.

'This is yours,' it said. It even sounded like Gregor. It seemed like the alien had control of the environment and had chosen it from my subconscious. This was worrying enough. The question was had it been trying to make me feel comfortable and chosen the wrong thing or was it trying to put me off guard, fucking with me?

'Is there something else we could be?' it asked, Gregor's voice flat, no feeling. I nodded and watched it turn. The low, sleek, black, off-centre humanoid shape of a Berserk. Its multiple limbs ending in long powerful claw-like fingers except the one that wore the bulky weapon glove with its splinter gun and other Swiss Army Knife-like weaponry accoutrements. The only difference was that Berserks were matt black; this one seemed to reflect the light, and like Gregor's eyes its skin seemed to contain the stars. It looked like a portion of space. That reminded me of the Ninja that had taken out the rest of the Wild Boys and infected Gregor.

'Yeah, that's better,' I said. 'Let's not forget what we both are.' It didn't say anything. 'Who are you?' I asked.

'We are Ambassador. Though you make us look like murder/slaughter.'

'What do you want?' I asked, trying to make sense of his words, perhaps it was having to deal with Vicar but I was wishing that I could just have a normal conversation with someone.

'We need peace,' it said.

'Yeah?' I said sarcastically, and then wondered if it understood sarcasm. 'Stop attacking us.'

'We cannot, until you do. You will not listen.' Suddenly I was moving towards it rapidly. Without seeming to have taken a step, it grew to fill my vision, and I hit it. It felt like I had flown through a thin veil of water and I was screaming as I seemed to fall through space. Quickly I managed to control myself and look around, rolling in apparent free fall as I did. In the distance I could see the blue marble of Earth. I could dimly make out the various orbital stations that formed a defensive ring around it. As a grunt there was no need for my spatial geography to be up to much, but I guessed we were in high orbit.

I spun around but Ambassador, or whatever it was, was nowhere to be seen. Then I saw the burn; it was a pale-blue colour. It was one of Their ships. There was no doubt about that, though it was a configuration I'd never seen before. Roughly conical in shape, it looked like a series of separate, aerodynamic seed pods joined together, attached to a faster-than-light engine unit. It was difficult to make out, because it was set up for stealth, only the burn of the manoeuvring engines giving it away. Space seemed to pulse. I could not make out what was happening but I saw part of the craft seem to crumple, flame from within, briefly and silently blossoming, before being sucked out into the vacuum and disappearing. The craft seemed to fall apart but it was just the engine system being jettisoned explosively. Each of the pods was a separate stealth re-entry Needle. All of them were heading for Earth. Space pulsed again and again, the light from distant stars disappearing and then reappearing almost instantaneously as more and more of the re-entry pods crumpled and silently blew themselves apart.

I had always found the silence of space battles eerie, a view I seemed to share with most of humanity judging by the rousing music and special effects they were enhanced with on news broadcasts. I finally worked out what the pulsing was. I traced it back and made out a stealthed craft, this time of human design but more sophisticated than most I'd seen. It was firing some kind of black laser, presumably similar to Their black light weapons. One after another, the re-entry pods were destroyed.

Earth's orbital defences probably would not even be able to detect this distant conflict. They did not seem to be fighting back. It looked like all of the pods were being destroyed but suddenly I found myself shooting through space. I did a bit more screaming before I managed to get a grip. I was in near orbit now. Just in time to see a damaged pod make it through the orbital defence cordon apparently undetected, which meant significant stealth tech, and flame flower briefly as it hit the atmosphere. I guessed it must have been read as a meteor or something. This was it; this was the craft I'd found in the park. The pilot was the creature that Vicar had downloaded. I felt disoriented to the point of nausea as I found myself looking at Gregor again on the plain of mud and dead trees.

'Why won't you let us talk to you?' it asked. Did I imagine a tinge of desperation in its voice?

'Aaagh!' It took a moment to realise it was me screaming. I was in the church again, very sudden, real shock. I doubled over and retched, a little bit of bile dribbling out onto the floor. Someone had just yanked me out. Vicar was stood behind me, cable in one hand, a heavy-calibre automatic in the other.

'What the fuck!' I managed.

'The red rider is here,' he said, the mad glint back in his eyes.

'What?' I demanded.

'The people you're hiding from,' Morag said. She had changed and was wearing some kind of hard-wearing but threadbare baggy trousers with many utilitarian pockets, a pair of boots which looked a little too big for her and a hoody bearing the logo of a band or music collective or product that I was unfamiliar with. She'd cleaned her make-up off and tied her hair back in a ponytail. She looked more like a young girl and less like a sex crime now.

'Rolleston?' I asked. Vicar nodded. I stood up, still feeling somewhat disoriented.

'Well?' Vicar asked.

'It said it wants peace,' I told him.

'Lies,' Vicar said, but even he did not sound sure of himself.

'No,' Morag said. She did sound sure of herself.

'Was that thing set up for infiltration and assassination?' I asked him. Vicar considered this.

'Infiltration obviously, assassination I don't think so, but it could be a psy-op,' he said, and I knew he was right.

'How long have we got?' I asked. Vicar smiled.

'They are nearly at the door.' He handed me the solid-state memory cube that contained Ambassador.

'What?' I said. 'What do you want me to do?'

'I am going to try and slow up Rolleston and the Grey Lady for as long as possible. Take this to Pagan, tell him this is the path to the one true God,' he said, as if that should mean something. 'In Hull,' he continued.

'Hull's gone,' I said.

'The Avenues. He'll find you.'

'Vicar?' Rolleston's voice asked smoothly from a nearby communicator. Vicar looked at me, his eyes almost sane. I nodded, unable to understand why he was sacrificing himself like this. I turned and headed for the hole in the stone floor that led down to some ancient crypt. I noticed that Morag was carrying a grey canvas shoulder bag as I stepped into the hole.

# 7
# Dundee

I reached up. Morag felt tiny between my metal and flesh hands; she seemed to weigh next to nothing as I lifted her down. The last of the light went as Vicar moved something very heavy over the hole. Darkness. Thermals did not help much as there was no heat down here. Then I made out the line of radioactive paint that pointed our way out. It was stale, cold and dry down here, the air thick with dust as I breathed in millennia-old dead people. I heard Morag whimper next to me.

'Don't worry, I can see,' I said, not entirely meaning it. She jumped at the sound of my voice in the darkness, even though she was holding on to me. I could make her out silhouetted in the red, oranges, greens and blues of the thermographics. I felt a strangely voyeuristic thrill at the beauty of a person's heat signature seen in the dark. I thought I could hear Vicar's heavily muffled raised voice above me.

'C'mon,' I said and began pulling Morag down the radioactive line of paint, banging my head and bumping into things as I dragged her after me.

The exit was a tunnel of poured concrete that Vicar must have made himself. I could smell the unmistakeable odour of sewage and pollution that was the Tay at the end of the tunnel. I could see large rodent heat signatures in the tunnel and, beyond, black waters and the intermittent heat signatures of the Rigs.

'Mind the rats,' I told Morag, not so much a problem to my various layers but the diseases they carried would do the girl no good. I made enough noise going along to try and scare them. They ignored me. I was the trespasser in their world. The plastic and metal they weren't interested in but they knew flesh. Eventually I ended up carrying Morag.

At the end of the tunnel I peered out, looking for Rolleston's people. We were beneath one of the raised toll roads, the multiple-lane motorway that headed out over the Tay towards Fife and more parkland. The water either side of the bridge was clear. The Rigs used to reach this far up the river, but like the old road bridge they had long since been rendered down into waste by metal- and concrete-eating microbes to make way for the toll roads.

Out on the Tay, east of the new bridge, I could see a police riverine patrol boat making its way towards the far bank and the lights of Newport-on-Tay. On dry land behind us, beneath the toll road, were the various dregs of Dundee: junkies, the odd traditional drunk, trash burners and assorted homeless – people like us. They all looked authentic enough; that kind of resigned desperation is difficult to fake.

'I'm going to have to put you down now,' I told Morag. She nodded. There was a sucking noise as her boots sank into the soft, polluted, foul-smelling Tay mud.

'Where to?' she asked me. She was obviously afraid but coping well. It was a good question. I was dead. Rolleston would just hunt me until I was dead, and he had the resources to make sure it happened. I leant against the wall and lit up my penultimate cigarette, dragging down a lungful of the wasted sweet smoke, my internal filters already removing all the poisons. My life would be spent on the run. A series of near misses, each one getting closer and closer until the Major, or more likely the Grey Lady, got me. I looked down at the frightened young girl beside me. She looked back at me expectantly.

'You got kin?' I asked her. She nodded.

'Where?'

'Fintry.' Christ, I thought, the Rigs must've seemed quite appealing to her. Even by Dundee's standards Fintry was a shit hole.

'They sold you into the life?' I asked. She nodded.

'They got quite a lot of crystal for me 'cause I was pretty and young,' she added by way of explanation. I didn't ask her how old she'd been. Fucking wonderful, I thought. This girl may have even fewer options than I did. I took another drag of the cigarette; the glow lit up my burnt face and I saw Morag flinch.

'You got people you can go to?' I asked. She looked like she'd been slapped. I turned and made my way through the sucking mud towards the intermittent lights of the Rigs. I heard her struggle through the mud after me.

'Hey,' she said. I ignored her. 'Hey!' I kept going. 'Fucking stop, you cunt!' she yelled. I stopped and swung round on her.

'I'm dead, do you understand me?' I asked. 'The people I've pissed off don't stop and never fail. Sooner or later they will find me and kill me. Now I don't know whether or not they know about you, but if they don't the best thing you can do is run and hide as best you can.' She looked up at me. I couldn't quite read her expression; the fear was gone and something else was there. She looked like she was going to argue and then suddenly the life was sucked out of her.

'So where are you going to die?' she asked. I hadn't really thought that through.

'Dunno,' I said. I hadn't got enough cash for the booths, though that would've been nice. Drifting away, becoming disembodied in spirit. The Grey Lady quietly entering the booth and snipping my silver cord with a bullet, blade or toxin. That would be peaceful. 'I guess I'll get some cigarettes, go back to my cube, put on some Miles Davis and drink as much whisky as I can before they come for me.' Morag nodded.

'Sounds kind of nice,' she said. I smoked my cigarette down to the filter and flicked it into the mud. I turned and headed back towards the Rigs. Morag kept pace with me. I let this continue for a while, before stopping again.

'What are you doing?' I asked her, thinking that despite my earlier impressions she was just in fact another dumb rig girl.

'Coming with you,' she said. I stared at her for a while, knowing that all she would see would be her own reflection in the black polarised lenses that use to be my eyes, but she stared back at me defiantly.

'I'm going to get killed. I don't think you understand. This is no media. These guys don't miss and have endless resources. To all intents and purposes it's the government after me.'

'What've I got?' she asked. And then it struck me – Ambassador, what Vicar had said, the trip to Hull. False hope or not, this was probably the only hope she'd ever had. If she wasn't already, then soon she would be old enough to get drafted and she'd end up a recreational worker, servicing the troops, officers first while her looks held up, then NCOs, then the squaddies. She would be used up by her early twenties. If she were lucky, sneaky, vicious and preyed on her fellow whores she would get NCO rank. Do unto others as she'd had done to herself. More likely she'd be discharged with no trade skills, not even the basic infantry skills of survival. If she dodged the draft it would be much the same, only in a more Darwinian environment. Coming back to my cube, drinking some whisky, listening to jazz and waiting to get shot in the head probably seemed like quite a good option for her.

'What about Ambassador?' she asked. It seemed to me she was trying desperately to keep the hope out of her voice.

'Darling, it's a pipe dream. The people it would need to speak to are the ones trying to kill it and us.'

'But we could go to Hull?' she asked.

'Yeah, we could die in Hull instead, but all things being equal I think I'd rather die in Dundee.'

'But if we could push this a little further, find out some more, maybe something'll happen?' she said, pathetic eagerness creeping into her voice. I was trying to decide what was worse. Destroying her hope outright or continuing down the road letting the hope build only to watch it crumble and die when they caught us.

Maybe it wouldn't come to that, I caught myself thinking as we resumed our trudge towards the Rigs. Maybe when the end was close enough and Morag had lived a little more than she should've with her assigned lot in life, a laser pistol to the back of her head would be kinder.

'I'll fuck you,' she said, offering the only currency she thought she had. I closed my eyes.

'Just ... Look, don't say that again,' I said.

'I'm sorry.'

'Don't fucking apologise!' I shouted, angry, not sure at whom, probably me. The offer to completely take advantage of her wasn't as abhorrent to me as it should've been. 'Just don't ... okay,' I said, more quietly. She looked scared and confused but I was relieved that it didn't look like she was going to burst into tears. 'Look, we don't have any money, no passes out of the city, no travel permission.'

'We have these,' Morag said, reaching into the canvas bag that Vicar had given her. She pulled out a bundle of paper cash. 'And this,' she said, holding up a pouch. I took it from her and looked inside. It contained rough, irregular-shaped yellow nuggets of metal. Probably Belt gold, not as valuable as the homegrown stuff but not something to turn your nose up at. 'And this.' She showed me a finance chip. I took the chip from her and plugged it into my chip reader. I let out a low whistle because it was an untraceable black chip, probably worth as much as the cash on it. More to the point it could be used with impunity even in corporate enclaves and Ginzas. In the big scheme of things we didn't have a fortune but we certainly had enough to be going on with. I wondered why Vicar had done this and why he'd martyred himself. What was so important about all this?

Peripheral vision registered the light behind me. I turned around to see the aircar float out from the city over the river, twin searchlights playing over the area. It looked like a high-end Mercedes. Despite its civilian configuration I didn't doubt for a minute that it was an armoured gun platform with an excellent sensor suite.

'Come on,' I said to Morag and dragged her under the rotting planks of what used to be the old commercial docks. We headed towards the riverside marketplace. They'd have thermographics and various motion sensors, both of which could be defeated if we were prepared to lie in the mud and crawl very slowly towards the Rigs. I was hoping to avoid that as the amount of toxic shit in the Tay would probably kill us in the long run, possibly the short run.

'Is that them?' Morag asked, out of breath.

I nodded.

'Why don't you just let them kill you?' she asked. I glared at her.

'Because I don't want to die in this mud,' I said. I'd had more than enough mud in my life. The Mercedes seemed to be searching further downstream. Perhaps they thought we were heading towards Perth on foot, or that Vicar had had the foresight to leave an escape craft of some kind, possibly even a submersible. In retrospect that wouldn't have been a bad idea.

We made it up into the bustling marketplace, hoping to lose ourselves among the other heat sources in the lines of stalls selling everything from tasteless vat protein mulch to dodgy black-market implants. The tarpaulin roofs of the stalls where blown about as the Mercedes took a low-altitude pass over the market.

A couple of times I saw people who stuck out, too clean, clothes too nice despite the effort to dress down. Occasionally they would seem to be listening to voices from elsewhere. Each time I was pretty sure we managed to avoid them. Morag was good, untrained but street smart and listened when I asked her to do something.

Eventually we made it through the market to the Rigs. We hurried onto a rickety catwalk of old pallets, the sludge of the river slopping around beneath us. We made our way up a scratch-built spiral staircase made of scrap metal. The staircase was about one quarter practical and three quarters dangerous self-expression on the part of its builder. We climbed up into the higher levels of the Rigs and headed deeper into the superstructure, both of us moving with the swiftness of long-term rig inhabitants.

I still wasn't sure what I was going to do. It would be so easy to take the money from Morag, maybe leave the girl with enough for her to indulge her own tastes for once or maybe just enough for her to survive for a while. I could go to the sense booths and just wait; the Grey Lady wouldn't make me suffer, she had no need to. It would be so easy I wouldn't feel a thing. I mean, this wasn't a media, I wasn't some guardian angel; I was just another arsehole trying to get by as best I could and now I'd failed. I was out of time. So fuck Morag, she wasn't my responsibility. But then she'd already offered that. I can't remember how I found myself outside McShit's and not the sense booths.

McShit's was a series of split-open cubes held by high-tensile wires around the central support of *Piper Dawn*, one of the older Rigs. The wire-hung cubes arrangement made for an interesting environment during bad weather.

Inside was the usual array of scavenged bar furniture you would expect from a rig pub. The bar itself was an inverted bulletproof screen from an old bank with a wooden counter haphazardly glued to the top. A mixture of flickering electric bulbs, gas-burning lamps and various naked flames provided illumination. A still bubbled away behind the bar.

The place was filled with the various rig denizens who could afford a vice that night and had settled on booze. The place was subdued, probably because of the orbital strike on the Forbidden Pleasure. Nobody paid us much attention.

I knew the barman. He was a Twist, one of McShit's kin. His name was Robby. Like all of McShit's kin, a generation or two back his familial genes had been screwed by some viral weapon, pollutant or too much exposure to depleted uranium, and as a result he was born stunted. This didn't stop them being used by humanity's voracious war machine. If their nervous system wasn't too screwed up then they would become chimeras – pilots for tanks, walkers, ground effects raiders and sleds, assault shuttles and even starships. A few of them were fast enough to become signalmen but most of them ended up like McShit himself: support and logistics. Robby looked up at me as I approached.

'Evenin' boss. Heard what happened?' Then he gave Morag a long hard look. I think he knew her from the Forbidden Pleasure. Morag tried to smile at him. I nodded in answer to his question. He turned back to look at me more slowly.

'Usual? The good stuff?' he asked, his tone neutral, his expression guarded.

'No. Er ... yeah, gimme a bottle and have you got any fags?' I asked. Robby's eyebrows rose. I could see his mind go into overdrive.

'You minted, like?' he asked, but reached under the bar for a bottle of the park exported single malt. I could feel Morag glaring at me. This wasn't what the money was supposed to be for.

I nodded uneasily at Robby's question.

'What fags do you want?' I gave him my brand, the expensive brand I liked. The brand normally smoked by officers, senior NCOs and rebellious corporate enclave kids. The brand I could normally only afford straight after I'd won a race or a pit fight.

'How many d'ya want?'

'Two hundred.' Robby stopped as he was reaching under the bar for the black-market cigarettes.

'Yeah?' he said, somewhat surprised. I nodded. He looked between the two of us.

'You score big tonight?' I almost started laughing hysterically at this but Robby brought out the cigarettes and named his price. I turned to Morag.

'Pay him,' I said. She looked like she was going to argue but pulled out some of the dirty notes and counted them off for Robby.

'New meal ticket?' Robby asked sceptically.

'Like fuck,' Morag muttered under her breath. I lit up another cigarette and resisted the urge to open the bottle of malt.

'Is McShit in?' I asked. I watched Robby's expression harden. Others in the bar were beginning to take an interest as well and not just the Twists.

'Now you know McShit's always out,' Robby said.

'How much till he's in?' I asked. Robby looked at Morag again.

'Tell me straight, boy, you in trouble?' he asked. I nodded. 'A lot?' I nodded again. He watched me, seeming to size me up. 'We're closed!' he shouted suddenly. 'Everyone out!' There was surprisingly little argument as people shuffled out, the cubes shifting slightly on their cables due to the mass exodus. A few of the Twists remained, making no secret that they were packing.

Robby opened a small door in the bar and beckoned us through. We followed him past the steaming, huffing still. Robby guided us to the tubular steel central support for the rig. The hatch that had been cut into the steel had been very well concealed. Robby must have sent a signal from his neural ware because the hatch popped open for us. Behind it was a red-lit world of corroded tube steel. Robby reached over and grabbed a rusted rung welded into the old metal and began to climb down with a practised ease that belied his stunted appearance.

The tube world inhabited by the Twists was an open secret on the Rigs. Everyone knew about it – you could hear them from time to time inside the supports. Off the Rigs it was a true urban myth, a grotesque hidden fairy-tale kingdom made up of all the shit things people say about the Twists: cannibals, stealers of children, that sort of crap.

All the lighting was red safety lighting, which gave the place an eerie glow. The distant echoes of other people's movements in the pipes further increased the eeriness, though many of the areas had cheap foam insulation to try and deaden noise. The Twists didn't want to advertise their presence; this was their place. The other inhabitants of the Rigs pretty much left them to it as the Twists were useful and they had their own niche.

Robby led us down into the concrete block at the base of the rig. Originally ballast, it had been hollowed out with the same programmable concrete-eating microbes that they had used for the old Tay Road Bridge. More supports had been added externally, both driven deep into the riverbed and attached to the neighbouring rigs.

*Piper Dawn* was on the east end of the Rigs, close to where the Tay led out into the North Sea. On the east wall of this damp, submerged concrete block was a home-made airlock. Home-made was never a phrase I liked hearing in connection with things like airlocks. There were a few rigs between *Piper Dawn* and the North Sea but the Twists had gone out in diving gear with torches and remotes and cut a channel. Now this was all that was left of the Port of Dundee.

This was how you came and went if you didn't have the influence and the means to use the motorways, the Mag-Lev, the sub-orbitals or own an aircar. McShit's Port of Dundee was for those who needed to leave quietly. The Port had a few uncomfortable-looking chairs in it and bits and pieces of equipment I guessed were for regulating the atmosphere inside, some of it maybe sensor-based. There were a couple of monitors that showed external views of the polluted riverbed.

Various Twists were working on the machinery or just hanging around. Again there were guns on display, as well as less than subtle security systems. Throughout the hollowed-out concrete block ran steel bars. They weren't supports but rather formed a kind of climbing frame that provided access to all areas of the Port. From part of this frame hung McShit.

McShit had been a chimera. Rumour had it that he could have had anything from a fighter to a starship but instead he'd chosen an armoured recovery vehicle and joined the Royal Engineers. Since being removed from the vehicle he had made himself a sort of small armoured cupola to hold him and his life-support requirements. The cupola was hanging from the frame by two powerful-looking waldos, making McShit look for all the world like a baby in some kind of machine-like cradle.

The top half of his tiny stunted body stuck out of the cupola, various wires extending from it to plugs in the base of his neck. His eyes were ugly, home-made but doubtless good-quality optics that stuck out from his skull like old-fashioned camera lenses.

The waldos swung the cupola along the metal frames in a kind of inverted loping gait until McShit came to rest in front of us both. He didn't look pleased. Robby must've texted him via an internal cellular link that we were coming and that we were hot. I hoped it had been encrypted.

'McShit,' I said.

'Don't you McShit me. You're fucking tracking mud everywhere, you radge cunt!' he snarled. I looked down at the filthy concrete floor. The only way he could know that we had tracked in more mud was because it was covering our boots.

'Sorry,' I offered.

'Robby says you're in a lot of trouble.' McShit glared in Robby's direction.

'I need to leave Dundee, get to—' I began. McShit held up a hand.

'That wasn't what I asked. Same people after you who did the Pleasure?'

I nodded.

'Lot of people dead, lot of people hurt. Too much. Nothing we can do about it in the community. There was a lot of steam, the water going meant some of the rigs got knocked about, people got crushed, lot of pain, and here's us with no resources.' He was shaking his head.

'Wasn't my doing,' I said, thinking it was half true.

'That's government trouble that is, or a major couldn't-give-a-shit corp,' he said.

'They've got special forces operators on the ground hunting for us. People I knew, bad types.'

'You're bringing me a lot of heat.' I was worried I couldn't read his expression. Suddenly the other Twists in the room all seemed to be paying attention.

'I'm not denying that.'

'Could be I'd do better handing you over to them – maybe a reward.'

'Probably, though they might just kill you, plausible deniability and all that,' I tried.

'You're from here, aren't you?' he asked.

'I live here.'

'They're not, are they?'

'They all live in nice places.'

'This is a nice place.' I cracked a smile at this. Good old-fashioned them and us negotiation.

'They be able to trace you here?' McShit asked me.

'They'd be able to trace us anywhere if they put their minds to it.'

'We need to get you out of here then.'

'We need to get to—' I began.

'Will you shut the fuck up?' McShit snapped. 'If what you say is right then some bad people are about to come and traipse more mud through my nice little world, and they're going to come with anger in their hearts, a poor general demeanour and the willingness to do me and mine harm. When that happens I am going to tell them exactly what I know about you. I am going to cooperate as much as is humanly possible for this twisted little body to do so. I will spill my guts.'

'Come on, he can't help us,' Morag said angrily.

McShit turned to look at her, a smile splitting his grotesque face. Then he swung the cupola back to face me. 'I don't have much of a neck and I'm not sticking it out for some dumb grunt and a whore.'

'Fuck you, dwarf!' Morag spat in anger born of fear.

'Shut up,' I told her quietly.

'So you see how important it is that I don't know where you want to go?'

'They could still kill you.'

'If they're professional then I will have to impress on them that it's far more trouble than it's worth to take me and mine out.' Once again his leering grin spread across his face. 'Now this is a deeply beautiful moment – workers unite in the struggle and all that – but how much fucking money have you got?'

# 8
# North Sea

'Why'd you have to give him that much?' Morag asked. We were sat facing each other leaning against the ceramic hull of the stealth submersible. It was eerily quiet as the sleek craft, propelled by nearly silent hydro jets, slipped through the cold depths of the North Sea. I'd had to make do with the bottle of whisky because I'd been told in no uncertain terms that I couldn't smoke on the sub. I'd gotten about a quarter of the way down the bottle. I looked up at the tired, frightened, street-smart girl.

'There's a good chance McShit won't make it,' I said.

'But he said he was going to grass us.'

'Rolleston'll probably still kill him and take out his operation,' I told her. 'Him grassing us is the only thing he can do. Even if he didn't tell them straight off they'd find a way of making him talk. What he just did may have been the kindest thing anyone's ever done for you.' Morag lapsed back into silence.

The sub we were on was making a run to the drug factories in the Secessionist Amsterdam Territories. McShit had arranged with the captain that she would drop us where we asked. McShit would tell Rolleston all this and he would waste some time looking in Amsterdam, and find the captain, who would then tell Rolleston that we were in Hull. We would have a day in Hull at the most before they caught up with us. I hoped that whatever Pagan had for us was worth it.

I looked back up at Morag; she was going through the bag that Vicar had given her. Dressed casually and without the heavy make-up, she looked like any other kid. Though Christ knows what that meant today, just more grist for the mill. She was pretty, probably too pretty for her own good, and although there was wariness there it hadn't quite become hardness yet. She looked back at me, suddenly self-conscious at my scrutiny despite the fact that when I first found her she'd been wearing very little.

'What?'

'How old are you?'

'Why? Is it important?' she demanded, sounding more like a teenager than a rig hooker now.

'Yeah, it is,' I said.

'Seventeen,' she said. I really didn't want to know when she'd started working.

'Old enough to be drafted,' I said. She nodded.

'MacFarlane fixed it for us. Bribed the Drumheads to hold off as long as possible so ... so ...' she struggled.

'So he got his pound of flesh.' She shrugged. To her there was nothing strange or horrible about this. She thought of herself, at least at some level, as a commodity.

'I want ... wanted to be a signalman,' she said. 'When I got drafted I mean.'

Everyone wants to be a hacker, I thought.

'You got religion?'

'Not yet. I'll get it in the net, when I begin to see,' she said with a gleam in her eye. There was something about the interface: somehow or other it triggered the same response in people that religion did. They saw things, hallucinated religious iconography out there in the net.

'You would've been posted to R & R,' I said. Meaning she would've been doing the same thing in the military as she did on the Rigs, entertaining the troops. I didn't stop to think just how cruel a thing it was to say. She stopped rummaging in the bag and looked up at me, her eyes meeting my lenses. I could plainly see her resolve.

'Not if I scarred myself. Not with a knife but with acid, something like that,' she said, and then went back to rummaging through the bag. I wasn't quite sure what to say next.

'You any good?' I asked, lighting another cigarette.

'At being a whore? Yeah, brilliant. You any good at whatever you do?'

'Signals, hacking,' I said, somewhat exasperated.

'I broke into MacFarlane's accounts once, had him donate some money.'

'That's pretty good for a surface hack with no implants.'

She shrugged. 'My sister taught me how – she was signals.'

'You've got a sister?'

'Had. Brain fried over some planet out there. Don't even know where. They didn't think it was important enough to tell us, burial in space. Had she been here, Mum never would've sold me on.'

'MacFarlane ever find out?' I asked. She smiled to herself and shrugged.

''Course. He hired a hacker to trace it and then scared some of the others into grassing on me. He had this guy, some wired-up kung fu type.' I nodded thinking of the fashionable bodyguard I'd beaten to death on the Forbidden Pleasure. 'Well he also had some other skills wired in, like how to hurt people without leaving a mark so you could still work. I got to spend a couple of hours with him.' I thought about this for a while.

'Probably won't make much difference now, but that guy's dead.'

'Yeah, I got that,' she scoffed. 'The boat blowing up was kind of hard to miss.'

'No, I mean I beat him to death.' She was quiet for a bit.

'Good,' she said quietly. Then we sat in silence for a while. I was desperately trying to think of something to say that wouldn't remind her of something horrible.

'Why do you smoke?' she suddenly asked. 'I mean you've got lung filters and stuff, right?'

I nodded. 'I like yellow fingers, brown teeth and the smell.'

'Oh.'

'We're not very fucking stealthy if you two keep on talking!' The Russian sub captain hissed at us through the door to the bridge. 'And I told you no smoking!' I put the cigarette out and the pair of us lapsed into silence again. I was kind of thankful for it.

I thought about what Morag had said, the way she'd said it. The human race could fly to the stars and this young woman felt she had to mutilate herself so she didn't have to service the troops. That wasn't right. I'd always known that things were fucked up but more than anything else this drove home to me that there had to be another way. After sixty years of war we needed hope, we needed the war to end. If what Ambassador had said was some psy-op head fuck then it would be the cruellest thing of all.

Duty was something they drilled into us in basic, something I got in 5 Para: duty to our leaders, duty to our fellow soldiers, duty as protectors of the human race. By the time I got to the Regiment we knew it was a joke, or maybe it wasn't but we were pretty cynical about it anyway. If, on the other hand, there was the slightest chance that we could do anything to help this war end, give us a chance to recover as a race so we weren't eating our young, then that was our duty.

See that was the thing that got me: what if the cure for cancer was lying dead in a trench? What if the child of Vicar's god was born on the Rigs? What if the man or woman who could bring peace to the universe was too attractive so they had to go to a service brothel? Nobody would ever know.

I had seen, done and experienced a lot of very fucked-up things but somehow what Morag said was the worst. I'd been going through the motions, just putting things off until Rolleston caught up with me. We had no chance, we were dead, but I had been trained to operate with these kinds of odds. Unfortunately so had everyone we were up against. I couldn't put the cork back in the bottle; it'd been thrown away. I was in this now.

'Why are you doing this?' I whispered. Morag looked up and shrugged.

'I didn't have much on,' she said. We both smiled. 'Besides,' she said more seriously, 'I think it was gentle.' I guessed she meant Ambassador. 'Doing what I do you very quickly get a sense of who's gentle and who wants to cause you harm. I don't think it wants to cause us harm,' she finished.

I laughed.

'What?'

'We're going to try and stop this war based on hookers' intuition.'

'I guess,' she said, laughing.

'You realise this could all just be a psy-op on Their part? Just another tactic in Their attempt to wipe us out.'

'I know,' she said quietly. 'But I don't believe it.' The resolve was there again. She looked me straight in the lenses. 'We have to try,' she said, echoing my thoughts. I nodded.

'You two can swim if you want!' the captain hissed again.

*I was looking forward to a downer-induced speed crash and then sedation in orbit. Natural sleep was a thing of the past, too many drugs, too much shit in the subconscious. Ahead of us we could see assault shuttles taking off, making their way to the fleet in orbit. In the pale Sirius B sky we could just make out the flashes of light. The 6th Fleet was catching hell in high orbit from Their fleet. As we approached the evac point we could see lines of soldiers waiting for transports. Waiting as the more valuable personnel and equipment was evacced first. I'd long ago stopped feeling angry about this. After all we were special forces so we were quite valuable.*

*'Douglas?' Amar Shaz, our signalman and hacker, said over our encrypted tactical comms link. He came from somewhere in the Midlands from a Sikh family. He'd not been particularly religious before he'd become a signalman, but now of course he'd found religion in the net. His faith renewed, he'd started attending virtual temple regularly, grown a beard and even started*

*wearing a turban and carrying a vicious-looking, sword-length kirpan on patrol. The turban was made of ballistic mesh. In true squaddie style he'd come to us with the nickname of Sharon already firmly in place.*

*'Yeah?' I asked, not even bothering with comms discipline.*

*'Orders to report to SOC,' Sharon told me. He hadn't done this over the communal band. He wanted me to be the bearer of bad news. There was no way we could go out again. The firebase we were using as an evac point was an hour or two away from being completely overrun. What did they want from us? I relayed the good news to the rest of the squad.*

*'Fuck this,' Mudge said, in front of me on the hover scout. 'I'm not in this fucking army. I'm a journalist. I'm out on the first shuttle.' I knew he'd be there with the rest of us.*

*We pulled the vehicles up just in front of the Special Operations Command bunker. I recognised the two figures stood there. Major George Rolleston was SBS, the Royal Marines equivalent of the SAS. They were a good regiment, the equal of our own, not that we'd ever admit it, but Rolleston was an arsehole. A black ops svengali who'd killed a lot of operators. His insignia-less uniform was rumpled but not dirty, so he hadn't left the bunker, though he had the trademark Spectre subsonic, suppressed gauss carbine slung across his chest. He was our immediate superior at SOC and responsible for the deaths of a lot of Wild Boys, as far as I was concerned.*

*Stood behind him and to one side was a legend in the special operations community, Private Josephine Bran, the Grey Lady, a sniper and assassin who'd come up through the Marine Commandos and the SBS. Everyone knew her reputation and she made me very nervous. It was probably her presence that had stopped Rolleston from getting fragged years ago. Nobody could figure out why she protected Rolleston – the normal conclusion was that they were lovers – but I think there was more to it than that. Her fatigues were a mess and the marks of camo paint and the huge bags under her grey artificial eyes told me she'd been working.*

*I climbed off the hover scout and stretched my legs. I felt like a zombie. I was so tired that much of what was going on didn't seem to be making sense to me.*

*'What do you want?' I asked Rolleston. The relationship between officers and enlisted was very casual in the special forces community but my insolence was pushing it. Rolleston let it go.*

*'I have a job for your Wild Boys,' he said, pronouncing our troop's, now our patrol's, nickname with contempt. Every troop earned a nickname. Whatever our troop had done to earn the name Wild Boys had happened so long ago that by the time I'd joined nobody was left alive that could remember. Now Gregor and I were the two oldest surviving members and we didn't know, but it stuck with us. Still, I'd heard worse names.*

*Someone had once told us that the name came from a pre-Final Human Conflict story about a group of homosexual assassins. Spinks had beaten the shit out of him – I could never work out why, must've been an Essex thing. Maybe he didn't like being called an assassin, though we were, sometimes. Oh yeah, Spinks was dead, I suddenly remembered. Rolleston was looking at me expectantly.*

*'What?' I demanded.*

*Rolleston cleared his throat and looked at Mudge, who was bobbing up and down gently on the hover scout.*

*'George, do you mind if I call you George?' I asked. He said nothing. 'We've been out raiding for eight days straight, trying and failing to do anything we could to slow this fucking push of Theirs. I am so tired that I can't think fucking straight, so anything even remotely subtle is going to fly right fucking past.'*

*'Get rid of the journalist,' Rolleston ordered.*

*'Go and fuck yourself, he's one of us,' I told him. I'd heard this before but couldn't be bothered with it right now. Rolleston and I glared at each other for a while. I could hear the squad shifting behind me, just in case things turned nasty.*

*'Fuck it,' Mudge said. 'Tell me later.' He gunned the hover scout and headed off.*

*'You will insert by stealthed gunship—' he began.*

*'Wait. Insert where? What are you talking about?' I began. Something was beginning to nag at the back of my skull. I'd assumed that we were going to provide a security element for the evacuation. Instead of answering, Rolleston gave me a grid reference. It was more than twenty miles behind enemy lines.*

*'This is a fucking joke, right?' Ashley Broadin, the bullet-headed driver of the other Land Rover asked in her harsh Birmingham accent. Rolleston pushed on with his mission brief.*

*'You will patrol that area attempting to avoid contact with Their forces . . .'*

*'And how will we do that if we fucking land in the middle of them?' Ashley demanded.*

*'Ash,' I said, and the tough Afro-Caribbean Brummie lapsed into silence.*

*'We have reason to believe that one of Their elite assassin caste bioborgs is operating in the area, hunting the remnants of a Foreign Legion behind-lines raiding party.'*

*'Bait,' Bibby Sterlinin, the other railgunner in the squad, muttered to herself.*

*'You are to capture the assassin bioborg and call for evac,' Rolleston finished. SOC had been making up shit on the spot throughout the war and we'd gone out on some pretty hazy mission briefs. This was the vaguest and the dumbest.*

*'We've saved you some ammunition, food and water. Resupply and I want*

*you ready to move in twenty minutes – that is assuming you still want to catch a shuttle off when you've finished.' None of us moved, none of us said anything. Rolleston waited, looking expectantly at us.*

*'What?' I asked. 'You expect us to take you seriously? Leaving aside the fact that Dog 4 is lost. Leaving aside that we're about to be overrun. Leaving aside that we're dead the moment we hit the landing zone. Leaving aside that we are all so tired and wired we don't know what we're fucking doing any more, and leaving aside that more than half the troop is dead. Going after a Ninja? We haven't captured a Berserk alive yet, what chance do you think we've got with one of those things?'*

*'You have your orders, Jake,' Rolleston said.*

*'Those aren't orders; it's a death sentence,' Gregor said in his soft Highland burr. 'Personally I don't think we'll get near the Ninja even if there is one out there. We're dead the moment we touch down. Besides, even if we were at full strength, well rested and on top form, we'd struggle to take one down.' We'd all heard about the Ninjas. They were Their answer to special forces, except one of them was worth a patrol of ours. Ninjas were known to have chewed up two SEAL squads, one SAS patrol and one of Germany's Kommando Spezial Kraefte squads.*

*'I'm used to hearing troopers whining but there is a war on. Could you please get on with it now?' Rolleston asked, smiling.*

*'Fuck you!' Ash was off the hood of her Land Rover heading towards the Major. I felt rather than saw Bran shift slightly. 'I ain't going out there!' There was murmured assent from Bibs, Sharon and even David Brownsword, our taciturn Scouse medic. Rolleston sighed and pinched the bridge of his nose between his forefinger and thumb. He looked at Ash.*

*'I'm not giving you a choice. You either take your chances out there as befits a soldier in the SAS or you get shot for mutiny right here and now.' Ash was incredulous. I didn't like the way this was going down. I felt the Wild Boys move from where they'd been sitting on the remaining Land Rover.*

*'Don't threaten my people,' I told Rolleston evenly. He ignored me. Ash took a few more steps forward. 'Ash,' I said warningly.*

*'Have a look around you, Rupert. I see a lot more of us than there are of you,' the Brummie said. I closed my eyes momentarily. Rolleston smiled. Bran lazily brought her Bofors laser carbine up to bear on Ash. I heard the rest of the squad bringing weapons to bear on Rolleston and Bran.*

*'Now why don't you just calm down?' I heard Gregor say from behind me. Rolleston was just smiling. He looked perfectly calm.*

*'You can't win this.' I told the Major.*

*'Yes, Douglas, I can and will,' Rolleston said. His voice was cold but the smile hadn't left his face. 'This will soon become a farce,' he added.*

*'She can't get all of us,' I said.*

*'She can with my help, though that won't concern you as I'll take you out first.' Again there was no trace of doubt in his voice; he just sounded bored.*

*'Why don't you be reasonable about this?' I asked him. I wasn't feeling quite as confident as the Major was.*

*'I am. I'm not going to court-martial and shoot Ms Broadin.'*

*'Fuck you!' Ash said unhelpfully. Rolleston was still staring at me, his cold blue eyes looking into my matt-black lenses. He seemed to be telling me that this was a no-win situation. I seemed to believe him. That's when I sold the squad out.*

*'We're going,' I said to the sounds of incredulity behind me. 'Put your weapons up.'*

*There was something wrong with Buck and Gibby, other than them still being here. Attached to Royal Air and Space Force 7 Squadron, British special forces bus drivers, they were on loan from 160th Special Operations Aviation Regiment, or the 'Night Stalkers' as they preferred to be called.*

*The two Americans barely looked like pilots. They were both jacked into the heavily modified, stealth-outfitted Lynx VTOL gunship. Gibby piloted the bus and Buck was co-pilot and gunner. The pair of them were all hair, leather, ratty dreadlocks, cybernetics, tattoos and old-fashioned, wide-brimmed cavalry hats that had no place in the cramped interior of a gunship. They looked more like a pair of cyberbilly degenerates, both their artificial eyes covered with cheap plastic sunglasses. The pair of them were much higher than the nap-of-the-Earth flying their bus was throwing us through.*

*Gibby had tricked out the cockpit with a keyboard. What plugs of his weren't wired into the gunship were wired into the instrument. Buck had slaved the gunship's weapons into his guitar and the pair of them accompanied our trip with the pounding, rhythmic, harsh strain of ancient country and metal riffs.*

*Had I not been so tired I would've questioned the stealth benefit of playing retro at high volume. On the tail of the irregularly shaped craft one of them had written, 'Jesus Built My Gunship'. Buck and Gibby were the kind that loved the war. To them it was just one long drug-induced guitar solo of miniguns and chaos surfing.*

*We'd taken more speed, more Slaughter, more ammunition and then out again. In the gunship nobody said anything, we were all too tired despite the amphetamines and Slaughter. The drugs woke up the body but our consciousness and the meat and metal of our bodies were two very different things. None of this was real. It was just bad news, drugs and dislocation.*

*Nobody would meet my eyes. I couldn't blame them. I'd sold them out. We'd talked about it in the past. At what point do we say no? At what point do the orders become so psychotic that we can't follow them? If ever there'd been a time we, I, should've said no that was it. The reason I hadn't said no was simple: fear. I tried to tell myself it was for the squad, that I really believed that Rolleston and Bran would've killed us all and I did believe that.*

*Rolleston did not strike me as the sort of person who bluffed or took risks beyond what his profession asked of him. He was too controlled for that and Bran may as well have been a force of nature. Besides, even if we had managed to take out Rolleston and Bran, what then? We were still more than eight light years from home on a planet that was about to be overrun, and sadly our only hope of getting off the world was the same military organisation that had put us in harm's way in the first place. At the back of my mind, however, was the nagging doubt that I'd done it because I didn't want to die. I'd bottled it.*

*In the short Sirius night we were aware of rather than saw the huge organic armoured advance on either side of us. None of us really wanted to look too hard.*

*'Listen up,' I said. The six remaining grudging faces of the Wild Boys turned to face me. Grudging except for Gregor; there was no judgement there. He was there for everyone in the squad, even when they fucked up. I looked at them and despite my fatigue I managed to feel something, regret for putting them back on the line and the need to try and make amends.*

*'We're going in hot. We will find the best place we can to hole up. Wait the least amount of time possible to make a bad impression and then call for extraction. We are not fucking around out there and we are certainly not hunting a Ninja. You see, hear, feel anything that strikes you as Ninja-like, or even if you just get a little bit scared, we are out of there, okay?' There were nods of agreement and even a few muttered affirmatives. Normally we'd hold a Chinese Parliament and refine the plan but nobody cared.*

*Across my internal comms link Buck sang some garbled slang and American military terminology at me that led me to believe we were approaching the LZ. I felt the four vectored thrust engines power back and saw the miniguns begin to rotate in their ball turrets.*

'Jake?' I arched an eyelid open and saw Morag looking down at me, concern on her face. I felt somewhat in awe that she could still be bothered to care about anything.

'Don't call me that,' I said. I opened the other eye and searched around for a cigarette. Then I remembered I couldn't smoke and wondered if the captain would actually throw me out of the sub if I sparked up again.

'What?' she asked, sounding slightly confused.

'Jake, my name's Jakob.'

'What's the difference?'

'One I like, the other I don't. It makes me sound American.' She stood up and smiled.

'What's wrong with that?' she asked.

'Nothing. I'm just not,' I said. I was never great when I was woken up. Something that even twelve years in the service never quite overcame.

'You okay?'

'Yeah? Why?' I asked, knowing why.

'You looked like you were having a dream,' she said.

'Know any vets who don't have problems sleeping?' I asked. Suddenly her eyes looked haunted.

'Yeah,' she said. 'The bad ones.' This war just reaches out and touches everyone. She shrugged it off quickly. 'We're here.'

# 9
# Hull

It was brown, very brown. It took a while to focus and realise that I wasn't just looking at a plain of mud, though the only difference was the swell, as far as I could see. There wasn't much in the way of landmarks to help either. Lincolnshire, although one of the least affected eastern counties after the Final Human Conflict, was pretty much a featureless green and grey.

There was the ruin of the Humber Bridge, two partially collapsed towers, steel, wire and concrete protruding from mudflats. Then there was Hull, the old port overrun with the brown waters of the Humber, not deep enough to cover it, just enough to turn it into an ugly mud-like industrial Venice that nobody wanted.

The submarine had broken the surface and we were walking along the deck to a rickety-looking, plastic-hulled water taxi that, despite the calm water, still looked like it was being too ambitious coming out this far. Morag and I clambered into the unsteady craft and waved at the Russian sub captain, who just glared at us. She knew we were going to cause her trouble. The boat headed away from the sub, towards the east of the city.

If our boatman thought anything strange about his human cargo and their manner of arrival he didn't say anything; perhaps he did this all the time. Then again perhaps he didn't say much at all. He was old and quiet, his face craggy and impassive. He seemed to show no sign of cybernetics (possibly he was old enough to have avoided the draft); his clothes were warm and well looked after, if somewhat threadbare.

The old man piloted us through abandoned half-submerged docks. Through streets of deserted factories, probably abandoned years before the waters rose, a testament to a very distant past. Everything was eerily still. The only sound was the gentle lapping of the waters. This was the ghost of a city long gone. It was hard to believe that anyone lived here at all, but then that was the thing about Hull: it gave you a chance to opt out if you didn't like the way things were going. Come to Hull and you got left alone because nobody wanted it.

We floated underneath the support of an old bridge, its road surface now under the water. We passed an old commercial section and on to what must have once been quite a wide road. Either side of it was a mixture of shops and housing. Now it was all deserted of course. Or almost deserted; on my thermographics I could see human-sized heat sources here and there. Presumably pickets for the Avenues. I didn't see the point in saying anything. The boatman wasn't talking and probably knew about them and all it would've done was make Morag uneasier.

We headed down the turgid brown water in this wide street for just over a mile and turned right into another similarly wide road, the ghosts of bars and shops on either side. Morag grabbed me by the arm. The people watching us were becoming more obvious.

'I know,' I said quietly. The boatman's craggy face was as impassive as ever. Ahead of us I could see something stretched across the channel/street. I magnified my vision and made out a net of vicious-looking spiked chains stretched across the water, blocking our way. On the right-hand side the chain disappeared into a house that presumably contained some kind of winch mechanism. On the left was a building that looked like an old hotel or apartment complex. Sticking out of that building from a hole cut in the first-floor wall was a rickety-looking jetty.

'Is this the Avenues?' Morag asked. The boatman inclined his head once, signalling affirmative. There were figures moving all around the area. Many of them seemed to be going about their everyday lives but a fair few were taking an interest in our little boat.

Off to my right, behind the chain, I could make out an area of open water, broken where stumps of dead trees breached the surface. The water looked cleaner there and it seemed to have been cordoned off with some thin plastic material that formed a wall to keep the dirty water of the Humber out. I assumed it was some kind of farm for fish or maybe kelp.

To the left I could see a water-filled road lined with partially submerged terraced houses. An ancient, battered and rusty sign on the end house read 'Marlborough Avenue'.

The boatman brought the boat to a halt about ten feet away from the jetty. Stood on it was a kid probably not much older than Morag. He had bad skin, a haircut that looked like someone had torn chunks out of his scalp, a badly decorated armoured leather jacket and a powerful hunting carbine that may have been older than the boatman. There was no sign of any cybernetics on him that I could see. He was unaugmented and judging by his age, a draft dodger. Good for you kid, I thought, best of luck. Up until he pointed the carbine at me. I wondered if there was a place you could go and not get guns pointed at you.

'That's close enough,' he said somewhat predictably. 'What do you want?' I decided to let him have some time staring at my polarised lenses.

'We're here to see Pagan,' I finally said.

'What about?' Now to be fair to him he may have just been doing his job or he may have been bored, but it seemed to me that I had put a lot of time and effort into getting this far and I couldn't be bothered with this crap any more.

'Just go and get him will you?' I told him brusquely. The kid smiled.

'No,' he said slowly, as if talking to someone a bit slow. 'I said—'

'I heard what you fucking said, kid. Look, we could have some kind of alpha male competition here that I win because I'm more violent, and then you feel humiliated and have to go and do the thing that I've asked you to do anyway. Just fucking tell Pagan I'm here and let him do the thinking for you,' I told him irritably.

'Good conflict resolution skills,' Morag muttered. I thought about the conflict resolution skills I'd learnt at Hereford. I wondered why so many people feel they have to force you to hurt them in order to just get them to be reasonable. Do they think courtesy to a stranger is a sign of weakness? Sadly, maybe it was. To the kid's credit he didn't look flustered; in fact he lowered his carbine.

All I really saw were teeth, big sharp-looking steel teeth. I was vaguely aware of the hugeness of the mouth that had broken the water and the power-assisted nature of its jaws. I heard the resounding snap as its jaws slammed shut in a demonstration of power inches away from our boat, showering us all in the brown muck of the Humber. I instinctively scrambled away from it, as did Morag. The boatman tried to make sure we didn't capsize the craft.

'Fucking dinosaur!' I screamed, dragging my pistols free of their holsters. Morag looked shaken; I was too busy with my own panic to register if she'd screamed. The cybernetically augmented alligator, which was so large it had presumably grown up on a steady diet of growth hormones, sank beneath the brown water with the sort of disgruntled dignity of a predator denied its prey.

'Vicar sent us to see Pagan. Just tell him Vicar sent us, please!' Morag said to the kid. Many of the people on the Avenues side of the chain who had been watching us were laughing now. I suspected this sort of thing had happened before. The kid was speaking to another armed man back in the old hotel on the corner of Marlborough Avenue. Then he turned back to face us.

'I know it may be galling for you to be questioned by someone of my age, but I live here, so when you come to visit, behave or you will get eaten.' This kid may not be quite the punk I'd taken him for.

'It's a fucking dinosaur,' I managed again. I watched nervously as another armoured reptilian back broke the surface of the water. There was more than one of those things. The other man nodded to the kid, who turned back to us.

'Okay, you can come in, but try not to behave like wankers, okay?' Morag nodded and smiled. I glared resentfully for a bit and nodded. It was going to take a little while for my bravado to return after my run-in with the alligator. It didn't seem to matter how well trained you are, or how much cybernetics you have, I reckoned, at some level humans are just scared of big lizards. We clambered onto the jetty.

'I'll show you the way,' the kid said and smiled at Morag. I'm not sure if it was some protective instinct, jealousy or just the urge to smack the smug little bastard in his pus that I felt. 'My name's Elspeth, by the way.' Fortunately he'd turned away and didn't see Morag and I trying to stifle laughter at this.

Elspeth led us through the building that I had initially thought was a hotel. Now I thought it must have been something more institutional. The whole place smelled of damp and the low-tide stink that I was already used to from living on the Rigs. We clambered up some stairs and onto the roof. From there we could see all the way down Marlborough Avenue.

'Pagan lives on Westbourne,' Elspeth said as if that should mean something to us.

The water came up to about the halfway mark on the ground floors of the pre-Final Human Conflict terraced houses. Most of the buildings were three or four storeys high, many of them with balconies or large window ledges, almost every single one of which had some kind of garden on it, most growing vegetables to my untrained eye.

I assumed that the majority of these buildings once had attics, but the roofs had been removed, flattened and then used as farms. Some of them were planted with crops and vegetables. Others had chickens, sheep and even a few cows and pigs grazing on them. There was even what looked to be a small orchard on one roof. All the houses had been shored up with material salvaged from the deserted rest of the city.

Between the two sides of the street, over the turgid Humber water, were a series of scratch-built, rickety-looking catwalks. Many of them had solar panelling strung between them. I could also see the smoke of stills and hear the rhythmic thump of alcohol-burning generators, and on some of the roofs small wind turbines added to the electricity generation.

'We've also got some wave-powered generators further out in the Humber,' Elspeth said. He was obviously proud of his community. Morag was looking around in awe. I saw some more of the clean-water pens fenced off from the dirty river.

'What are you farming there?' I asked.

'Not sure in that one. We've got different ones, a fair amount of kelp, various types of shellfish. We've had less luck with fish though.' I was impressed despite myself. This was quite an undertaking. 'There's more pens back in Pearson Park,' he said, gesturing back to the open body of water that we'd seen on the way in. 'And more at what used to be the Spring Bank West Cemetery.'

I'd also noticed the trunks of dead trees sticking out of the water, but these had been carved into various shapes and forms. I was looking at one that seemed to be an angel holding a globe. It looked ancient and pitted.

'Those were sculpted before the FHC and the rivers rose. We're doing our best to maintain them,' he said.

'Why?' I asked, almost involuntarily. The practical side of me was saying that they had more pressing things to do. Elspeth just looked at me disdainfully as he took us out over the river on a corroded metal catwalk that shook with every step. It probably would've bothered me if I hadn't lived on the Rigs. We passed by a couple of cows that paused from grazing to look up at us with their sombre, watery eyes. We crossed from the roofs of Marlborough Avenue and onto the roofs of what was presumably Westbourne Avenue.

The set-up of Westbourne Avenue was pretty similar only more of the rooftops seemed to be given over to greenhouses and what looked to me to be hydroponic gardens, though again they'd had to scavenge what gear they could find.

Below us in the water-filled avenue an off-white monument of some kind stuck out of the water. It looked to me like a giant chess piece, like a bishop or something. Two people standing in a boat seemed to be cleaning it. The monument or whatever it was stood in a circle of houses with a flooded road leading off opposite from where we stood.

Elspeth took us towards a house just past the little circle, which had presumably once been a roundabout. We climbed down a metal ladder bolted to the side of the house and through the remains of a window. As well as the ever-present smell of damp and the Humber there was a strong earthy smell here. The roof garden above was supported by a reinforced ceiling and further shored up by supports made from scavenged steel beams. There were cracks where dirt had spilled through.

'These things ever collapse?' Morag asked, half joking.

'Every so often, though nobody's died in over a year in a collapse,' Elspeth answered in a matter-of-fact tone. 'Actually the main problem is salvaging the earth afterwards,' he added as we headed down a flight of stairs to the house's first floor. It seemed that the house had at one point been converted into separate flats.

'Huh?' I said intelligently. Once again Elspeth gave me a look of condescension that only cocky teenagers are truly capable of giving.

'Good soil is actually quite difficult to find,' the precocious little sod said. 'We had to search quite far and wide for it – we even sent out raiding parties.'

'Outstanding,' I said. Elspeth and presumably the rest of the inhabitants of the Avenues seemed very proud of their community, and grudgingly I could see why.

We came into a hall that had been extensively decorated with a mural of some kind. I couldn't really make it out, but it seemed to be a series of interconnecting spirals bordered with knotwork. I could hear raised voices on the other side of the door. I probably could've tried to listen in if I'd boosted my hearing but I decided against it. Elspeth hammered on the door and the voices stopped. He turned and raised his eyes at us and took one last lingering look at Morag, which caused my blood to boil. She smiled nervously back at him and he left as the door opened.

If someone was going to call themselves Pagan I would pretty much expect them to look like Pagan did. The face that greeted us from the door was old, tanned and leathery. His features were pinched and angular but the half-smile beneath the black lenses that replaced his eyes went some way towards softening the hardness of his face. Half his head sprouted fiercely orange dreadlocks. The other half was the restructured ugly military tech of his integral computer. Tattooed on his face and disappearing into the neckline of the tatty, dirty T-shirt were spirals of knotwork. I later found out that the knotwork was made from implanted circuitry.

He wore a leather biker's jacket that I assumed was armoured, and some old combat trousers. In his ears were the rather predictable multiple piercings, though he didn't have any others that were visible at least. The biggest and most obvious affectation was the gnarled wooden staff held in his left hand, various fetishist objects hanging off it. It was tribal but had an old look. It reminded me of Buck and Gibby, the two cyberbilly Night Stalkers on Dog 4. My initial impression was: trying too hard.

He looked us both up and down, nodded to himself and opened the door wider. His expression had become worried.

'You Pagan?' I asked. He nodded.

'Tea?' Behind him I heard what I could only assume was cursing in German.

Morag and I followed Pagan into a lounge area. The damp and earthy smell mixed with the pungent aroma of burning incense. The room looked like a museum: it was filled with clutter, old armchairs and a suite with its stuffing spilling out. Books, actual real paper books and a lot of them, lined one wall. Pictures of fantastical landscapes and creatures covered another. Lying around was a mixture of high-tech and what I could only assume was ritual paraphernalia. My second impression was that this guy was pretty far gone.

Stood in the middle of the lounge glaring at us was a tall, raw-boned, athletic-looking, black woman with a Mohican. Her eyes were polarised lenses like mine. She wore a leather top and I could see she only had one breast. The other, presumably, had been surgically removed.

'This is Jess,' Pagan said politely and then looked expectantly at us. While I tried to decide whether we had anything to lose by telling them our real names, Morag introduced us both. Pagan smiled and disappeared into the tiny kitchen and began making tea.

'Where you been?' said Jess, asking the standard vet question. She had a thick German accent.

'Around,' I said. 'Spent some time on Dog 4.'

'Special forces?' she asked. I told her yes by not saying anything.

'You?' I asked.

'Luftwaffe. Proxima, a little in Barneys.' Barneys was what the military fraternity called Barnard's Star.

'Jess was one of the Valkyries!' Pagan said from the kitchen, an unmistakeable hint of pride in his voice.

'That was your crew who took down one of Their dreadnoughts?' I asked. I'd heard of the Valkyries. They were a hardcore all-female fighter wing that flew off the *Barbarossa*, one of the German carriers.

'Lost more than three quarters of the wing doing it,' she said.

'You on that?' I asked. She nodded. She was still looking at me with outright hostility. Pagan bustled out of the kitchen with four radically different steaming mugs of brew.

'Make yourself comfortable,' he said. Morag and I cleared away enough strange debris to sit down together on the slowly exploding settee.

'Where you been, Pagan?' I asked.

Pagan smiled. 'Mostly Barneys.'

'Signals?' I assumed. Pagan shook his head, his dreadlocks flailing.

'RASF, combat air/space controller.' I was impressed. RASF combat controllers were one of the few units in the British military alongside the SAS, the SBS and one of the intelligence units that got special forces pay. With a similar skill set to signalmen and -women, they tended to be attached to special forces patrols and used as forward observers to call in air and orbital strikes. They also tended to be first on the ground during an assault from orbit to guide in the shuttles. It was a hairy job. I tried to fit what I knew about combat controllers with this oddball in front of me. Of course he could've been lying. Some people tried to claim what they saw as the glamour of special forces work for themselves but I didn't really get that from this guy. I didn't think he could care less what I or anyone else thought of his war record. I guessed that like most hackers he'd got religion in the end.

'This Vicar who sent you,' Jess said. I guessed there were no secrets in the Avenues, which bothered me. 'He's in Dundee, yes?'

'Not any more.'

Pagan looked up sharply from his tea. 'Dead?'

I nodded. I saw the momentary grief of a soldier who had lost yet another of his friends cross his face before he did what we all had to do, put it to one side and get on with the task in hand.

'Lot of trouble in Dundee,' Jess said. I nodded again.

'Who killed him?' Pagan asked.

'He killed himself,' I said. 'He didn't want to fall into Major Rolleston's hands.'

'Who is this Rolleston?' Jess asked.

'SBS, intelligence, black bag, dirty ops type.'

'This Rolleston after you?' Jess asked dangerously.

'There's a day at the most before he catches up with us.' Jess started swearing again. I sat there and let her.

'The orbital strike, that was to do with you,' Jess said. I nodded again. More German swearing, then she rounded on Pagan. '*Christus!* An orbital weapon, that's too much trouble. We cannot have them here.'

'It's too late,' I told them. 'They're going to come here whatever. You need to just cooperate and tell them what they want to know.'

'And what if they just hit us with an orbital weapon?' she asked.

'They'll want to come in and make sure first. They need to confirm we're here.'

'Besides,' said Pagan, 'the political fallout from the stunt they pulled in Dundee will make it difficult for them to do that again.' Jess glared at us and stood up.

I held up my hand. 'Where're you going?' I asked her.

'I'm going to warn people.' The operational security element of what we were doing was a real mess but I couldn't find it within myself to stop her. This was after all their place and it was Morag and I that'd brought the trouble. She walked past me.

'Why is this Rolleston after you?' Pagan asked. Suddenly I found I was going to have real trouble explaining this, especially to another vet. Like me he'd spent the majority of his adult life fighting Them, and to all intents and purposes I had just betrayed my entire species by aiding one of the things that had probably been responsible for the deaths of many of his mates. For all I knew, I could tell him what I was carrying and he could just shoot me and destroy the memory cube.

Pagan was looking at me expectantly.

'You may as well tell him,' Morag said. 'We've got nothing to lose and they deserve to know why we've brought all this shit down on them.'

It took over an hour and one more cup of tea, but we told Pagan everything, finishing with Vicar's message.

'He actually said that, did he?' Pagan asked, examining the solid-state memory cube. 'That this was the path to the one true God?' I nodded. Pagan smiled to himself.

'Vicar was always given to the melodramatic,' he said, sounding slightly sad. 'Was he still quoting Revelations?'

'Until the end,' I told him. Pagan was taking the news that we were carrying a downloaded one of Them, and in doing so committing high treason, quite well.

'Never quoted another part of the Bible, you know,' Pagan mused.

'It's a big book. Maybe he didn't memorise anything else,' I suggested.

'He had it in his memory; he downloaded it onto his visual display when he was preaching. Probably had sub-routines set up to find appropriate quotes for any given situation.'

I just said nothing.

'What does it mean?' Morag asked. Pagan looked at her and smiled benevolently.

'I'm not sure yet. May I?' he asked, holding up the cube. I looked at Morag and she shrugged. I nodded. Pagan grabbed his stick.

'What's that for?' Morag asked. To me it just looked like a sturdy dead bit of tree. I'd assumed it was an affectation or possibly for support.

'I cored it and filled it full of solid-state memory not unlike the cube Vicar gave you,' Pagan said as he began wiring in his plugs to Vicar's cube. 'Lot of memory in there. Some of my more sophisticated software, stuff that would take up too much room up here.' He tapped the ugly military cyberware that stuck out of his skull in a way that put my teeth on edge. 'There's also some backup for some of my other software. I've run sensors all the way up and down the staff for an instantaneous link,' he said, holding up his left hand, which had a palm link embedded in the centre of it. Not too dissimilar to the smartgun links on both my palms. 'Between that and the upgrades I've made to what the RASF have put in my head, I'm just about managing to stay ahead of the game.'

'Have you got a ware doc here?' Morag asked. Pagan looked up frowning. I turned to look at her too.

'Why?' he asked. I was interested in knowing as well. Morag began to pull items out of the grey canvas bag that Vicar had given her. They were small vacuum-packed items. I recognised them as cyberware: she had plugs, neural interface, CPUs, visual display – everything needed to cut and chop your brain and become a hacker. By the look of it, it was top of the line. Most of it had come from the equator, high-end designer stuff from the Spokes. If she used it her head wouldn't end up looking like Pagan's and Vicar's, with their ugly military tech protruding from their skulls. Pagan looked up at me. I wanted to object. I wanted to stop her from polluting her real flesh, but at the end of the day it wasn't my decision.

'We've not come here for this,' was the best I could manage.

'I can pay,' Morag said.

'With what?' I asked.

'The money Vicar gave me.'

'Oh, gave you now, is it?' I asked. 'I thought it was so we could deliver this.' I nodded at the cube.

'Why do you think he gave me the ware?' she asked me.

'Look, you don't understand ...' I began, sounding just like I was about to give Morag the same kind of pompous adult lecture that pissed me off when I was her age. On the other hand, if I had to be honest I should've listened to a few of them, especially the ones about draft dodging.

'It's not your decision. It's not your business. In fact it's got nothing to do with you.' And once again I could see the resolve in this quiet, apparently shy girl. Pagan was looking between the two of us nervously. He actually cleared his throat before he spoke.

'She's not the only one who should see the doc,' he said, looking at me. I reached up to touch the burnt ruin of my face. I'd kind of forgotten about it.

'I've got a wound in my leg as well and I need my transponder removed,' I said, searching for the aching reminder of the Grey Lady's playful warning among the other aches and pains.

Pagan was smiling. 'We've become quite good at removing transponders.'

'Look, whatever we do we're going to have to do quickly,' I said, conscious of how little time we had.

'We're a poor community. You're going to have to pay your way,' Pagan said.

'Speak to my accountant,' I said nodding towards Morag, who glared at me. Pagan held up the cube. 'Do whatever you want,' I said.

'What're you going to do after this?' Pagan asked. And that was a good question. What were we going to do? Run until they caught us? Find a place to die? Kill ourselves in such a way to avoid pre- and post-mortem interrogation? I glanced at Morag; again I felt the urge to protect her. The last thing I wanted was for her to fall into Rolleston's hands.

'Run,' I heard Morag say.

Pagan looked at the pair of us thoughtfully.

# 10
# Hull

Morag went under the knife, or more likely the laser. She was kind enough to pay for someone to clean and knit new flesh to my face. They also sprayed on new skin and saw to my leg wound better than I'd been able to back at Vicar's place. While we were doing this Pagan had an audience with Ambassador.

The ware doc worked from what looked to me to be a stainless-steel cube assembled in a larger room on the ground floor of one of the terraced houses. It was watertight and you entered it through a hatch in the ceiling. You could hear the Humber lapping against the side of it. When I opened my eyes and felt my new tender flesh, Morag was lying on the other operating chair next to me, still under the anaesthetic. Her head was shaved and covered in a network of fresh scar tissue. I could just make out a couple of new plugs in the back of her neck. It was the girl's down payment on her humanity as she tried to become something more than she was. It seemed a waste as we were probably both dead soon anyway.

The ware doc loomed over me. He had ancillary arms sprouting out of his shoulders that ended in various surgical tools. It made him look like a surgical-steel preying mantis.

'Pagan wants to speak to you,' he told me.

I hated the net. Maybe that's strange coming from someone who spent so much of their time in the sense booths. The technology was similar, total sensory immersion hard-wired through a neural connection, called a sense link, directly into the brain. This made the sensory input seem real to the extent that you could die from neural feedback, and thousands of hackers did every year. As did other users who got caught in the crossfire.

The vast majority of people at one time or another accessed the net, either through education or if you didn't get education then through military training. If you wanted to communicate with anyone who didn't live within walking distance then one way or another you used the net. You also had to access it for much of your entertainment.

I could see its uses but I still didn't like it. In terms of virtual geography you could interact with through your icon, the net was supposed to be potentially infinite. To me it always looked so crowded and jumbled. Maybe it was because as a casual user I'd only ever been to the popular bits. Virtual architects didn't have to conform to the laws of physics, so sites could look like anything from a normal building to a giant mushroom to a huge, constantly galloping alien horse. The highways, the equivalent of their city streets, ran at all angles to each other. Often you would look up and see a highway with its sites inverted above you or shooting away at a disorienting angle, and of course, because its main users were hackers there was a huge amount of garish religious iconography. Maybe it just offended my almost ordered atheist mind, but I never wondered why hackers were so weird. What really got me was that the net was our dream world. It had the potential to be an uplifting counter to the painful realities of humanity's ongoing conflict, but instead it was just as garish, crowded, unpleasant and mercenary as the real world.

Dinas Emrys almost made me rethink my views. I'd found Pagan in an immersed trance, a note scrawled on sub-paper asking me to join him; it was taped around a plug attached to an independent CPU/modem unit. With some reluctance I plugged myself in.

It took a while for me to enter the site; I assumed that this was due to the heavily encrypted transport program that took me to my destination. I appeared in a curved stone corridor that looked like something out of a medieval sense program or media, except it had the trademark net look of well-rendered animation rather than being completely naturalistic. The corridor had a low ceiling and was lit by atmospherically flickering burning brands. I looked down and found myself in the bland mannequin icon of the casual net browser, an androgynous vaguely human form with the most basic of facial features.

At the end of the corridor was a thick wooden door reinforced with iron bands. To the right of the door was a set of stone steps leading up. Behind me the corridor went on endlessly. I could see other doors but I guessed I had been brought to where I was for a reason. I headed towards the door, trying to come to terms with the initial disassociated strangeness of mentally moving my icon until my mind accepted the new reality of the sense link. The icon was nowhere near advanced enough for smell and touch but this site looked like it was pretty well written.

I reached the door and was slightly irritated to find that it was locked. At the top of the stairs I could see what looked like some kind of gallery. Moving up the stairs I found myself looking through arches down on to a large, circular stone chamber with a domed ceiling. Burning brands also illuminated the chamber. As I reached the top of the stairs I was suddenly aware of chanting in a language that was both strange and somehow familiar.

In the centre of the chamber was a strange, constantly moving amorphous black blob. It seethed and roiled, reaching out with pseudopods that grew. It was probing some kind of barrier that seemed to hold it in the centre of the chamber before disappearing again. Around this information form was some kind of intricate circle pattern containing strange symbols inscribed on the stone floor. Presumably this was the source of the barrier and some kind of quarantine or isolation program.

Around the circle stood a number of figures, all of them wearing hooded robes of various hues from black to a constantly moving paisley. The robes disguised their wearer's icons. I tried to count them but something kept on playing with my perception, moving them around, presumably another high-end security function of the site. They stood completely motionless. The only sign of any movement was an occasional transparent scroll appearing and unrolling in front of them, unreadable symbols scrolling across it as they received information.

I watched this for a few minutes, according to the mannequin's clock, then the figures began to leave. Some disappeared, others just faded slowly out, a few exploded in a variety of different colours, one was enveloped by shadows and a couple simply used one of the doors in the chambers. Finally only one figure in a very off-white robe was left. The figure turned to look at me and beckoned me down.

Pagan's icon came as no surprise. It was a man of a similar age to Pagan, his hair cut into some kind of tonsure. He wore tatty and authentic-looking robes and carried various tools and fetish items that made him look like he had just stepped out of a history documentary. He of course had a long beard and a staff. I stood with him in the now otherwise-empty circular chamber looking at the contained information form.

'That's it, isn't it?' I said. Pagan smiled and nodded. I noticed the chanting had stopped.

'What was with the chanting?' I asked.

'Manifestation of our anti-surveillance software.'

'So you wanted me to see but not hear?' I said.

'You weren't our main concern and what you saw was designed to engender trust,' he said.

'Where is this?' I asked. I looked around. From inside the chamber I could see that the walls were covered in many shelves, each containing bundles of scrolls. This was some kind of huge library of information.

'This is my sanctum, Dinas Emrys,' Pagan said. I detected a hint of pride in his voice. I was impressed despite my dislike of IT. A site as secure as a sanctum was an impressive bit of programming, something that took time beyond the instant gratification that most hackers sought.

'Who are you people?' I asked. Pagan gave this some thought. It looked like he was trying to find the best approach to explaining something complex. It was the slightly patronising look I'd seen before from hackers and signals types when they had to explain something to the uninitiated.

'Do you believe in a god or gods?' Pagan asked. I almost turned and walked out. Though that was potentially futile in a controlled realm. I'd heard this sort of thing from hackers before.

'I'm sure your religion is very nice, but I'm not a hacker and I haven't had my religious gene tickled,' I said, hoping that the mannequin managed to translate my irritation. Pagan's icon sighed. It was a good icon.

'Jakob, I couldn't care less what you believe in or whether you believe in anything at all, and I certainly have no interest in trying to convert you to my own rather private beliefs,' he explained patiently. 'What I want to know is, do you believe in anything?' I gave this some thought.

'Beyond self-reliance, not really,' I told him. 'If there's a god even you'd have to admit that he doesn't appear to give a shit.'

'So what do we see in the net?' he asked.

'They're just hallucinations. The overactive imagination of a brain that's receiving too much information through its ware.'

'Perhaps you're right, but does that matter?'

'Whether God or your gods are real? I would've thought it was pretty key to your faith,' I said.

'No, faith is pretty key to our faith. It doesn't matter if they are gods and spirits that have somehow come to live in the net. It doesn't matter if they are information forms that have developed pseudo-sentience and taken on the identity of our cultural icons, or if they are aliens, or as you say just a hallucination tickling the old religious gene. All that matters is how we respond to them, what we choose to do with them. Personally, I see them as manifestations of worthwhile concepts that we should respect and work with, such as communication and creativity, or our scarred and beautiful Earth.'

'That would seem to prove my point that they're not real,' I said. Pagan opened his mouth but I cut him off before he could speak. 'And don't fucking ask me what's real,' I warned him. One problem with working with signals personnel was often when there was nothing else to do you ended up debating religion.

'I wasn't going to say that. The visions we see on the net seem very real to us. We have to deal with that reality. In a sense their origins do not matter subjectively.'

'But it's your mind playing tricks on you,' I said. Pagan considered this.

'Do I strike you as a particularly gullible or stupid person?' he asked. I managed to get the mannequin to shake its head. 'And I know of the various explanations for the visions or encounters.' I nodded again. 'But I am still, for want of a better word, religious. Though I prefer the term spiritually inclined.'

'I just don't see the point,' I said.

'To help,' he said.

'Who?'

'Me initially. It helped me make sense of things.'

'Things make no sense,' I said.

'No, probably not, but a tool to help you try and understand is a useful thing. Or rather a tool to help you put things into a perspective so you can process them, handle them.'

'So what cultural icon do you worship?' I asked. I was trying to decide how to bow out of the conversation. Being really rude was rapidly becoming the option I was favouring.

'I am inclined towards a modern interpretation of northern European paganism, of the kind practised by the Celts.' I'd heard of this brand of paganism but it really didn't mean a lot to me. 'I have a relationship with, rather than worship, Oghma. I see him as a totemic figure, inspirational iconography.' I shrugged; it meant nothing to me.

'And you believe this Oghma is alive and well in the net?' I asked.

'Oghma brought writing to Britain. I believe he is out there, still inspiring creativity, still writing, but now he's writing code.'

'In your head.'

'I don't care about his objective existence.'

Then I remembered something that Vicar had said to me. 'Vicar didn't believe in God, he told me.'

'You said it yourself: our gods are cultural icons,' Pagan said.

'So?' I replied, searching for a point.

'So we create them.'

'What's that got to do with that thing?' I asked, pointing at Ambassador.

'The ultimate act of hubris. We want to make a god but in a way that is indisputably not in our head, but obvious to all.' I turned to look at Ambassador in its containment program.

' You're going to worship that thing?' I asked in amazement. Suddenly my treason didn't seem so bad.

'No, we're just going to make it God. Or rather use it to help create God. Nudge the net, something that has evolved almost organically, into true sentience. A life form made of information that is near omniscient.'

'And this was Vicar's plan?' Pagan nodded. 'What a total fucking waste of time,' I said. Clearly this particular group's religious mania had gone beyond the pale. Morag and I were going to die on a fool's errand. I looked around trying to decide how best to leave before my poor IT skills reminded me to trip the escape function.

'Please wait,' Pagan said. 'Just hear me out.' I hesitated. To be perfectly honest I had nothing better to do until Rolleston caught up with me.

'What you witnessed was a meeting of a think tank of some of the best hackers on the planets. The vast majority of them vets,' he said. I nodded. Fortunately I'd long given up on any kind of operational security. Everyone seemed to know about the alien now.

Great, I thought, let's get this over and done with.

'For some years now we've been working on an idea. Have you heard people call Them demons before?' he asked me.

'Vicar called them that, he had a rationale for it. I've heard others say it as well,' I said, and to be perfectly honest the concept made a degree of sense if you were that way inclined. They seemed to exist for no other reason than to cause us suffering. Though my initial meeting with Ambassador had suggested there was more to it than that. Especially if Ambassador wanted peace, as he claimed.

'We decided that if our gods are created by us then we would commit the ultimate act of hubris and make a god that was capable of defeating Them,' he continued.

'You had a group psychotic episode?' I asked. For the first time it looked like I'd irritated Pagan.

'Don't take everything so literally. God was just our name for it.'

'For what?' I asked. 'You couldn't have known about Ambassador then.'

'We didn't, that was providence.'

'Divine providence?'

'Arguably all providence is divine. Would you prefer luck?' I shrugged. 'But your Ambassador may be the key to what we are trying to accomplish.'

'Which is?' I asked, becoming interested despite myself.

'We are trying to develop an AI management system that would be capable of nudging the net into sentience,' he explained. I didn't understand.

'What are you talking about? Writing a program that controls the net?' I asked.

'No, we will not control it. We are talking about giving the net self-awareness, making it sentient, turning it into God.' I was really struggling with this.

'An AI?' I asked, but Pagan shook his head.

'A new kind of life, beyond us, better than us.'

'That's insane. What if you create a monster?'

'Worse than this? Worse than ongoing war? Besides, we would create certain parameters to protect ourselves.' I thought back to a young girl telling me, quite seriously, that she was going to scar herself so they wouldn't use her any more. Pagan was insane but he may have had a point.

'I don't understand, how would that defeat Them?' I asked. I wasn't sure if I was confused or just taken aback by the scope of Pagan's mania.

'Because it would be greater than the sum of all its parts. It would have access to nearly all the knowledge of humanity. It would have processing power beyond what we could even imagine. This is as near to actual omniscience as we can artificially create. We are talking about an intelligence beyond what we can comprehend.'

'Godlike,' I said, getting the point. Pagan nodded. 'And you hope that this god will show you the path to defeat Them and end the war?' I said.

Pagan smiled patiently and nodded. He seemed pleased that I'd managed to understand him.

'Seems a long shot to me,' I said, unable to fully express just how ridiculous I thought the whole thing was.

'Well there's more to it than that, and as I said there will be certain governing parameters.'

'So you will control it?' I asked, 'I mean hypothetically.' The one reassuring thing about this craziness was it seemed unlikely to ever actually happen. This was the real problem with the religious mania of hackers: nerds though they may be, all you needed was one charismatic one and you had a cult on your hands. The government had feared the consequences of letting vets with special forces enhanced cybernetics back on the street. With our training and heightened abilities we were capable of causing havoc if we wanted to, but we weren't the real danger. The real danger were the people who made magic with information.

'No, it will control itself, but it will have certain moral guidelines – like don't murder everyone on the planet,' Pagan said, and funnily enough that was one of my worries. In theory this pet god of theirs would have access to just about every automated system connected in some way to the net. This included orbital defence platforms. Military and high-end corporate sites had the highest security our technology was capable of, but I got the feeling that wouldn't stop something that was omniscient, wouldn't stop this new life form we seemed to be talking about.

'What you're talking about is the world's biggest computer program designed to defeat Them?'

'It could have so many other applications, help us in so many other ways.'

'For example, help us build more advanced weapons?' I asked.

'It's going to be programmed for general benevolence.'

'Aren't most religions? How many people died in the FHC?'

'Two hundred and fifty years since the last religious war.'

'Still, it's going to have to be pretty aggressive to find a way to defeat Them,' I said. This was beginning to smack of the usual religious hypocrisy.

'We're less concerned with defeating Them than with stopping the war. Perhaps conflict is not the answer,' Pagan said. I considered this. In many ways it was a worthy cause as long as it didn't result in getting our entire race eaten or something. Then I remembered that this was all nonsense.

'But isn't that the problem with all you religious types?' I asked. 'You want your god to act as a magic wand, make everything all right either now or in the afterlife.'

'But, don't you see this god would be real with tangible power?' said Pagan. I wasn't sure whether it was fervour or enthusiasm I saw sparkling in his icon's eye. It was a really sophisticated icon.

'It's still abrogating your responsibility to something else to sort out your problems,' I pointed out.

'No,' said Pagan matter-of-factly, slightly deflating me. 'We're doing what humans have always done. We're creating a tool to help deal with the problem at hand.'

'What problem, a lack of faith or Them?'

'Whichever.'

'And if God doesn't make it all right and kiss it better for you?'

'Then we, by we I mean humanity, will think of something else, though somebody else may have to do that.'

'But you want to be the saviours of humanity?' I asked. Pagan actually stopped at this. If I was reading him properly then it looked like I'd actually hurt his feelings.

'What are you doing to help?' he asked, sounding angry for the first time. 'There is a problem; we may have an answer, we may not.'

'You may make things worse,' I pointed out.

'We may but we don't think so. You mentioned abrogating responsibility earlier on. Well if not us, then who are you hoping will make things all better for you? The corps? The military? The government?' Now *I* was beginning to get angry. This was starting to sound like arrogance.

'Oh please, save me,' I said sarcastically. 'Are you Christ?' Pagan leaned in towards me. He must've triggered a cantrip, a minor program designed to provide special effects for his icon. His hair seemed to catch in a non-existent wind and lightning seemed to play across his features. Heavy-handed it may have been but I was reminded that this man could kill me in here.

'We are God's parents, as all humanity have ever been. What are you afraid of?' he asked. I took an inadvertent step back and would've sighed if my icon had been sophisticated enough. What was I scared of?

'It's just too big,' I said. I think that was when I maybe started to believe in it as a possibility, or rather wanted to believe, but I also knew I had to resist the disappointment that followed hope.

'At some point someone has to do it,' Pagan leaned back. The storm passing, he seemed back to his more benevolent self.

'Why us?' I said before I'd even realised I'd included myself.

'Nobody else is stepping up, and if we don't nothing happens.'

'I'm not a hacker.'

'Sadly, Jakob, men capable of violence are always useful.'

'We can't stay here, you know that. If we do we'll just destroy everything you have here.'

'Perhaps, but everything is about to change and you have nothing to lose.' He had a point. I had nothing else to do.

'What's this got to do with the alien?' A horrific-sounding gravelly voice asked. It sounded like someone was trying to speak and chew glass at the same time. My response was embarrassing. The hardcore special forces veteran jumped. Thus probably disgracing three hundred and fifty years of regimental history. What made it worse was that the mannequin was so primitive there was actually a delay between my urge to jump and the mannequin obeying me.

Pagan was looking past me and smiling. I turned to see who was making that horrible sound. The icon looked as bad as it sounded. It was just about identifiable as human. It had a stooped back, a long face with a long sharp tongue and a mouth of squint and irregular but vicious-looking teeth. There were elements of it that looked like a stereotypical witch icon of the type popular in the net at Halloween, for those who could afford it, but there was something about its deathly pale-blue skin, wiry musculature and nasty-looking claws that gave this icon a much more primal and sinister aspect to it. It wore what looked like a simple, ragged black sackcloth dress tied at the waist with a rope.

'Have you decided how you want to be addressed?' Pagan asked.

'Black Annis,' the hag said.

'Well I'm sure Jakob will disapprove because of its religious connotations.'

'That's religious?' I managed, pointing at the grotesque thing in front of me. 'What kind of religion do you follow?' Everyone ignored me.

'No,' the hag-like figure said. 'For me, it's a fairy tale. This is what I almost had to become. It could've been the other way around.' It was then I realised.

'Morag?' I asked. The Hag nodded. If she'd had to make herself ugly to become a hacker then her icon would've been beautiful. To her this was the payment of a karmic debt.

'Not the Maiden of the Flowers then?' Pagan said, sounding both amused and pleased. Annis shook her head, almost shyly, I thought. 'Religious or not, it has resonance with me. I congratulate you. It is a very sophisticated avatar,' he said. Annis seemed to beam with pride.

'The hardware helped a lot,' came that horrible voice again. The hag was looking around the chamber, its face a picture of grotesque wonder.

'First time?' Pagan asked.

'First time jacked in, first time feeling,' Morag said.

'That was quick,' I said, both impressed and suspicious of Morag's presence in the net.

'Clearly there is a degree of natural talent,' Pagan said. With the arrival of Morag I'd suddenly started to feel weary. I realised that Pagan had been sucking me into his insane plan; now his spell was broken.

'What about the alien?' I said, repeating Morag the Hag's question. 'You said it was key.' Pagan was suddenly serious again, speaking to both of us.

'Along with the information form, Vicar also put the result of the tests he'd run on the alien in the memory cube. What he found was that Their physiology is all integrated; there are no separate organs. The brain runs throughout and is compatible with the rest of Them when they rejoin each other to form one consensual hive mind,' he said. Again this was something that had been theorised before.

'Then it's a biological machine?' I said somewhat patronisingly, probably more for Morag's benefit than mine.

'Yes,' Pagan said. 'In the same way humans are, but they do not differentiate between what we would see as technology and themselves.'

'Bioborgs. So?' I said. This was actually nothing new.

'Pagan said they were like a biological liquid equivalent of nanites,' Morag said. Pagan nodded.

'That's right, but the important thing is that Ambassador's processing power is remarkable, and it seems able to learn as instantaneously as we can manage to measure it.'

'So?' I said.

'So it would be able to manage information on the scale required for Pagan and his friends' plan,' Morag said.

'You heard?' I asked appalled.

'I sent her the files of our discussion when she entered the library,' Pagan said.

'Jakob, you've no idea. The hardware enables me to process and understand so quickly. I know so much; I can learn so quickly,' she said. Her enthusiasm would've been more infectious if I could stop thinking about the metal and plastic that seemed to infect us all these days. I'd had enough of this.

'Okay great, you've got your pet alien. Best of luck. This has nothing to do with us,' I said, not even thinking. Black Annis turned to look at me. Was that amusement I saw in the black orbs that passed for eyes? 'Me,' I said pathetically.

There was the sound of breaking glass as the alien burst through its containment program. Black tendrils exploded out through the roof of Dinas Emrys, through the cracks in the ceiling. I could only see more blackness, which meant we were in an unpopular part of the net, the virtual middle of nowhere. The main body of the alien information form seemed to remain within the circle. I instinctively ducked down but Pagan was already working. Scrolls appeared and disappeared in front of him as streams of translucent blue light issued from his hands forming coronas of energy around Ambassador's black tendrils but seeming to have very little other effect.

'Out now!' Pagan shouted in a commanding voice at odds with his normal gentleness. Not being used to the environment, I began looking for an actual exit before I remembered the escape function. The tendrils began to convulse like a snake swallowing a meal, the convulsions becoming more and more rapid.

'Yes,' I heard Morag all but whisper. I turned round to see who she was talking to, as did Pagan, his eyes widening in shock. The Black Annis icon's face was a picture of strangely grotesque wonder. A thin black tendril shot out from Ambassador and pierced the head of the hag-like icon.

'No!' I was vaguely aware of myself shouting as I moved towards her, before I realised that here I had no way to help whatsoever. The Black Annis icon was lying on its arched back, shaking as if it/she was experiencing a powerful seizure. The black tendril had pierced the virtual skull and was also convulsing rapidly.

'Out! Now!' Pagan shouted again. Years of military conditioning compelled me to obey. I knew I was becoming part of the problem. I spared one more glance at Black Annis and then felt the disorienting pull of reality.

# 11
# Hull

It seemed to take a long time for the information I was receiving to make any kind of sense. Though it was probably no time at all. The world glowed a flickering red. There was a keening noise, but that was cut off suddenly. I eventually recognised the sound as some kind of old klaxon. Then came the seemingly constant soundtrack of my life, gunfire and the screams that always seemed to accompany gunfire. My guns were in my hands. I was not aware of having drawn them.

Pagan was still sitting on his tatty couch, still in his jacked-in trance, his face a mask of effort and concentration. More worrying was the newly skinhead Morag lying on the couch next to where I'd been sitting, jerking and twitching but on her face a strange look of contentment.

I wanted to help but there was nothing I could do. Morag was jacked over a wireless link, she wasn't plugged in, and I couldn't disconnect her. I could feel a strange sense of panic building in me. Later I would think that I didn't cope well with being responsible for non-combatants. I had to put that aside and focus. Begin processing the information I was receiving.

I could hear a mixture of weapons being fired, everything from pistols and shotguns to old-sounding automatic weapons. These were being answered by the unmistakeable sound of the Vickers advanced combat rifle. A weapon I had intimate knowledge of, as it was standard issue in the British army. I could also hear the sound of 30-millimetre grenades being fired from underslung launchers and then exploding.

Thermographics were almost a waste of time. I saw lots of humans moving quickly, lots of momentary blossoms of gunfire. Then I saw the dragon. There was a streaming arc of flame from a machine in the middle of Westbourne Avenue moving towards us. The arc touched a building and there was a roof top garden on fire. I saw the multi-hued heat signature of a burning human jumping from the roof.

The flames burning colder but still burning as the Humber's murky waters engulfed him.

I switched to low-light optics and edged over to the window and peeked out. Further up the Avenue I could see a flat-bottomed riverine patrol boat. The green optics flared as the deck-mounted zippo sent another stream of napalm into the terraced houses on the same side of the street as me. I magnified my optics. On the deck I could see soldiers in British uniform. I tried to make out their insignia; failing that I managed to decipher the boat's serial number. They were a guards unit of course, the Coldstream Guards. Fortunate Sons.

I backed away from the window, glancing over at Morag and Pagan. They were still jacked in but Morag's seizure seemed to have stopped.

Every single vet hated the Fortunate Sons. Every nation in the world and the colonies had them. In Britain it was all the guards units. The worst thing about it was when you joined the army you got all the death and glory histories beaten into you during indoctrination. Most of the regiments that had become the Fortunate Sons had a proud history. The men and women who had died serving in those regiments would probably be sickened to see what had been done to their legacy.

The Fortunate Sons were the children of the wealthy and influential. Sons and daughters of corporate executives, the independently wealthy, civil servants and other government functionaries as well as their own officers. A convenient self-perpetuating tradition. Obviously the draft had to be seen to be fair, but the good people of the world didn't want little Timothy or Samantha to be sent to die in a meat grinder under some alien sky, so they bravely took up the task of keeping Earth safe. I'd also heard them described as latter-day praetorians, as most of their duties tended to involve 'counter-insurgency' work, like this. In other words shooting civilians that the government considered inconvenient.

Vets had a lot more respect for draft dodgers. Needless to say, Fortunate Sons and proper soldiers didn't tend to share messes, as that would've led to considerable bloodshed. The problem was that the Fortunate Sons still knew what they were doing.

What I couldn't figure out was how they'd found us so quickly. It was too soon unless the sub captain had sold us out, or McShit had or someone here had. Clearly they were here for us. There are however, worse ways for a veteran to die than fighting Fortunate Sons, and I had every intention of killing a lot of them.

My pistols were levelled before the door to the flat had finished bursting open. Elspeth may as well have been shuffling, he moved so slowly. My laser pistol had drawn a bead on him before he could bring his ancient hunting carbine to bear. Jess on the other hand was wired as high if not higher than me. She had her surplus Kalashnikov in my face, my Mastodon in hers. Recognition reached my brain before I fired.

'You,' Jess hissed out, her features seething. 'You've brought them here.'

'Way too quickly; one of your people must've sold us out. They brought this down on you,' I said, my tone more calm and even than I felt.

'Both of you, cut it out!' Pagan shouted from the couch. I didn't take my eyes off Jess, nor she me. 'We've got more to worry about. Help me!' With one final look at Jess I raised both my pistols; she hesitated and then did the same with her Kalashnikov.

I turned to look at Pagan. He was inserting a jack connected to one of his own plugs into one of Morag's, in a manner I found inexplicably obscene. I moved over to them, kneeling down beside her. I could hear the whooshing noise as the zippo was fired again. It sounded closer.

'What's wrong with her?' I asked.

'The Ambassador information form burst free. As far as I can tell, it seemed to effortlessly penetrate a number of different databases. I think it tried to pass some or all the info on to Morag. Her systems were overloaded and there must have been some kind of information bleed.' He talked as he worked.

'Is she going to be okay?' I asked.

'Come on!' Jess hissed at us.

'I think so. She's going to be disoriented for a while. She'll have to come to terms with a way to sort and process it.'

'They're getting closer,' Jess said urgently. Then it hit me.

'Pagan,' I said. He ignored me, presumably receiving information via the connection to Morag's plugs. 'Pagan!' I said more forcefully.

'What!' he snapped irritably.

'Is this it? Is this what They planned? Have we unleashed some kind of viral weapon on our net?' I asked. Pagan turned to look at me, I could tell the same thing had already occurred to him.

'I don't know. Ambassador's back in his box,' he said. I was impressed despite myself.

'How did you manage that?' I asked. Pagan was no longer looking at me, concentrating instead on the job at hand.

'Well,' he said, obviously irritated at my questions. 'After I tried every offensive, coercive and entrapment program and sub-routine I could think of, I asked it nicely.'

'Oh,' I said.

'For fuck's sake, leave the bitch!' Jess shouted. I turned round to glare at her. She ignored me. I turned back to Pagan.

'Was it traced?' I asked. Pagan unplugged the jacks.

'She's going to be out for a while. We have to move her.' He reached under Morag to pick her up. I grabbed his arm.

'This is important,' I said to him evenly. 'Obviously we've been compromised but I need to know if you were traced.'

'Where we going to go?' came a terrified voice I belatedly recognised as Elspeth's.

'We'll take her to Fosterton,' Pagan snapped, and then turned to me. 'I can't be sure. That thing went through every conceivable countermeasure we have and penetrated some heavy databases. All of them will try and trace an invasion like that and it wasn't subtle.'

'So they'll have traced us.'

'They had Dinas Emrys but it's gone now. I destroyed it and they'll squabble over the ruins for a bit. I don't think they traced it back to me or Morag, but I can't be sure.'

'C'mon, c'mon!' Jess said through gritted teeth, and then fired through the wall as she dived to the filthy carpet. I barely had time to register the huge shadow outside the window when the ruby-red light cut through the building at what would've been waist height. I was already down low, as were Pagan and Morag, but I saw Elspeth's torso begin to smoke. I don't think he had time to realise what was happening to him. He just sank to his knees and then the top part of his body collapsed and he hit the carpet face first.

Pagan scooped up Morag and ran for the door. The wall above the window looked like it was being systematically chewed away. My aural filters reduced the constant supersonic roar of the multi-barrelled, rapid-firing railgun to a manageable level. The window shattered and the wall disintegrated. Outside I could see the twenty-foot-tall mechanical form of a Walker combat mech.

Jess didn't bother wasting any more ammo, she just ran low out of the flat. I followed her, clambering over the remains of Elspeth. The supersonic roar came again and chunks of masonry began to fall on me, as did more than a little earth. It occurred to me that the Walker was aiming high, suppressing us. If it had wanted us dead we would not have presented much of a problem. That meant they were after us specifically. I was also worried that enthusiastic suppressing fire could bring the earth-filled roof garden down on us. Suddenly I was less impressed with the Avenues community's farming accomplishments.

Out on the first-floor landing things were no better. Pagan was gone, I didn't know where, and he'd taken Morag with him. I didn't have time to think about that as the house shook from an explosion beneath us. I assumed it was the front door being blown in. I could hear the splashes of Fortunate Sons wading through water. I looked over the banisters and fired both my pistols down into the waterlogged ground floor, my independently targeted shoulder laser quickly joining in. The smartgun links showed me where bullet and beam were going to hit the body-armoured soldiers. The murky steam of the Humber mixed with the red steam of blood where my lasers penetrated through armour and flesh and into the water below, superheating it.

I was peripherally aware of Jess laying fire down the stairs as well. To their credit the Fortunate Sons didn't panic, despite leaving some of their mates face down in the murky water. Instead they knelt or took cover. Parts of the walls and stairs around me exploded as I was forced back by accurate, presumably smartlink-guided, fire.

I moved away from the edge of the landing. Holes were appearing in the floor from the gunfire below me. I reloaded the Mastodon and fired back through the floor, moving back towards the top of the stairs. The carpet began to smoulder from the heat of my lasers. The Mastodon was empty again. I ducked down, emptying the spent cartridges and reloading from a speed loader, and then I holstered both my pistols. From outside I could hear the mixed gunfire of the Avenues' dwellers become more intense. They had managed to mount a counter-attack.

Jess changed the clip in her Kalashnikov and fired down through the floor. I took advantage of this and sprinted towards the top of the stairs and threw myself down the stairwell. My shoulder laser targeted and fired independently as I extended the four knuckle-claws from each arm.

I hit the lead Fortunate Son, and the pair of us went sliding into the dirty brown waters of the Humber on the partially submerged ground floor. I repeatedly ran him through with the nine-inch long ceramic blades before he could grapple me. I barely registered his blood changing the colour of the water.

The next Fortunate Son was moving rapidly, trying to get a clear shot to help his mate. I burst out of the water, sweeping my left-hand blades up with sufficient power to destroy the Vickers ACR he was trying to bring to bear on me. The blades penetrated his armour and slid into his stomach and I forced them up into his chest cavity, lifting him off his feet.

The next soldier's fear overcame concern for his dead squad mate and the first of the 9-millimetre long rounds caught me in the side, knocking me back. One penetrated the armour of my coat and was only just stopped by my dermal plating. I spun away from him into one of the ground-floor rooms, moving as quickly as I could in the foot and a half of murky water.

I swung my claws through the door frame of the room, sending plaster and rotting wood flying as the ends of my claws caught the Fortunate Son hiding behind it in the face. It was a superficial wound but enough to cover her face with blood, hurting and shocking her. I continued swinging, catching another one, hiding on the opposite side of the door opening, in the shoulder. He screamed and dropped his Vickers, but tried to draw his sidearm. I repeatedly punched him in his unarmoured face with the claws on my free right hand.

My shoulder-laser stabbed out twice, the split-screen targeting system showing me a third Fortunate Son on the other side of the high-ceilinged room. The walls all around me were being chewed away by automatic weapons fire, more and more rounds were finding me. I staggered back, bleeding into the water as a couple penetrated my dermal plating.

The Fortunate Son I'd blinded with her own blood staggered to her feet, her back to me. I stepped behind her, using her as cover, as her squad mates fired into her. As she fell back into me I grabbed 30-millimetre grenades from her webbing. The grenades could either be fired from the underslung grenade launcher on the Vickers or activated manually. Holding her now dead body up with one hand I armed the grenades. I threw one behind me against the external wall, the rest through the door and the holes in the wall towards the front of the house. I could hear swearing, commands and panic as the Fortunate Sons tried to get away from the grenades.

'Jess, get out now!' I shouted, but there was no reply.

Someone tried to jump in through the window, silhouetted by the flickering red light behind him. There was a momentary ruby-red connection between him and my shoulder laser and he fell into the water. I hunkered down next to the wall and pulled the two nearby dead Fortunate Sons over me as the first of the grenades I'd thrown went off. It blew a hole through the wall from this house to the next. The explosion soaked me and covered me in debris. The compression wave created a small tidal wave that rammed me against the interior wall, which bulged from the force but didn't quite give way.

Fragmentation from the grenades tore into the corpses I was using for cover, some of it embedding in my armoured coat.

I pushed the two corpses off me and ran towards the newly made hole between this building and the next as gunfire rained all around me, blowing holes through the walls and making contrails in the water. Another bullet caught me square in the shoulder but I continued to stagger through the water as quickly as I could manage. I dived through the hole as the other grenades began going off behind me in quick succession.

I waded as rapidly as I could away from the explosions. I went through the room I found myself in as I heard the structure of Pagan's house begin to creak. The grenades as well as the rest of the considerable damage done to the old house were beginning to take effect on the building, and with the roof garden it was top heavy.

I made my way towards the window and glanced out. It seemed like the entire Avenues were on fire. The patrol craft was just about level with me but receiving fire from multiple positions as people from the Avenues fought back hard. As I watched, a Fortunate Son standing waist deep in the water was snatched under. Moments later a huge steel-toothed reptilian maw erupted out of the water and tore a chunk out of the side of the patrol craft and a Fortunate Son standing on the deck.

In front of the house I'd just left I could see the Walker still firing its rotating-barrelled, rapid-fire railgun, raking it up and down the terraces. It had long, thin, powerful legs that made the armoured barrel-like torso, containing the jacked-in operator, look like it was perched on stilts. Around the torso the various weapons systems moved. Its head was the mech's sophisticated sensor array.

The crash would've been deafening for those who didn't have audio filters, as the front of the house collapsed. The weight of the soil from the roof garden caused it to tip forward, engulfing the Walker. I watched the servos and gyroscopes on its legs try to compensate but failed, and it collapsed under the earth. That wouldn't hold it but it would slow it down.

There was a huge explosion, and I was thrown across the room, slamming hard into the back wall, cracking it and some of my armour. I fought for air, my head ringing and my ears popping as the room turned orange. I got another mouthful of the Humber and realised I was looking up through water at a room filled with flame.

I screamed and inhaled more water as something heavy landed on me. I fought my way to the surface, stabbing whatever was on top of me repeatedly with my blades, though I was having problems penetrating the thing's hide.

Spitting polluted water out and sitting up in about two feet of water, I saw that the room had been burnt from the fiery explosion that had thrown me under, but it was only actually on fire in a few parts. The thing that had landed on me was floating nearby. It took me a moment or two to work out that it was the badly charred headless corpse of one of the cyber alligators.

I staggered to my feet. Outside the water was covered in a sheet of fire. It was strangely beautiful. The patrol craft had gone. Presumably one of the alligators had penetrated the zippo's fuel supply.

Another explosion shook the house and sent me to my knees. It sounded like a man-portable, light anti-armour missile detonating, Laa-Laas as we used to call them. I hoped that was the mech being taken out. I lurched out of the room, eager to get away from the heavy munitions.

The shot took me full in the chest, knocking me off my feet and sending me back beneath the Humber. I didn't think it'd pierced my coat. It felt like a shotgun. Stupid, stupid, stupid. I shouldn't have been caught like that. No excuses, just a long time since I was in combat this intensive.

I was back up on my feet. It seemed like it took for ever but I was moving faster than anyone. The Mastodon was in my hand. I saw the two feet of muzzle flash from the revolver's barrel before I recognised that the guy with the shotgun wasn't a Fortunate Son.

As our mutual friendly fire incident escalated, time slowed down and with my boosted reflexes I could almost see the bullet. It took him in the chest, piercing his second-rate armour. It seemed like an age as he fell back into the water. Still I didn't know him.

'I'm on your side, you stupid fucking cunt!' I screamed at his corpse, angrier with myself for being caught out despite just having experienced multiple concussion waves.

As I staggered away from the corpse I could see into another room across the hall. Again it was large, with a high ceiling and about a foot and a half of water in it. Inside were three people surrounding a fourth. The three were obviously locals. The fourth was a small man with his back turned to me. He had dark hair and wore a black combat jacket and trousers. Not the kind you would wear on active duty but the kind you'd buy in a shop and wear on the street, or some people would.

The small man had his hands clasped together above his head, a shotgun pointed at his face; a lever-action hunting rifle on one side and an SMG older than I was on the other. My blue-on-blue incident had distracted the two men and a woman covering the small man. My boosted reflexes allowed me to assimilate this data very quickly. I could see what was coming as the small man began to move.

'No!' I shouted as I tried running through the water towards the group. The small man pulled his hands about ten inches apart and brought them down in front of him so quickly I could barely follow – he was at least as fast as I was. The barrel of the shotgun held by the woman in front of him fell into the water, as did her forearm, and then the front of her face slid off. It took me a moment to realise he had some kind of monofilament weapon.

He swung his arms out as my boosted leg muscles carried me into the air, and I made yet another serious mistake in this league. The top of the man with the SMG's skull came off, bisected by the weighted monofilament. That meant the weapon was in his right hand now. Committed to the kick I moved myself into position in mid-air, the sole of my boot aiming for the base of his spine. Hopefully with enough power to damage even a reinforced skeletal structure.

From the left-hand sleeve of his combat jacket a compact 10-millimetre Glock appeared. He triggered a quick burst from it and the man with the lever-action rifle's face disappeared.

The small man's three victims were falling away from him and I was about to catch him square in the base of his spine when he appeared to flip backwards without even bending his legs. Suddenly he was inverted in the air, his boot travelling at my face with some velocity.

He kicked me so hard my internal visual display jumped. My nose disappeared into my face and I felt my facial dermal plating and reinforced skull give slightly. I had no idea how he'd powered the kick. He stopped the momentum of my flying kick and the pair of us plummeted into the water, and I went under. Again.

I raked up with my blades but he was gone. I sat up in the water, my blades withdrawn back into their forearm sheaths, my pistols suddenly in my hands. The small man was running away from me towards a window in the back of the room. He had a compact Glock in each hand and he was firing alternate bursts from them. I think it was supposed to be suppressing fire but it was disturbingly accurate as I felt bullets penetrate my coat, lodge in my dermal plate and then explode, knocking me back into the water. I was not going to be able to take much more of this. All over my internal visual display were red warnings from internal diagnostics.

I rolled, tried not to think about getting the Humber into my wounds and then sat up. The little man was gone but I'd seen his face. He was Nepalese, an ex-Ghurkha and either a member of 22 SAS or an ex-member reactivated like I'd been. His name was Rannu something or other. The other thing I remembered was that he'd been the regimental kick-boxing champion. I groaned and lay back in the water. I'd never met him but I'd heard stories about him taking money off people in illegal fights in the cargo hold of troop ships bound for Proxima Centauri.

Rolleston must've sent him but I couldn't work out why they hadn't come with more operators. Why just him and the Fortunate Sons? If they'd wanted the job done properly then three or four like Rannu would've done it. What got me about this was everything I'd heard about Rannu suggested he was sound, and we'd been pitted against each other by a bunch of wankers. A guy I'd probably rather buy a drink had just beaten the shit out of me.

# 12
# Hull

I managed to stagger to my feet. I had to find Morag and get out of here. There was no chance that the Fortunate Sons hadn't reported the situation. Reinforcements would be en route. I was in a bad way but I didn't have time to revisit the doc, assuming he was still alive and his facilities hadn't been destroyed.

I tried not to think about the humans I'd killed. It was easy killing Them. They looked different and were normally pretty enthusiastic about killing us. Obviously I'd killed people before: in the regiment we went after 'terrorists' or people who disagreed sufficiently with the powerful. Terrorists like the people who lived in the Avenues, I guessed. We weren't supposed to war against each other. That was what we were supposed to have learnt from the Final Human Conflict and the havoc we'd wreaked on the world. Not that that ever stopped us from feeding off each other on the streets.

From the other Avenues I could hear more gunfire. The Fortunate Sons must have been trying to clear all the Avenues, not just Westbourne. My communications icon was flashing. I was receiving an encrypted message. The code was an old special forces one that I had fortunately kept the key for. It would give whoever was running signals for the Fortunate Sons pause but they'd crack it quickly. It was like everything else about me, I thought, remembering the effortless kicking I'd received at the hands of Rannu moments before: obsolete.

'Yes?' I said tersely, answering the comms message.

'Where are you?' Pagan's icon asked.

'Still on Westbourne, not far from where I started. Be aware there is at least one operator on the ground. What is your situation?' I asked as I began climbing up the creaking, damaged stairs in the house, hoping to find a way across the roofs and out of the Avenues. I left the bodies where they had fallen, floating. Those that had a face were all staring up at the ceiling.

'We're mopping up the last of them ...' Pagan began.

'We still need to get out of here; they'll be coming mob-handed now. Do you have any prisoners?' I asked, the patrol leader in me taking over. Pagan seemed to pause. I think he was trying to decide whether or not he wanted to seem to be obeying my authority. The conflict was momentary.

'Yeah, some, but they're not going to last. People are pretty angry.' I could hear screams from behind him accompanied by the spite-filled enthusiasm of an angry mob. I couldn't really find it in myself to feel much sympathy for the Fortunate Sons. They'd burnt these people's homes, everything they'd built, and many of the people here were vets, not the biggest fans of the Fortunate Sons in the first place.

'What's your position?' I asked.

'Where you came in,' Pagan said.

I had reached the rooftop gardens. All around me were flames. I made my way carefully across the roofs. The gardens weren't burning as badly as other parts. There was an explosion to my left as a still launched itself violently into the air. I made my way across to Marlborough Avenue. I felt like falling over: my wounds were making me weak and nauseous. I grabbed one of the walkway's railings with my left hand and then quickly removed it. The metal was burning hot.

On Marlborough I could see the ruins of another patrol craft. Every so often I saw a huge armoured reptilian back break the surface of the water.

'Can you keep your pet dinosaurs off me?' I sub-vocalised to Pagan.

'You're safe, they won't attack you unless we specifically tell them to,' he replied.

'Good,' I slurred out loud, and then half fell, half jumped the four storeys down into the water. It was a messy landing and for the amount of time I'd spent beneath the unpleasant waters of the Humber I may as well have become an amphibian. I'd knocked the wind out of myself and more red warnings were appearing in my visual display telling me I'd damaged components – metal, plastic and the ones I'd been born with.

I clambered to my feet and, spitting out the filth I hadn't swallowed, started wading down Marlborough Avenue, the water up to my waist. Corpses bumped into me. Every so often I was shot at and once hit; I had to scream at my attackers that I was on their side. The worst of it was watching the guard alligators breaking the surface here and there, knowing that they were in the water with me, largely unseen.

*

I'd clambered up onto the small jetty at the end of Marlborough Avenue with the help of two angry-looking inhabitants of the Avenues. Pagan was stood in the institutional hotel-like building. Morag was with him but looked a little unsteady on her feet, though not as frightened as I thought she'd be. Sadly she was probably getting used to this. I noticed she was cradling a fifty-year-old Sterling SMG in her arms.

A large man and woman wearing ragged and wet working clothes, both obviously infantry vets from their bearing, had a Fortunate Son on his knees, hands on his head, in front of them. He was young and, under all the grime, probably blandly attractive in the way the scions of the middling wealthy tend to be. He was scared but mastering it.

I managed to climb unsteadily to my feat. Morag opened her mouth to say something but Pagan grabbed her arm and she lapsed back into silence. Clever boy, I thought. Don't let her say anything in front of the Fortunate Son. I staggered towards the young officer, mustering my angriest look. God knows what I looked like, probably a mess. I half collapsed onto my knees in front of him.

'Look, kid, you know that everyone breaks eventually. Spare yourself the pain and tell me what you were doing here.' The kid looked up and attempted to grin defiantly, trying to mask his terror.

'You don't have time to break me,' he said. I gave this some thought. My head was ringing and I didn't feel like I was thinking clearly.

'You're probably right,' I said and swayed back on my knees drawing the Mastodon and levelling it at the centre of the young lieutenant's forehead. He did the only reasonable thing he could in the circumstances and wet himself. Sad really, he'd probably played this moment over in his head and saw himself as the stoic type. I tried to move out of the way of the stream of urine without waving the revolver around too much.

'Believe me son none of it's worth dying for.' And I pulled the hammer back, largely an act of intimidation on a double-action revolver.

'Okay!' the kid shouted and started weeping. I leant in towards him, again trying to avoid the piss.

'Don't worry,' I said. 'Nobody's going to know but us and we don't matter. Why'd you come here?'

'Orders,' he said.

'To do what?' I asked.

'We were given your details and told you had a girl with you,' he said. Shit, I thought, they were on to Morag.

'How'd you know we'd be here?' I asked. He looked bewildered and frightened. I don't think he had an idea of how to answer that question.

'You need to help us, son,' I said, drunkenly waving the huge revolver about.

'I don't know, I don't think they did,' he said in a tone of panic.

'What do you mean?' I slurred.

'Guards units have been mobilised all over the country, searching places like this. They're looking everywhere for you.'

'This sweep was done on spec?' I asked, somewhat incredulous. I thought Rolleston would send operators, maybe a task force like the one that had hit the Avenues, once he knew where we were. We must have him really worried, not to mention his masters, if they'd mount an operation of this size and unleash their praetorians on the populace.

'You mean this is going on all over?' Pagan asked. He sounded as surprised as I was. The lieutenant nodded.

'In places like this,' the lieutenant said. He meant neighbourhoods not renowned for doing as they were told; any place where people could go to ground and hide. It was sheer luck they'd stumbled on us.

'Why are you looking for him?' Pagan asked. The lieutenant craned his neck around to look at the scruffy hacker. For the first time I noticed that Pagan was bleeding from a head wound.

'We weren't told.' He turned back to me. 'But you must've done something really bad. I think you're working with Them.' He spat, his previous defiance coming back. I swayed in towards him until my mouth was by his ear.

'Listen, if you ever get the balls to go out and face Them instead of making war on your own people, people who have gone out there and fought, then you and me can talk about Them, understand?' The Fortunate Son swallowed and nodded. 'What makes you think it's to do with Them?' I asked.

He hesitated. I could see him holding something back.

'You've just upset me,' I told him. 'Now would be a bad time to start pissing me about.'

'Because of the Nepalese guy,' he finally said.

'The Ghurkha?' I asked. He nodded. 'What about him?'

'He was what we call XI.' The lieutenant said. 'It means—'

'I know what it means.' I laughed bitterly. Rannu was just like me, another victim of Rolleston. I pushed myself to my feet.

'You finished?' the woman guarding the lieutenant asked. Then something occurred to me.

'What the hell made you come in hard like this?' I asked him.

'We didn't,' the young lieutenant said. 'We came here with authority to search this place,' he said bitterly.

I looked up at Pagan. 'You declared war on the British government?' I asked incredulously.

'This is our home, we've paid our dues,' the woman who was guarding the lieutenant said. 'We see an invasion, we fight. All we wanted was to be left alone.' There was a kind of logic to it but I'd been taught to pick my fights wherever possible. 'You finished now?' she asked again. I nodded, not really thinking. The shot rang out and the lieutenant slumped forward and slid off the jetty into the water.

'Hey!' I shouted, moving towards the woman. She looked at me, her face a mask of hate.

'Fuck him!' she spat. 'You know what that was,' she said, pointing at the floating corpse, then she and the man with her turned and walked away.

'We need to get out of here,' Pagan said.

'And do what?' I demanded.

'This has to count for something,' he replied, gesturing at the destruction all around.

'You know better!' I said, stabbing my finger towards him. 'It never counts, never makes a difference.'

'Jakob, please,' Morag said quietly. I relented. I just wanted to lie down.

'Did Jess get out?' I asked.

'We haven't been able to raise her,' Pagan said quietly. I looked up. He looked old and wizened, as if he'd shrunk.

'I'm sorry.' I said. 'Ambassador?' Morag rummaged in her bag and held up the solid-state memory cube.

'Are you okay?' I finally got round to asking her. We were on a boat piloted by Pagan, back on the deceptively placid brown plane of liquid that was the Humber. The hacker had produced his staff, folded in two, from his pack and put it back together; it seemed to provide him with a sense of security.

'No,' she said. 'Those people didn't deserve that.'

'Nobody deserves it. Well, maybe that's not true.'

'What are they going to do?' Morag asked, turning around to look at Pagan. The hacker shrugged.

'I don't know. Maybe leave, maybe hide in other parts of the city; perhaps some will start again.' He shook his head. 'We'd come so far; we'd really made something there.' He lapsed back into silence.

'I meant in there,' I said, pointing at her head. She shrugged.

'I've still got the worst headache ever, and my thoughts feel so jumbled I don't know what's me and what's new. Pagan's teaching me how to write sub-routines to sort it,' she said.

'Where'd it go?' I asked her. She shrugged but Pagan answered.

'Lots of different places, some innocuous, some not. It seemed to be taking huge random samples of information.'

'Like where?' I asked.

'Everything from literature libraries to major equatorial corporations,' he said.

'That the worst it did?' I asked. Pagan shook his head.

'No, I'd say that the NSA and GCHQ were the worst of it.' I felt cold. Even I knew that the National Security Agency and Government Communications Headquarters were supposed to be as near impenetrable as was possible.

'Oh shit,' I said. Pagan said nothing. 'You've got some of that info in your head?' I asked Morag.

She shrugged. 'I guess.'

'How well did you cover your trail?' I asked Pagan.

'Pretty well, but as you can imagine we've got those two organisations on us in the net and they're both justifiably shitting themselves so they're probably going to throw a lot of resources at it.' I felt he'd understated the problem. 'Rolleston would've already had people in the net looking for us, but now everyone will be.'

'And there will be bounties as well,' I said. Pagan nodded. I lapsed into silence. This felt pretty hopeless.

'Did it do any damage?' I asked. I still wasn't convinced it wasn't a strike against Earth's communications infrastructure by Them.

'Not as far as I can tell. It just took information.'

'Was it looking for anything?' I asked. Pagan looked at me like I was too stupid to understand.

I began to tend to my wounds, trying to keep my mind off the enormity of the events I was caught up in. I did what I could, cleaning and knitting or at least sealing the wounds with the pretty basic med kit I'd managed to find in the Avenues before we'd left. I was a broken machine, and without a good technician I was not going to be operating at what passed for my best these days.

'What's with this?' I asked Morag, pointing at the SMG.

'Jess gave me some combat skillsofts – small arms, small unit tactics, unarmed stuff,' she said. At the mention of Jess I could see tears in her eyes. I wondered how long before those stopped. How long before she knew more dead people than she had tears.

'Hey,' I said. 'Those things are all right as far as they go but they're no substitute for real skills and experience.' She nodded, blinking back the tears. 'You also need to acclimatise to them, break them in.

I'll run you through it when we have time and space.' She nodded again. My old prejudices against skillsofts were coming back. I'd used them – you can't learn everything after all – but I really thought that people should learn to fight properly.

The place was called Fosterton. It was basically a series of large rusting barges secured together on the Humber over what had been part of north-east Lincolnshire before the waters rose. It was a private port, cranes and cargo-handling mechs unloading everything from hydrofoils to small ships and sleds. It was obviously a smugglers' haven.

Pagan was talking to the owners of the place, three generations of a family that had probably lived round here for hundreds of years. None of them had military ware that I could see, just the cybernetics they'd need to run a place like this. I don't think any of them had done military service. I felt a pang of envy – a close-knit family, a place to call home. Their lack of military ware notwithstanding, it would've been foolish to cause trouble here, as they were obviously capable of controlling a place like this and the people who used it.

Pagan had clearly had dealings with them before but they did not look happy. He was trying to book us passage somewhere, anywhere, but the owners of Fosterton just kept on looking over at where Morag and I were slumped resting against a packing crate. I wondered if they knew. Had they heard about the bounties that were presumably now on our heads?

'Who's Howard Mudgie?' Morag suddenly asked, using a name I never expected to hear from her mouth. I turned to stare at her.

'Where did you get that name from?' I asked her.

'Do you know who the NSA are?'

'Yes,' I answered. It was difficult not to know who they were in the line of work I'd been in.

'Some of the information that Ambassador gave me, it connects your name to this Mudgie.'

'How?' I asked.

'You're listed as a known associate is all. I think it's been flagged by someone outside the NSA but I can't tell who,' she said. That would mean someone with a lot of pull, I thought.

'Howard was a member of the Wild Boys—'

'The Wild Boys?' She was smirking. I sometimes forgot that the names that had such powerful resonance for us often just sounded silly to the uninitiated.

'The SAS troop I served with,' I said, trying to imply that I didn't want the piss taken out of the name. 'He wasn't even army; he was a journalist, but after so long in the field he was as good as any of us and developed a taste for it.'

'He liked being a soldier?' she asked incredulously. I gave this some thought.

'It's not that simple,' I finally said. 'He, a lot of us, we just couldn't put it down. After a while you get so good at it that it becomes normal ...'

'And you enjoy it?' she asked. I turned to look at her. She was looking up at me with concern.

'You worried that I'm some kind of psycho?' I asked. 'Do you think I enjoyed it back there?'

'I may not be some war hero but I know enough about psychos,' she replied coldly.

'Yeah, I guess you do,' I said, nodding. Again I couldn't shake the feeling that I should apologise to her for the state of things. 'Look, as bad as it's been here and in Dundee, this is nothing like being out there. I know this sounds patronising, but until you've done it some of the things we think aren't going to make much sense to you. I don't know if there's anything wrong with me – I'm just trying to cope with stuff as it comes – but you don't have to be afraid of me.'

She smiled at me and then gave me a hug. 'I know,' she whispered. I wasn't quite sure what to do. I didn't reciprocate. She felt me tense up and let go.

'But this Mudgie, he didn't have to be there?' she asked, trying to break the awkwardness that had suddenly built up.

'I guess,' I said. 'But he was one of the good guys.'

'Who?' Pagan said, coming back to us.

'Any luck?' I asked. He shrugged.

'Depends on what you mean by luck. We can get a sled into Russia.' Both Morag and I stared at him. Russia was effectively a huge and very dangerous criminal empire that controlled most of the black market in northern Europe. It was no surprise that Russia was a possible destination, as it was Russians, like the sub captain McShit had arranged for us, who controlled the illegal transport economy in everything from people to heavy farm machinery to the drugs made in the Dutch factories.

'What's your plan?' I asked.

'Money talks in Russia. We buy some privacy and finish work on God. You provide us with security in the real world,' he said, leaning heavily on his staff. Pagan now had an old surplus BAE laser rifle in a scabbard secured to his back, a sidearm at his hip. He'd presumably grabbed them during the Fortunate Sons' attack.

'What about Mudge?' I said, turning to Morag.

'The journalist?' Pagan asked.

'You've heard of him?' I asked, turning back to look at the aging hacker.

''Course. He was the journo that blew the story on them dumping the special forces vets. You know him?' I nodded. Morag was watching me again.

'He served with him,' she said to Pagan.

'Yeah? Good guy,' he said. Mudge's story had probably prevented a lot of special forces operators from ending up dead. 'Wait a second.' I saw what was coming. 'You were Soldier A,' he said. 'The mutineer, weren't you?' I sighed.

'What's he talking about?' Morag asked.

'A while after I got out of the service,' Pagan began, 'the government realised that they couldn't risk having a lot of ex-special forces types on the street, as even with decommissioned cybernetics they were still potentially very dangerous.'

'Besides,' I added, 'those who had their cybernetics removed were being hired and re-outfitted by the corps, the syndicates, various mercenary outfits and even the better-financed street gangs.'

Pagan nodded. 'It was a major security risk. Now, what some enterprising soul did was discover a loophole in the law that basically meant that the government were in no way culpable for anything that happened to their troops in unclaimed space.'

Morag looked appalled. 'You mean they were just going to dump these guys in space?' she asked. I nodded.

'He was one of them,' Pagan said, pointing at me.

'A lot of the troop carriers are converted freighters,' I began quietly; this was never something I'd enjoyed talking about. 'Their cargo holds are modular and easy to cut off from the main body of the ship. They just had to blow the airlocks and we were gone.'

'After you fought for us?' she said.

'Yeah.' I surprised myself; I no longer felt angry at the betrayal, just sad.

'But they didn't space you?' she prompted.

'Oh, they tried,' I said.

Pagan was smiling. 'The problem was that they were trying to kill some pretty resourceful people. Soldier A here and some others resisted and took over the troop transport.'

'And killed some people,' I added.

'Soldier A?' Morag asked.

'During a hearing or a court martial, special forces operators are referred to like that to preserve their identity for operational security,' I told her.

'They court-martialled the people responsible?' she asked, sounding a little more reassured.

'No,' I said.

'They court-martialled you?' she said incredulously. I nodded. 'Why?'

'Because legally we were in the wrong. I'd mutinied and committed murder. They found me guilty and I was going to be shot, but Mudge had been with me, part of the mutiny. He used his contacts to make sure the story got everywhere.'

'Real scandal,' Pagan said. 'Actual public outcry.'

I shrugged. 'Everyone's a vet now. Could've just as easily been them. Mudge saved my life, again. Instead of being shot I was dishonourably discharged.'

'Really?' Pagan was laughing. It was difficult to get dishonourably discharged these days because troops were needed so badly. By the time you did something bad enough to warrant it you were more likely to just get shot. Everyone wanted to be dishonourably discharged.

'Mudge disappeared about eight months ago,' I said. 'He was looking for another friend of ours.'

'I know where Mudge is,' Morag said.

## 13
# The North Atlantic

'We're going to New York,' I said with what I hoped was finality.

'Are you crazy?' Pagan asked, apparently missing the finality.

'Isn't New York supposed to be a bad place?' Morag asked.

'Compared to what? The Avenues? Yeah, when it's not being attacked. The Rigs, probably. Dog 4? I don't think so,' I said.

We were riding at just under the sound barrier about ten feet above the North Sea, heading up the coastline. Up past where Morag and I had started off in Dundee. We were in the cramped converted hold of a fast attack sled. I think it had probably started life as a Lockheed but the vehicle had been so extensively customised and presumably rebuilt after taking damage it no longer resembled its original form that much.

It was a long, grey, armoured wedge of a vehicle, somehow managing to be aerodynamic and ugly at the same time. To aid with its stealth capabilities there were no right angles on it, and at the moment its weaponry was retracted behind concealing panels. It looked like the lump of ugly, utilitarian metal it was.

The Russian pilot had introduced himself via a loudspeaker. His name was Mikael Rivid, and he assured us that he had piloted sleds like this for the Spetznaz, but then I got the feeling that every Russian sled driver said that. Pagan had said that Rivid was okay but according to his friends at Fosterton a little mad, but then everyone said that about Russians, and sled drivers. In fact, it seemed quite likely that Rivid was a little mad: he was, after all, flying at about ten feet over the North Sea at just under seven hundred miles an hour, a feat that only someone with very good enhanced reflexes was capable of.

Typical of pilots of low-level, ground-effects vehicles like this, Rivid was a chimera. He was directly wired into the vehicle, a requirement because of its speed and the amount of handling it required. Rivid, like many chimeras, was severely disabled. He existed cradled in a technological womb secured on a complex series of gyroscopic mounts in the front of the sled.

The womb took care of all his needs. His food came in a drip with many tasty flavours; a disturbingly visible catheter removed his waste. His sense link was as close as he was ever going to come to feeling the touch of another person, his external world a hallucination of ghost people piped in from the net. I was momentarily envious before I realised that even for me that was taking self-pity too far.

The sled was Rivid's body; he was wired in so deep that he had developed an intimacy with the machine that most people never achieved with their lovers. It was far beyond what I felt jacked into my bike. Chimeras were so good at what they did because if their vehicles went down they had no way of escaping. That tended to focus the mind.

'It will be a little more to travel to New York,' Rivid said. His voice was tinny from the cheap speaker, though still heavily accented. 'More fuel and more ... excitement. We will have to stop at the Faroe Islands.'

'Have you been there before?' Pagan asked. There was static over the cheap loudspeaker which I realised was actually laughter.

'Of course! I've been to Barney's World! Why wouldn't I go to New York as well?'

I wasn't sure I followed his logic. 'Is it as bad as they say?' I asked.

'Worse! Very bloody! Very ... exciting! Dangerous unless you're a pirate.'

'Do you want to go there?' Pagan asked Rivid.

'Why not! More money for me.'

Pagan seemed to sag and then turned back to me in the cramped quarters. We found ourselves pushed back up into the bucket seats, as the sled's compensators didn't quite remove all the Gs. We were banking hard to the left and I was against the right-hand bulkhead. I found myself looking down at Pagan and Morag strapped in opposite me.

'Sorry,' came the cheerfully unrepentant-sounding voice of Rivid.

'Look,' Pagan began. 'We risk everything if we go there. Let's just go and finish our project,' he said, meaning God.

'You think Russia will be any safer?' I asked. 'Like you say, everything's for sale. They'll be able to outbid what you pay for privacy, and you know it. Also, the Russian authorities, criminal or not, will cooperate with the people who are looking for us in a way that Balor's lot won't.' Morag shivered at the sound of Balor's name. Like most people her age, she knew Balor's reputation as a criminal bogeyman. A cyborg transformed to look like some mythical sea monster that ran his pirate kingdom from within the ruins of New York City.

Pagan and I knew more. Balor had been special forces, SBS. He may even have served under Rolleston.

Some soldiers, most of them originally street punks, had themselves altered to look like monsters. There were entire units made up of werewolves, goblins, even things from old medias like the Klingz. Often it wasn't just cosmetic alterations. A werewolf would have his olfactory senses enhanced, claws, fangs, etc. Needless to say, while this sort of stuff may be useful on the streets it had been pointless in the war. In squaddie circles people doing this were thought to be trying too hard and considered something of a joke. They rarely made it into any special forces. Balor and his crew were the exception. He didn't give a shit what people thought of him. He just wanted to be different. He did not want to be human. He wanted to be the sea.

Balor spent most of his operational existence fighting on Proxima Centauri, deep in the cold dead oceans of a cold dead planet. He had been extensively rebuilt for submarine operations at incredible depths. Pretty much most of his body had been replaced. At the same time he had his body sculpted to resemble some primordial sea demon from mythology. The body sculpt had been so good that it gave me pause the one time I'd seen him. There seemed to be nothing human about him: it was as though he was as alien as one of Them. There also was a rumour that he'd undergone neurosurgery to change his thought patterns into something that was no longer human.

And then there was the eye. While it may have been an affectation, a reference to obscure ancient mythology, there were more damn rumours about that eye than there were about Them. An experimental weapon, self-mutilation, Themtech, even some particularly unpleasant sexual practices involving eye sockets were suggested, though probably not within his earshot.

Balor had been a senior NCO, I forget what rank. His outfit was called the Fomorians. The majority of them had been navy divers and not Royal Marines like most of the SBS and they loved Balor. He commanded their total loyalty. Most of them were transformed for deep ops and most of them also had themselves sculpted to look like sea monsters.

Again it was only rumour, but apparently he stopped listening to the officers and started making up his own missions. Command became worried first and then scared about their inability to control Balor and his people. He was asked to leave the service. The Fomorians went with him and nobody tried to stop them. They disappeared.

That was ten years ago. Three years later they turned up again. They were at the head of a coalition of maritime-based criminals and veterans chosen from various navies and maritime special forces. Units like the SBS, Navy Seals, Italy's San Marco Marines, the US Marines Maritime Special Purpose Force and Russia's Naval Spetznaz. They took over the ruins of New York, pushing out the existing gangs and nearly feral tribespeople, who had lived in the city since it had been evacuated in the wake of rising waters. They fortified the partially submerged city, turning it into a maze-like death trap for any who entered without their permission. Under Balor's control it became a free port, a base for piracy, smuggling and just about every other criminal enterprise imaginable.

There had been a few half-hearted attempts by the American government to retake the city, but in the end it proved to be more trouble than it was worth. Again rumour had it that the American government cut a deal with Balor. They rerouted what shipping they could and paid protection money for what shipping they couldn't, like everyone else, and learned to tolerate the self-styled pirate king of New York.

See, that was the problem when talking about Balor; he based himself on myth and all anyone really knew about him was rumour. However, by far and away the scariest rumour that I had ever heard about him was that he had been the Grey Lady's lover. For some reason I found that more worrying than the atrocities, the general weirdness and his ability to scare governments.

'You ever meet him?' I asked Pagan.

'Balor? No. You?' he said, still not looking happy.

'Saw him once. He was coming back, I think for the last time. I was shipping out to Sirius for the first time. I saw some really hard men and women get out of his way.' I thought for a while about the eight-foot-tall monster I'd seen in the disembarkation lounge of the Kenyan Spoke. It still sent a shiver down my spine. I looked at Morag's concerned expression. I don't think the two ex-special forces operators accompanying her were being particularly reassuring.

'Still,' I said. 'We won't be having anything to do with Balor himself. We'll just keep our heads down, find Mudge and then decide what to do.'

'I don't like this,' Pagan said. 'Morag, what do you think?' Morag looked surprised that she was being asked her opinion. She thought about it for a while.

'I think the program's the most important thing,' she finally said.

'The God thing? You serious?' I said, surprised.

'Do you think this Mudge can help?' she asked me.

'Help what? You guys find God? Not really.' I was beginning to lose a point of reference for the conversation.

'Maybe we should go to Russia then.' She sounded unsure of herself.

'Look, you guys do what you want. I'll make my own way to New York and find Mudge myself. Besides, I think New York is the one place that Rolleston may have some problems killing me,' I told them. I was pissed off for no good reason I could think of. Morag looked away from me and an awkward silence followed.

'I'm going with Jakob,' she suddenly announced. Pagan looked between the two of us. It was obvious that he was not happy with her decision.

'Well I guess we're going to New York,' he said.

*Hot LZ. I could hear Buck's guitar solo accompanied by the near-constant whining rhythm of the gunship's six slaved minigun turrets. It seemed strangely calm as my audio dampeners kicked in, taking out the worst of the noise, and I watched the tracer light display fill the air with disinterest.*

*Beneath us was a plain of mud, bodies and the wreckage of various armoured vehicles, all ours. Even in the gunship I could feel a warm wind blowing across it. We debussed almost looking like a military unit as we rolled into the trench network. Training, common sense and experience pushed through a haze of drugs and fatigue, telling us where the best places to hide and point guns were as we found overlapping defensive positions.*

*I became vaguely aware of taking light fire from the moment we landed. I barely noticed the gunship take off, peripherally aware of vectored air pushing down on me as it climbed away from us. We leapfrogged from covering position to covering position. We did everything we could to avoid contact as we were right in the middle of Their push, and more importantly we really couldn't be bothered to fight. Not that They were trying too hard to find us.*

*Their mechanised push was going on above our heads. Every time one of Their heavy troop-carrying tanks went over, the honeycombed energy matrices glowing blue, we would take cover, bury ourselves in mud or simply remain still. All we really had to worry about were Their Walkers and any loose Berserks. There were relatively few of both as this was mainly an artillery, air and armoured battle, or more accurately a rout.*

*The sky was infrequently lit by Their energy beams and black light. Our return fire – plasma, various HE rounds and missiles – was even further away and more infrequent. Every so often a flight of Their fighters would scream overhead, coming back from a distant massacre.*

*

*I was lying on my back all but submerged in the mud, watching the underside of one of Their heavy tanks float overhead, admiring, not for the first time, the beauty of the energy matrices. It seemed to take a while for me to register the events around me as dangerous and then quantify them further as incoming enemy fire, though it was probably a lot faster than it felt. Wired reflexes and nerves, along with slaughter, warred with near-total physical exhaustion to create this bizarre, twilight half-world in which I seemed to exist.*

*One of Their Walkers, ten feet of organic mech, had one foot in the trench we were living in for that moment. Power-assisted, liquid-looking tentacles reached out for David Brownsword, the quiet Scouser who was running point for us. Brownie made life difficult for everyone by dropping a multi-spectrum smoke and ECM charge from his pack before making a sprint straight for us.*

*Split-screen visual info from the rest of the squad told me that there were Berserks entering the trench, debussed from a heavy tank behind us. I didn't bother with orders. They knew what they were doing. My shoulder laser tore through the easy-release clips on the inertial armour at my shoulder. The beam stabbed out superfluously at the Walker but acted along with my smartlink to form a lock for one of my pack missiles before Brownie's grenade took full effect.*

*I turned away from the Walker in front of me and brought the H&K SAW up to fire through my squad at the enemy infantry coming from behind us. The light, high-explosive, anti-tank missile launched itself from one of the twin tubes on my pack. I was barely aware of the heat as its rocket engine kicked in ten feet above me.*

*Bone-like biological penetrator rounds filled the trench from the Walker's shard cannons. Multiple hits against my solid-state breastplate and helmet flung me to the ground. One round even beat the hardening inertial armour undersuit and embedded itself in my cybernetic arm.*

*From prone I pushed myself into a firing position and continued firing through the squad using the SAW's smartlink to target the enemy infantry flanking us in the trench. They were Berserks. Hunched, hulking, four-armed, vaguely humanoid forms made of chitin and black liquid. Each of the aliens' four limbs ended in some kind of weapon attachment. With something approaching disinterest, I began placing bursts of armour-piercing, hydro-shock rounds into them, each burst getting a little push from the gauss booster on the end of the barrel, sending the bullets deeper into the supersonic.*

*Behind me the HEAT warhead's explosion shook the ground and sprayed mud everywhere. I had no idea if my missile had hit, been confused by Brownie's ECM or been taken out by the Walker's black light anti-missile defence.*

*Overhead my audio dampeners compensated for one long hypersonic boom as both Gregor and Bibs began firing overlapping long bursts from their railguns, aiming by dead reckoning where they thought the Walker was, their optics confused by the multi-spectrum smoke.*

*Brownie slid into the mud next to me, sending a grenade perilously close to the railgunners to impact at the back of the advancing squad of Berserks. He swore as his grenade launcher jammed. As he tried to work the pump he was suddenly wrenched off the ground. I felt warm wetness rain down on me as the Walker's tentacles tore Brownie apart in mid-air. Where was my adrenaline? Can you wear out the glands?*

*I rolled over, triggering the microwave emitter on top of my SAW, as the Walker bore down on me. It had the weird, warped, off-centre look to it They get when they're injured. The minor millisecond pause the microwave emitter gave me was enough as I triggered the rest of the SAW's magazine into it at point-blank range, probably not doing a great deal of harm. However, it was staggering as hypersonic round after hypersonic round impacted into it. Gregor advanced until he stood between it and me. The Walker finally toppled over, beginning its rapid sludge-like dissolution to join the local mud. I barely registered that there was a red mess from a shard round where Bib's face used to be. I walked past her as she slid to the ground. Now They would want us, now They knew we were here.*

*I ejected the spent cassette from my SAW and replaced it with another vacuum-packed two hundred rounds. It didn't matter that Bibby Sterlinin was dead. It didn't matter that the sum of the experiences that went to form her existence as a sentient being was over. It didn't matter that the thrill-seeking corporate brat who could've easily joined the Fortunate Sons or dodged the war altogether had been my friend and even on one very drunk occasion my lover. What mattered was we needed her ammunition.*

*'Get her ammo,' I said to no one in particular. If we'd had the time we would've stripped her of ware as per our standing orders. At least with the planet being evacuated the Carrion units wouldn't get to her and harvest her body for implants.*

It hadn't even felt like sleep. More like a broken machine running down, but the dreams had come anyway. I'd woken up alert, aware of the sled's high-pitched whine. The internal clock in my head was at least working. I'd been asleep for just under eight hours. I couldn't risk using my internal GPS in case its signal was traced, but that had to put us close to New York. I knew I was going to have to find a cyber doc.

I looked around the cargo hold. It smelt pretty ripe now. Especially as we hadn't had time to clean up after the attack on the Avenues, and in my case I'd been dumped in what I could only assume by the smell was raw sewage.

Morag was asleep. Pagan was in a net trance, presumably working on his God program. I tried not to watch Morag sleep.

'Rivid,' I said quietly.

'Yes, my friend?' His amplified voice boomed out. Morag stirred.

'I miss the Faroes?' I asked.

'Yes, we got fuel there, we didn't stay long. You were very tired, I think.' Even through the cheap Russian amplifier he sounded distracted. Morag was awake and bleary-eyed.

'Everything okay?' I asked him.

'I am not sure,' he said.

'Whass going on?' Morag asked sleepily.

'I've been tracking something, a big signal currently twenty or so miles to our north. I detected it a while back and didn't think anything of it, but it has changed its course to an intercept with us.'

'Will it?' I asked.

'No, too large, too slow.'

'Morag, can you link to Pagan and tell him we need him out here? What is it?' I asked Rivid.

'Not sure.' The jolly Russian was gone; there was only concentration in his tone now. 'The signal's confused. They're either trying to jam or it has stealth capability, sub-surface though.' I didn't like the sound of this. The capabilities involved were beginning to sound very military.

'Could you—'

'Multiple incoming! Secure for manoeuvres!' the tinny amp suddenly screamed at us. We banked so suddenly I could have sworn I felt us touch the waters of the Atlantic. I heard servos whine as they struggled to open the hatches for the weapons pods.

'Can we help?' I shouted at Rivid.

'Pagan, they are attempting to hack into my systems. I need you on comms!' Rivid shouted. Pagan was still in his trance. I turned to Morag to find out why she hadn't contacted him.

'It's all right. He knows and he's on it. I'm going to help,' she said, anticipating my question. Suddenly the bulkheads came to life. They were papered with a kind of thin viz screen. I could see various images from the cameras around the sled as well as sensor data. Heading towards us from the north were the contrails of two missiles. I'm not sure that witnessing the attack was doing my sense of helplessness any good.

'Do you want me to jack into the weapons?' I shouted over the sled's screaming engines as we suddenly banked hard again. My only answer was a tirade of badly distorted Russian. I watched as beams of harsh red light from the sled's laser anti-missile defences bisected the sky. It looked like a nearly constant grid of light as the missiles threw themselves into a series of defensive manoeuvres to avoid the lasers.

I knew that Pagan and Morag would be trying to repulse any electronic warfare attempts while simultaneously trying to jam or control the missiles. One of the missiles went up. All around me on the bulkhead screens everything seemed to be orange. The compression wave battered into the sled and I screamed, hating that I was in someone else's hands. It was a conventional warhead but a large one. I thought the sled would flip. Instead it spun across the choppy grey Atlantic like a skimming stone thrown by a child. I still have no idea how Rivid managed to regain control of the sled. Though I couldn't help but notice that the catheter had been used once he did. I knew how he felt.

'Fuck you! Fuck you!' Rivid's tinny-sounding voice screamed. Mid-spin I was vaguely aware of him launching several surface-to-surface missiles of his own. I knew he'd link to Pagan and have him provide electronic cover for them, jam our unseen enemy's countermeasures so the missiles would have a chance of hitting.

The problem now was the second missile. Even if the laser or the chaff and decoys that Rivid was now firing off brought the missile down it was too close and would probably still destroy us.

'Three, no four, craft have been launched. Copters by the look of it. Making heavy burn for us,' Rivid said. I didn't see what he was worried about. Surely the missile was the more pressing concern. I could see on the bulkhead screens the missile coming towards us and on the sensor display the four incoming copters. Judging by their speed their rotors were stowed and they were just using jets.

Then the missile just dropped into the ocean. A moment later there was an explosion but the water dampened much of the force. I felt the sled rise and buck violently from the underwater blast but Rivid rode it through.

'Nice one, Pagan,' I muttered to myself. Hacking a missile in flight was more than a little impressive.

Ahead of us the bulkhead screen showed what was left of Staten Island and Brooklyn. We were approaching the headland at over five hundred miles an hour, the copters gaining on us. I saw a missile lock warning appear on the screen and then another.

We were through the Narrows. I could see the copters clearly now on the screen. I recognised them as US Navy. A missile lock warning disappeared, presumably jammed, but I saw a blossom of flame from one of the copters as the remaining locked missile was fired. Chaff exploded from the sled and laser cut the air again. Ahead of us New York was a grey city of broken spires reaching out of the water.

Rivid banked suddenly. Again the craft was at ninety degrees to the dark water. My audio implants dampened the sound of railgun rounds bouncing off the sled's armoured body. The laser caught and destroyed the incoming missile and I heard the pointless return fire of the sled's own railgun.

Suddenly we were in New York. The light dimmed as we shot down lower Broadway, the ruined buildings too much of a blur to make out anything about them. I only barely caught the explosion behind us as one of the copters went up.

'What was that?' I asked, meaning the copter's destruction.

'One of the city's SAM emplacements,' Rivid answered. I wondered if they had a reason not to target us.

Rivid weaved in and out of the partially submerged buildings as railgun rounds and exploding rockets covered us in debris. We played hide and seek through water-filled steel and concrete-walled canyons. We were chased under bridges made of collapsed skyscrapers. I was able to get a look at the lean, predatory, insect-like form of the copters following us, their forward-facing twin railguns reminding me of mandibles.

In the middle of a rocket barrage Rivid mangled the front of the sled as he crashed through a pile of debris into a building. Fire chased us through deserted and destroyed offices and out the other side as we dropped back down into the water. He shot uptown again. The sled was slowing down; its handling seemed less smooth. There were still three of them on us. We'd seen other missile emplacements and various other defensive systems but it seemed that the inhabitants of New York were not going to provide us with any further help.

'Jakob, my friend,' Rivid's voice slurred from the cheap loudspeaker. 'Do you think this is our swansong?' I assumed the question was pretty much rhetorical. I mean I could've asked to be let out, and the copters may not have noticed us, but that seemed unfair to Rivid, who was presumably only in this situation because of us.

'You could let us out,' I suggested, sounding like a coward and a hypocrite to my own ears.

'You disappoint me,' Rivid said. He sounded sad. 'I thought we'd go out fighting, yes?' Problem was I hadn't done any. The last time I'd felt this helpless was during a disastrous night drop on Dog 4. We'd watched our assault shuttle being overtaken by other burning shuttles tumbling out of the sky. Shot down by Them AA emplacements.

Rivid didn't wait for an answer. He banked tightly around the corner of Seventh Avenue and West 34th Street. The copters were back on our tail, kicking in their afterburners, as we crossed Sixth Avenue. Rivid throttled down hard, the damaged engines screaming as he cornered north onto Fifth Avenue so fast he went halfway up the wall of a building in a wash of water. He shot up Fifth, throttled back and turned into a crumbling debris-strewn building that looked like it was once some kind of multi-storey car park. He gunned the protesting sled up a spiral ramp, using the weight of the armoured vehicle to knock ancient burnt skeletons of cars out of his path as he made his way to the roof.

On the roof Rivid brought the sled to a halt.

'This is your plan?' I shouted.

'There's very little planning going on,' Rivid had time to say as the first copter rounded the corner of Fifth some two hundred feet above us. I could hear the muted thunder of railgun rounds impacting on the sled's armoured hull. Two, then three missile lock warnings appeared.

'What's going on?' Morag shouted as she and a worried-looking Pagan came out of their trance. I could hear multiple supersonic bangs become one constant thunderous roar, my audio dampeners reducing the sound to a manageable level as Rivid fired the sled's own railgun. I felt, heard and saw on the screen Rivid launch a surface-to-air missile as rockets exploded all around us and one finally hit. We were thrown about in our straps, and the sled shot back from the force and battered into a concrete pillar.

My head ringing, I only just caught the copter that had hit us disappearing back around the corner of Fifth Avenue followed by the SAM. The explosion blew the side out of the building on the corner as the burning copter dropped into the waters beneath it.

'Yes!' I shouted. Morag looked terrified.

Pagan glanced at her. 'How many SAMs left?' he shouted at Rivid.

'That was it.' There were still two more copters out there. 'Still, not bad for a sled versus copter, I think?'

'Pretty good,' I said. I looked at the radar images projected on the bulkhead. The two copters were circling us using the surrounding buildings as cover. Presumably they were being a bit more cautious since Rivid had taken one of them out. I smiled, finding myself just across the road from the broken but unbowed and still impressive Empire State Building. In either direction I saw the bridges. They ran in a network all across Manhattan, spanning the canals of New York from the most structurally sound buildings. On Fifth I could make out small, fast-moving craft heading towards us from either direction.

These would be Balor's people. I'd heard about these tactics: they preferred to do their fighting in the sunken maze-like warrens of the city streets.

Proximity warnings from the sled's motion detectors showed there was movement all around us: from nearby buildings, on the bridges, climbing out of the water. The problem was they were probably just as pissed off at us as they were with the naval aviators. The only thing we had going for us was that the aviators were Fortunate Sons, else they'd be working for a living on the seas of Proxima at Barney's.

Then something beautiful happened. The first copter came low out of 35th Street just north of us. Missile lock warnings appeared and the hull reverberated to the sound of railgun rounds. From the top of the building on the corner of Fifth and 35th I could see something thrown off the roof. It seemed to blossom and expand as it fell. It took a while for my brain to understand what it was, surprised as I was by this low-tech approach. It seemed to happen very slowly as the high-tensile steel net opened and landed on the rotors of the copter, tangling itself in them. The copter seemed to hang there for a while. I watched it try and fold its rotors away and move to jet, but the blades were too entangled. The copter dropped, battering itself off the side of the building in a shower of rubble, before disappearing into the water beneath.

Then I saw one of the most insane things I have ever seen. The final copter, its nose down, predatory, crept around the Empire State Building at about level with the sixtieth floor. I saw the missile lock warnings appear one after another. It was over Fifth Avenue now. Rivid caught what was happening on one of the sled's external cameras and zoomed in so we could see perfectly. A figure exploded through plate glass sixty floors above the ground, about fifty-five storeys above the water. The three of us in the back watched in shock.

The figure cleared the sixty or so feet to the craft and grabbed the fuselage of the copter. Rivid closed in on the figure. It did not look human but I recognised the monster clinging to the side of the aircraft. I could see the terrified face of the jacked-in aviator. I could see where the monster's claws had dug into the copter's armour, providing him with purchase. Balor leant back. In his free hand he held some kind of collapsible spear. I watched as he rammed it through the armour and into the cockpit. I saw the pilot scream. Balor pulled his spear out through the hole he'd made. The copter lurched violently and began to spin towards the east side of Fifth away from the broken-topped Empire State Building.

We watched as Balor let go of the copter and dropped, positioning himself into a dive and disappearing beneath the water. Achingly slowly, the copter seemed to cross Fifth and fly into another building, transforming itself into wreckage before it plummeted into the water, bent and broken. That more than anything drove it home to me that Balor was maybe more than just a scary-looking cyborg.

'Uh, guys,' Morag said. I looked at the bulkhead screens. I could see figures closing in on us from all sides. Moving tactically, surrounding us.

'You can get out now,' Rivid said. Was that disgust I heard in his voice?

# 14
# New York

Rivid had done his bit. We had to face the music. Out of the sled, the three of us down on our knees, covered by pros as we were searched and then secured. Then face down on ancient pitted concrete looking at webbed feet.

'Find their heads, spike them and add them to the rest,' said an impossibly deep and inhuman-sounding voice. It came as a relief when I realised that Balor was talking about the aviators and not us. A little while later I heard the sled leave. I was pleased. Rivid was a good guy and had presumably cut some kind of deal.

'And them?' I heard a female voice that was used to command ask. She had an American accent. Initially I found the growling that responded unnerving but I realised it was just Balor thinking.

'Show me the girl,' Balor's voice answered. I heard Morag being dragged up for Balor to look at.

'Leave her ...' I managed to say before getting kicked in the ribs.

'Shut up!' Pagan hissed at me.

'Get them on their feet,' Balor ordered.

We were dragged to our feet. Balor towered over me. He was around seven and a half feet tall, his face strangely angular and his mouth too big for even a head that size. His smile revealed rows of shark-like teeth. His height was in proportion to his muscled build, though as powerful as he looked he still gave off an air of wiry speed. His skin was blue, black and green overlapping scales, as much lizard as it was fish. I knew that his armoured skin and reinforced skeleton were capable of surviving the crushing depths of the freezing oceans of Proxima. He was dripping wet from his dive and the only clothes he wore were a pair of cut-off old combat trousers. His hair looked like dreadlocks made of black seaweed but my understanding was they were some kind of sensor aid to help with echolocation. His large, powerful, long-fingered hands ended in sharp vicious-looking claws. He carried the collapsible long-bladed spear I'd seen him use on the copter pilot, now no more than a cylinder of some super-hard metallic compound from the Belt. Strapped to his leg he had a very functional-looking diver's knife. At his waist he wore what looked like a Benelli twelve-gauge shotgun pistol. It was a sidearm that only power-armoured troops and the largest heavy conversion cyborgs could use because of the size of its magazine.

Of course the most striking thing about him was the eye. The eye had as many myths about it as the man himself. His right eye was a black pool, yet it still looked organic, despite the fact I knew it to be artificial. It was his left eye that all the fuss was about. The sharkskin eyepatch was engraved with an ornate knotwork design and seemed to cover half the left side of his face. You would assume that this would limit his peripheral vision but I could see he had what looked like small glass studs that circled his head providing him with 360-degree vision.

'Put them in a cage,' said the monster, pointing two clawed fingers at Pagan and me. I looked at the circle of hard faces around us. I didn't know them but I recognised them. Balor had done his work well. He'd recruited from the best. They were dirty and ragged, but their kit, though old, was clean and well looked after. We didn't stand a chance here but I didn't want to be separated from Morag.

'The girl?' the American woman asked. Balor took his time looking Morag up and down in a way that made my skin crawl.

'Bring her to me,' Balor said finally, and turned to leave. It was the perfect time for me to shout no and start struggling but I knew that would have been a pointless gesture in this league.

'Mr Balor sir?' Morag said, her voice sounding somehow tiny and scared. Balor stopped and turned to look at her. 'I really don't want to be raped or eaten,' she said. There were a couple of sniggers from the gunmen and -women surrounding us but most of them looked less than impressed, and although Balor's strange features may have been difficult to read he seemed to be one of them.

'I'll bear that in mind,' he rumbled. I was desperately looking around for an opening but finding nothing, when I saw someone I recognised. She was short but heavily muscled, a lot of upper-body strength. She wore tatty but still-functional armour and a telltale bandanna across unkempt short hair. She was carrying a Metal Storm gauss rifle slung horizontally across her torso.

'I know you?' I said, desperately trying to place her face.

'Yeah, you know me,' she said in a resigned manner. She sounded like she came from the Arizona coast. Then I placed her.

'You were on the *Santa Maria,*' I said. She seemed to consider this for a while. Balor was watching her. Everyone in the special ops community knew the significance of the *Santa Maria*, the cargo ship we were on when they tried to dump us into space.

'Yeah. Yeah, I was,' she finally acknowledged.

'SEAL, right? I'll have your name in a second,' I said. Balor looked at the ex-SEAL and then back at me, his expression unreadable.

'Cage,' he reminded the people guarding us.

'Our gear?' Morag asked. I groaned inwardly. Balor turned to regard her for a moment, just long enough for the monster's gaze to make her really uncomfortable.

'Bring it to me,' he finally ordered. 'If there's anything really good it'll get split.' Morag had inadvertently tipped them off that we were holding something worthwhile.

'Bollocks,' I said with some feeling. On the one hand I wasn't dead, which meant I'd lived longer than I thought I would with Rolleston on my trail. On the other hand I was still less than pleased about being in a reinforced cage waist-deep in freezing-cold water. The irritating thing was that the locks were solid, heavy duty and mechanical so Pagan couldn't even hack them. Nor had boosted muscle been able to bend the bars. It was almost like they didn't want us to escape. We didn't even know what part of New York we were in. Our only frame of reference was the occasional dead rat floating by.

We were in a series of partially submerged cages that formed a kind of grid. There were some other people in here but they didn't show much interest in talking to us. I clambered down from the cage and held myself as I shook from the cold in the water.

'How's our girl doing?' I asked Pagan, assuming that he'd link with Morag.

'Don't know, they've got too many other hackers keeping an eye on us,' he said. He seemed pissed off. At me, I mean.

'If it makes you feel better you can tell me we should've gone to Russia,' I said.

'Chinese parliament,' he said. 'I raised my objection but in the end agreed to come with you – can't complain about it.' He didn't sound like he meant it. Balor had taken the solid-state memory cube that housed Ambassador. The pair of us lapsed into silence.

'Good work on that missile,' I eventually said. Meaning the one he'd dropped into the Atlantic before it had gone off.

'Wasn't me.' That got my attention.

'What then? Malfunction?'

Pagan shook his head. 'Morag did it.' I stared at him for a while.

'Even I know that's a pretty sophisticated hack. She doesn't have anything like the experience.'

'I agree,' Pagan said. He had a funny look on his face.

'She scares you, doesn't she?'

Pagan gave this some thought. Eventually he answered, 'I'm not so sure it's her so much as her and Ambassador.'

'It's helping her?' I asked, worried by this alien influence over Morag.

'Don't get me wrong. She's good, she's definitely got the talent and will be a brilliant hacker, better than me probably, but yeah, to do what she's doing she's getting help.' I wasn't sure what to make of what he'd said. It was so beyond my scope of experience. Was she still Morag?

'You sure this isn't an attack by Them?' I eventually asked him. He considered my question, shivering in the cold water.

'I'm not sure of anything – seems an unlikely way to go about it,' he finally said. He looked up at the network of corroded pipes and the pitted concrete ceiling above us.

'He'll sell us to Rolleston, won't he?' Pagan asked. I shrugged.

'I honestly don't know. I don't think he thinks like anyone else. He could do anything.'

'What do you think he wanted with Morag?' Pagan asked. I just looked at him. I felt that was a pretty naive question for an ex-special forces operator. Pagan had just as much knowledge about these kinds of things as I did and I was trying really hard not to think about it. Co-opted by an alien, and now Balor himself had her. I was trying not to think that maybe it would've been better if I'd put a bullet through her head a while back.

We heard the clanking of an ancient freight elevator. Moments later webbed feet stood above us on top of the cage.

'Balor wants to see you,' said the strangely modulated voice of one of the Fomorians.

We were under heavy guard. I could barely stand but it made me feel better – it's nice to get some respect. Outside it was muggy and close, the air ionised, black clouds rolling in above the spires of the partially submerged city. When the rain started it was hot, the pollution making it feel greasy, like being sweated on. We were in what used to be called Times Square. We made our way over surprisingly well-made catwalks towards what looked like some proto Ginza writ large. Neon signs leaked dust from ruptured tubes. Huge viz screens had been hung over the scarred facades of old buildings. They seemed to be showing wildlife documentaries about sea life.

Craning my neck I could just about make out various defensive emplacements around the square, concealed and otherwise. This area was well protected. The well-armed denizens of New York seemed to be congregating in the square. Below us in the water, powerful speedboats, hovers and hydro-bikes were landing at small jury-rigged jetties. In the centre of the square held up by high-tensile steel cables, was part of the flight deck of the USS *Intrepid*, an ancient naval aircraft carrier that had once been moored in New York. Apparently the *Intrepid* was now suspended inverted between two crumbling buildings further uptown. The pieces of suspended flight deck were the focus point for the crowds assembling in Times Square. Hovering cameras floated around it and I could see on one or two of the smaller screens pictures of the empty platform from the cameras. On the one hand I had a sinking feeling, on the other it didn't seem possible that all this attention could be for us.

We climbed up ringing metal steps. The rain was beginning to worsen now, but I was already wet and cold. We headed towards what was once a semicircular lounge in the Marriott Marquee above the waters in Times Square. The roof of the lounge had long since gone and it was now open to the elements. Seated back in the Marquee, sheltered from the open air, a string quartet played something understated and pleasant.

In the lounge itself I was relieved to see a frightened but uneaten Morag. She was sitting at an expensive-looking, long, dark wood table that had been polished to a fine sheen. With her was Balor, who was helping himself to what looked to be a well-prepared meal. He seemed oblivious to the rain. There were several people with him, including the ex-SEAL woman whose name I just couldn't remember, and a number of his Fomorians. All the Fomorians had been extensively altered to adopt the sea-demon persona of their boss man but none to the extent of Balor. I was trying to decide on an approach but nothing was really presenting itself to me.

I was less than pleased to see Rannu, the Major's man, sitting at the table. It was the first time I had had a good chance to study the small Nepalese. He was compact but heavily muscled, though his movements suggested that his surprising bulk did not slow him down. He was doubtless augmented, but I suspect he had been fast before he'd been turned into a cyborg. Sunglasses presumably covered lenses not unlike mine. His features were unreadable though he seemed to radiate a kind of passivity. His expression didn't change when he saw

Pagan and me but I knew he was sizing me up just as I was sizing him up.

'You eat well,' I said to Balor.

'I work for it,' he said without looking up. At the same time I messaged Morag, asking her if she was okay. One of the other people at the table, a nondescript individual wearing practical faded-grey overalls and with half his head replaced by hardware, looked over at Balor and nodded. Balor looked up at Pagan and me. Pagan was shivering.

'I'm fine,' Morag said.

'You think we're monsters here?' Balor asked. There was some chuckling from round the table. The SEAL woman didn't laugh. Reb, her name came to me. Presumably short for Rebecca or Rebel. Knowing the SEALs, it was probably the latter.

'I thought that was the point,' I said. Balor's toothy grin disappeared; I was quite pleased by that, I didn't like his predatory mouth. He looked between Morag and me.

'Let's keep everything out in the open, yeah?' he told us.

'You sure you want that?' Morag asked, her voice sounding surprisingly even for the situation she was in. Balor turned to her, fixing her with what they described on the vizzes as his baleful eye. Morag looked down immediately. Oh, well done, you cunt, I thought, intimidate a seventeen-year-old girl, my anger taking me by surprise. This sort of shit is much easier when you really don't care.

Balor stretched out both his arms expansively, gesturing at the fine, but increasingly soggy, meal in front of him.

'In the seventeenth and eighteenth centuries, pirate crews would go out of their way to make sure they had a good cook on board. Food was one of the biggest bones of contention on any ship. Pirate captains didn't have the authority that the regular navies or even merchants had over their crews, so good food was one of the ways they kept their people happy.'

'Kept them in line,' Pagan said suddenly. I glanced to my side. He looked old standing there shivering in the warm rain. 'Making it worth their while was one way pirate captains kept their crews in line, the other was fear,' Pagan had no problem meeting Balor's eye.

'And fear is based around ...' Balor began.

'What you have to lose,' Pagan finished for him. I found the expression on Balor's monstrous face difficult to read. He was either irritated by Pagan or impressed. 'You're trying to provide us with motivation.' I wasn't sure I was entirely following the conversation.

'Not you,' Balor replied. 'Him.' He nodded towards me. I felt that sinking feeling. I really didn't think I deserved this. I pointed at Rannu without looking at the solidly built Nepalese. Balor smiled, reached out and tapped his wicked-looking claws on the solid-state memory cube that contained Ambassador.

'This is bollocks. Let's discuss this, make a deal. You're a commercial operator. This pantomime demeans us all,' Pagan said, quite eloquently, I thought. Rannu had already beaten the shit out of me once. I didn't fancy it happening again, especially not in front of several thousand pirates. I didn't think I had a particularly large ego, but these things got around and I could live without spending the rest of my life getting the piss taken out of me by every vet I met for such a public beating. Maybe Balor wanted to humble me for some reason. Weird really. I already felt pretty humble.

'No, what demeans us is reducing everything to commerce,' Balor said, his one visible eye rolling up in a disconcerting manner. 'I am not some fucking merchant and you obviously need to remember that you are alive.'

'A nice dram and a night with a beautiful woman reminds me I'm alive,' I said with some resignation. Balor turned to look at me. He took his time, just looked at me until he'd decided I was good and uncomfortable.

'You are a victim,' he finally said. I gave this some thought. I had to agree there was an element of truth to what he said. 'You do it to yourself,' he continued. I was less sure about that. I hadn't set these events running. We were dealing with powerful people and institutions way beyond my control. 'You behave like a worm and as a result you will be treated like one.'

Fuck this. I moved towards the table expecting some of Balor's people to shift in case I proved to be a threat. They didn't. That was more worrying.

'I see what you're saying,' I told him. 'I should just fucking kill you and walk out of here.' It was only later I realised that the pause was Balor deciding whether or not to kill me right then and there. Balor stood up. I took a step back. Balor climbed onto the table, knocking plates of food and wine glasses over. I took another step back.

'Bluster and temper are no substitute for courage,' he said. I glanced over at Reb as Balor began walking down the table towards Rannu. The ex-Ghurkha watched him approach impassively.

'I'm not a coward,' I told Balor. I was never going to take unnecessary risks but I could function when the fear came, and that was what it was about after all. Balor pointed towards Reb.

'I know. I know that you are Soldier A, and Reb told me what you did on the *Santa Maria*.' He reached Rannu. I noticed Rannu shift slightly, ready in case something went down.

'Then cut me some fucking slack,' I told Balor's back.

'Why?' Balor asked, turning to look down on me.

'The people here are mostly vets, right?' Pagan asked, gesturing around at the multitudes beginning to line Times Square. 'Special operators, yes?' Balor nodded. 'I refuse to believe that after lifetimes of violence these people will be impressed by this tawdry spectacle.' And he was right: if you'd gone toe to toe with a Berserk, watching two guys beat the shit out of each other was going to be pretty tame, especially if you have the same skills.

'This is just a decision-making process,' Balor told us, the shark grin back. 'Why did you come here?'

I looked at Rannu and said nothing. Balor followed my glance, then looked back at me.

'You know, long ago you could be executed for talking politics in private. You had to have the guts to say what you believed in front of the whole tribe or they knew you to be a low person,' he said.

I was getting tired of this shit. 'So I'm a low person,' I said.

'And *you* have secrets,' Morag said. I looked over to her and she was pointing at Balor. She looked scared but she also looked angry. Both Pagan and the other hacker were looking between her and Balor. What had gone down here? Had she just sent him something? This was the second time she'd implied that Balor needed to keep something quiet.

'You up for this bollocks?' I asked Rannu. 'I've heard of you – you're not supposed to be a wanker.'

'I'm here for the box and you three. I don't care what condition you're in and I don't care about anything outside my orders,' Rannu said. His English was good; he spoke quietly and evenly with just a trace of accent. 'At the moment this would seem to be the easiest way to complete my mission.' He shrugged. There was not a trace of doubt in his voice that he could beat me.

'Working for Rolleston?' Pagan asked. Rannu said nothing. Pagan looked up at Balor. 'What about you? You were SBS, you must know what he's like. You going to do his bidding?' Balor walked back down the table towards Morag and stood over the box containing Ambassador.

'Well, that's why we require a decision-making process.' He pointed at me. 'I know that you were once a warrior.' I shook my head. Warrior creed bullshit. I heard Pagan groan behind me. 'I know what you did for your brother soldiers. I know that once you weren't a low man, a worm ...'

'I was trying to fucking survive. I was shit scared,' I told him, possibly not helping my case.

'And I worked with Rolleston on Proxima. He is no coward but I know what kind of man he is.'

'So give us the box and let us go,' I said.

'But I also know what's in the box,' Balor said. I had a sinking feeling. Without looking I could feel Pagan tense up behind me. Suddenly I was aware of the expressions on the faces of Balor's men. They were expressions of barely contained anger. 'You see,' Balor said, jumping off the table, 'to some it would seem that you have betrayed your own race.' He was standing next to me all but whispering in my ear. He smelled of the sea, in a bad way. 'I will not be a slave but I am no friend to Them.' There was the smell of meat on his breath. I turned around to face him.

'You think we are? You think we're selling us all out? You think our experiences in the war were different to yours? Think They came and made us a brew and gave us some cake?' I asked.

'Think about it, Balor. What would make you deal with Them?' Pagan said. Balor never took his eyes off me. Why me? I wondered.

'I wouldn't,' Balor growled. I was sick of this. What Balor probably thought of as courage was just me deciding I didn't give a fuck any more.

'Fuck you!' I told him. 'We're—' I managed before he grabbed me by my neck. I had seen him begin to move and tried to get out of the way but he was deceptively fast. He picked me up and held me about four feet off the ground. Great in a viz, very intimidating, but my subcutaneous armour went rigid, and I could still breathe, and even if he had crushed my windpipe I still had a small internal air supply.

Instinct overcame intimidation. Suddenly my claws were out and I was punching into him with all eight of my blades. Panic started when I felt my blades sliding off armour and artificial physiology designed to withstand the incredible pressure of oceanic depths. I was flung across the semicircular balcony, sliding through the collected rainwater and coming to a stop when I hit the low wall. I started to get up but a foot stood on my chest and slammed me back into the ground with tremendous force. I looked up. Balor looked angry, really angry.

'Do not,' he said, his voice sounding like two mountains grinding together, 'ever disrespect me in my house.' I bit back my angry replies. Past Balor I could see Morag on her feet looking over at me, eyes full of fear. Pagan was off to my right, presumably aware of the futility of our current predicament.

'Listen to me,' I said through gritted teeth. 'We're not fucking traitors, and I think you know that. There's more to this, and I think you're smart enough to know that as well. But if my only way out of here with the box and my people is through him,' I said, looking over at Rannu, 'then I'll play your stupid fucking game.' Balor just looked down at me and nodded before taking his foot off my chest. 'Any chance of a gunfight?' I asked. 'I'm not feeling my best today.'

# 15
# New York

It wasn't going to be a gunfight and I'd taken a battering in the Avenues. There were still a lot of warning icons on my internal visual display. I'd patched myself up with what little I had and my internal repair mechanisms were doing the best they could but I was a broken machine. I needed a doc and some replacement components. My armour had been pierced in several places and the flesh and machinery beneath it damaged, but my biggest concern was my cracked chest plate. One good blow to that could make a real mess of my internal organs and systems.

Rannu on the other hand looked fine and well, fast and dangerous. Everything I didn't feel like myself at the moment. The platform swayed slightly on its high-tensile cables. Rannu was stripped to the waist and going through some simple exercises. He was obviously heavily augmented but he had no visible prosthetics. He turned his back to me and did some more stretching exercises. Beneath the four plugs in his neck a tattoo covered most of his back. It was a stylised rendering of a black, biomechanical, multi-armed goddess with a weapon in each of her arms. I didn't know a great deal about religion beyond the conversations I'd had with various signals types, but this was ringing alarm bells in my head.

I recognised the image: it was Kali, a Hindu goddess. I knew there was more to her but the figure was often connected with images of death and destruction. She was the patron goddess of a murder cult called the Thuggees. They had originally existed before the FHC at a time when Britain had apparently ruled India, as difficult as that was to believe today. About twenty or so years ago some vet signalman from Leicester had decided to revive the cult. See, this was the problem with hackers: they were geeks, but you got one with charisma and a bit of imagination and you ended up with a cult. Pagan was a pretty benevolent example of this type. Berham wasn't. He had perverted Hinduism and recreated the Thuggees using the cult's tactics of ritualistic murder to take over Leicester's criminal economy. He was one of the most notorious criminals in Britain. He'd killed police, corporates, politicians, and ruled through fear and intimidation. Much of his organisation had been taken down recently in a complex sting operation, but Berham had escaped and several high-ranking policemen, along with members of the Home Office, had been targeted in revenge killings, as had their families.

This kind of made sense. Many Ghurkhas were Hindus; I guessed that Rannu was one who'd gone bad. It explained the weighted monofilament I'd seen him use in Hull. The Thuggees' signature weapon was a monofilament garrotte that they used to decapitate their victims. I also noticed that his kukri was still at his waist, a curved knife about sixteen inches long, the traditional weapon of the Ghurkha regiments. I'd even heard of Ghurkhas going toe to toe with Berserks with only their knives. I did fleetingly wonder why Rolleston was employing a Thug or why a Thug was working for Rolleston, but I figured that wankers were just naturally drawn together.

The rumbling sound took me by surprise until I realised that it was the cheering of the crowd, and suddenly I was nervous beyond the impending fight.

Rannu moved towards me, closing the distance between us. His purposeful stride became a stepping front kick to my stomach, knocking me back. I did the same to him, neither of us blocking as we exchanged kicks, almost a handshake as we tried to gauge each other. I showed nothing on my face, but I suspect he was kicking me a lot harder than I was kicking him as we forced each other around the old flight deck.

His first sidekick took me by surprise, lifting me off my feet, but I recovered quickly. He was in the air now, spinning to power a kick that looked like it would take my head off. I rolled under him, his foot snapping out and just missing me. I could hear the crowd cheering as I came to my feet. He'd already turned and was in the air again. I stepped hurriedly out of the way, putting myself off balance as he landed crouched low with a powerful elbow strike to where I'd been. I threw a hurried sidekick that caught him on the shoulder. It was like kicking stone. I then moved back out of his way to get my balance and correct my stance.

Rannu stood up across from me. Times Square had gone quiet again. We'd finished the initial playful exchange. We both knew what we needed to know: it did not look that good for me. The two things I had going for me were that he would commit to any attack and liked powerful blows, presumably because he was used to fighting other heavily armoured cyborgs. The problem with blows like that was you had to take some punishment to land them as they were slower than lighter blows. That said, he seemed capable of taking the punishment required. The other thing I had going for me was that he liked being in the air. Yeah, this fight would be easy if he wasn't so fast, strong and skilled.

We were on again. The noise of the crowd slipped from my mind as we traded turning kicks and blocks, sliding round in a near circle as we did so. We weren't even trying to hurt each other though the kicks would've dented steel. We were looking for an opening.

I saw my opening as I skipped inside his kick and straight-armed him in the face. My knuckles just touched his skin as he slid to the side and elbowed me in the head so hard that my internal visual display jumped. Then he did exactly what I didn't want him to do and kicked me hard in the chest, sending me flying to the ground and sliding across the rain-slick flight deck. There were more warning signals on my flickering internal visual display. Now I knew he would be in the air. I threw myself forward with no grace whatsoever. As I felt, rather than heard, him land I kicked out with all the force I could muster from the ground. The lucky blow caught him in the base of the spine with more than enough force to break the back of a non-augmented person. I saw Rannu lifted off his feet and thrown over the edge of the deck.

I stood up. As my hearing returned, along with a new ringing sound, I could hear the crowd again. Some of them were booing, which I didn't think was fair. I didn't look over the side at the place where Rannu had gone over. Instead I walked along some twenty feet and then peered over the edge, hoping to see him swimming. As I did so he swung back up onto the flight deck, landing low and steady, knees bent with an easy grace. He was about thirty feet from where I stood. He quickly moved towards the centre of the deck. I jogged backwards, hands in a loose guard, to join him. Still, I had the feeling my best trick had gone.

He skipped forward and was in the air again as his knee hit my chest and his fists hit me on either side of my head so hard that they would have crushed an unarmoured skull. I staggered back. My visual display became a line and then blinked off, leaving me in darkness. It came back in time for me to see another boot flying towards my face. Darkness again. I flung myself away in a manner I hoped was so random he wouldn't be expecting it. A glancing blow on the shoulder knocked me to the deck; the knees of my jeans were torn as I hit it. I assumed he was in the air and rolled backwards coming to my feet as

I heard his combat boots hit the flight deck in front of me.

My vision returned grainy and interspersed with static. Rannu was turning towards me. I leapt into the air, somehow managed to grab his head and powered my knee into his face with enough force that I heard something crunch. It was one of the most satisfying blows I'd ever landed. He staggered back as I landed but stayed on his feet. I leapt up again, this time bringing both knees up to his chin, while bringing both my elbows down on the top of his head. And he punched me. I did that to him and he should've died, armoured cyborg or not, and he had the presence of mind to fucking punch me.

The blow caught me solidly in the stomach and threw me back as I'd still been in mid-air. He was hurt. His face was covered in blood. It had that strange split look that comes from damaged subcutaneous armoured plate, his features distorted. I stepped forward hoping to press what little advantage I may have still had. I swung at him again but he wasn't there. I made the mistake of looking up instead of just moving as his boot axed into the top of my head and drove me into the flight deck. I tried to get up and another kick hit me in the head. I hit the deck again and expected him to finish me but nothing happened.

I managed to climb onto my hands and knees. I spat out blood and overrode the warning icons on my flickering internal visual display, as they seemed to be filling my vision now. Rannu had backed off. He was standing some twenty feet away from me, just watching, because he'd figured out something that I hadn't yet. It came to me when I heard the tribal chanting and cheering of the crowd. This was entertainment. Maybe the jaded veterans watching had seen it all before but so what? After seeing your squad torn apart by the tentacles of an alien Walker you weren't going to be all that impressed by what was on the viz. After all, Roman legionnaires had still gone to the Colosseum and vets still went to pit fights. It was a lot safer to see others fighting than have to do it yourself, and I had to admit it I was a pretty good kick-boxer, entertaining to watch.

Rannu was better, but here was the thing: when two guys of comparable skill go at it, the hungrier guy wins. I was the hungrier guy. I was almost certainly fighting for my life as well as Pagan's and Morag's. Now I liked Pagan but he had the potential to even further complicate my life, and I guess Morag did as well, but at this moment, more than anything, I really did not want to see her hurt. The intensity of that surprised me. I was fighting for my life and this guy still felt he was able to put on a show.

I'm not sure if I could've beaten him in my prime but he was younger, faster and stronger than me, and if I was being honest probably had fewer bad habits. That got me. I was only thirty – kind of old in our brave new world – and Rannu was proving that I was obsolete. Maybe this was what Balor was talking about. I had all these augmentations and skills. Even in a society completely geared towards war I had to be considered among the more dangerous, yet I was at the mercy of people like Rolleston, the Grey Lady, Balor and now this punk. That was depressing. And now I could barely stand up.

Rannu was in the air again. I didn't move. He landed with his knees on my shoulders, his elbow about to hammer down on my head. It would be a good finish, something for all the fight fans. I was going to have to take the elbow strike, got to give a little to get a little. My claws shot out of the internal sheaths in my arm and I rammed them up into each of his thighs. I felt the resistance of his subcutaneous armour and then it gave as I pushed them into him, a sense of satisfaction before the darkness.

I wasn't sure whether I'd blacked out or my internal visual display had gone down again, but when my vision returned I was staggering around dangerously close to the edge. I lurched away from it, spinning round and overcompensating as I tried to find Rannu. I was nearly overcome by nausea and the pain. I guessed I'd exhausted the abilities of my internal pain management systems and my reservoir of powerful painkillers over the last couple of days.

Rannu was on his feet but bent over holding his bleeding thighs. Why was he standing up? I think I may have even muttered that. I could hear more booing. Fuck 'em. Rannu looked up at me. The fucker didn't even have the common courtesy to look angry.

Suddenly I was aware that the huge figure on many of the viz screens around the square was me. Though it didn't look like me. The figure's features were misshapen and he was wet, bloody and breathing heavily. I looked at the figure and wondered why he was still fighting. Some strange part of my brain couldn't help admiring the composition of the shot.

There was cheering as Rannu drew the kukri at his side. It looked old and sharp. I spat some blood out. Rannu seemed battered and tired, or at least I hoped he did. I walked towards him with what I thought was purpose. I meant to do him harm but I may've just been staggering at him. Why was I still standing?

We traded kicks, ineffectually slicing at the other's legs with our blades, hitting armour and sometimes cutting through. That was about as far as we got with skill, we just started to slash at each other. He was good with the knife. He parried my attacks and slashed at me.

I caught the vicious-looking knife on my blades and countered. The thing is I had two weapons to his one, and although he was fast and managed to parry many of my attacks, more of them were getting through. Like a good kick-boxer he knew he had to take his licks to give them. Neither of us broke. Both of us were red.

Finally I noticed that I was slowly pushing him back. A slash to his forehead bled into his eyes. He swung just a little wide. I don't know how I had the presence of mind to realise his mistake and push my advantage. The blades on my right hand pierced his right wrist. I all but heard the crowd's intake of breath. With some satisfaction it was also the first time I heard Rannu cry out in pain. The kukri flew from his hand. I punched forward with the blades on my left hand and he bent backwards so far that they shot over his face. Somehow I was peripherally aware of the kukri sliding to the end of the flight deck and tipping over, falling towards the water.

With my blades still in his arm he kicked me in the face. I staggered back, spitting more blood. I heard another cry of pain from Rannu as my blades were torn out of his arm. His forehead was coming towards me. There was a crunching noise from my nose. I staggered back but managed to recover sufficiently to punch forward with my right. He caught the prosthetic, twisted his arm around it and elbowed me repeatedly in the face with his other arm. That was when I knew the fight was finally over. Rannu kicked my legs out from under me. I hadn't done so bad, better than I thought. I hit the deck. Shame I'd let everyone down. Blacking out would be good. Will he just kill me now? I thought I was beyond pain until I felt the tearing at my right shoulder. I found the energy to scream. Why wasn't I unconscious?

I rolled around on the wet flight deck. Just as I saw the bloody stump of my prosthetic arm flying towards my face I saw the weirdest thing on the viz screen. The figure on it wasn't me or Rannu. It was Morag. She looked really upset, like she was terrified and had been crying. It was like a reaction shot from an old viz. I got hit with my own arm. Nothing.

# 16
# New York

I wasn't sure whether I was more surprised or disappointed to be alive. I felt I needed a rest and this wasn't it. Smell returned first, antiseptic, which was good as it suggested a hospital. There was the faint rotting smell of low tide, so I was still in New York, and the familiar friendly smell of tobacco.

'Fag,' I croaked. I was trying to decide how I felt about opening my eyes. I came to the conclusion that doubtless something bad would happen to me when I did. I felt a cigarette placed between my lips and heard the wheel of an old-fashioned lighter being flicked. It sounded very familiar. A brief warmth on my face and I sucked in the smoke. I didn't even cough as my internal filters went to work. ''S my lighter?' I asked.

'Mine now,' a voice said. It sounded familiar. 'Tell me, have you ever won a fight?' I cracked an eye open. I was surprised that my vision seemed to be working just fine. It took a moment for me to recognise his slightly off-kilter features as he'd grown a rather wispy and slightly sad-looking beard and dyed that and his hair dark brown. He was huddled in a parka drinking from a bottle of expensive-looking, proper Russian vodka.

'Fuck off,' I said by way of greeting. Mudge smiled, the corners of his eyes turning up round the expensive camera-lens eye implants that he'd used to shoot the war. He took the cigarette back and took a drag on it as he kicked back in the chair. Beneath the jeans he was wearing were, I knew, a pair of top-of-the-line prosthetic legs. He'd always boasted he could run faster than anyone in the troop and would do if things ever got really bad, and he could move really fast when correctly motivated, but he never ran.

'Did that cunt really tear my arm off?' I asked. I couldn't really feel any pain but I was trying to ignore that in case I was paralysed.

'You mean Mr Nagarkoti?' Mudge asked, pointing past me. I turned my head and saw Rannu in a bed less than four feet from me. He was awake and watching me, his face impassive as ever. He had medgels and -paks all over his face and the top part of his body. I felt good about that. I answered a lot of questions about how I was feeling by trying to crawl out of the bed to kill him.

'Easy, tiger,' Mudge said, grabbing me and pulling me back into bed. The fact that he could do this suggested I wasn't quite back to my old self just yet. Rannu seemed to find this funny, further infuriating me.

'Get me a gun, get me a fucking gun!' I demanded.

'Shut up,' Mudge said. 'And to answer your question, yes, he tore off your arm and beat you with it. It was pretty fucking brutal, man. He just kept beating you with it. Balor had to swing in and stop him. Nobody's quite sure why you're alive.'

I turned around to glare at Rannu. His face was impassive again. Then something occurred to me. 'You saw it?' I asked.

'You getting your arse kicked?'

'I didn't do that bad.'

'No, you came a close second. Yeah, I saw. I was driving the media deck.'

'You filmed us?'

'Hell yeah. Not every day you can profit from seeing a close friend get beat mostly to death.' He grinned and the pair of us lapsed into silence. I had a closer look around. We were in some kind of hospital ward, all peeling paint and old beds, but the linen was clean and all the medical equipment couldn't have been more than twenty or thirty years out of date. There were about a dozen or so beds in here but Mudge, Rannu and I were the only people in the ward. White curtains were pulled across the windows but a pale light shone through the thin material.

'How long was I out?' I asked. Mudge took another generous sip from the bottle of vodka and offered me a mouthful. I shook my head but hoped Morag was alive and more importantly still had my whisky. You have to learn to prioritise at a time like this.

'Three days,' Mudge said.

'Jesus!' Now I was really surprised I wasn't dead. Why hadn't Rolleston gotten to me? Why hadn't Rannu killed me, or failing that, the Grey Lady? I looked down at myself. Like Rannu I was covered in medgels and medpaks. The scar on my chest told me that my cracked subcutaneous chest armour had been replaced. I wondered who'd paid for that. It took me a while to get up the courage to look at my right arm. I was relieved to see it had been reattached. Pak-controlled gel running all the way around the join, knitting flesh to metal.

I was in very little pain and an internal diagnostic told me I was still banged up but healing.

'Who?' I asked.

'Balor,' Mudge answered. 'He's providing shelter for you and your mates, just like he did for me.'

'He paid for this?' I asked.

'More sort of stole it all. Says you're under his hospitality. He's got some funny ideas.'

'But Rolleston ...' I began.

'Your friends told me what happened in Hull. This ain't the Avenues. Rolleston can't just walk in here.'

'The Grey Lady can.' Mudge considered this.

'Yeah, yeah, she can,' he admitted, looking down at the bottle he held between his prosthetic legs before looking back up at me. His lenses whirred in their sockets. 'Your friends tell me you came to New York looking for me.' I nodded. He gave this some thought. I was suddenly very aware of Rannu in the bed next to me. 'You trying to get me killed, Douglas?' Mudge asked evenly.

I began to answer, but as I did the door to the ward opened and Pagan appeared with Morag. Morag was wearing similar clothes to what she'd found in Vicar's charity bin. A hooded top and combat trousers, but they looked newer and cleaner. Her shaved head now had a covering of light fuzz. I was relieved that her hair was growing back. Pagan looked surprisingly happy to see me awake, or perhaps even alive. Morag smiled and I suddenly felt a lot better.

'You look a lot better than you did a couple of days ago,' Pagan said.

No shit, I thought.

'You okay?' Morag asked. I held her gaze just a little too long and then nodded. She smiled.

'What's going on?' I asked. 'And can someone get me a gun so we can kill this guy?' I said, nodding towards Rannu.

'That won't be necessary,' Pagan said.

'He's with us,' Morag said. I let this sink in.

'Says who?' I asked.

'We've discussed it,' Pagan said. I couldn't believe it.

'That's great. You trust him? Do you know what he is?'

'You mean the tattoo?' Pagan asked. I nodded.

'I was never a Thug,' Rannu said from the other bed. I turned to look at him. There was edge in his voice. He'd said Thug with distaste.

'No? What, you just like the look and the monofilament garrotte?' I asked.

'After I left the Regiment I joined the police—'

'You're not really filling me with confidence here,' I said.

'Jakob!' Morag said. I turned to her.

'What?' I said both angry and surprised.

'Just listen to him.'

Rannu was waiting patiently for the interruption to be over. 'They wanted someone with a covert ops background to try and infiltrate the Thugs; I was chosen. High pay, one-off job. I was under for a year getting known in Leicester before they finally let me in.'

'You must've done some bad things,' I said, perhaps a little pettily. I caught the flinch before his impassive mask returned.

'Anyway, I made my way up the organisation, getting enough to tear them apart. Getting enough to go after Berham. We were just about ready to go when Rolleston approached me.'

'About us?' I asked. Rannu shook his head.

'About some domestic wetwork. I said I couldn't. He insisted. I explained the situation. He told me his work was more important. I said no again and he burnt me,' Rannu said. He said it matter of factly but I could see the emotion beneath the surface. This guy hated Rolleston as much as I did. Or he was a good actor. I let out a low whistle. To burn someone's cover while they were deep was just about *the* cardinal sin in covert ops.

'How'd it go down?' I asked.

'How'd you think? Badly. Lot of dead people. I only just made it out. Two months in hospital being rebuilt and another month in recovery after that.' I knew that to do that amount of damage they must've tortured him.

'So when Rolleston came to speak to you again you went to work for him?' I asked. I heard Mudge's sharp intake of breath. I watched Rannu as he struggled with his composure.

'You know the score,' he said. 'We don't have much choice.'

'But now you're all turned round?' I asked.

'Now I appear to have an option,' he said, looking at Morag. I felt a surge of anger, maybe something else.

'Good story, but by your own admission you're an experienced undercover operator. How do we know you're not just trying to infiltrate us?' I asked.

'For what purpose?' I could see him beginning to get irritated now. 'I won. Balor will hand you over to me now if I ask him. I already know your plan. I have everything I need to complete my job, so what do I have to gain? I believe the girl can set us free.' That was weird. Morag was looking down and blushing. I wondered what was going on.

Still red-cheeked, Morag looked up at me and took my hand, the left one, the one that was still flesh.

'I think he's on the level,' she said earnestly.

'Hooker's intuition?' I said before I could stop myself, but she just smiled.

'Something like that.'

Mudge looked down at my hand in hers and raised an eyebrow. She blushed again and let go. I glanced over at Rannu but he showed no reaction.

'We could be forgiven for thinking that you're just pissed off he so thoroughly kicked your arse,' Mudge said, smiling.

'It wasn't that thorough,' I muttered before turning to Rannu. 'So you kick my arse and now you've turned over a new leaf and want to work with us.' He shook his head. I noticed Pagan and Morag looking distinctly uncomfortable. 'What?' I asked.

'I decided while listening to Morag at Balor's table,' Rannu said. I just stared at him, trying to master the ability to talk again.

'Before the fight!' I shouted. Rannu nodded. I spent another couple of seconds speechless. 'Then why the fuck was there a fight?' I demanded.

'Two reasons,' Rannu said calmly. 'The first was I don't like not completing missions, so I needed to know I was capable of it, which I was.'

'Hey, you're in hospital too, pal.'

'Yeah, but not because you pulled off his arm and beat him half to death,' Mudge said, grinning. I glared at him. 'Sorry.'

'And the other?' I asked.

'To save Balor's face,' Pagan said. I didn't get it. 'If Rannu had joined us straight away then we would've been the only party responsible for bringing trouble down on New York and he would need to make an example out of us. With Rannu still apparently representing Rolleston, he could pit the two sides against each other and to his people he would still seem to be in control.'

'I got made an example of!?' I protested.

'But we were in control of that,' Pagan said. 'Well, we were supposed to be,' he said, glaring at Rannu.

Rannu shrugged. 'I was upset when I lost my ancestral kukri.'

'And you don't think tearing my arm off and trying to beat me to death with it was an overreaction to a lost knife?' I screamed at him.

Rannu considered this. 'Not in context. I'm still upset about it.'

'Looked good on the viz,' Mudge said. The thing was, even if Rannu was on the level, and I was beginning to think he was, you just couldn't walk away from the kind of violence that Rannu and I had done to each other. You can't just shake hands and let bygones be bygones. Every time I looked at him my shoulder ached. I mulled this over. I didn't like the way the others were looking at me, as if they were waiting for my approval. I decided to change the subject.

'What were you saying to Balor about secrets?' I asked Morag. She smiled slyly.

'Something I found sifting through the data Ambassador stole when he got free. Balor cut a deal with the CIA to get left in peace in New York. He does a bit of work for them here and there, let's them use New York when they need to. None of his people know and he wants to keep it that way.' I could see why. His reputation was that of a free agent able to defy governments. I'd even heard him described as a one-man nation state.

'And how's God coming along?' I asked. Pagan said nothing and just looked at Mudge.

'Never fucking ends,' Mudge said. I guessed he was referring to always being kept out of military briefings.

'Oh, come on,' I said. 'If the Leicester Strangler over there is in and you've told Balor and probably half of New York, I don't see why my mate should be excluded. I'll vouch for him: he's solid.'

'He's a journalist,' Pagan said.

'Whereas pirates and someone who you thought was working for Rolleston are trustworthy?' Mudge asked, taking another swig from his bottle of vodka before offering it to Morag.

'Different situation,' Pagan said.

'I think operational security's a bit fucked,' I said, watching with some amusement as Morag took a big swig of vodka.

'Besides,' Mudge said, taking the bottle back from a resistant Morag. 'I know what you're planning. Sounds fucking stupid to me, but don't worry, you won't have seen my byline on much recently.'

'So now we've established that we're all friends, how's God coming along? Are we all saved yet? Can I go home and get drunk?' Which reminded me. 'Have you got my whisky?' I asked Morag.

'I drank it,' Morag said apologetically.

'All of it!' I was coming to the conclusion that I preferred being unconscious. Judging by the way Rannu was glaring at me I might soon get the chance again. I wondered what his problem was now.

'Balor helped,' Morag said. 'It was my birthday.'

'Fucking Balor!' I spat incredulously.

She shrugged and looked quite uncomfortable. 'He's kind of cute when you get to know him.'

'Can we discuss boys later?' Pagan asked. 'In between Morag's whisky binges we've made some good progress.'

'You've been helping?' I asked her. She nodded. Pagan looked uncomfortable. 'How long?' I asked Pagan.

'I don't know,' he said. 'I would hope sooner rather than later.'

'Assume there won't be a later,' I suggested. 'So what do we do?'

'Balor says you can stay as long as you want,' Mudge said.

'Rolleston knows we're here?' I asked Rannu. The ex-Ghurkha nodded. 'So why not just hit us with another orbital?'

'The political fallout from Dundee was too heavy,' Rannu answered. 'He will not get access to another orbital strike.'

'Besides,' Mudge continued, 'if he didn't kill everyone he'd spend the next twenty years fighting terrorist insurgency from vengeful special forces types, and I think that Balor's got an ASAT nuke somewhere. Basically it's more trouble than it's worth.'

An anti satellite nuke, a ground to orbital weapon, I gave this some thought. 'Even Balor wouldn't do that,' I said.

'He wants to burn brightly and be famous, of course he would,' Mudge said. I saw Pagan nodding in agreement.

'Conventional forces?' I asked, already knowing the answer. Mudge let out a humourless laugh.

'Nightmare scenario, heavily defended city with enough supplies and booby traps to fight an indefinite guerrilla war. Balor and his Fomorians could fight it from underwater, as could a lot of the other vets here. Again more trouble than it's worth.'

'Rolleston could buy us,' I suggested.

'Balor's given his word,' Pagan said.

'Well that's reassuring,' I said sarcastically.

Mudge sighed. 'Look, Balor's unquestionably fucked in the head but he keeps his word. It's one of the reasons he commands so much loyalty. You're under his protection. He'll die for you if he had to and do it smiling.'

'Suddenly we have so many friends. So all we have to do is stay here and try not to get assassinated?' Mudge and Pagan nodded. This was beginning to sound good to me. I could get drunk and wait for the Grey Lady to come in relative comfort. Maybe they even had some sense booths here. We couldn't stop the Grey Lady; in fact I wondered why she hadn't already killed us all. Then I remembered why we'd come to New York in the first place.

'Why are you here?' I asked Mudge as he lit up another cigarette. Morag stole it from him and I stole it from her before she could take a drag. Mudge lit another one and looked around at the assembled people. I sighed. 'Have we not already decided that we are all friends?' I asked.

Mudge shrugged. 'Sure you want to hear this?' he asked, the tip of his cigarette glowing as he took another drag.

'No, but we've come a long way and nearly died twice doing so, so we might as well.'

'I think Gregor's still alive,' he said. He took another drag on his cigarette and watched my expression. I suppose I'd known I was going to hear about Gregor but I guess deep down I'd assumed he was dead. Maybe it would've been easier that way because I wasn't obligated to a dead man.

'Where?' I asked.

'I don't know.'

'What makes you think he's alive?' I asked. The others were quiet.

'Because Rolleston really wanted someone infected by a Ninja. After your trial I asked around, spoke to a couple of German guys who'd been in the KSK and a Delta operator. They'd both been working with squads taken out by a Ninja. In both cases the Ninja had left one of the members of the squad alive after somehow infecting them.'

'Just like Gregor,' I breathed. Mudge nodded.

'In both cases Rolleston and the Grey Lady show up soon after, looking for the infected guys, but in both cases the infected guy was totally fragged when he was found. Neither Delta or KSK were taking any chances.' Rolleston had wanted someone infected and that was why he'd dropped us in the mincer.

'Why were they infecting people and then leaving them to be found? Germ warfare?' I asked.

'Most probably,' Mudge said. 'But who knows how they think?' I couldn't help but glance over at Morag when he said that. She didn't notice but I felt Pagan looking at me.

'So Rolleston's got Gregor somewhere, infected by an alien germ?' I asked.

'I don't know, maybe,' Mudge said, taking another long pull from the bottle of vodka.

'But you don't know where he is?' I asked.

'Nope.' I felt some relief. Even if MacDonald was alive it sounded unlikely that there would be any point in rescuing him; in fact it would make things worse. I was relieved that I was free of the obligation. In my head I could hear myself apologising to my absent friend. 'But I think I know who does know,' Mudge finished. I heard Pagan groan. I think he saw what was coming.

'Who?' I asked.

'Everywhere Rolleston and Bran went looking for those infected by the Ninja they were flown—'

'By two degenerate fuckwits,' I finished for him, Gibby and Buck, the two cyberbilly Night Stalkers from the 160th SOAR. 'You think they know where Gregor is?'

'I think they would have transported him for Rolleston. It was what they were doing when we last saw them.'

'Let's just stay here, finish the job at hand and worry about this later,' Pagan said in what I guessed he hoped was a reasonable-sounding voice. Truth be told it was a reasonable request, very reasonable, and I wholeheartedly agreed with him, but some things just aren't reasonable.

'Good idea,' Mudge said.

'You know where they are?' I asked Mudge. He took another mouthful of the vodka. I wondered how drunk he was, how many bottles he'd had today.

'Knew where they were,' he said. 'I was on their trail. Fully ready to beat what I wanted to know out of that pair of cunts when the Grey Lady caught up with me and made it perfectly clear that I should drop the matter.'

'See, it's old info. They'll have moved on by now,' Pagan pleaded.

'Where are they?' I asked. Thinking I'd like to have a violent little chat with them myself.

'They deserted the 160th—'

'They probably got killed by Rolleston,' Pagan interrupted.

'No, they definitely deserted. They made it to Crawling Town.' Mudge upended the vodka bottle, draining the rest of it and tossing the bottle into a bin.

Crawling Town was a place as infamous as Balor's New York. Well, not exactly a place; it was a city-sized, always-moving convoy made up of disparate gangs, road tribes and other disenfranchised people. They were left alone by the authorities because they travelled the Dead Roads, the line of heavily polluted and irradiated land that ran down the east side of the US from Lake Eerie to east Texas. An area considered largely uninhabitable by what passed for sane people these days. Pagan could see what I was thinking.

'Have you not learnt?' Pagan asked. I looked up at him.

'You're here now doing your thing. We need to do our thing, and we'll go and do it whether you help or not. You're safe now. Stay here, complete your little electronic god. Besides, New York seems to have worked out well for everyone but me.' I didn't add that it had worked out better than if we'd gone to Russia, but I think Pagan got the message.

'You're going out into the wasteland to chase a months-old lead to find someone who's probably infected by something virulent and highly fucking dangerous. Will you listen to yourself?' Pagan asked.

'Yeah, we should stay here while you make God, because that's more sensible,' Mudge said. He sounded distracted. I think he was looking around for more booze. Pagan glared at him. Thing is, Pagan was right. The shots were too long, even for us. If we did find Gregor, chances are we'd just have to do him a favour and put a bullet through his head anyway.

'Jakob, we need your help. We need your protection and we need you running interference for us. If the Grey Lady comes, you and Rannu are the best hope Morag and I have.' It didn't seem like much of a hope but I liked the way he'd emphasised that Morag needed me. Manipulative cunt. I looked at Mudge. He'd found another bottle from beneath my bed. He was watching me again, waiting for my response, his lenses moving in their sockets. I reached over and took the bottle from him.

'You recording this?' I asked him, and took a long swig of the vodka, enjoying it burn down my gullet.

'Hell, yeah,' Mudge was grinning.

'Brilliant,' Pagan muttered.

'He's right, you know?' I said to Mudge.

Mudge nodded. 'I know.'

'Maybe we can do something if this works?' I said, sounding pathetic even to myself. I tried to cover it by taking another long swig of vodka.

'You going to give that back?' Mudge asked. I held the bottle out to him but Morag took it. I suddenly noticed how flushed and nervous she looked. She took a long swig from the bottle.

'You okay?' I asked her. She nodded.

'I think we should go to Crawling Town,' she said. 'And I don't think your friend is diseased.'

'For fuck's sake,' Pagan muttered.

'What makes you say that?' Mudge asked. Morag didn't say anything.

'This is bullshit,' Pagan said.

'Losing your religion?' Mudge asked. Pagan glared at him.

'Look, Morag,' the old hacker began. 'I know a lot has happened to you, and you think that you know—'

'Don't fucking patronise me,' Morag said. That resolve of hers was back. I wished it wasn't in this case. I didn't want to go to Crawling Town. 'He's not infected. They were trying to communicate.'

'How can you know that?' Pagan asked, but I think we both knew the answer.

'Just believe her,' Rannu said. 'I'll go with you to Crawling Town,' he added, sounding very formal. I looked over at him incredulously.

'What the fuck's it got to do with you?' I demanded.

'More the merrier,' Mudge said. He'd taken the bottle of vodka from Morag and raised it to Rannu, who bowed.

'Pagan, why don't you stay and work on God? We'll go. Balor will protect you,' I said. He looked very uncomfortable with my suggestion.

'I'll come,' he said finally.

That was when I realised two things. Pagan was happy when we were doing his insane things but not when we wanted to do ours. After all, going to Crawling Town wasn't any madder than trying to make God, in fact probably less so, and if there was a chance we could help Gregor then I owed it to him. The other thing I realised was that Pagan really needed Morag's help. That worried me.

'This is insane,' Pagan muttered again.

'What is?' A voice growled from the doorway. I looked up to see the massive and alien figure of our host standing in the entrance to the ward. He was dripping wet and leaving a trail of unpleasantly foul New York water behind him. He held Rannu's kukri in his left hand. I think it was the first time I ever saw Rannu looking happy, but then again I hadn't seen his face when he was beating me unconscious with my own arm.

'You found it,' he said, grinning. Balor walked over to the ex-Ghurkha's bed. He didn't smell very nice; only Mudge and Rannu seemed not to mind.

'You deserved it back,' Balor said.

'He's pretty much been searching for it non-stop for three days,' Mudge said.

'He's got a lot of time on his hands then?' I asked.

'I think it's sweet,' Morag said. I wondered what the mischievous look was about as I tried to ignore a sudden surge of emotion I didn't want to analyse too deeply.

'I think it's obsessive,' Mudge suggested.

Balor stuck out a thick reptilian tongue that was sort of a bruised purple colour.

'Very attractive,' I muttered. Morag glared at me.

Balor ran the kukri blade across his tongue, drawing blood. All of us watched this in surprise.

'Why?' Mudge finally managed to ask.

'Because the kukri cannot be put away before it's bloodied,' Balor said, blood dripping from his maw, and handed the curved knife back to Rannu. He seemed just as surprised as the rest of us.

'It did draw blood – mine,' I said.

Balor turned to me. 'Do you feel more alive now?' He seemed to be serious.

'What, are you fucking mad? I just got near beat to death! Strangely that doesn't make me feel more alive, just fucking sore!' I shouted, sitting up in bed and getting pushed back gently by Mudge. Balor loomed over me, his face distorting with what I assumed was anger.

'What did I tell you about respect in my house?' he growled at me.

'Oh, I respect you. As a fucking psycho!' I spat before my sense of self-preservation kicked in. He considered what I said. I assumed he was just going to reach down and do something violent to me.

'Good,' he finally said, but not before I was covered in cold sweat. 'You are all welcome, just tell me what you need.' And he turned and walked out. I suddenly felt very tired, too tired. I realised I was crashing and crashing hard. I turned to look at Mudge. He was smiling at me.

'You stimmed me?' I asked. He nodded. I faded quickly. Like moving backwards quickly down a black tunnel. Further and further away from them all. The last thing I heard was Pagan berating Mudge for his irresponsibility.

*The SAW ran dry. It had been my last cassette for the weapon and I'd long ago exhausted grenades for the launcher so I just dropped the weapon in the mud. I turned and jumped over the remains of a low wall. We'd been fighting a retreat since we landed. We were now in what had once been a small town. It had been some kind of centre for the surrounding rural communities when people had been able to grow things here. Now it was just a series of maze-like low walls sticking out of the mud, traces of the buildings that had once housed a community. It was mostly night; Sirius B was low in the sky. Fire and manoeuvre was rote now, we didn't even really think about it.*

*I tore the Benelli assault shotgun from the smartgrip back scabbard strapped to my pack and started firing three-round bursts at the Berserks sprinting towards us. The flechette penetrators burrowing into their hardened chitinous bodies before their explosive cores detonated. It was like watching them get chewed up from within. I was going through the motions. Crosshairs from the smartgun link over the next alien, fire, repeat until it was time to reload. Ignore the fact that what little cover I had was being eaten away by their returning fire. Ignore my multiple wounds. Ignore that we were dead anyway.*

*I watched Gregor sprinting towards me. I covered him as best I could. He turned and my audio dampeners kicked in as he fired a long burst from the railgun at the charging Berserks. I watched as several of them seemed to explode into liquid mid-stride. Gregor hit the quick-release catch on his gyroscopic harness. The whole rig along with the gun and ammo pack fell into the mud. Gregor was running again, pulling his personal defence weapon from a holster on his thigh, unfolding it as he ran. Leaping over the wall, sliding into the mud nearby before scrambling back to join us and then opening fire.*

*Like most signal types, Shaz favoured a laser. I could feel the heat from its beams as he fired bursts of bright red light into the remaining Berserks. The Tyler Optics laser carbine was set at a frequency designed to superheat what it hit rather than burn through it. Where he hit the Berserks I saw their solidified liquid flesh turn to a greasy black steam. I could hear him through my access to the command net requesting air and artillery support for an immediate evac. I could hear the hopelessness in Shaz's voice. We were getting nothing from command. I understood the necessity of sacrifice but there seemed to be no gain in sending us to die like this.*

*Behind us I could hear Ash's SAW firing long bursts accompanied by Mudge's AK-47. The AK-47 was a replica of a pre-FHC weapon chambered for 9-millimetre long that he insisted on using. They were all around us and closing. We kept on taking Them down, thinning their numbers, but They kept on charging at us. The uneasy joke had always been that if They ever learnt tactics humanity was really screwed.*

*Concentrated shard fire had Shaz, Gregor and myself duck down into the mud as the low wall was chewed away and they were on us. I managed to get off a shot point blank into one of the eight-foot-tall monstrosities before dropping the Benelli and extending my knuckle blades. I rammed the blades up, sliding under chitinous plates like they trained us, augmented muscle and prosthetic driving the plates apart as black liquid poured all over me.*

*With some effort I heaved the dying alien to one side. The Berserk behind him swung a limb, ending in some kind of spiked weapon, into my rigid breastplate. It hit so hard it cracked the plate, causing the inertial undersuit beneath to harden. I landed on my back in the mud, retracted my knuckle blades, drew my laser pistol and the Mastodon and fired a lot. It seemed to take a while but the advancing Berserk fell back into the mud.*

*I managed to get to my feet before the next one tackled me and sent me sprawling back down. I dropped the pistols and just stabbed repeatedly into it as its power-assisted claws tried to peel me out of my armour. I was still stabbing a long time after it had stopped moving and had leaked all over me. It smelt like burnt plastic.*

*Eventually it dissolved over me. Gregor was there to pick me up, as ever. It had gone quiet. I retrieved my weapons, watching as Gregor cleaned black ichor off his sword bayonet. Shaz was doing likewise with his kirpan. Mudge was changing a clip and Ash was just looking out over the low wall.*

*'What's going on?' I asked. It seemed very quiet. It was now nearly dark. We were entering the short night of a planet in a binary system.*

*'They're just standing there,' Ash said shaking her head. Mudge stood up.*

*'Get down!' I hissed, Gregor and Ash doing the same.*

*'They're not doing anything,' Mudge said. He studied them for a while. I wondered how wasted he was and what it was this time. I crawled over to where Mudge was stood, cradling my automatic shotgun in the crooks of my elbows. I peeked over the low wall. Mudge and Ash were right. The Berserks were standing, swaying as if in some unfelt wind about two hundred metres back. Between them and us were a multitude of black, viscous oily puddles that showed where we'd killed their mates. A feeling was making its way through my fatigue, something not felt for a while – interest.*

*'You ever heard of anything like this?' I asked Mudge, who was intently studying the sky. I'd asked him because Mudge was one of the few of us who took an active interest in the rest of the war. He shook his head.*

*'Can't see it being anything good for us,' Ash mumbled in her thick Brummie accent.*

*'What do you want to do?' Gregor asked. I had no idea. There were obviously too many of them for us to fight. I shrugged.*

*'Get yourselves sorted. Patch yourselves and your armour up as best you can, check your ammo, ready secondary and tertiary weapons. Shaz, I know it's a waste of time but keep on the command net. Got any time after that, we'll have a brew.'*

*'Then what?' Ash asked. I could hear Mudge giggling.*

*'If they haven't killed us and they're still playing silly buggers then we head back to the firebase and see if we're in time for the last shuttle.'*

*'Or we're sharing the planet with a lot of angry demons,' Shaz said.*

*'Where's Ash gone?' I heard Mudge say. Then I saw the look of horror on Gregor's face and Shaz screamed. I swung round bringing my shotgun up. I found an awestruck Mudge staring at a bit of what I can only describe as dark air.*

*'She got sucked in,' Mudge whispered.*

*'Mudge!' Gregor shouted as he brought his PDW up to cover the dark air. 'We need you in this world!' This seemed to bring Mudge out of it. He staggered back bringing his AK-47 up to cover it. A red beam lanced out turning part of the dark air into greasy steam.*

*'Cease fire!' I shouted. 'Shaz, you watch our backs. I want to know what the rest of them are doing.' Shaz stood there staring. 'Shaz!' He looked up at me, his eyes wide around his lenses, and then he nodded. Through the split screen on my internal visual display I could see through Shaz's helmet camera.*

*The Berserks were still holding off in their rough perimeter. The dark air hadn't move. It still stood where Ash had stood.*

*'Mudge, what happened?' I demanded, cursing, though not blaming, the journalist for choosing to get high now. The war was easier for him as a hallucination. I could see his knuckles whitening on the grip of his assault rifle.*

*'Mudge, do you want me to come over there and beat the shit out of you?' Gregor asked quietly. This seemed to shake him out of it. I guess we all listened to Gregor no matter how wasted.*

*'It moved up behind her,' Mudge whispered, but I was hearing it across the patrol's tactical net. 'And just yanked her in.' On my internal visual display I saw Shaz's helmet camera turn from the perimeter and back to the dark air.*

*'Shaz,' I said. The signalman turned back to the perimeter. Mudge giggled again. I resisted the urge to shoot him.*

*'It was like a spatial anomaly,' the journalist said, 'a little spatial anomaly.' Gregor and I exchanged looks. Ash fell out of the dark air, what was left of her. She was covered in her own blood. Her body looked like one big wound as if she had been pierced in every part of her flesh. We lit the night up with our muzzle flashes.*

Back again. There was just one person at the end of the bed this time. Just Morag. She appeared to be checking over an auto pistol. She had her legs crossed on the bed and I could see a holster strapped to her upper thigh.

'Where'd you get that?' I tried to say, but it came out a slurred mess. She looked up at me, made the gun safe and holstered it.

'Balor gave it to me,' she said. 'I don't know why.'

'People tend to give pretty girls things,' I slurred. I was slowly beginning to sound a bit more like I was speaking English. Whatever I said it was the wrong thing, judging by her expression. I glanced over at the bed next to me. Rannu was gone.

'Where's the Thug?' I asked, sounding petty even to my own ears. Morag looked up. She seemed kind of angry.

'He's away being a warrior with Balor somewhere.' And she began to get up.

'Morag, wait.' She stopped and turned to look at me. 'You get a cutlass with that?' I said, nodding at the pistol. 'Maybe an eyepatch?' She cracked a smile but didn't sit back down. 'How long have you been sat here?'

She shrugged. 'A little while.' She sounded half pissed off and half coy.

'Prefer it when I was unconscious?' I asked.

'You're nicer,' she said, smiling again.

'You okay?' I asked. She nodded.

'I was worried about you,' she managed to say and then looked embarrassed.

'I was worried about me too.'

'I didn't like seeing what happened to you.' For all the violence I knew she would've seen just by growing up in Fintry and the Rigs, somehow she'd not managed to become inured to it. Then I realised what she was really trying to say. I'd been really stupid.

'You didn't like watching me do what I did?' I said. She considered what to say next but it was written all over her face.

'Morag ...' I began.

'I'm being selfish.' She stood up.

'Wait,' I said, and she stopped. 'Morag, look at me.' She wouldn't. 'Please.' I couldn't make out her expression. 'I would never hurt you. Do you understand me?' Finally she nodded. 'Please sit down, stay with me.' I tried to keep the pleading tone out of my voice but she sat down again. Not surprisingly there was an uncomfortable silence, then she looked up at me.

'I wouldn't let you,' she said, her voice full of that steel-like resolve. It was a declaration. She was never going to be a victim again. Initially I was taken aback. I didn't want her to think of me in the same light as all the other arseholes she'd met in her short life, but then again maybe I was. Finally I nodded and smiled.

'So, you like Balor then?' I asked as casually as I could manage a little while later. Morag let out a little laugh.

'I was winding you up,' she said. Good job, I thought.

'What's with you and Rannu?' I asked.

'I think he thinks I'm some kind of prophet,' she said, seeming partly embarrassed and partly amused by this.

'Oh,' I said. 'That'll piss Pagan off.' She shrugged. I could feel myself fading again but more naturally this time. I was just tired.

## 17
# Crawling Town

Crawling Town was not going to be difficult to find. Balor had given us access to a satellite he bought time on to track the huge convoy. Besides, we couldn't miss the irradiated and polluted dust cloud kicked up by that number of vehicles.

We said goodbye to our psychotic benefactor on the banks of what was left of the state of New Jersey, near where the city of Newark had once been. Balor had provided us with vehicles, hazardous environment gear and some other bits and pieces that would come in useful. The vehicles, like most of our gear, were treated with a serious anti-corrosion finish or they wouldn't last a day in the Dead Roads. I think he was helping us because we had the potential to piss people off and maybe even cause some chaos. In fact he'd been pretty good to us except for the bit where I'd had to spend five days in hospital.

I watched, straddling the low rider that Balor had provided for me, as Rannu drove the armoured muscle car off the flat-bottomed boat. Mudge was sitting in the passenger seat of the car, bottle of vodka in one hand, some inhaled burning narcotic in the other. I wasn't best pleased at Rannu's presence, but I knew first hand that he was capable, and sooner or later we were going to need all the guns we could get.

Balor and Pagan came to stand next to me. Neither of them said anything. Balor just favoured me with one of his disturbingly toothy smiles. I think he thought he'd taught me some valuable life lesson. He had: if I were ever to tangle with Rannu again I'd shoot him in the back, a lot, preferably while he was sleeping. I noticed Balor was watching Morag now as she walked off the flat-bottomed boat towards us.

'Balor,' I said, deciding I had to know something. He turned his monstrous head towards me. 'There's a story about you. I've got to know whether it's true or not.'

'Which one?' he growled.

'Did you ever see the Grey Lady? I mean—'

'I know what you mean,' he said. Pagan was watching us both, a look of slight concern on his face. Morag was just about with us now, her clothes and the armour she'd managed to scavenge covered by the poncho part of her hostile environment gear. Balor seemed to be considering my question. We were all dressed in anti-radiation/pollution chic, we had on either ponchos or, as in my case, dusters to keep the worst of it out.

'She scares me,' he finally said. Not really what I wanted to hear, probably served me right for trying to be clever. 'Besides, I only have eyes for Magantu.' He was looking at Morag. Then he turned and walked back towards the water.

'Who's Magantu?' Morag asked, only hearing the tail end of the conversation.

'It's the name of a great white shark from a Polynesian legend,' Pagan said. We watched as Balor waded into the water. It was a clear but colourless grey day. Opposite us, across the water, we could see the broken spires and grey canyons of New York. Balor disappeared beneath the water. I fixed the filter over my face and then clipped the goggles to it. Rannu gunned the four-wheel-drive muscle car up the small dirt slope that led away from the water. Balor's people began reversing the flat-bottomed boat away from the shore.

I plugged a connecting wire into one of the sockets in my neck and pushed the other end into the bike's vehicle interface. Both the car and the bike were typically American, all style and muscle, no handling.

'Come on,' Pagan said to Morag. 'We can work in the car.' Morag didn't say anything to him. Instead she fastened her mask and goggles and climbed on the low rider behind me. Pagan was obviously pissed off but didn't say a word. He headed towards the car and Mudge got out to let him in the back seat. I felt good. Morag clipped her PDW to the bike on the opposite side to the Benelli assault shotgun I'd bought in one of New York's many arms bazaars. Then she wrapped her arms around me.

'I'm driving in the afternoon,' she told me as I gunned the engine and we took off into Jersey, the others following in the muscle car. I heard a cheer from Mudge.

This was a scarred land. It had been hit pretty hard during the FHC as the corporations and the equatorial states had gone after what was left of America's heavy industry. They'd used nukes as well as biological and chemical weapons. Those, along with the pollution from the deregulation of industry that had taken place before and after the FHC – a desperate attempt by America to hold on to its failing economic power – had left a wasteland nobody wanted. So the people nobody wanted had moved in.

Most of the land was covered in a white ash-like dust. The colours in the sky were vivid and unnatural, and everywhere we passed, from distant tower blocks and empty suburbs, to abandoned refineries and power stations, was eerie and deserted. It was like being alone in the world. I found myself liking it. I liked Morag's skillsoft driving of the low rider less. Though not as much as Rannu and Pagan disliked Mudge's driving, and when he and Morag decided to race each other I had to agree with them.

We headed west, further into America. Progress was slow, most of the routes were still partially blocked by debris. All the vehicles that had been abandoned on the Dead Roads had been pushed to the side, presumably by the passage of Crawling Town. There were, however, still craters, rubble too heavy to be moved, downed bridges and the general poor repair of the road to deal with. The satellite info told us that the slow-moving convoy was heading towards the ruins of a city called Trenton, near the New Jersey–Pennsylvania border. This was a border held and violently defended by the US proper.

I knew there were people who lived out here other than the inhabitants of Crawling Town. I knew there were tribes living in some of the towns. I knew there were packs of dogs and swarms of rats, but we saw nothing and no one. It was the evenings I liked best. The sun going down as we rode towards it. The strange half-light before it got too dangerous to travel and we had to stop. The only sound was the throbbing of the two engines as our vehicles became silhouettes. I wondered if Rolleston knew it was us. Was he tracking us? In many ways we were at our most exposed, yet this was the happiest I'd been since it had all begun. Actually it was the happiest I'd been in a long time.

On the first night we stopped and set up the tent. It had an airlock mechanism and we had to maintain decontamination discipline. Morag and Pagan worked on God, tranced into the net for hours at a time. Rannu, Mudge and I took turns on guard, setting up an OP away from the tent. Rannu was uncomplaining about taking the middle watch, which always meant a disturbed night's sleep, and I doubted if Mudge, who was usually drunk or high, was a great deal of use. When they'd finished working on God for the night and my watch was done, Morag would curl up next to me. Mudge looked amused,

Rannu was as impassive as ever and Pagan looked disapproving but never said anything. I just held her while she slept.

It was my favourite time of the day when we first saw it. In that strange, unreal, twilit half-light we saw a huge dust cloud that obscured the western horizon. Unspoken, we brought our vehicles to a halt. I magnified my vision. Suddenly the huge dust cloud was much closer, filling my vision, impenetrable, though I saw a few outriders on bikes and trikes disappearing in and out of the haze.

'The city rides for a week and then makes camp,' Pagan said over the comms net.

'You picking up anything?' I asked.

'Nothing much, though there is some heavily encrypted stuff going on.'

'Military?' I asked.

'I would imagine so; the town's getting very close to the border,' Pagan answered. America's Fortunate Sons would be out keeping a close eye on the convoy.

'So when are they due to camp?' Morag asked.

'Well, they're either going to have to stop soon or change direction, which can't be easy for a convoy that size, or invade America,' Pagan said.

'Then what?' Morag asked.

'Then Rannu and I go in and have a look,' I said.

'It'd be better if I go,' Mudge said. 'I'm better at finding people.'

'I need you to stay here and provide security for Morag and Pagan.' They would need it if they were going to be working on God. Working on God, I couldn't even begin to imagine what that would entail, but somewhere along the line I'd begun to accept it. Maybe I had more faith in Morag than in Pagan.

'And I would be better providing security,' Rannu said. What he didn't say was that he would be better able to stay close to Morag.

'Guys, please, help me out here, yeah?' I said. There was no reply. I had my reasons for taking Rannu. Mudge was right – he was probably more capable of finding Gibby and Buck – but I wasn't sure he wasn't just going to shoot the pair of them when he found them. I couldn't really blame him; I was only slightly surer I wasn't going to do the same.

We'd called it right, and Crawling Town had come to a halt on the outskirts of the ruins of Trenton. They'd formed a huge circle of their articulated lorries and land trains, most of them huge five-axle rigs pulling multiple trailers. Many of them were covered in neon patterns that Pagan had told me were veves, Pop Voudun occult symbols. These trucks belonged to one of the biggest gangs in Crawling Town, one of the founder groups at the core of the huge convoy. They were Haitian and Jamaican Yardies who'd muscled their way into the haulage business a couple of hundred years ago. They called themselves the Big Neon Voodoo. They were popular subjects for lurid sense experiences and shock documentary makers, many of whom ended up dead. I also noticed that some of the trailers had huge viz screens running the length of them.

The dust cloud above the convoy had seemed static for a while but it was beginning to come down now. It coated everything and made the air little more than a thick grey fog as Rannu and I headed towards the parked vehicles. The powerful headlight on the bike barely cut through the murk. As we approached we could hear the sound of over-revved engines. Sporadic gunfire provided brief illumination through the dirt and the larger vehicles were just shadows that suddenly loomed out of the murk at us.

They were all here, all the bogey gangs I'd seen on vizzes, be they documentaries, sports programmes or horrors. All the stories that grow out of places like this, all heard second hand. Gangs like the all-female Nicely-Nicely Boys in their pinstripes and bowler hats, or the Electric Circus. There was the ghoulish, literally, Bad Faeries. The infamous First Baptist Church of Austin Texas, in their pastel-coloured dress suits, dead-skin masks and armoured station wagons, a militant prayer group with a serial killer in charge of them. I reckoned that if Buck and Gibby were going to be anywhere they'd probably stick with their own people. They'd be with some cyberbilly outfit like the Hard Luck Commancheros. For all the stories about the convoy, we'd survived New York, despite nearly being killed, and I couldn't see it being much worse than the Rigs.

An hour later I was less than pleased to find myself naked, securely restrained and hanging from some kind of metal cross attached to the back of an armoured dune buggy. The dune buggy had a stylised swastika crudely painted on the top of it. They'd pegged me for an outsider as soon as we'd rode in.

Rannu and I had made it past the perimeter of encircled trucks and into the impromptu town itself. There was every conceivable kind of civilian vehicle capable of traversing rough ground there, many of them still on the move through the streets of tents and parked vehicles. We swerved to avoid a monster truck, though we could've probably ridden between its huge wheels, and only narrowly avoided colliding with a half-track that looked like it could've been pre-FHC. Its armoured hood was painted with the face of a cartoon swamp monster. Everything smelt of burning alcohol, and the sound of powerful engines provided the ambient soundtrack.

Through the thick, settling dust we could see that all the tribes were out. Those that had hazardous environment gear had heavily modified it to display their colours and show their allegiance. There were many there who didn't have any HE gear, either through choice or poverty. Sense programs and vizzes had made much out of the so-called wasteland mutants that made up Crawling Town. The sad fact was there were just a lot of deformed and otherwise very sick people. They were the real mutants.

We'd heard screams and gunfire and even seen a drive-by, which somehow struck me as redundant in a place like this. Crawling Town was not unified. It was made up of many disparate and antagonistic groups that somehow managed to travel together. We kept our heads down. The town was some eighty to a hundred thousand strong so it was going to take a while to find Buck and Gibby unless we were really lucky. Initially we would need to just get the lie of the land.

'We should split up,' Rannu suggested. 'Cover more ground.'

'That means one of us on foot.' There was screaming as a man was dragged past us on a chain behind a quad bike, his skin being flayed off by the corrosive dirt. 'This doesn't strike me as a good place for pedestrians.'

'You keep the bike, I'll go on foot,' said Rannu. We found a garishly decorated mobile home that looked like it had put down roots for the time being. We used it as a fixed point, or as much of one as we were going to get in this place. We memorised the position. It was still too dangerous for us to use GPS.

'Four hours and then back here,' I said.

'Comms discipline?'

'Tight burst once per hour. Use the crypts that Pagan gave us. Signal to me and back to Morag and Pagan, agreed?'

'And we hit trouble?'

'Quick burst to me, or me to you, but if possible exfiltrate first. Some of these gangs are well organised and they'll have some serious hackers. We can't compromise the others,' I said.

'Agreed.' He seemed reassured by what I'd said.

'What're you carrying?' I asked.

'Just sidearms. They'll be enough for a quick recon.'

I nodded. I had my pistols and the assault shotgun clipped to the side of the bike. I looked up and he was gone. Disappeared into the settling dust.

I had been sloppy; there was no other explanation. I'd noticed them pretty quickly. Their rad gear was old but well maintained. Their gear was a dust-covered black colour and they had a red cross on their left breasts over the heart. They were difficult to miss. They'd started following me in a monster truck, heavily armoured and decorated in their colours. Vicious spikes of scrap metal and the barrels of military surplus heavy weaponry protruded from the truck. I was going to be able to outrun that easily. I was a bit more worried about the motorcycle outriders and the fact that they presumably had a better knowledge of what the configuration of Crawling Town was tonight.

I was so concerned about the ones behind me that I hadn't noticed them getting in front of me. I should've but the place was full of people so there wasn't a great deal I could do. Even checking on thermographics would only have shown me what I already knew, lots of people and hot engines. Even so I don't think this would've happened had I been on my game. The jeeps slid from either side of the crossroads ahead. They had enough discipline for their gunmen to competently cover me. I got out of the way of the first net. The second only clipped me and somebody died with a round from the Mastodon through their skull. The third net got me and they pumped enough current through it that even my systems weren't able to cope. I hope I cost them a fortune in energy. I was too busy being electrocuted to send out a distress message to Rannu and too unconscious to do it when they'd finished electrocuting me.

They were called the Wait. They were a skinhead monastic order that'd been evicted from their commune in Oregon and subsequently joined Crawling Town. It'd taken me a while to figure out the whole skinhead swastika thing. They were Nazis, a political ideology from back when people had them, which promoted white supremacy – as ridiculous as that might sound. It was a pre-FHC idea that apparently had resulted in quite serious wars at one point. I was surprised to find that people like this still existed. I guess that in times like these people needed to find something to hang on to, to try and make sense of things. Even if that thing is old and foul and pointless. Also I doubted they'd been able to make out that I was a quarter Thai, so I did wonder why they'd picked on me.

To give them credit, they knew how to secure someone properly. They'd attached a spinal clamp, effectively paralysing me. They'd stripped me and taken all my gear but otherwise I was in pretty good shape. I just felt embarrassed and more than a little angry with myself. I'd tried to send a comms message out to Rannu but I could feel some kind of inhibitor jacked into one of my plugs.

The skinheads had set up a compound of sorts. They'd run electrified fencing topped with programmable razor wire between several huge armoured mobile homes. They'd also set up several other security measures and were patrolling the compound relatively professionally. Thing is, I got the feeling that few if any of them had ever seen service. These were hate-filled children playing soldiers. I always wondered why people like this never joined up. I mean if they really felt the need to wallow in hate-filled pseudo-military bullshit?

From out of the mobile home, which I guessed was supposed to be Command and Control, I saw three of them exit and head towards me. Two of them wore black rad ponchos with the red cross on them. They carried replica Schmeissers chambered for 10-millimetre caseless. The guy in the middle did not have a rad suit on. He wore a spotless, pressed black tunic with matching trousers and high black boots which actually looked like they'd once been part of an animal's skin. They were very black and shiny. He wandered over to where I was crucified and looked up at me.

'Hi,' I said. His head was totally shorn of hair. In fact he seemed to have no hair anywhere on his head and I couldn't work out why he seemed to be wearing purple lipstick. Across his scalp, just beneath the skin, I could see a complicated network of circuitry. It was high-end expensive stuff. This guy was obviously a hacker. I didn't like his eyes; they were blue and multifaceted like an insect's. It wasn't right. He just watched me for a long time. I could see multiple images of myself reflected in the eyes.

'What do you want?' I finally asked, irritated at being unnerved by someone I guessed wasn't much more than a kid.

'We have everything we want.' His voice was so cold and expressionless, I was sure it was modulated. This guy was so image conscious he had to be young.

'Why am I up here?' I asked.

'Are you Anglo-Saxon?' he asked, as if the term had any meaning whatsoever.

'Yes.'

'Your accent sounds Scottish; the Scots aren't Anglo-Saxons.'

'I'm still white,' I said hopefully. I was planning on choking the life out of the little shit when I got down. The insect-eyed Nazi went quiet.

'You still haven't told me why I'm up here,' I said eventually.

'To suffer.' That didn't sound good.

'Any reason?' I asked.

'To suffer for the crimes the lesser races have inflicted on the master race. To show God that some of his chosen people still care. So you can feel an iota of what our Lord Jesus felt when he was brought low by the likes of you.' Something struggled through my memory. Some half-remembered conversation with a Christian signalwoman attached to my first squad when I'd joined the Paras.

'I'm not Roman,' I told him, pretty sure that was right. 'I've never even been to Italy.' He ignored me.

'For *untermensch* you are strong, yes?'

'I don't know what that means.'

'I think you will last a long time and your sacrifice will be great.' I came to the conclusion that there probably wasn't going to be a great deal of reasoning with this guy.

'Oh bullshit, you whiney little cunt. This isn't about ideology or religion, this is about your own fucking inadequacies. You're weak and frightened so you have to fucking act out. Try and get people under your power. Get people to fear you because respect and love are beyond you. You know as well as I do that if you guys hadn't got the drop on me you wouldn't last ten seconds in a locked room with me. Don't you, don't you!' I screamed at him. I think I saw a flicker of annoyance, but to give him his due he retained his composure quite well.

'Cook him. Take him to the craters,' insect-eyes finally said.

For a while it wasn't too bad. They drove the dune buggy over rough ground, and because I'd been restrained with my arms outstretched every bump put a lot of stress on my back and arms, causing pain despite my reinforced physiology. Pretty soon that was the least of my worries. It was the dust. It was corrosive and stung. Filters or no filters, I felt the dust filling my nasal cavity and throat. I tried to keep my mouth closed, opening only to scream when I was jarred particularly painfully. As my head nodded down I saw that I was covered in blood. My skin and flesh were being slowly stripped down to the armour as the dust sandblasted me. I felt like I was disappearing, being peeled back layer by layer. When I tried to scream I just choked on more dust.

It felt so pointless. Insect-eyes could've stripped me down for parts, maybe even sold my flesh; instead there was just this suffering, the point of which was beyond me. Pretty soon it wasn't me up on that frame atop the dune buggy. It was just a lump of suffering flesh that wasn't capable of the higher forms of thinking. It was a mindless wounded animal, a broken machine. The form and the mind were mutually exclusive, neither able to identify with the other beyond the electric signals from screaming nerve endings. I would've passed out, but every time I tried I was jarred awake by the pain in my back and arms.

Really the last thing I remembered that made any real sense was the feeling of panic, a reassuringly human sensation at the time, as the dune buggy inched precariously over the side of a huge crater. It felt like it was going to turn over but the driver, in his radiation-proofed vestments, held it as we drove down into the crater at a shallow angle, leaving a dust cloud of hot dirt behind us. The crater seemed huge and a pool of reddish liquid had collected in its centre. I couldn't work out the reason for this hole.

## 18
# Crawling Town

*Over and over in my head I could hear Shaz's voice repeating our grid coordinates and requesting, practically begging, for immediate evac. It was more slender than the Berserks; it moved with more grace and it looked more humanoid, more like us. You couldn't look at it straight on for some reason. It didn't seem to make sense that way, some kind of camouflage effect that affected even our sophisticated optics. Fire, realign target, fire, realign target, fire again, reload. It just stalked among us, rarely getting hit, and the few times it did it just seemed to stagger back slightly and then move on.*

*Mudge went down first. He was behind it, I think, or maybe he was in front and we were behind. I'm not even sure it mattered. I could see the flickering light of Mudge's AK-47, when the alien just reached out towards him and something black, sharp and slightly impossible-looking detached itself from it at speed and then seemed to accelerate. I watched as Mudge's AK-47 came apart in his hands and he was thrown off his feet into the air. It looked like the upper left part of his chest was trying to separate from the rest of his body. He seemed to be in the air for ever as I watched him, high on my boosted reflexes, Slaughter and amphetamines. Finally he hit the ground and remained still.*

*Suddenly the thing was gone again. Shaz had no head, the stump of his neck a brief red fountain before he slumped to his knees and then forward onto the ground. His urgent comms request for an evac still echoed in my head. I fired the remainder of the rounds from my shotgun magazine over Shaz's body at absolutely nothing.*

*It was standing next to me. I swung round to face it. It was holding Shaz's head. For some reason it occurred to me he was studying the head sadly, trying to find answers. I don't know how I had the time to think of that or where it came from, but it was an impression I couldn't shake.*

*The head dropped, forgotten. My shotgun exploded as it swept its claw-like hand through the weapon as if it didn't exist. The alien pierced a solid breastplate, a hardening inertial undersuit and subcutaneous armour with little apparent effort. I could feel it inside me. Panic made its way through training, conditioning and combat-grade narcotics as its hand split apart into what felt like thousands of tendrils that flailed through my chest cavity.*

*Gregor was in the air. I'm not sure that made sense to me. The muzzle flash of his PDW seemed welcoming, a friend to me. The impact of the bullets on the alien looked like ripples on the surface of a dark pond. Gregor body-checked the somehow solid alien, knocking it back. Its arm slid out of me. The alien's liquid flesh had separated into many thin, swaying tendrils that, inanely, reminded me of a sea anemone as I sat down hard on the mud. I had no idea what to do.*

*Gregor was all but on top of the thing. He scrambled off it, throwing aside his empty PDW and grabbing desperately at the Tyler Optics laser pistol on his right hip. He put himself between the alien and me.*

*The alien sat up, reconfiguring itself in a way that made my head hurt, as bright red beam after bright red beam stabbed through it, creating greasy black steam. It was like the alien was melting, collapsing in on itself like a mountain of mud, but it was still moving towards Gregor when his laser pistol's battery ran dry. Gregor flung the weapon at it and reached for his sword bayonet just as the alien surged forward. Part of it seemed to be falling away, dissolving into the murky black puddles of the useless junk genetic code we had come to expect from Them. The rest of it was separating into more thick tendrils. Gregor screamed, a noise I somehow couldn't connect with him, a noise quickly cut off as a tendril forced itself into his mouth, his eyes, ears and nostrils. I saw his face contort and bulge as his veins stood out, turning to black as the thing forced itself into him. I could make out his skin moving beneath his inertial undersuit. He slumped back into my lap, dead. No, not dead, still breathing. His eyes were solid black pools and all his veins were black also. I stared at him.*

*'This is Kilo Two Zero requesting a sitrep from call sign Wild Boys, over.' Rolleston's calm, well-enunciated voice over the command net was so incongruous as to be meaningless. I had no idea how long I sat there cradling Gregor in my lap. I laid my friend down in the soft mud and stood up, walking over to Shaz as Rolleston repeated his message.*

*Shaz had no head. He was still dead. Shaz was dead, Gregor may be worse. I was aware, at some level, of movement among the perimeter of Berserks, but they were not approaching yet. They seemed so normal, so commonplace.*

*Ash, Ash was still dead as well. Didn't have to worry about Ash, only Gregor, but didn't want to think about him. I went back to Gregor and closed my eyes, reaching down blindly, every movement causing me to leak more blood from my wounded chest cavity. I couldn't make sense of the information I was seeing regarding the wound on my internal visual display. I felt the still-hot barrel of Gregor's laser pistol and picked it up. I opened my eyes and looked at it. I tried to work out what it was and what it meant. Eventually I ejected the spent battery into the mud. I bent down, searching for spare batteries, trying not to look at black eyes and black veins.*

*Mudge groaned. I felt irritation but that went away when I realised that I would have something to do, something to take my mind off Gregor. Rolleston's message came across the command net again. He sounded angrier, more demanding, but it was still just ambient noise to me.*

*Clean the wound. Apply the medgel and a medpak to drive it, then a stim to wake him up. Pain for Mudge as he sits up. A stricken expression on his face as he sees Ash and Shaz and asks me about Gregor. I ignore him. I can't answer him, wouldn't know how. Rolleston's voice becoming more annoying now. I commit only a little act of treason by giving a journalist access to our command net.*

*I walk around for a while. Mudge all but has to wrestle me to the ground to get me to lie down. I can feel his hands on and in my chest. All the while he is requesting an immediate evac. I can hear sporadic shard fire. Mudge is hunkered down low over me as he tends my wound. He is still screaming across the comms connection at a Rolleston reluctant to come and get us. Fine, we die here, big surprise.*

*Heavier shard fire now, Rolleston wants information. Wants to know exactly what happened to Sergeant MacDonald. Mudge isn't telling him what he wants to hear. I can hear the Berserks charging across the mud towards us.*

*'I don't know! I wasn't fucking conscious!' Mudge shouts.*

*'You want to know? You want to know!' I hear a hysteria-edged voice that isn't Mudge scream. Everything seems to come into sharp relief. 'It's inside him. It forced its way inside him!' I realise I'm screaming even though the comms connection is sub-vocal. I realise I'm weeping, but it's dry, no tears when you have machines instead of eyes. I half-heartedly draw Gregor's laser pistol and take aim towards the Berserks closing in on our position.*

*Everything stops. There's a really bright light. It's sort of blue and white at the same time. Mudge and I are no more than silhouettes now that everything has become a bright circle of light and the ground seems to want to climb into the air. There is no noise. Then there's a rushing sound and there's all the noise at once. Am I screaming?*

*Then I am burnt and blistered and standing, somehow, on a plain of brown glass. Mudge is on his knees close by, crying. I doubt he could tell you why. That sound is the sound of a gunship coming into land. The guitar riff is suitably sombre so it doesn't jar more than a little bit. I turn and walk towards it. Rolleston and Josephine Bran jump out of the craft with an energy I can barely remember. Rolleston moves quickly to Gregor and begins examining him. I don't like this and raise the laser. There's shouting. I'm aware of the miniguns on this side of the gunship swivelling towards me. They are already rotating, up to speed. Buck's fingers are poised over his fretboard; he's the most tense I've ever seen him. One of the most dangerous people I've ever met is pointing a laser carbine at me as well.*

*Mudge is standing next to me and pushing the laser pistol down, but that's no use, how will I shoot Rolleston now? I think Mudge is saying something to me. I watch Rolleston move Gregor, easily slinging him over his shoulders and moving him into the gunship, where there's some kind of small glass technological coffin. It's not dead, I think, and then correct myself: he's not dead. Later I'll realise it's a secure biohazard isolation chamber.*

*Gregor's in the coffin now. Mudge pulls me towards the gunship, telling me we're going home now. Leaving Dog 4. But as we approach the gunship the weapons remain up, covering us. They won't let us on board. They are businesslike and polite but we are not being let into the gunship. I am actually surprised that Mudge has the energy for a pointless argument, screaming at the gunship as the blast of their take-off forces us backwards.*

*It's actually quite beautiful watching the gunship bank towards Sirius Prime, rising massive and seemingly close on the horizon. I realise that despite the thing inside Gregor, I don't want Rolleston taking my friend away. I wish I'd shot him, in the head, with his own laser – Gregor, I mean.*

I woke up screaming. I don't think anyone noticed. I was hoping to die soon as I didn't want another day of this. I hung from my frame looking down at the skinheads going about their business as I swayed in the wind, making noises that didn't sound particularly human to me.

I watched the gate open and a figure walk in. He was wearing a rad duster not unlike the one I used to have. He wore a wide-brimmed hat and a mask that had a series of fetishist charms hanging off it. Dreadlocks spilled out of his hat, reaching halfway down his back. That meant something. He walked over to a group of skinheads. They began talking and I saw the dreadlocked figure remove a small pouch from the pocket of his duster. I heard myself start to make what I can only describe as a wet roaring sound. The skinheads and the guy with the dreadlocks and duster looked up at me. He moved closer to me, peering up. It was him all right. Despite feeling like my skin had been flayed off, despite the fact that I barely felt human and definitely had more important things to worry about, I was taken aback by how much rage I felt towards Gibby.

'Jakob?' So I was still recognisable, that was something of a relief. I could see insect-eyes emerging from the C&C mobile home. He was watching this intently. Gibby turned to the skinheads he'd been dealing with.

'You need to kill that guy,' he said. I could've sworn I heard a bit of panic in his voice. The skinheads shook their heads, shrugging in a manner befitting low-level thuggery confronted with a problem.

'Fuck it, I'll do it myself.' The pilot flicked open the duster. An ancient Colt Navy .44 he'd added a smartlink to and modified for accuracy and modern ammunition appeared in his hand. Insect-eyes was walking towards us. Gibby cocked the hammer needlessly on the revolver. This would be better.

'Stop him,' insect-eyes ordered. A skinhead grabbed Gibby, dragging his gun hand down. Insect-eyes walked up to the restrained pilot and slapped him hard, knocking Gibby's sunglasses and mask off. Gibby's head snapped round with the force of the blow. When he turned back I could see the lenses that had replaced his eyes and a look of anger.

'Who is this?' insect-eyes demanded, meaning me.

'You out of your mind, Messer?' Gibby asked, fixing insect-eyes with a stare. So the little Nazi punk had a name. Messer, I'd have to remember that.

'I asked you a question,' Messer said dangerously.

'Let me go,' Gibby said. Messer nodded to the skinheads holding him. They let Gibby go but kept him casually covered. Gibby spun the pistol and slid it back into its holster. He pointed up at me.

'Get rid of him or we will,' he drawled.

'You're in no position to—' Messer began, but with a final glance at me Gibby stalked out of the compound. He looked scared.

I was fading in and out. Nothing really seemed to hurt any more.

'I thought it was just skin.' A voice I recognised from what seemed like long ago. I was in a grotto, a magic cave of ultraviolet magic symbols and medical equipment. I'd been chanted over in a language I didn't understand though I recognised some of the words. I'd been painted in blood and had things that rattled shaken over me. And then they'd painted new skin on over flesh flayed down to the armour.

'He's received a pretty high dose,' said a voice thick with an accent I'd normally be able to identify.

'Can't you do anything for him?' a worried-sounding Morag said. I tried to say her name but it sounded more like someone drooling themselves to death.

'He'd need all his systems replaced, internal decontam for his organs, new blood and then only maybe. If we had facilities like that here, Crawling Town would be a much healthier place.' It was a Caribbean accent of some kind, I decided, proud that I'd worked it out.

'New York?' she asked.

'I checked. Even Balor doesn't have the gear,' the first voice said. Pagan, I knew him as well. I felt nauseous.

'What you want to do?' the heavily accented voice asked.

'Patch him up, get him back up on his feet,' Morag said decisively.

'Why don't we just make him comfortable?' Pagan said. Fuck off, Pagan. Make me comfortable for what?

'Just do it,' Morag said.

I remember very little of it. I remember everyone coming in, but most of it I got from Mudge's viz recording. He thought I'd want to see my rescue. I remember Mudge moving with a narcotic jaunt in his steps, his AK slung across his front. I remember Pagan, staff in hand, looking for all the world like the ancient Druid he so obviously wanted to be. I remember Mrs Tillwater, lilac skirt suit, very smart, the suburban matron from all those soap operas and sitcoms from long ago, except for the dead-skin mask from her last victim, unworn and tucked in the top of her skirt. She'd been an officer in the US Rangers until she'd crucified a column of refugees on Proxima Centauri for refusing to help her platoon hold back a Them advance. Dishonourably discharged, she spent some time in prison, but somehow she had been released and now she ran the First Baptist Church of Austin Texas. Of course I couldn't forget Big Papa Neon and Little Baby Neon.

Big Papa Neon was perfectly attired in glowing graveyard finery, from top hat to tails. His dreadlocks had glowing circuitry woven into them and left fractal patterns in the air as they moved; one eye was covered by a glowing UV monocle. Like Pagan he carried a staff but it was a stick of pale blue luminescence.

Little Baby Neon was something else altogether. Rumour had it that Little Baby Neon was Papa Neon's younger brother. Little Baby Neon was huge and mainly made of metal. If there was anything of his original body left I couldn't see it. He was so augmented that there must've been very little remaining of his humanity. We were all estranged from our flesh once we started replacing it. Little Baby Neon was divorced from it. He was to all intents and purposes a machine. I'd heard him called a cyberzombie. There had been a mutiny on Proxima. Papa and Baby Neon and some of their people had deserted the Haitian Marines and hijacked an Earth-bound transport. However, some of Baby Neon's proclivities had become too much even for the Big Neon Voodoo, and Papa Neon had just kept having ware added to his brother. Baby Neon's metallic hide was covered in the luminescent sinuous figures of veves. Pop Voudun protection from Papa Neon for his near-mindless brother.

And then of course there was Morag. Wearing a black tunic not unlike the one that Messer wore and trousers that looked damn close to leather. Nobody was wearing his or her hazardous environment gear. No Rannu. Took me a while to realise he'd be out on the town somewhere, covering this little meeting. Also, the presence of the Neons notwithstanding, Rannu being Nepalese probably would've excited these throwbacks. It was thinking along those lines that made me realise that Morag with her recently shaved head and new costume could've passed for one of these fucks.

I hadn't wanted her to see me like this. Pagan had glanced up at me, Mudge hadn't, and neither had Morag. She was striding across the Nazi compound like she owned it and she looked angry. There was something very un-Morag about her. If she was acting then she was doing a very good job. Later I would realise that all the time that she was working on the Forbidden Pleasure she would've been playing a role. I watched as Messer and a group of his skinheads met Morag and the others.

The rest I got from Mudge's recording. His camera eyes were mounted on stabilised balls to compensate for the movement of his head, but even so it was a strange first-person perspective. Mudge was striding forward, Morag just in front to his right and Pagan on the other side of her, walking with the Neons and Mrs Tillwater. According to Mudge, Pagan was on very good terms with the Neons, and Mrs Tillwater had been asked to come along because the Wait respected her all-white gang of serial killers, despite them being Baptists. Pagan had friends. Indeed he seemed to be walking with the lords and ladies of Crawling Town.

I saw Messer gesture towards Mudge's eyes. One of the skinheads moved forward, holding his hands up to block Mudge's recording. Mudge grabbed the skinhead's hand and twisted it, forcing the skinhead to bend forward at the waist. Mudge had his Regiment-issue SIG Full Auto in his hand. He pushed the barrel into the skinhead's shorn skull and looked straight at Messer. The other skinheads brought their weapons to bear. Pagan and the Neons stopped and Mrs Tillwater kept walking around Messer and the group of skinheads, flanking them. From Mudge's perspective I could see she was carrying an M-19 ACR, the standard assault rifle of the US Army.

Morag, however, kept walking. She walked right up to Messer and backhanded him hard enough to draw blood from his stained purple lips. Watching the recording I was somewhat taken aback by this. Mudge was chuckling, but when Messer turned round I could see that she'd managed to make him lose his composure. Needless to say there were a lot of gun barrels being pointed at her. So she slapped him again. Watching this played back, I burst out laughing. I laughed so much I threw up blood. Messer's face was now a mask of rage.

'You are a disgrace to your race!' Morag spat at him. I watched his eyes widen and the crystal of his multi-faceted eyes turn red. I realised Morag's strong Dundonian accent had gone.

'Who are you, woman, to come here with niggers and say that to me?' Messer demanded, his voice shaking with fury. Baby Neon stepped forward but Papa Neon laid a hand on him and muttered something in patois that I didn't understand. It was an interesting approach to negotiation – not sure I would've taken it.

'We being niggers or not, you need to remember where you are, boy,' Papa Neon said. A lot of the skinheads were spending their time looking nervously between Baby Neon and Mrs Tillwater. Morag softened and stepped in, running her hand down Messer's face, causing him to flinch.

'You are a good soldier, Messer,' she said and then pointed at me. Mudge glanced up. I was a mess. 'But that is mine and I want it back,' she said, and then she became all coquettish. 'And if I don't get it you will make my masters very unhappy.' Then she grabbed the skin on the side of his face and was all authoritarian again. 'Do you understand me?' Messer looked over at Mrs Tillwater.

'Mrs Tillwater?' It was clear that despite Mrs Tillwater being a member of the weaker sex, according to this guy's fucked-up ideology, she was seen as a kindred soul. It was kind of pathetic really. It was all the more pathetic that these violent little children had taken me down.

'Well it's up to you, Messer,' Mrs Tillwater said, as if she was addressing a Sunday school lesson. 'But if I were you I'd do what the nice young lady asks.' I didn't like the look on her face though. It was as if she wanted to see something. Messer pointed up at me.

'That is my gift to God,' he snarled. That upset me; I liked John Coltrane.

'The gods have other uses for that one,' Pagan said. Messer's head snapped round to look at his fellow hacker. I could sense Messer appraising the bizarre tattooed and pierced figure he saw in front of him.

'And you are?' Messer asked.

'Pagan.' Mudge did a close-up reaction shot of Messer. I could see the punk Nazi's eyes widen round the red crystalline lenses. He'd heard of Pagan. Pagan held Messer's stare. You could tell that hacker patriarch was a role he felt comfortable with. It was a bit like watching

Messer get spanked. 'Your god is coming and when it does all the niggers will feel his wrath,' Pagan said, though it was obvious he was trying to master his distaste. Papa Neon looked over at Pagan with an expression of amusement on his face.

'The space niggers as well,' Messer said, looking up at the sky, though mostly all he would see was dust. He was sounding more and more like a desperate child. Mudge had to stifle a laugh as Pagan nodded benevolently.

'The space niggers as well,' Pagan said. This was clearly a ridiculous ideology that Messer had discovered. It was difficult to imagine anyone ever having taken this seriously.

Morag sauntered up to Messer, seemingly oblivious to the guns covering her. She stepped behind him and, smiling, leant forward to whisper in his ear.

'Let me have him back,' she whispered. It seemed to me that Messer actually flinched. I found out why later: the whisper was the signal for Pagan to send him an encrypted message saying that if he didn't release me they were going to take me anyway and his people would lose all their respect for him. The only thing he could really do was try and save as much face as possible. I could see him looking between Papa Neon and Pagan. They were the two big-name hackers there. He knew he was outclassed.

'Conflict is good – it feeds Ogu Bodagris – but boy, you push too hard, both here and in the spirit world. You need to calm yourself,' Papa Neon said. I could see Messer swallow like he wanted to say something but had decided against it. He ordered me to be taken down.

I saw myself being got down, barely able to stand. Mudge was helping me. Somehow I managed to walk aided by Mudge. I didn't remember this, but as I walked past him I grabbed Messer. I was holding myself up by my bloody grip on his tunic.

'I'm going to kill every single last one of you,' I managed to mumble. Messer said nothing as Mudge pulled me off him.

The rest of the viz was me being carried by Mudge and Mrs Tillwater to the back of a pickup truck and driven through the transient streets of Crawling Town. We stopped to pick up Rannu from where he'd been watching my rescue along the barrel of a gun. The ex-Ghurkha glanced at me but said nothing. I noticed that Pagan had fortunately had the presence of mind to retrieve my personal belongings from the Wait. They took me to one of the Day-Glo articulated lorries that belonged to the Big Neon Voodoo. Morag was shaking like a leaf.

'You did fine,' Pagan told her. Mudge mumbled his agreement. The back of the lorry they had brought me to was a garishly decorated infirmary. I must've been hallucinating by this point because Mrs Tillwater was wearing her mask of somebody's flayed face.

'Welcome to America,' the grinning mask told me. I may have screamed.

## 19
# Crawling Town

It was kind of a baseline nausea. Like the day after you've had a lot to drink, and although you're capable of functioning the sickness in your stomach tells you that you overdid it the night before. It was like that but all the time. Just reminding you that there was something wrong, something corrupt in your body at a basic level. Other than that I felt fine.

In the trucks and land trains of Crawling Town there were stabilised trailers with protein vats and hydroponics farms, but they didn't provide enough for self-sufficiency so Crawling Town raided and traded. One of its main cash crops was drugs. Ironically they made more from selling medical drugs on the black market than they did selling the cheap and readily available recreational drugs. This was one of the reasons that Papa Neon was a genius. It was also where the initial supply of drugs that was going to keep me functioning until close to the end came from.

In the mirror I looked the same, pretty much. They'd even ironed out some of the creases for me. Was this my face? It had been rebuilt so many times I felt a bit like the broom who'd had its handle and its brush changed. The hair had to go, which pissed me off. It wasn't vanity. I was vain enough to not want to see it fall out but I didn't want to end up looking like the bald-headed bastards who'd done this to me in the first place.

It was written all over their faces when they came to see me in the Big Neon Voodoo's ritual infirmary. By this time my hair had been shorn and I had a bandanna tied round my head and sunglasses on. I felt like I was in the American army. There was that awkwardness you have when nobody wants to mention something awful. Weird really, when you consider that several of the people in the room had probably killed more people than they could remember, but they couldn't bring themselves to say radiation sickness. Well, except for Mudge.

'So you're dying then?' He'd spent some time looking confused by the forced politeness in the room and apparently become bored. There seemed to be a collective sharp intake of breath. I paused long enough to make everyone uncomfortable and then started laughing as Mudge offered me some vodka.

'A bit faster than everyone else,' I said.

'Sure you just don't like us all coming to see you in the hospital? I think you like the fuss,' he said. I was about to drink from the bottle when I stopped.

'Is there no chance of you ever drinking whisky?' I asked.

'Oh,' said Morag and searched around in her bag. She pulled out a bottle of single malt, one from the park distilleries. I was impressed.

'Where'd you get that?' I said.

'Found it,' she replied simply.

'Spent a long time searching for it,' Pagan said. To his credit there was only a little bit of resentment in his voice. Presumably she'd been looking for it when she should've been doing her God homework.

'Nice rescue, guys. Not sure that was the approach I would've taken,' I said. I would've killed them all.

'I was scared shitless,' Morag said, glancing at Pagan.

'I told you, people like that are always scared of women. If they weren't they'd respond to people better,' he said. So it'd been his plan.

'Ever done any psy-ops, Pagan?' I asked. Pagan said nothing.

'When are we going to kill the Wait?' Mudge asked once the silence had got kind of awkward. I was touched that I could see Rannu nodding.

'That will not happen,' Papa Neon said. Mudge's head didn't move but I saw one of his eyes rotate to look at the gang leader.

'They're going to die before my friend here does,' Mudge assured him. 'I'll film it and everything. We can show you after, if you like.'

'Oh, for fuck's sake,' Pagan said. 'Papa Neon has helped us out a hell of a lot here. Can you not show a bit of respect?'

'I thought we'd be doing him a favour. The Wait didn't seem to have anything nice to say about him and his people,' Mudge said. I could see him getting irritated now. I took a sip of the whisky. It was good, a smooth burn. I watched Pagan and Papa Neon. I was beginning to see why Mudge and Rannu hadn't gone in shooting when they came to get me.

'They are Crawling Town, you are not,' Neon said.

'What I've seen of Crawling Town amounts to a small fucking war going on,' Mudge said.

Papa Neon shrugged. 'Several wars. We are a city; like all cities we have social problems. Though our biggest killer is traffic accidents rather than gang warfare. But it doesn't matter. We can wipe each other out. If it gets out of hand then steps are taken, but we will not tolerate threats from outside,' he said with a sort of laid-back finality.

Mudge looked around at everyone else. 'You're kidding right?'

'Mudge,' I said softly, 'Pagan's right. Papa Neon's done right by me. He's done a lot of shit he didn't have to and we've probably been a huge pain in the arse to him,' I said, looking at Papa Neon. He just smiled. 'Besides, he's one of Pagan's little conspiracy of God builders, yeah?' Pagan started; Neon didn't show any reaction. Morag looked up at Papa Neon as if seeing him anew.

'It is true. I would see Obatala brought back into this realm and I will dance for him,' Papa Neon said.

'You were one of the robed figures in Dinas Emrys,' I replied. Papa Neon nodded.

'Could've maybe mentioned this before, Pagan,' Mudge said.

'He didn't want to risk exposing his contact, did you?' I asked.

'With good reason,' Pagan said.

'Pagan's right,' Morag said.

'How's that?' I asked, trying to decide how pissed off I should be. If Pagan had contacted Papa Neon in the first place this would've gone down very differently.

'Crawling Town is being overflown almost constantly by recon drones,' Pagan said.

'Fortunate Sons?' I asked. Pagan nodded. 'We are pretty close to the US,' I said.

'There's more to it than that,' Pagan said and looked at Papa Neon.

'You're not the only ex-special forces type that's been picked up in town recently,' the gang leader said.

'Rolleston's people?' I asked.

'They're XIs,' Rannu said.

'You sure?' I asked.

'The two that broke were, before they were broken down into their constituent parts,' Papa Neon said. I could see Rannu shifting uneasily at this. 'And this isn't New York,' he added. He meant that he couldn't or wouldn't protect us like Balor had. I didn't really blame him. I climbed out of bed and started getting dressed. I didn't feel too bad, except for the nausea.

'Dude, should you be out of bed?' Mudge asked. I looked at him and grinned.

'I'm gonna need a lot of drugs.'

*

Mrs Tillwater would not shut up but I was a little too disconcerted to ask her to be quiet. She was interspersing the most banal day-to-day conversation with descriptions of sadistic violence. Some people would do that just to try and freak you out, but I wasn't getting that from her. She genuinely seemed ill.

I was riding shotgun with her. Papa Neon had asked her to act as our native guide to the white-trash element of Crawling Town. She had gently scolded him and agreed to do it. I'd chosen to ride with her because I'd been getting tired of seeing the look of sympathy on Morag's, Pagan's and even Rannu's faces.

I'd been right: Gibby and Buck were riding with one of the cyberbilly gangs, the biggest and most powerful one, the Hard Luck Comancheros. Mrs Tillwater was taking us out to see them. Apparently they'd left the town and driven into the ruins of Trenton. We were all suited up. Mrs Tillwater's hazardous environment gear was lilac, which appeared to be her favourite colour. It had scalps hanging off it. We were in her armoured, four-wheel drive station wagon. Morag was following on the low rider with Rannu, Pagan and Mudge in the muscle car behind her.

'Of course, there are tribes in the ruins of the cities on the Dead Roads,' Mrs Tillwater was saying. 'Little more than savages really. File their teeth, wear human skins, barely human themselves.' I looked at this woman. Other than her augmentations, the plugs in her neck, replacement eyes, she looked every bit the suburban matriarch. She wore slightly too much make-up, was ordinarily attractive for a woman of a certain age and seemed to take a lot of care with her disconcertingly banal appearance.

'I hear some of them eat human flesh,' I said, pretty sure I could defend myself if this got out of hand. She didn't miss a beat.

'Yes, but they don't prepare it properly ...' She went into quite some detail about how to properly prepare human flesh. I began to worry when I found my mouth watering. I was relieved when I started to hear engines ahead of us.

The outskirts of Trenton, the industrial part of the city, had been hit by a low-yield nuke during the FHC. It was probably that crater that the dune buggy I'd been attached to had driven through. The nuke had killed the majority of the city's population. Those that didn't die probably succumbed to the radiation and burns not too long after the blast. The city itself had been pretty badly banged up. Mrs Tillwater was steering round piles of rubble and the four-wheel drive was definitely coming in useful. I was a bit worried about Morag but she seemed to be getting better with the bike. On either side of the road, damaged high-rise buildings reached up towards the unnaturally red sky like broken fingers. Many of the buildings were covered in freshly painted graffiti depicting complex but abstract patterns. Others had murals depicting stylised tribal heroics and what I guessed were hunts. Much of the graffiti was quite beautiful.

'Those done by the tribes?' I asked, pointing at one of the abstract designs. The serial killer sitting next to me nodded.

'Territorial boundaries. The murals are histories,' she said. 'I mean, why can't they do something useful like clean the place up a bit?'

'Yeah, tidying would be the way forward,' I said. Mrs Tillwater turned to look at me.

'I do understand sarcasm, Mr Douglas, I just choose not to lower myself to use it.' Suddenly the constant patronising sympathy of the others didn't seem so bad.

'The tribes wouldn't mess with us, would they?' I said, trying to change the subject.

'Why on Earth wouldn't they?' she asked, sounding surprised. 'They attack convoys much larger and better armed than ours.' I looked out the back window to see Morag riding behind us, her poncho flapping in the wind. Suddenly she seemed very exposed.

We turned into the ruins of what we would've called a scheme back in Dundee but I think they were called projects over here. Basically it had been a large and ugly estate of state-provided housing. Now it was an empty crumbling mess. There was a large, rubble-strewn open area; beyond that were rows of terraced flats and beyond them a series of ugly high-rise buildings.

Parked in the open area were a lot of different vehicles, most of them muscle cars, heavily customised, all four-wheel drive. There were a few pickups and vans, also heavily customised, and lots of bikes and trikes, most of them low riders or chopped, with a few performance bikes here and there. There was even the ancient half-track with the cartoon swamp creature painted on the bonnet that we'd seen on the first night. Everything was customised. I couldn't help but stare at the machines. The noise of the various engines hit us like a solid wall of sound. I overrode my audio dampeners. I wanted to hear this.

'Boys will be boys,' Mrs Tillwater said cheerfully. People glanced up as we pulled in. Everyone there seemed to be wearing a duster and wide-brimmed hat, though many of them didn't have their masks on. Most were bearded, even some of the women, and like Gibby and Buck, dreadlocks seemed to be the order of the day. They had the degenerate cowboy look of the cyberbilly scene. I could just about make out the sounds of heavy western guitar riffs playing through a powerful sound system somewhere. The singer was grunting about his one true love stealing his car.

As we pulled into the area, our beat-up vehicles getting looks of scorn from the assembled cyberbillys, I wondered how they managed to get their cars and bikes to look this good in such a corrosive environment. I saw the start of a drag race, two of the muscle cars accelerating so quickly that their front wheels came off the ground, flames shooting from their exhausts as they raced up part of the remaining and very unsafe-looking raised road system. A cheer went up from the onlookers. I almost felt like I could live this way.

Mrs Tillwater found a space and fussily parked in it, I wasn't sure why. I fixed my mask and goggles in place and climbed out. Morag came to a halt nearby and Rannu pulled up next to us. Mrs Tillwater headed over to a group of the cyberbillys. All of them had the aces and eights of the Dead Man's Hand painted on their clothes somewhere, the colours of the Hard Luck Commancheros. There were some glances our way but finally she signalled to us and started across the concrete square. We followed, doing our best not to get run over by speeding bikes or cars. It was kind of gratifying to see Pagan, Rannu and Mudge form a loose formation, watching all around. I'd found myself doing pretty much the same thing.

We were heading towards the street of terraced flats, where a crowd of the Commancheros was gathered. There were a couple of cars and a pickup, but this mostly seemed to be where the bikers where hanging out. Suited me. Mrs Tillwater signalled to me and then pointed up to the road embankment that ran along one side of the square. Stood on top of the embankment watching us was a figure. I zoomed in on her. She wore an outfit of skin, possibly human, and looked lean, tough and athletic. Her hair was tied back tightly and what I could see of her skin was covered in ritual scars. Her mouth was open in a grimace and I could see her filed-down, steel-capped teeth. She carried a compound bow that looked like it had been made from salvaged metal and had a wicked-looking curved blade stuck through her belt.

'If we can see her then that means there will be others around that we can't,' Mrs Tillwater said over our tactical net. It was like the tribeswoman was challenging us. It was strange. I got a thrill from seeing her. I knew she was another human being but it was like the thrill I got as a kid when I was out with my father in the park and we saw a stag or bear tracks, or even heard wolves howling when we had to camp. The tribeswoman looked feral and degenerate but she also looked noble, unafraid and somehow unpolluted. She hadn't surrendered her humanity to machinery and war. There was little difference between her tribe and one that had cars and guns except maybe honesty. I think I envied her.

'Will they attack?' I asked Mrs Tillwater. I could see her shake her head as the answer came back over the net.

'No, they're just letting us know whose neighbourhood we're borrowing.'

We'd reached the crowd of cyberbillys and I saw them both. I glanced to my left and saw Rannu making his way round that way; I glanced to my right and saw Mudge. I let Mrs Tillwater and Pagan go ahead of me and kept my head down. Morag was next to me. Buck was straddling a low rider, revving it. Gibby was kneeling down next to the engine, fiddling with it. The pair of them looked up as we approached. Neither had their masks on, just plastic sunglasses, though their faces were largely covered by beards anyway. Buck nodded at Mrs Tillwater, then I saw Gibby look to my left – he'd made Mudge. A word passed between Gibby and Buck. Gibby stood up, both of them reaching for their old customised .44s. I came round from behind Mrs Tillwater, the Mastodon in one hand, the Tyler in the other. I couldn't use my shoulder laser because of the radiation duster.

'Don't do it!' I shouted. Mudge had his SIG drawn and was moving in on the pair, the fully automatic pistol levelled at Gibby. Pagan and even Morag had their pistols in their hands but kept them down waiting to see what the crowd was going to do. Rannu had disappeared somehow despite being the only Nepalese present. He suddenly appeared again, one of his Glocks levelled at Buck and Gibby, the other held down at his side ready to fire into the crowd if need be.

Mudge was still moving up on Buck and Gibby. He didn't look happy. I wasn't either. I could still remember them flying away from us, leaving me standing with the corpses of two of my friends. Mudge walked up to Gibby and wrapped his hands round the ex-pilot's greasy dreadlocks before digging the barrel of the gun painfully into his skin.

'Hello, Gibby,' Mudge said. 'Jakob, we only need one of these cunts to talk, right?'

'Calm down, Mudge,' I said. The crowd was edgy. I was sure that weapons were being drawn out of sight. The cyberbilly closest to me tried to pull a cut-down pump action out of her duster. I moved the Tyler to cover her. 'Do that and I'll turn your head to steam,' I said. 'Okay, everyone, just take it easy. We just want to talk to Buck and Gibby.'

'I don't,' Mudge said helpfully.

'Except for Mudge, who wants to torture them to death,' I muttered to myself. There were a lot of Commancheros here and lots close by. If it came down to gunplay it would get futile very quickly.

'Jakob,' I heard Morag say. I didn't like the tone in her voice. 'Ow, fuck!' I turned round to see Mrs Tillwater with an automatic held to Morag's head. It looked like she'd just bitten Morag's ear through the hood of her poncho – I could see it bleeding through the material. I moved the Tyler to cover Mrs Tillwater.

'You have been told once,' she said evenly. The suburban matriarch gone, she was all military commander now. 'They are Crawling Town; you are not. Now lower your guns,' she ordered. More of the Commancheros had their weapons in their hands now.

'Fuck her,' Mudge said. 'Shoot her in the head.'

'I will eat her,' Mrs Tillwater said, and I believed her. I lowered my weapons. Rannu and a relieved-looking Pagan did the same. Obviously Mudge didn't. The cyberbilly whose head I'd threatened to turn to steam tried to take my Mastodon out of my hand. She found herself lying on the ground with my foot on her throat.

'Let's not get carried away here. We lower ours, you guys lower yours, and we'll see if we can make it through the next ten minutes without any of you getting killed,' I said. Always negotiate from a position of strength, even when you obviously don't have one. Mudge still had his gun levelled at Gibby.

'Mudge!' I said. I saw one of his eyes swivel towards me. Finally he lowered his gun. I turned to Mrs Tillwater.

'Now let her go,' I said, holstering my two guns. Mrs Tillwater released Morag, who spun away from the serial killer as she was putting her automatic back in her handbag.

'What did you have to bite me for?' Morag demanded.

'Sorry, dear,' Mrs Tillwater said unapologetically.

Morag punched her. It shouldn't have connected with a vet like Tillwater, but it did. I guess she hadn't been expecting it; I know I hadn't. It was hand-to-hand stuff from Morag's softskills but she'd obviously been practising enough that her body had properly integrated the software. She caught the side of Tillwater's jaw with her fist and knocked her back a bit. Tillwater's head snapped back and she looked furious, as did Morag. I got ready to draw my pistols but Mrs Tillwater just smiled, nodded at Morag and turned away.

'Hell, that was tense,' Buck drawled. Mudge pistol-whipped him so hard it knocked him off the bike. Even I cringed as the bike hit the concrete, scratching the electric-blue paint job on the alcohol tank. Gibby helped Buck pick the bike up.

Buck was bleeding from the mouth. He spat out blood and a tooth. The crowd was getting restless again.

'What the fuck!'

Gibby looked at the ruined paint job. 'Fuck this! Everybody kill these people,' he said. Weapons were drawn again.

'Buck, Gibby,' Mrs Tillwater said, as if she was talking to two naughty boys, and she kind of was, 'both myself and Papa Neon would appreciate it if you would talk with Jakob and his friends.'

'But look what they did to my bike!' Buck moaned. Mudge didn't help by grinning at him.

'Everyone!' Mrs Tillwater said to the Commancheros. 'Shall we give these old friends some time together?' Then she turned to me. 'I'll be just over here with all of Buck and Gibby's friends, so I want you to play nicely,' she said sweetly. 'Understand?' All trace of sweetness gone.

I nodded. 'Everyone put your guns away,' I said over the tactical net. Eventually even Mudge holstered his SIG.

'Come on, everyone,' Mrs Tillwater said, as if she was organising a picnic.

'We ain't going nowhere,' one of the Commancheros said. 'Who the hell are you to tell us what to do?' Mrs Tillwater walked over to him. He towered over her.

'I'll come and find you and we can talk about it tonight?' she said and then smiled up at him. I was pretty sure I saw him blanch behind his goggles.

Finally, once everyone had stopped being macho, the five of us were left alone with Buck and Gibby. Gibby at least had the common courtesy to look a little nervous. Buck just looked pissed off.

'We need to talk,' I said to the pair. As soon as I opened my mouth Buck revved the engine on the low rider, drowning me out. 'That's pretty childish,' I said, and predictably he revved the bike again.

'Fuck it. Let's shoot him and torture Gibby,' Mudge said as my audio dampeners kicked in to drown out the bike engine's throaty roar.

'We're wasting our time,' Pagan said and again the bike engine was revved.

'We don't want to talk to you. Fuck off an leave us alone,' Gibby said. He was looking pretty scared. I didn't think it was because of us.

'You know Rolleston's going to find you sooner or later,' I told him.

'Yeah, because of you, you fucker!' he answered.

'Rolleston's always known where we are,' Buck said angrily. 'And that was fine as long as we didn't talk to anyone.'

'Well, whether you talk to us or not he's still going to kill you,' Mudge pointed out.

'So fucking what? You know anyone over forty?' Buck asked. Maybe Rolleston, I thought, but decided to keep that observation to myself.

'That's no reason not to talk to us,' Morag said.

'And it's no reason to talk to you,' he replied. 'Unless you wanna work it off, darlin',' he said, grinning. I felt like hitting him. Morag didn't; she felt like kicking him. I was worried that she was getting too violent. However, Buck managed to lean out of the way of the kick. Morag looked pissed off and Buck just grinned at her.

'Maybe you want to watch the mouth—' I managed to say before Rannu kicked Buck so hard it picked him up off the bike and knocked him to the ground. I cringed as the paintwork got another scratch.

'Fuck!' Gibby shouted. He sounded genuinely distressed.

'Thanks,' Morag said to Rannu. Buck clambered back to his feet looking livid.

'You boys play nice now!' Mrs Tillwater shouted from where she was standing with the rest of the Commancheros, presumably swapping recipes or something. Buck picked the bike up again, grimacing as he looked at the paintwork.

'We're finished here,' Buck said. 'You ain't getting shit from us.'

'You owe us,' Mudge said.

'How you figure that?' Buck asked.

'You fucking left us there to die.'

'We didn't like it none,' Gibby said. 'But we didn't really have much of a choice.'

'And so fucking what? That was then, this is now. I'm over it,' Buck added.

'You fucking over it if I come back and bugger you to death with an exhaust pipe?' Mudge asked. Suddenly we were all looking at him. 'What?' he asked. 'It's a threat.' Buck revved the engine again.

'Like I said, we've all gotta go sometime,' the cyberbilly said.

'Yeah, but an exhaust pipe?' Gibby said, looking a little disturbed. Buck gunned the engine.

'This,' he said, patting the bike, 'this is what it's all about.'

'Look, I like bikes as much as the next guy, and that's a sweet ride,' I said, momentarily distracted. 'But there's more important things at stake here.'

'No. There's nothing more important. I know this and that's why I'm free,' Buck said.

'Yeah, I've seen your freedom,' Mudge said. 'You guys are free to die of cancer, free to die of respiratory problems, free to have deformed kids and slowly rot away.'

'Live free and die of cancer – John Wayne taught us that,' Buck said.

'Who?' I asked.

'I ought to have you horse-whipped,' Buck snarled.

'Can we talk or not?' I demanded. Buck's live free and die young crap was almost as irritating as Balor's warrior crap. I wondered why people, men usually, couldn't make it through life without developing some kind of crackpot code of ethics.

'Maybe we should, man,' Gibby said. 'We're fucked anyway. These guys might be jerks but Rolleston's a real fucker.'

'Rolleston never done marked up my bike,' Buck said.

'If you guys help us there's a chance, a slim one, but a chance that things could change sufficiently that Rolleston might not be a problem any more,' Pagan said.

'You wanna talk to me?' Buck said. I nodded. 'Go get your bike. We'll talk up there.' He pointed up at the most distant high-rise.

# 20
# Trenton

Why was nothing ever simple? Why did everyone have to turn simple things into competitions? Didn't anyone want a quiet life? I'd taken one of the pills and then a stim to pep me up a bit.

'Well, that went well,' Pagan said. 'Did you have to try and kick him?' he asked Morag. 'I thought he was about to open up.' I'd brought the bike back over to where we were standing. Buck, Gibby and some of their friends were standing round Buck's bike.

'Which conversation were you listening to?' Morag asked. 'Besides, everyone else gets to be a macho arsehole.'

'Not everyone, just Mudge,' I said as I ran a diagnostic on the bike. It was a good bike as far as it went, but it wasn't set up for racing like Buck's would be. I wished I had my Triumph with me. I was a pretty good racer and could hold my own in scheme races back in Dundee, as long as I picked who I raced carefully, but if Buck rode like he flew then I was outclassed both in ware and skills. Still, could be fun, I thought, looking at the course.

'Rannu kicked him,' Mudge pointed out in his own defence.

'Yeah that helped,' I said.

'He was being disrespectful,' Rannu said. Morag smiled at him and gave him a hug. Just concentrate on the bike, I told myself.

'If we went around attacking everyone who was disrespectful we'd never get anything done and you'd have to kill Mudge,' I told Rannu.

'Hey, I'm not you. I would've kicked his arse in New York,' Mudge said, apparently seriously.

'See!' Morag said. I was as ready as I was going to get. The starting point looked like a ramp leading up onto the roofs of the terraced flats. There was a ramp on either side of the street. Buck had the right side of the street; I was expected to take the left.

'What's the betting he's given himself the easier side of the street?' I asked nobody in particular. Straddling the bike, engine idling, I walked it over to the starting line accompanied by fast-paced, heavy western guitar riffs and pounding drums. Buck didn't even bother looking at me.

'Try not to fuck up,' Mudge said encouragingly.

'What's the signal to start the race?' Morag asked while Buck roared up his ramp and onto the roof of the terraced flats, as one of the cyberbillys fired a flare into the air. I gunned the low rider up the ramp, accelerating so fast I was only just able to keep the front wheel down on the deck. The bike jumped slightly as I hit the top of the ramp onto the flat roof about three storeys above the ground. I then had to swerve violently to avoid a huge hole in the roof. I'm sure that would've been hilarious for the crowd.

I was heading for a low wall at speed. I noticed there was a small metal ramp up against it over to my right, I veered hard, only just managing to straighten up as I hit it. I was airborne again, the bike bouncing on its shocks when I landed. I could see Buck ahead of me and off to the left. Basically the roof of the terraced flats was a straight sprint. All I had to do was avoid debris and holes and use the ramps over the low dividing walls. Then Buck disappeared.

I changed up a gear as the bike accelerated, spending more time in the air off the ramps and bouncing further when I hit the ground. Plugged into the bike I saw its performance in numbers on my internal visual display and could feel it in my head. I tried to get the feeling of merging with it like I did with my Triumph, but this wasn't my bike and it wasn't as elegantly engineered as the Triumph.

I hit the next wall and screamed as there was no roof on the other side of it. I hit a down-sloping ramp fighting for control of the low rider. The ramp took me into the interior of the flats. I hit the bottom of the ramp, swerving to avoid an interior wall and then riding through the next in an explosion of plaster, again only just staying on the bike. Ahead of me I could make out the course, a series of chicanes defined by interior walls and holes in the floor. I swerved from one side to another, getting down as low as I could in the cramped space. I didn't like the give the floor had beneath my bike. Then I remembered I was dying anyway and sped up. Leaning down low over one of the holes in the floor, I could see it went down further than two storeys and into the sewers below. I swerved the other way, the top of my head just clipping the interior wall. I barely felt it. Part of the floor gave way behind my bike, and I felt it slow, but the wheel caught and I was away. I realised I was smiling as I hit the up ramp. I soared into the air as I came out of the flats back onto the roof. Buck was closer now.

I throttled down as we approached an intersection in the road. I hit the ramp at speed and was in the air over some of the crowd, who cheered as both of us went by overhead. Buck landed first, I landed soon after. There were vehicles keeping pace with us; I noticed that our muscle car was one of them.

On the new roof the dividing walls had narrow passages knocked through them, the holes had been patched and there was little rubble. I pushed the bike faster, coaxing it as I saw red lines appear in my vision. This was going to be the last chance to really get my speed up. The terrain became a blur around me. I had enough presence of mind to make sure the way was clear; the rest of it was focused on the ramp ahead. I was sure I was grinning now, the nausea a distant memory, the first sores on my scalp as meaningless as pissing blood this morning.

I hit the ramp. I felt like I was in the air forever: everything slowed down as the tower block loomed larger and larger in my field of vision. The jarring bump, the bounce, the fight for control – don't lose speed. I was in the high-rise building for seconds, if that. The path that had been cut and cleared through the building was just a blur as I hit the next ramp and was in the air again.

Then the next tower block and the next, each time throttle down, keep speed as high as possible. Each time going a little higher, each time bouncing as I landed, trying to control the bike and not hit the ceiling. Sometimes I was aware of Buck's bike to the left of me in the same building or as we flew through the air – he seemed a little closer each time I saw him.

This was what my boosted reflexes were made for; you couldn't do this without augmentation. This was why we were different from the herd. Maybe Buck was right: this was what mattered. Land, control, throttle down, speed up, not even thinking about how high off the ground we were as we leapt from high-rise building to high-rise building.

The hole in the side of the tower block coming towards me was too low. I was too high. I'd taken off too fast. I slammed myself down on the bike, cursing the high handlebars on low riders. I felt my duster scrape against the top of the hole. I was going too fast but if I braked now I'd wipe out. I'd seen people do it in the schemes in Fintry, just jump straight into a wall at one hundred-plus miles an hour. The wheels bounced and finally found traction as I sped between the supports of the building.

I was in the air again. Buck was behind me somehow. It happened so slowly I had the time to take in the view of the ruins of Trenton below me and appreciate just how high forty storeys up was. It was the roof of the last tower block I was heading for. I overshot, landing in the middle of the roof, moving at speed towards the edge, way too fast to stop. I didn't think, I just ditched the bike. My bike was moving away from me in a shower of sparks as I slid along, the rough concrete roof going though my duster, then my clothes, then my skin, yet again. I heard protesting tyres skidding behind me as I followed my bike off the edge of the tower block.

The bike flew in a long graceful arc out over the city. It seemed to take a long time to fall. I was watching it fall away from me. I slid off the roof, just managing to grab a piece of the rusted metal frame that ran through the crumbling concrete. I stopped suddenly. Had I grabbed it with my left I would've gone over but I'd grabbed it with my right and locked the metal fingers of my prosthetic arm around the metal. The metal tore itself out of the concrete in a shower of dust and I dropped, but it held. As did my arm, but only just. It was still healing from when Rannu had torn it off and I felt the gel around the new join give, as did the join itself slightly, and blood was running down my neck and chest.

More concrete dust showered down on me as Buck skidded to a halt on the roof's edge in time to see the end of my bike's swan dive. I think I spoilt his enjoyment at seeing my bike smash through the roof of an old bus station by screaming a lot. He lit up a joint and dragged deeply.

'A little help, please,' I gasped. Buck looked down at me.

'Oh yeah.' He pushed the kickstand down with a cowboy boot, got off the bike and knelt down on the edge of the roof. He leant down and placed the lit joint in my mouth.

'Thanks,' I said around the joint.

'Let's talk,' he said, grinning.

One of the Commancheros had been a medic on Lalande. I think I needed to get my own medic to follow me around.

'Can you do anything without fucking yourself up?' Mudge asked. I had to admit that Mudge's sense of humour was beginning to get on my nerves. We were sat back in the concrete square. The right side of my body had been cleaned, the bits of clothing, roof and rad-proofed material picked out of the wound. The gel and the pak on my shoulder join had been reset and much of me was covered in new skin and medgel.

'Hey, I won,' I pointed out.

'Almost beat me to the ground as well,' Buck said, smiling. 'Joe, give us a moment,' he said to the medic once the guy had finished. The cyberbilly nodded at me and headed off. We were sitting round a jet-black muscle car with tinted windows. Air intakes stuck through the hood and the suspension was heavy duty and raised. The car belonged to Gibby judging by the way he fussed over it. Buck and Gibby were with us. Mrs Tillwater had gone back to rejoin Crawling Town after we'd assured her that we were going to play nicely. I sat on the bonnet despite Gibby's complaints. Mudge sat on some rubble nearby with Rannu and Pagan. Morag seemed both worried that I'd hurt myself again and pissed off that I'd destroyed the bike. Buck was still sitting on his bike and Gibby had sat down on the ground with his back to one of the car's polished wheels.

'So let's hear it,' Mudge said.

'What do you want to know?' Gibby asked.

'Where's MacDonald?' Mudge asked.

Buck looked at him as if he was an idiot. 'How the hell are we supposed to know that?' he asked.

'Okay, let's not get ahead of ourselves,' I said. I wanted to hear this from the start or maybe I just wanted to put off a decision I would have to make about Gregor. 'Why were you ferrying Rolleston and the Grey Lady around?' I asked.

'They'd received intelligence that when the Ninjas went in they would try and infect at least one of the people they attacked,' Gibby told us.

'What did they infect them with?' I asked.

'You tell me,' Buck said. 'You saw as much as we did, more. Looked like they infected people with themselves.' He was right.

'Did Rolleston know why?' Mudge asked.

Gibby shrugged. 'There were a number of theories: some kind of disease-based warfare, to take them over, breeding ... Who knows? There's a reason we call Them aliens. I'm not sure we're going to help you fellas.'

'What did Rolleston want with an infected human?' I asked. Buck answered me this time.

'When they turn into puddles their genetic make-up is junked and they destroy themselves rather than be captured. Rolleston figured that if they infected a human then at least part of them would be intact—'

'And they could study them,' Pagan finished. Buck got up, went to the back of Gibby's car and popped the boot.

'Beer?' he asked everyone. Even Rannu said yes.

'I don't get it,' Mudge said when we all had our beers. 'Why'd he ask a pair of degenerate cocksuckers like you to do his driving?' I had to wonder about his interview technique – I mean professionally, as a journalist. I wasn't really surprised that he'd never ended up interviewing celebrities or politicians.

'Your mother recommended us,' Buck said.

'I could see my mother recommending you have a bath, but really. I mean why use Yanks?'

''Cause the 160th are good,' Buck said. This wasn't just trans-atlantic banter. Mudge had a point: why hadn't Rolleston kept it in the family?

'So's 47 Squadron and the CHF,' I said, meaning the Commando Helicopter squadron.

Gibby sighed. 'They are.' Buck glared at him. 'But we were air and space force before we transferred into the army. Part of the Special Operations Wing.'

'So?' Mudge asked. Sometimes I forgot that Mudge wasn't actually military.

'I get it,' I said. Mudge and Morag turned to look at me. Pagan had already worked it out and Rannu didn't seem to care.

'They don't just fly gunships and copters; they're trained to pilot spacecraft as well,' Pagan said.

'And interface stuff like assault shuttles,' Gibby added.

'You can fly spacecraft and you chose to fly gunships?' I asked. Flying spacecraft was the more prestigious job. Gunship pilots at the end of the day were just infantry taxi drivers. Buck let out a snort of derision and Gibby smiled.

'Spaceships are boring. Here's some black, here's some more black,' Gibby began. 'But flying two metres above the ground at six hundred-plus clicks, watching a tracer firework display with crystal setting your veins on fire, that's fun.' Buck nodded his agreement.

'You boys miss the war?' Morag asked. At first I thought Buck was going to take offence – it wasn't a question that most vets like to hear – instead he smiled.

'Naw, miss the toys though.' He lit up a cigarette and I nicked one off him.

'Rolleston take you out-system?' Mudge asked.

'Couple of times, but you know how fast information moves out there. I think he had other teams in the other colonies looking for the same thing. It was mostly in-system stuff and we were always too late until that Foreign Legion unit went down and he decided to use the Wild Boys as bait,' Gibby answered.

'Who was he taking orders from?' I asked. Gibby shrugged but Buck answered.

'We don't know, but I'll tell you this: he was outside the chain of command. I once saw him give a full air force colonel an order and get it obeyed. He didn't like working with us none, though.'

'No?' I asked.

'Can't imagine why,' Mudge said. 'Two such sweet guys like you.'

'Son,' Buck said, 'you keep banging your gums together like that and I'm going to kick your ass so bad you'll get to wear it as a hat.'

Mudge opened his mouth to counter threaten. I said, 'Mudge, give it a rest, will you?' He looked like he was going to argue but decided to remain quiet. Buck was busy staring at Mudge so Gibby took up the story.

'Like I said, we had the skill set he needed, but I think they were setting up their own people.'

'A private army?' Pagan asked, leaning into the conversation and taking an interest.

Gibby shrugged. 'Mebbe. He definitely wanted to keep it in-house.'

'Like the XIs?' I asked. Buck and Gibby looked at me blankly.

'The whole XI thing doesn't seem to be working too well for Rolleston,' Pagan said, nodding at Rannu and me. I had to agree with him.

'So why hasn't he sent his army after us?' I asked. 'Why just the XIs?'

'Because we're not important enough,' Pagan said.

'So what is?' I asked.

'You feeling unwanted?' Mudge asked.

'Not really,' I said.

'It would suggest that this God thing is all bollocks,' Mudge said. Pagan glared at him. 'I'm serious, man. The alien is dead, that seems to be all he cares about. We're just loose ends that the XIs and the Fortunate Sons will deal with eventually. If Rolleston wanted you dead you would be. Thinking you're more important than that is just delusions of grandeur. You've pissed him off but you're not the big threat you think you are.'

'Whereas you are?' Rannu asked. Mudge turned around to look at the Nepalese.

'I don't know. The Grey Lady comes to me and asks me to mind my own business or she'll kill me, and I tend to believe her, but that's the thing, see? I'm a pain in the arse.' I found myself nodding with everyone else present. 'Not a huge threat. I think we may have lost some perspective.'

'Maybe,' I said. 'But we are running around with an alien, even if it's only an alien information form. That is potentially a serious threat to Earth security.'

'You've got a what?' Buck asked, swapping a look of confusion with Gibby.

'I guess Rolleston either doesn't care or doesn't know about that,' Mudge said.

'So what do you suggest?' Pagan asked.

'Keep a low profile and die of liver failure,' Mudge answered. That appealed to me. Even coming to some kind of an accord with Rolleston appealed to me.

'So what happened to your friend?' Morag asked. I turned to look at Buck and Gibby.

'After we left you guys—' Buck began.

'To die,' Mudge added. I glanced over at him. He just shrugged but remained quiet.

'We had a mid-air rendezvous with a transport shuttle. In orbit we docked with Rolleston's ship—'

'He had a ship?' I asked, surprised. Pagan let out a low whistle. That was serious resources. Buck looked pissed off with yet another interruption.

'What was the name of the ship?' Pagan asked.

'HMS *Steel*.'

'Frigate class, fitted out for stealth operations,' Pagan said. It was the sort of ship that special forces types tended to operate off.

'Anyway,' Buck tried again, 'we were still in orbit waiting for clearance to set sail. We were using some of the bigger ships for cover from Them's fleet and surface bombardment when the call comes through that you two had made it off Dog 4.' I already knew this. Rolleston had given the command to dump us.

'So what? Tell me about Gregor.'

'Thing you've got to know is the gunship and the transport shuttle, all of them, were set up for bio containment. They were ready for what happened to your friend.'

I flicked the cigarette away, resisting the urge to cough in case I didn't like what came up. I was feeling quite weak; I'd need another stim soon.

'So where'd you take Gregor?' Mudge asked.

'Back to *Sol*, the Atlantis Spoke,' Gibby answered. 'We took the whole of the transport into the biggest cargo elevator.'

'That the last you saw of it?' I asked. Gibby nodded. I could see the disappointment on Mudge's face. It meant nothing. The Spokes were entrepots. They were connected to the entire transport infrastructure of Earth. If Gregor was still alive he could be anywhere. I heard Pagan sigh.

'Give me the exact date and time,' Pagan said in a resigned tone of voice.

'Can you do anything with that?' I asked him.

'Maybe.'

'Do you want help?' Morag asked.

'It'll just be sifting through data, little hacking involved, pretty boring.'

'I have to learn that too.'

'That it?' Mudge asked. He was visibly pissed off. Buck and Gibby gave the question some thought and seemed to come to an unspoken agreement.

'Not quite,' Buck said. We all turned to him expectantly.

'Go on,' I urged.

'Look, man, your friend is more than likely fucked. Why you doing this?' Buck asked.

'Stupid question,' Rannu said.

I pointed at Gibby. 'He goes down in a burning gunship, what do you do?' I asked. Buck nodded.

'MacDonald might still be on the Spoke, or at least I'm pretty sure he was kept there for a while,' Gibby said.

'Why?' Mudge asked.

'For one thing, the elevator took the transport way down below sea level. It went straight past the flight decks, and docks.'

'So?' I asked. 'They could've taken him out by submarine, slow but stealthy.'

'Or used the Mag Levs,' Mudge suggested.

'And there were people there waiting for us,' Buck added.

'That doesn't mean anything either,' Mudge said.

'Maybe so, but I overheard one of them mention the facility. Way he said it made me think that it was in the Spoke,' Buck said.

'That's pretty thin,' Mudge said. Buck shrugged.

'I'll see if we can corroborate any of this,' Pagan said.

'It is pretty thin. Thing is, Bran overheard this guy. I saw her look between him and me,' Buck said. Silence followed.

'So?' Morag said finally.

'She was going to kill him,' I said. Buck nodded.

'That's when we decided to haul ass,' Gibby said.

'That was when you deserted?' I asked. The pair nodded. We all lapsed into silence for a bit, just thinking, or at least I assumed everyone else was. Gibby went to the cool box in the boot of his car and got everyone another beer.

'So what do we do with this?' Mudge asked finally. The sky was beginning to darken and we were being treated to an incredible light show of purples and reds in the pollution. Some of the cyberbillys were heading back to Crawling Town. The rest seemed to be intent on partying in the ruins of Trenton. Campfires started to appear as the vehicles were parked so they could be better watched. I looked over at where I'd seen the tribeswoman, but of course she'd gone and my tolerance for cyberbilly music had been reached and breached some time ago. Didn't these people have any pre-FHC jazz?

'If I were you, I'd mourn your friend and let it go,' Buck said. 'There's no good result I can think of for what happened to him.'

I was beginning to think he was right.

'Maybe not,' Morag said. I looked up at her. She had a thoughtful expression on her face but I found myself wishing that her hair would grow back faster. That said, even with her hair that short she was very attractive. And very young, the muted voice of my conscience managed to remind me.

'Morag, I don't mean to be rude but what could you possibly know about this?' I asked.

'Intuition?' she suggested hopefully. There was a snort of derision from Mudge.

'You've been talking to it again?' Pagan asked disapprovingly.

'Talking to what?' Gibby asked suspiciously.

'Maybe we should discuss this later,' I suggested.

Mudge pointed at Morag. 'She's got an alien in a box, and he,' Mudge pointed at Pagan, 'wants to use it to make God.' Pagan came off the ground, his face livid with anger.

'What the fuck are you trying to do?' he demanded. I felt pretty pissed off myself.

'It's a fucking stupid idea, a fantasy. Who gives a fuck? Nobody's going to believe us, and even if they do they're just going to assume that we're mad.'

'Mudge, you've made your point. Just keep your mouth shut, okay?' I told him.

'Yes, sir,' he snapped.

'We should listen to the girl,' Rannu said.

'Are you boys like a cult or something?' Gibby asked, he was sounding even more confused.

'You're only a couple of consonants out there, as in shower of,' Mudge said.

'Are you finished?' Morag asked. Mudge nodded. 'Look, I don't know anything for sure. When we try to communicate it doesn't always make sense,' she said.

'What doesn't?' Gibby asked, completely bewildered.

'Assuming it's not trying to influence you,' Pagan said.

'What do you mean you're all trying to make God?' Buck asked.

'You must try to seek understanding from what it says. It chose you for a reason,' Rannu said.

'It got delivered to the same whorehouse – whoreboat!' I shouted as I found myself unable to put up with this pseudo-mystical bullshit.

'The girl's a whore?' Buck asked, his face lighting up as he finally found something he could understand. Both Morag and I glared at Buck.

'Shut up,' I told Buck.

'I think it was trying to communicate,' Morag said.

'Are you boys a cult that worships a whore?' Buck asked with a look of dawning enlightenment on his face.

'What?' I asked him, unable to follow his reasoning. 'No, we're not a fucking cult.'

'And stop calling me a whore,' Morag added. 'Or, or, or I'll do something violent.'

'Well now I'm scared,' Buck said, grinning. 'How much, darlin'?'

'I'll do something violent,' I said. Rannu also sat forward, ready to move.

Morag turned on me. 'I can look after myself!' I was somewhat taken aback by this; I was after all just trying to help.

'What makes you think it was trying to communicate?' Pagan asked, trying to steer the conversation back to something productive.

'Ambassador said that what we call the Ninjas were an earlier form of what he was. They were designed to try and communicate with us.'

'Who's the Ambassador?' Gibby asked.

'The alien,' Mudge answered.

'Then why kill Ash and Shaz and have a good try at taking Mudge and me out?' I asked. I remembered it holding Shaz's head in its hand, studying it.

Morag shrugged. 'I don't know.'

'You all got an alien?' Gibby asked. I nodded, not even thinking about it.

'An alien whore?' Buck asked. Mudge started laughing.

'What?' I turned to the redneck. He looked confused.

Buck pointed at Morag. 'Did she fuck the alien?'

Mudge grinned and turned around to look at Morag. 'What an interesting question,' he said, ignoring my glare.

'No!' Morag shouted. 'I didn't fuck the alien, okay!' Some of the cyberbillys at a nearby campfire looked in our direction.

'All right, keep it down,' I hissed, and then pointed at Buck and Gibby. 'You two shut up and Mudge, stop winding Morag up.'

'It makes sense,' Pagan said.

'What does?' I asked incredulously.

'If all you know is violence how would you try and communicate?' he asked. My mind reached for this concept. It was a bit more complex than my usual relationship with Them. Fortunately it seemed to catch Mudge's attention.

'But why kill everyone else?' he asked.

'To find someone worthy,' Pagan said. I could see Rannu nodding.

'Why try and communicate?' I asked.

'Because they want peace,' Morag said.

'The alien whores want peace?' Buck asked.

'You high?' I asked.

'Normally.' Gibby answered for him.

'So are you. Give him a break,' Mudge said. He'd wanted to kill them a couple of hours ago.

'Or they've gotten smart,' I said to Morag, trying to ignore Mudge again.

'It would be a strange attack. With what I saw Ambassador do in the net it could've made a real mess if it chose to,' Pagan said, and I had to agree with him.

'Only if it properly understood the concept. They're alien; maybe they just don't understand the net and its importance,' Mudge pointed out.

'Assuming you're right,' I said to Pagan and Morag, 'what does that make Gregor?'

Pagan shrugged. 'At a guess, a hybrid trying to find a way to facilitate communication.'

'Hands across the stars, beautiful really,' Mudge said.

'That's some guess,' I said.

I received an encrypted comms burst from Pagan: 'It is and isn't. I believe that MacDonald was a physical version of what is happening to Morag. In effect Morag is a beta and cerebral version of MacDonald.' I stared at him.

Morag saw me staring and turned on Pagan. 'You think I'm a hybrid?' she demanded. Pagan looked shocked and then appalled.

'You broke that?' he asked. His voice sounded small. He was genuinely scared. 'How could you have broken that?' he said more to himself than any of us. From what little I knew of hacking, if she had done what Pagan said she'd done then it was possible, hard but possible. The thing was it took a very long time. Morag stood up. She had tears in her eyes.

'Is she an alien whore?' Buck asked, pointing at Morag. This time he wasn't quick enough to get out of her way. I heard his nose break and saw blood squirt down his beard.

'Fucking bitch!' he howled.

'Here we go again,' I muttered.

Buck reached for one of his revolvers. Rannu had a Glock in each of his hands. One was pointing at Buck, the other wasn't exactly pointing at Gibby but was close enough for Gibby to get the message.

Morag turned on Rannu. 'I told you I can look after myself!' And she stormed off. Rannu let her get a way off and then started to follow at a safe distance, which I had to admit made me feel a little better. Mudge watched them go.

'So?' he asked.

'What you want to do?' I asked.

'I want to go and get Gregor but I want to do it on more than the say-so of a teenage whore,' he said. I felt angry but I felt more tired. I reached into what was left of one of my pockets, removed another stim patch and slapped it onto the wrist of my left arm.

'Feeling all right?' Mudge asked.

'Brilliant. Don't call her a whore again,' I told him.

'Your judgement's affected. You're not thinking straight.'

'Fucking bitch broke my nose,' Buck whined. We ignored him.

'That'll be the radiation sickness,' I said.

'No, that'll be the girl,' Mudge said. Gibby was watching us intently. 'Look, even if she's right and Gregor's a hybrid, so what? That doesn't mean he's benevolent, that doesn't mean he's Gregor. It means you've got a trained special forces soldier with some of the capabilities of one of Their Ninjas. You want to release that?'

'No I want to go and see it, him. Look, if that's the case they'll have him contained. We'll put him out of his misery. It won't be like Dog 4,' I said. Mudge considered this and pointed after Morag.

'We don't even know whose side she's on,' he said. I think on some level I knew he was right. I also thought that this was one of the reasons I liked Mudge: he could be a wanker but he did force you to look at the truth.

'I trust her,' I said. It sounded false even to me and I wanted to believe it.

'No, you want to fuck her, which is different.'

'You fucking pussy,' Buck said, pinching his nose to stem the blood.

Mudge looked up at the cyberbilly. 'What?'

'You go into Atlantis, what's the worst that happens?' he asked. 'You get killed.'

'No,' Mudge corrected him. 'The worst that happens is we get captured, get put into a sense booth and tortured for the next hundred years.'

'So we shoot ourselves first,' I said, grinning. 'We're not doing anything better.'

Mudge sighed and went to get another beer from Gibby's cool box. 'I really, really want to die of liver failure,' he said as he opened the beer and downed it in one before helping himself to another.

'You still have your original liver?' I asked him.

'No,' he said. Which would mean his artificial liver would be much more efficient at breaking down alcohol, like mine. It still let you get drunk because if it didn't the British army would've mutinied in its entirety years ago, but it stopped the alcohol from doing permanent damage.

'So how are you going to die of liver failure?' I asked him.

'I'm going to try very hard,' he said. 'We're going to need Balor's help.'

'To die of liver failure?' I asked, momentarily confused. Like I said, I wasn't feeling the greatest. Mudge stared at me like I was an idiot.

'We'll help,' Gibby said. I looked up at him in surprise, as did Mudge.

'The hell we will!' Buck shouted.

'Oh come on now, Buck, she's not the first whore who bust your nose,' Gibby said.

'Could everyone please stop calling Morag a whore?' I said angrily.

'Yeah, thanks for the offer, guys. You were so helpful the last time,' Mudge said sarcastically.

'You know we didn't have a choice. You had to follow Rolleston's orders when he gave them as well,' Gibby said.

'He's right,' I said.

'Can we leave them somewhere dangerous?' Mudge asked.

'Fuck them!' Buck shouted. He looked appalled at Gibby. 'We ain't helping them.'

Gibby turned on him. 'We sold them out, man, you know that.' Buck said nothing. 'We have to make this right.' Buck looked like he was about to argue but didn't. Gibby had surprised me. I could understand me and Mudge and even Rannu being up for this. Mudge had his loyalty to the Wild Boys and Rannu to the Regiment, and that was something that rightly or wrongly we were indoctrinated with. Presumably Gibby had similar loyalty and indoctrination, but not to us, and that wasn't what he was talking about anyway. He wanted to help us because he thought it was the right thing to do. He had nothing to gain from it. I wasn't used to that kind of morality. Most of the time it was every man for himself, and most of the time it had to be that way to survive. The surprising thing was that Buck seemed to agree with Gibby, even though he was pissed off about it. I wondered where these two had picked up their values. Maybe they weren't quite the arseholes I'd taken them for. We could probably use them if we were going to Atlantis – if nothing else, we'd need taxi drivers. I was beginning to form a plan but I'd need more intel.

'Mudge?' I said after thinking for a while.

'Yeah?'

'Can you stop trying to piss everyone off?'

'No,' he said, smiling. I looked over at Pagan. He was quiet and I assumed he'd been in the net, but he hadn't. He looked scared.

'You okay?' I asked him. He just looked at me. I wouldn't have been surprised if he'd asked me to burn Morag at the stake.

I found Rannu standing away from one of the fires. Casually concealed.

'Where is she?' I asked. He nodded at the fire. Morag was standing by the fire but away from the rest of the people warming themselves. I walked towards her.

'Jakob?' Rannu said. I turned on him, assuming he was about to say something about Morag.

'I don't want to hear it,' I spat. He was mostly getting my spite from the previous conversation with everyone. Rannu remained as impassive as ever.

'I was going to say ... the sickness,' he said.

'What about it?' I asked.

'It's no way for a warrior to die.' I wasn't sure: maybe he looked sad or maybe it was the flickering shadows thrown by the fire.

'Thanks,' I said. 'And call me a warrior again and I'll shoot you in the back just to prove a point.' Rannu smiled. 'Can you leave us?' I asked him. He seemed to ponder my request and maybe he was considering me and the kind of person I was. Whatever he was thinking, it seemed like a long time before he nodded and walked back towards Gibby's car.

'Hey,' I said as I approached the fire. Morag looked up; she'd obviously been crying.

'What?' she demanded. 'Come to spend some time with the hybrid whore? Give me five hundred euros and I'll suck your cock.' She turned back to the fire blinking away tears. With impact-resistant plastic instead of eyes, I wasn't able to cry; hearing that I wished I could. I sat down cross-legged next to her and drew a burning stick from the fire, using it to light a cigarette. I thought about what had happened. She was eighteen years old, and a group of men with a combined age of over one hundred and fifty had effectively ganged up on her to give her a hard time. That wasn't what it had seemed like at the time, but in retrospect that was what had happened. Why would they, why would we, do that?

'They're frightened,' I said, looking up at her. She glanced down at me but went back to staring in the fire. 'We're frightened,' I corrected myself. 'Well maybe not Buck and Gibby; they're just arseholes.'

'Mudge is as well.'

'Yes, but he'll die for you,' I said with certainty.

'Huh?'

'He's just like that with his friends. I suspect he tries to keep their numbers low by behaving like a prick, and he's also frightened.' She turned and looked at me.

'Do you think I'm a hybrid?' she asked.

'You're prettier than Them,' I said, and straight away knew I'd said the wrong thing. How was it she was eighteen and smarter than me?

'And that's it, isn't it? I shouldn't fucking bother trying to make things better for myself or anyone else. I should just lie on my back and be happy with the ... the ... fucking commodity that I've got, yeah?' she spat.

'I'm sorry.'

'Tell me something, Jakob. Do you miss me being afraid? Do you miss the frightened little made-up girl-whore you found on the Rigs?'

I hadn't realised until she said it that it wasn't the hooker I missed, but the feeling that I was protecting her, looking after her. It must have been written all over my face.

'You cunt,' she said, shaking her head, and turned to walk off. I sat up slightly and swept the legs out from under her. She cried out as she landed on the concrete on her arse. We were beginning to draw attention from some of the others around the fire. I stared at a couple of them; my eyes would've been black pools not even reflecting the flames. People went back to their own business. I hadn't been paying attention and only just managed to block Morag's straight-arm strike.

'Okay, great, Morag. You've got some hand-to-hand softskills, we're all very impressed.' I turned to look at her. She was angry now.

'Out of my league, am I? Want to teach me a lesson in helplessness? Do you not think I've had enough of those?'

'I'm sorry!' I shouted more out of desperation than anything else. 'What do you want me to do about it? Sometimes we're all going to be helpless in situations that we can't do anything about, and in the circles you're travelling in at the moment I'm afraid you're going to meet a lot of people more dangerous than you.'

'Only physically,' she said. 'It wasn't so long ago that you were the helpless one and it was me that was doing the rescuing and, guess what? We managed it without violence.' She was right. The hackers were the dangerous ones; all I was was a weapon.

'And we're back to where we started. We're scared of you,' I said softly, and lapsed into silence. We sat there staring at the fire for a while. Eventually Morag produced my bottle of whisky from her bag.

'You left it back at Crawling Town,' she said, taking a swig and passing it to me.

'That was careless of me.' I took a long pull. I welcomed the burn down my throat; my stomach was less sure but I bit down on the nausea. I reached into my pocket for one of the pills that Papa Neon had given me to help cope with the symptoms, keep me going to the last. I hoped that Morag hadn't noticed. I washed it down with another pull of whisky.

'You want to fuck me,' Morag said. It wasn't a question, she almost sounded resigned. I shook my head. I was starting to feel angry.

'What am I supposed to say to that?' I asked her.

'You could admit it – admit that you think I owe you.' I turned to look at her. She was watching me, the glow of the flames reflected on her pale skin.

'I want you. You don't owe me a fucking thing,' I said and got up. I wasn't sure who I was more disgusted with. Yes, I was. It was me. How was she supposed to respond to this? How was I any different to any of her old johns? I was just another dirty old man and I needed to stay away from her. I started to walk away.

'I'm not an alien,' she said. I stopped. 'Bring the whisky back.' I sat back down, weak in every way. 'Will you hold me?' she said. I pulled her close. Was this what I wanted? She felt so small and vulnerable. I realised that I didn't want her to be scared or hurt. That was pretty much the best I could do. I didn't know what it meant. 'We talk, or we try to,' she said, confusing me.

'Who?' I asked, wondering if she meant us.

'Ambassador.'

'You realise you can do things you shouldn't be able to,' I told her. She looked up at me.

'I'm good, I mean really good. It's not just Ambassador; I was born for this,' she said.

'I believe you, but Pagan's not just professionally jealous, he's genuinely scared. He thinks that Ambassador is, I don't know, changing you or controlling you.' She didn't say anything. 'Morag?'

'Ambassador's just information,' she said. 'Pagan thinks I'm possessed or something.' She was hiding something. 'He thinks I'm the Whore of Babylon,' she finally said.

'Huh?' I asked, sounding ever so intelligent.

'That I have truck with demons.'

'You mean Them?'

She nodded. Well she did have truck with Them. We were just gambling that They weren't as bad as we thought They were. Even though that flew in the face of everything I knew about Them.

'It's a hacker myth, a sort of anti-Messiah who betrays us to Them. Judas to the entire human race. Vicar said the same thing,' she said.

'When?'

'"And the woman was arrayed in purple and scarlet colour, and decked with gold and precious stones and pearls, having a golden cup in her hand full of abominations and filthiness of her fornication." It's from the Christian Bible, Revelation, I looked it up,' she said, her voice flat and emotionless. Fucking hacker religious mania. Fucking Vicar.

'Vicar was always quoting from Revelation. Besides, he was insane.'

'You know, I don't think he was,' she mused. 'Papa Neon said something similar when you were out of it. He tried to pass it off as a joke but I got the reference.'

'What the fuck has voodoo got to do with Revelation?'

'There's no such thing as voodoo, that was made up for the vizzes. Papa Neon practises a religion called Vodou.' The word sounded the same to me. 'Which is west African religious practices influenced by Catholicism.'

'Really embracing the religious side of hacking, huh?' I asked.

'He sees Loa, spirits in the net, and talks with them,' she continued.

'And they've been talking about you?'

'Apparently.' How could I tell her that this was all bullshit? That it was just one story feeding another. We weren't much beyond burning witches. How much pressure could we bring to bear on this one teenaged girl?

'And Pagan thinks you're this ... ?' I didn't want to use the word.

'Whore? Everyone wants to call me a whore.' As if she didn't have enough to deal with at the moment. 'He hasn't said as much but I can see it in his eyes.' Then she looked a little embarrassed. 'Besides, I know he's been researching it in the net.' That was odd.

'And he doesn't know you know?' I asked.

'Nope.' That meant that she had outwitted an experienced hacker like Pagan. Spied on him and hadn't been caught. No wonder he was frightened. No wonder we all were.

'Morag, do you think Ambassador has changed you?' I asked more forcefully than I'd meant to. She looked up into my lenses.

'Of course it has, how could it not? And the cyberware in my head's changed me, and you've changed me, and Pagan's changed me. Ambassador doesn't control me, he's so gentle. I don't think I could explain what it's like talking to him.' This was beginning to sound worrying.

'Ambassador's in the cube, yeah?' I asked, trying to keep the mounting concern out of my voice.

'I think there's a ghost of him in my neural ware.' My eyes widened. 'Relax,' she said, seeing my response. 'Its scary, a bit, but all he does is help me with the things I can do. He doesn't control the way I feel or how I think.'

'He?' I asked. She shrugged.

'Just started thinking of him like that.' I wasn't sure how I was feeling about this. I was pretty worried and also jealous of the incredibly intimate relationship she had with this male entity.

'So you want to have me thingied?' she asked.

'What?'

'That thing where they drive demons out.'

'Exorcised?' I'd seen it done in the schemes and the Rigs. Usually some wannabe hacker, who'd gotten in over their head when they'd had their first vision and brought something back in their cheap neural ware. Sometimes their religious revelations were just too much for them to handle.

'Yeah, I really do,' I said honestly.

'Why?' she asked as she took the whisky bottle back from me and took a swig from it. I couldn't help but think of that as a dumb question.

'What do you mean why? You have an alien living in your head,' I said, sounding more reasonable than I felt.

'So? You didn't have time to get to know me before, so maybe me is me and Ambassador.' This was making my head hurt. 'I'm hoping that's the Morag you want. Unless you're like every other fucker, and you don't know me, and you've just made this image of me in the shape of what you want in your head.' She was looking at me accusingly.

'Fucked if I know, darling,' I said laughing. 'As far as I know it's you I want.'

'Well that me comes with an alien in my head, so judge me like you would anyone else you meet. Decide whether you trust me or not,' she said, and I realised I did. Despite the fact that I probably didn't trust anyone else other than maybe Mudge. 'You realise you're probably the first man I've ever actually wanted to have sex with?' she said. I had to laugh. 'Don't laugh at me, you bastard.' She slapped me on my bandaged wound. My scream caused a lot of the assembled cyberbillys to look our way. Morag was giggling.

'You shouldn't say things like that to men,' I said through gritted teeth as the pain subsided.

'Why not?'

'Makes us even more full of ourselves.'

'I want to be honest,' she said. 'Because I need you to know that and bear it in mind.'

'Half my skin's falling off,' I said.

'Somebody had just set your head on fire the first time I met you; besides, your skin's not that pretty anyway. Just put it down to me being less shallow than you are.' And then she kissed me. 'We need to go somewhere,' she told me.

I was searching through the boot of our car for the bivouac and the ultrasound rat deterrent. Isn't romance in the wasteland grand? I found what I was looking for and closed the boot. Mudge was stood there.

'Pagan okay?' I asked.

Mudge nodded. 'We're getting drunk, taking the night off. You?'

'Same. We need some privacy.' Mudge smiled.

'What, you don't want Rannu to come and watch you? Hell, Buck and Gibby would probably join in if you ask them nicely enough.'

'Well, I'm never going to have another erection,' I said.

'Probably sterile from the radiation as well,' Mudge said grinning. Then it hit me: what if I wasn't capable? Mudge must've read the expression on my face because he started laughing.

'You utter bastard.'

'Funny thing is you probably would've been fine if I hadn't put the idea in your head,' he said, laughing more.

'I will be fine,' I insisted, but this just made him laugh harder. I turned to walk off.

'Hey, Jake.' He knew how much I hated that name.

'What?' I said, turning on him, but he was serious now.

'You sure about this, man? She's very young.' I thought for a while. Maybe I was being selfish, but I would be dead soon anyway – that was assuming we didn't get killed by Rolleston or anyone else. I knew I'd regret it if I didn't. I guessed my motives were about as pure as you could hope for in the situation. Not that pure, but I didn't think I was taking advantage.

'Yeah,' I said. Mudge nodded. I turned to head back to the fire and Morag.

'Jake?' I stopped and took a deep breath before turning back.

'Mudge, you're preventing me from getting to a beautiful young woman who wants to have sex with me.'

'Despite the fact you're half man half tarmac at the moment?'

'I can shoot you. Besides, you should be down on your knees thanking God for people who'll have sex with ugly men,' I said. He grinned, then his face hardened again.

'When we're done with all this, we're going to come back here, to Crawling Town, take care of unfinished business, yeah?' I could've told him that he didn't have to but it would've been a platitude and it would've pissed him off.

'Yeah,' I told him.

It was on the second floor of one of the terraced flats near a big hole in the floor. It wasn't the most romantic place ever. We were after all in the middle of a polluted wasteland. I put down a groundsheet and set up the bivouac. Morag switched on a lamp – she didn't have my low-light vision after all – and unrolled two of the sleeping bags and connected them together.

'Do you want to know me?' she asked as she pulled something out of her bag. I took a closer look. It was a highly illegal biofeedback device, basically a box with eight wires extending from it, each wire ending in a plug. They were used either to enhance sex or as a torture device. The box was effectively a small sense machine. Each of us would feel what the other one did. It was about the most intimate thing I could imagine. I could fight in a hundred different firefights but it took a teenaged girl to really frighten me.

'Where'd you get that?' I asked.

'New York.' That figured. I swallowed and then nodded.

It would be a waste of time trying to describe what it was like to be surrounded by her and then feel what she felt, to feel every touch and its reflection echoing. We remained joined after, just holding each other. It was the release I'd sought but never received from the booths, the loss of self but without the dislocation. It felt like becoming more than just me.

It was only after that it occurred to me that I had given Ambassador access to me. It was only in the morning that my mind had to sabotage this. I guess I just couldn't accept something so good happening to me.

# 21
# New York

*I could hear Them singing. How could I hear Them singing in vacuum? It wasn't in my ears. It wasn't even in my head. It sounded like wind blowing through impossibly loud chimes, somehow discordant and beautiful at the same time, a choir of off-key angels.*

*They/It was beautiful as well. From where I hung in space I could see Their spires rooted deep into the asteroid, towers of a bioluminescent, coral-like material. They looked like a huge and perfectly still, tranquil city. I hung in space, naked and whole, no machinery in me any more, watching Them/It.*

*A whisper that came from deep within imparted to me that this was Them, that this was all They were. That this had been Their existence and They had been content because They had never known or wanted more.*

*I thought I could watch Them for ever and listen to Them for ever. Something at the back of my mind wondered how I could be in vacuum again and not be dying. I saw a flash image from a nightmare. Cold, so very cold, veins exploding, blood leaking around the plastic that filled my eye sockets. Gone again as I forced it down, a memory from another time, another life, and I just hung there and watched and listened.*

*I didn't know how long I'd hung there, never growing bored or restless, and I don't know what made me first realise that something was wrong. Maybe it was an old instinct. I looked around as much as my fixed position in the sky would allow. Eventually I found some of the stars were missing then more as the craft came closer. I recognised the configuration if not the actual ship itself. It was a light cruiser, the sort that had been manufactured around eighty to a hundred years ago. Because of the prohibitive cost of spacecraft many were still in service today. Though huge and seemingly ungainly, I'd always thought spaceships strangely graceful. Its manoeuvring thrusters silently and continually corrected the cruiser's course.*

*This was a warship, a human one, and I could see what was about to happen. I started screaming at it – somehow I could hear my own voice – but it did no good. The barrage of missiles had so far to fly it was like they were moving in slow motion, their engines burning harshly. The red light of laser batteries stabbed out, joining the cruiser to the beautiful alien spires again and again, scarring and burning wherever they touched. It was the cruiser's particle-beam weapon pulsing blue and white every time it was charged that did the most damage. I watched spires split and burst and float into space and then the rockets blossomed, covering the alien city in the brief fires of their plasma warheads.*

*Ice clung to my face from tiny frozen teardrops. I could not understand this. There was no point. It seemed like an attack on something beautiful for the sake of it. The worst of it was that I could still hear them, the same way I had heard their singing, but they weren't singing any more.*

*The asteroid seemed to spin in front of me. It took a moment to realise that it was me who was moving. We were on the opposite side of the asteroid. The cruiser was above me now, making minute alterations with its thrusters to hold it in place. From its hold came two heavily armed assault shuttles – again they were older models. The assault shuttles escorted a much larger transport shuttle. I couldn't remember the designation for the transport shuttle but it was one of those models that was basically an engine and a cockpit with a framework in the middle that could be filled with modular cargo loads. In this case it carried a portable base set up for deep space.*

*I watched as the assault shuttles landed and a squad of exo-armoured troops disembarked from each, setting up a perimeter for the transport shuttle. The base was tethered and set up. It was a large one but I couldn't make out what it was for. It wasn't a mining operation; besides the Belt resources were nowhere near exhausted and much easier to get at. It wasn't an OP, as they'd destroyed the only other thing on the asteroid. It was too small for a garrison and didn't have enough spacecraft with it, and the cruiser was a much better choice for a base.*

*I had no reference for time but it seemed to me that the base was set up very quickly, or rather the bare amount of set-up was done and it was abandoned. The transport shuttle and one of the assault shuttles were left there as the final assault shuttle took off. They'd also left all the exo-armoured troops on the asteroid. Then something really weird happened. The assault shuttle did not dock with the cruiser. Instead it set another course away from the asteroid at maximum burn. The cruiser began firing its escape pods on the same trajectory as the assault shuttle.*

*There was obviously some concern from the troops still on the asteroid. Then they started firing. Whatever they were firing at was behind me. Still floating in space though I was, I managed to swing round. Over the small horizon of the asteroid I saw it come. It looked like an oil slick, as it seemed to surge across the cold rock. It was huge, covering the ground, I could see splashes from where the armoured troops' railgun rounds impacted, but it still came on, tendrils and pseudopods reaching for the soldiers. I recognised this black liquid – it was what I'd seen beneath the chitin of a thousand berserks. It was the same stuff the Ninja had been made from when it had forced its way into Gregor, violating my friend, and it was the same material that had made up Ambassador. The city was Them.*

*Tendrils grabbed the armoured soldiers and simply prised open their armour. The soldiers inside the powered armour died when they were exposed to vacuum but the tendrils still pierced their flesh. The semi-solid black liquid surged into the shuttles and then penetrated the base. I found myself able to move, trying to ignore the panicking, dying humans around me as I moved, or was taken, into the base.*

*Corpses of military cyborgs hung in the air. It looked like they had tendrils of their own blood growing out of them. The base seemed to me to be more of a warehouse. It was full of weapons – everything from a space fighter to a laser pistol, but only one of each. There were surface-to-space missile launchers, self-propelled artillery, a sled, a tank, assault rifles and railguns. The newest of these weapons was about seventy years old.*

*The liquid seemed to reach out and touch it all, even the dead cyborgs; it was like it was tasting everything. Through the massive torn-open airlock door I could see what looked like a tree branch made of liquid reaching up towards the now inert and drifting cruiser. After all, if they were going to go to war they would need to learn to travel interstellar distances.*

*My eyes flickered open. I was lying in her lap. She was gently cradling my head. A familiar tendril of black liquid flowed from her mouth and into mine. Her eyes were gone; black liquid pools had replaced them. Suddenly I was choking and I could hear whispers inside me.*

I sat bolt upright. There was an uncomfortable yank from the sockets on my neck as our connection was broken. Morag cried out and sat up.

'What're you doing?' she cried. I was almost surprised to find myself in the dusty ruins of the old terraced flat.

'What am I doing?' I demanded, pulling the last remaining plug from the biofeedback device. 'What are *you* doing?' I was shouting now. 'In here!' I tapped the side of my head. She looked stricken, but I was too angry at my violation, at the revelation that flew in the face of everything I'd always known.

'But you said—'

I stabbed my finger at her. 'To share, with you. Not so you could fucking brainwash me! You let him in! You gave him access to my head!'

'What are you talking about?'

'You know it doesn't make any difference?' I told her.

'What doesn't?' she demanded, getting angry.

'Whether your pimp is human or alien!' I shouted. I think I expected her to burst into tears. She didn't; she just looked cold, distant and very angry.

'Go away,' she said through gritted teeth. Straight away I knew I was being an arsehole, straight away I knew I'd woken up afraid, but I tried to ignore that weakness and hold on to my pride and anger. I grabbed my clothes and my gear and went to find a place to dress.

I guess Mudge noticed my face like thunder as I returned to where we'd parked. The cyberbillys were beginning to break camp and head out. Dust filled the air again.

'Went well then?' he asked, smirking. He was smirking less when he found himself lying on his arse with his mouth bleeding.

Mudge jumped back to his feet. 'What the fuck!' he shouted.

'Not now,' I told him, and he had the sense not to push it further. Pagan was stood a little way from us, leaning on his staff, watching me. I couldn't make out the expression on his face.

Gibby skidded his car to a halt next to me, kicking up dust and causing me to cough. I slapped on another stim and knocked back some more of Papa Neon's pills with water. Buck pulled up on his low rider.

'What's the plan?' he asked.

Something exploded in the air over the square. We all instinctively ducked and weapons were drawn. I saw bits of debris rain down on the ground around a small group of complaining cyberbillys. Whatever it was hadn't been big.

'What d'you reckon?' Buck asked. 'Recce drone?' I nodded. I could see Morag striding angrily across the square towards us carrying the camping gear. Shame and anger were warring within me. I think shame was winning but anger had pride on its side.

From the embankment I could see Rannu walking towards us. He had removed the magazine from, and was folding in half, a shotgun/sniper rifle combo weapon.

'Recce drone?' I asked. He nodded, sliding the folded weapon into a long sheath strapped to his thigh. Morag was with us now, talking quietly to Buck. He did not look happy.

'Rannu just took out a recce drone, which means that we're compromised,' I said. Everyone continued to look at me expectantly except Morag. 'We're going to head back to Crawling Town and swap the vehicles if we can.' I was looking at Buck and Gibby. Gibby swore but Buck nodded. 'And then make our way as fast as possible back to New York. Is that okay with everyone?' There were nods and muttered assents.

I turned to the muscle car and climbed into the driver seat, ignoring complaints from Mudge. Rannu and Pagan climbed into the cramped back seat and Mudge took shotgun. I saw Buck get off his bike as I plugged myself into the car's interface and the engine growled into life. Morag climbed onto Buck's low rider and Buck got into Gibby's car. The suspicious and unpleasant part of my mind asked how she'd talked Buck into loaning her his bike.

We kicked up dust as we joined the rest of the Hard Luck Commancheros heading back to Crawling Town.

I drove the car through suburbs that looked more deserted than ruined. It gave them an eerie feel, as if all the people had just left. The sun glowed red through the polluted air. Every so often we saw feral dog packs roaming the rubble-strewn streets. We didn't talk much. Gibby's car was ahead of us and in front of that Morag rode alone. I could feel Pagan staring at the back of my head.

'What is it, Pagan?' I asked when I finally got fed up with the feeling of his eyes on my neck.

'You slept with her?' he asked. Mudge gave me a sideways glance. He was grinning. He seemed to have forgiven me for punching him.

'That's none of your business.'

'That depends,' he said.

'This should be good,' Mudge said exaggeratedly, making himself comfortable in his bucket seat.

'Do you know what a hierodule is?' Pagan asked me.

'You know I don't.'

'Oh come on,' Mudge said, shaking his head. 'A temple prostitute. You're not serious?' Every so often I forget that Mudge is actually quite well educated.

'I think she is possessed and I think she will do anything for what possesses her.' This sounded familiar. Pagan was starting to sound like Vicar. The thing is I wasn't sure he was wrong.

'It would certainly explain why she was prepared to sleep with this wanker when someone like me was on offer,' Mudge said, still grinning. I didn't say anything. Mudge looked over at me. 'You're not buying this shit, are you? She may have some funny ideas, probably thanks to this arsehole,' he said pointing his thumb at Pagan, 'but a one-hooker alien invasion she is not.' I still didn't say anything. I just concentrated on the road. Mudge was staring at me now.

'Jake?' he said.

'I don't know, man. Some things happened,' I said. 'Weird shit.'

'Cool. Did she lick your arse?' Mudge asked. This was why it was sometimes difficult to remember that he was educated.

'Was it her or the alien?' Pagan asked.

'Does she have tentacles?' Mudge enquired.

'Shut up, Mudge. I don't know. The alien, I guess.'

'But she seduced you?' Pagan more sort of stated than asked. Interesting question: did she seduce me? It didn't feel like a seduction but then maybe that was the beauty of it. She was after all an experienced hooker.

'Losing your religion, Pagan?' Mudge asked.

'What?'

'Listen to yourselves. You're turning a young girl – sorry, woman – into some kind of alien sex demon. What happened to the licentiousness of paganism? Hmm? You sound like one of those old-time pre-FHC fundamentalists. All women are evil. You're just pissed off because she's better than you. Don't worry. I don't think she'll be interested in playing John the Baptist; you'll get the glory for creating God,' Mudge said before turning to me. 'And you, you're lucky that Ash and Bibs aren't around because they would've taken you off and given you a right hiding by now. Grow the fuck up.'

'Mudge, you weren't there—' I began.

'Shame really. Even I wouldn't have been as big a prick about it as you are. Maybe there's something going on with her, so what? You keep second-guessing her and you'll make yourself miserable and I'll probably get punched more often. Take it at face value until you know better. You both just sound fucking frightened. In fact, fuck it, when we stop I'll go and ride with her, see how she feels about a real man. Yeah?'

I didn't want that, I definitely did not want that, but I did want to hit Mudge again.

'No, I didn't think so,' he said as he watched my knuckles turn white. 'You know, if we had more women with our merry band I wouldn't have to listen to this bullshit.'

'You're woman enough,' I assured him.

'Perhaps dressing it up in religious terms is hyperbole but the fact remains—' Pagan began.

'That she is reacting to what is happening to her; she has not found and adapted a belief system to herself. Hers is a natural reaction, whereas yours, like every religion, is man-made,' Rannu said.

'You've been thinking about this,' I said to him.

'I think when things do not go well between a man and a woman, the man and his friends sit around and damn the girl,' Rannu said. 'You are both just finding her more difficult to manipulate.'

'I'm not trying to manipulate her,' Pagan said. 'I have concerns.'

'Really? Fucking least of mine. The lovely Josephine Bran may be looking through a smartgun link at my pretty face right now,' Mudge pointed out.

'And if we inadvertently destroy the human race?' Pagan said. Mudge started laughing; even to my ears it sounded ridiculous. 'I'm serious,' he insisted. 'We get this wrong, we could hand over our system to Them.'

'Don't get it wrong then,' Mudge said. 'I still don't see how it'd be Morag's fault.'

'Have faith,' Rannu told him. We lapsed back into silence. If Rannu and Mudge were right, and I think I'd always known they were, then I'd screwed up big time. Not only that but I'd said the most hurtful things I could to her. It also meant that what I'd dreamt or what Ambassador had told me might be true. If that were the case then it would seem that not only had we started the war but we had also provided them with the means to make their own weapons. That, however, didn't make any sense. I couldn't think of a single good reason to throw humanity into a war like this. I couldn't understand the gain.

Back at Crawling Town we had a hurried meeting with Papa Neon and Mrs Tillwater. The moving city was getting ready to pull out. They'd had more incursions, serious ones this time. The Fortunate Sons had assembled a full armoured brigade across the border in Pennsylvania with air and artillery support. The Commancheros provided us with new vehicles: two pretty utilitarian pickup trucks (much to Buck and Gibby's disappointment) and a dirt bike to act as a motorcycle outrider. Mudge had taken the bike and invited Morag to ride with him, probably just to piss me off. She had accepted. It was working. I was pissed off but mostly angry with myself and very sorry.

Pagan sent out a heavily encrypted message to Balor. Rolleston, if he was still interested, could break it in time, but the phrase was random, prearranged with Balor when we'd set up our comms procedures. The Commancheros and the Big Neon Voodoo had both agreed to send out small convoys to confuse anyone surveilling us and to confuse satellite observation. Pagan was running scans and ECM attempting to either find or confuse recce drones and other methods of detection they might use. He'd also swept the vehicles and us for bugs but found nothing. We discussed nothing more about our plans on the journey back.

We drove through the night. Mudge ditched the bike but neither he nor Morag was badly hurt. I kept going through the pills, the stims and some rather good amphetamines that Mudge had. I'd known he would have some somewhere. Things were pretty quiet in our truck.

Balor himself met us by the water, a different rendezvous point from where we'd last seen him. There was a speedboat waiting for us; we were to leave the trucks. He greeted us all like old friends and Morag like visiting royalty. I think Buck and Gibby may have found him somewhat disconcerting.

Over the water I could see parts of New York were burning, the flames reflected in the cold grey water. Smoke was rising from other sections of the city.

'Problems?' I asked somewhat redundantly.

'Nothing for you to worry about,' Balor said. 'You are my guests.'

'Is this because of us?' Morag asked.

'I don't know; we didn't stop to ask them.'

'Who were they?' Mudge asked.

'They insulted me by sending a marine expeditionary force of Fortunate Sons. As if Fortunate Sons would be a match for my vets. Still, they did have a lot of aircraft,' he growled, sounding generally angry that they had not properly challenged him.

'Balor, they could level the city if they wanted to,' I said evenly. Balor turned to me.

'I think my evil eye would weep. I love that city.' He looked sad but then he laughed. 'I was told they tried to assemble a SEAL team to come into the city, but they all refused and then contacted some of their friends who work for me. That was how we knew they were coming.' He grinned his unnerving shark grin.

'If this is Rolleston he's painting with a pretty big brush,' Mudge said. I nodded.

We went to work, though I spent a bit of time in the hospital getting my skin patched up again. I wrote down what we would need and gave it to Balor. He read it, ate it and then asked me for another, memorised that one and then ate that too before complaining that I would bankrupt him. I was asking a lot from him but he came through. I couldn't help but be impressed when he showed me the ten Wraiths. They were one generation back but they were what I'd been trained on in the Regiment.

'You got the deep-water conversion kit?'

'Got all the conversion kits, deep water, deep space, toxic atmosphere, high gravity, you name it. They've never been used; they belonged to a Fortunate Sons unit before we boosted them.'

'You know we can't pay for these.'

'They attacked my home. You know I'm coming with you.' I looked up at him sharply and then nodded. He would be useful, very useful indeed.

'And I won't be needing one of these,' he said, gesturing at the Wraiths.

Pagan and Mudge went to work trying to find corroborating intel for Buck and Gibby's story. Pagan used the other world of the net and Mudge reached out to all his old journalist contacts. Morag worked on God, researched the actual Atlantis Spoke itself and either avoided or ignored me, not surprisingly.

Rannu helped me with an assault plan, which wasn't built on very much information. He was also teaching Morag to fight, helping her integrate her softskills, running simulations for her, that kind of thing. He'd added a smartlink to both her laser pistol and her personal defence weapon and provided her with glasses that would act as a heads-up display and show her where the crosshairs were. The guns were linked through a glove that was wired into the glasses. They also provided low-light vision. It wasn't as good as having it all hard wired but it didn't involve replacing any more of her flesh.

Rannu and I also worked on the Wraiths. We ran diagnostics, did the deep-water operations conversion and attached insulating foam to help keep their EM and heat signatures to a minimum.

Buck and Gibby took in the sights and got drunk and high. When Balor provided them with a transport flyer, they complained about it but went to work improving it as much they could and breaking it into their way of flying.

I was leaning against an acoustic tile, wearing only a towel just like the rest of us.

'If you're going to talk don't lean against the tile; have as little contact with the floor and walls as possible,' Pagan said.

'Should I stand on one leg?' Mudge asked. I thought Balor looked ridiculous with a towel wrapped round his waist but all our clothes were outside the clean room. I didn't think Morag looked ridiculous only wearing a towel. I was trying hard not to look at her. Pagan had checked us all thoroughly for surveillance devices before we entered. Worryingly, he'd found a couple on Buck and Gibby, presumably picked up while they were sightseeing.

I pushed myself off the wall and onto my feet.

'What've we got?' I asked. My question was aimed at Mudge and Pagan.

'A lot of smoke,' Mudge said. 'There are rumours about a facility deep below the surface. Couple of journos I used to know went missing looking into it. There have been a couple of deaths connected to it, one a hacker allegedly burnt out on their security countermeasures, and another a geneticist who'd contacted one of my missing journo friends. Rumour was he was going to blow the whistle. There are some wild stories about it from some of the more conspiracy minded. Usual stuff – the government has captured Them down there, that sort of thing. Nothing solid, but if I was looking for a story and didn't mind getting killed I'd look into it. Not sure if I'd plan an assault on the strength of it.'

'Any ideas as to where this facility might be?' I asked.

'I've got three sub-surface locations,' he said. Morag unrolled the schematics she'd found. Pagan hadn't allowed a monitor into the clean room. He'd said it was bad enough that we all had internal electronics. Mudge looked down the long, thick stem of the Spoke and found the three locations.

'Here, here and here.' He tapped the deepest one again. 'This being the one that was most recommended, but like I say it's all speculation.'

'How deep?' Balor asked.

'Five hundred metres. What difference does that make?' Mudge asked suspiciously, glancing over at me.

'That's the abyssal zone,' Balor said. 'No light, very cold.'

'Pagan?' I asked.

'I think there's something there. I found similar stuff in the more conspiratorial areas of the net. More importantly I confirmed most of Buck and Gibby's story. The *Steel* was docked when and where they said it was. There's a significant drain of power to that area,' he said, pointing at the third possible location, the one that Mudge had favoured. 'Some major kit has been delivered and then disappeared, as have a lot of supplies.'

'What kind of kit and supplies?' Rannu asked.

Pagan shrugged. 'Lab gear, bio-hazard stuff, big containment stuff, genetics equipment, general lab supplies, food and enough gear for a not insignificant security force.'

'Estimate?' I asked.

'Platoon strength at least.'

'Heavy-duty gear?' I asked. Pagan shrugged.

'Unknown,' he said finally. 'They could be reinforced from elsewhere on the Spoke,' he suggested and he was right. The Spokes were crawling with security, corporate and otherwise, soldiers returning or shipping out. Most had a garrison of Fortunate Sons, not to mention the Spoke Police, who would have a well-trained C-SWAT unit probably made up of vets like us.

'So we have to move quickly. Couldn't get into their net?' I asked, knowing the answer.

'It'll be isolated from the net, a completely separate system, never the twain shall meet. They'll have external communication in a separate net but it will be AI encrypts. I wouldn't be able to break them if they're even breakable at the moment.'

'Who's paying for this facility?' Mudge asked Pagan.

'Ostensibly a logistics company, but that's just a shell corporation. If I had the time I could find out, but judging by the sophisticated way they've covered their tracks I would imagine the logistics company is an intelligence agency slush fund.'

'Any idea whose?' I asked. Pagan shook his head.

'Okay what's here?' I asked, tapping the preferred location of the facility.

'Airlock,' Morag said. 'Submarine loading dock.' This surprised me.

'You sure?' I asked. She bit back a reply and nodded.

'External defences of the Spoke?' I said. There was shifting and muttering in the room. Spokes were thought to be near impregnable; since they'd been built there had always been paranoia about terrorist attacks.

'Forty feet of reinforced concrete, in theory enough to deflect a nuclear-tipped torpedo's blast. Full spectrum scans, motion sensors, automated steel guns, seeker torpedoes, probably augmented guard fauna, fast-response patrol submersibles,' Morag said. I wasn't the only surprised one; everyone was looking at her now.

'Sounds fun,' Balor said, grinning. 'I think I've always wanted to attack a Spoke.' He gave this more consideration. 'Yes, I have.'

Pagan looked furious. 'I've been wasting my time when I could've been working on God,' he said. 'What you're suggesting is suicide.'

'It does sound like an invitation to a cluster fuck,' Buck said. Rannu, who had helped me form the plan, just smiled.

'We're not going to attack the Spoke,' I said, trying to calm everyone down. 'All I'm suggesting we do is enter this facility from the ocean.' Balor looked disappointed.

'We have to stealth their security as much as possible, then all we have to do is keep them off our backs long enough for Pagan to get us in,' Rannu said.

'And while we're in the airlock they form up their security force and waste us,' Pagan said.

'Not if you're quick enough,' I told him.

'I don't have control over how fast water is pumped out of an airlock. Besides, how're you planning on getting to that depth? Submersible?'

'Wraiths,' Rannu said. Everyone stopped and considered this.

Mudge let out a low whistle. 'That would certainly give us an edge over their security force.'

'Can they even operate at that depth?' Pagan asked.

'Yeah,' I said. ''Course.'

'Just,' Rannu answered more honestly. 'Look, the plan is interesting as far as it goes but we don't even know for sure if there's anything there.'

'The plan's insane,' Pagan said.

'I like it,' Balor said.

'You're insane,' Mudge told him. 'Even if your highly implausible breach works, we still don't know what we'll be facing inside. That's if there's even anything there. For all we know this could be an expensive and dangerous assault on a laundry.'

'It's there,' Morag said.

'More hooker's intuition?' Mudge asked.

'No, but there's a hole in the information there.' She pointed at the third possible location on her schematic, the one that both Pagan and Mudge had favoured. She looked up at Pagan and her eyes glazed over.

'I said no comms traffic!' he shouted at her.

'They won't break it. Check my info,' Morag said. Pagan went quiet. We all watched him expectantly. A few minutes later he seemed to deflate.

'She's right,' he said. I think he must've felt a bit like I did when Rannu was beating the crap out of me – the realisation that you'd just been utterly superseded.

'So how come you didn't work that out?' Mudge asked innocently.

'Leave it, Mudge,' I told him. From underneath the schematics of the Spoke Morag took a second set of schematics, unfolding them and laying them on the floor.

'What's that?' I asked.

'I used the floor plans I could find and wrote a program to fill in the blanks. This is the area that we are dealing with. These,' she pointed at walls and supports, 'are internal walls and structural supports that have to exist or the Spoke will fall down. As to what's actually inside

I don't know, but as near as I can work out this is the shape of the area.' We were all silent; Pagan looked stricken.

'You sure?' I asked.

'Would you ask if Pagan had told you?'

'Pagan's done this kind of work before,' I said.

'Yeah, I know, and I'm just a stupid rig whore.'

'I didn't say that.'

'Well, not today anyway. Get him to check my work.'

'Whose work?' Pagan managed to say.

'Don't start that again,' Rannu said menacingly.

'Pagan, can you check that?' I asked him. He nodded. Morag sent the information to him and he drifted off, running over her work. It took him a bit longer this time.

'I think she's right,' he said.

'We still don't know what the layout will actually be,' Mudge pointed out.

'So as soon as we're in, Pagan raids their systems for a schematic,' I said. 'Look. Nobody said this was going to be perfect, but you know as well as I do that as soon as you hit the ground the first thing that goes for shit is the plan.'

'Not a good reason not to have one,' Pagan pointed out.

'We've all gone out on shakier grounds than this,' I said.

'Rarely ended well,' he said.

'Mudge, are you up for this?' I asked him. He just shrugged.

'Yeah, whatever.'

'I can do it,' Morag said. I turned to her.

'Do what?' I asked.

'When we get inside, I can raid their systems, bring up the floor plan, that kind of thing.' Pagan and Mudge both looked at her and then at me. Morag caught their looks. Buck and Gibby were looking uneasy as well. 'What?' she asked.

'You're not going,' I told her.

'What do you mean, I'm not going?' She seemed so surprised that she wasn't angry yet.

'Morag, you've proved yourself in tight situations again and again, and the info you've given us today is brilliant, but this is a mechanised assault in a hostile environment. We can't afford to have anyone down there that doesn't have the training, experience and the ware for this kind of thing. Besides, you don't know how to pilot a Wraith,' I said.

' I know how to pilot a Wraith,' she said triumphantly.

'How?' I asked, as I looked suspiciously over at Rannu. He remained impassive as ever.

'Softskills. I've run simulations.' I was glaring at Rannu now but I turned back to Morag.

'I've tried to tell you before, softskills aren't the same. Even if they're properly integrated they just give you the basics. You need experience and training, like I said. If we have to be thinking about you as well as what we're doing we're just going to get ourselves killed. We're going to have to look after Pagan when he's tranced anyway. One we can handle, two we just don't have the shooters for.'

'So let me do the running, and keep Pagan as backup for me and as an extra shooter. I'm faster than him anyway.' She turned to look at Pagan. 'I'm sorry but I am.'

'You mean you're better than me,' he said. Morag didn't answer.

'Look. Doing a run in combat is different—' I began.

'Actually it's not,' Pagan said. 'Once you're in the net you're in. Doesn't matter what's going on in the real world, you get hit, you get hit.' Morag grinned triumphantly. I glared at Pagan.

'Look, Morag,' Mudge said. 'You're good at what you do, real good, but you've never seen combat. You don't know how you'll react. You may freeze up. It's not just your life on the line; you could get us killed as well. When I first saw combat I used to piss myself all the time and shake like a leaf for several hours after.'

'You've stopped doing that?' I asked Mudge. ''Cause I was little worried that you might drown in your Wraith.' Mudge gave me the finger and then considered what I'd said.

'It's a possibility,' he finally allowed and then turned to Morag. 'Look, darling. I don't doubt you could do this given time, and I'd happily walk into a firefight with you, or at least as happily as I'd walk into any firefight, but this is just a bad job to learn on.'

'She won't freeze up. I'm happy to stake my life on it,' Rannu said. I felt anger surge through me.

'You are. What you don't have the right to do is stake mine and everyone else's here on it,' I snapped at him. I was furious that he was encouraging Morag.

'If we're talking about dropping people from the mission, what about you?' Rannu asked quietly. I felt like he'd punched me again.

'What are you talking about? I'm one of the most experienced soldiers here and I've done breaches before. Not to mention I was piloting Wraiths before you lost your virginity, sunshine.' I was trying not to shout.

'You piss blood this morning?' Rannu asked. I stopped. I felt cold, and he was right, I had.

'He's right,' Mudge said. 'You're pretty much being kept upright by drugs and the metal and the plastic in your body.'

'I'll be fine,' I snapped.

'So will she,' Balor said. I was astounded. I turned on Balor and Rannu.

'You guys know better!' They didn't say anything. 'You know what this will be like and you know you can't do it—'

'Without training and experience,' Morag said sarcastically. I turned to her.

'Do you really think I'm just saying this to be a cunt?' I demanded. 'Fine. You want to go? How about this? Let's say you manage to pilot a Wraith adequately, let's say you don't freeze up and get the rest of us killed, you ready to kill someone else?' I was shouting now. 'Because I'll tell you: the men and women we'll be shooting at and who'll be trying to shoot us, they won't be bad people. They'll be just like us, probably nice people just trying to make a go of it, do the best they can. The kind of people you could happily go for a pint with if we weren't so busy trying to kill each other. Instead you'll see their faces for a very long time, and then, worse, they'll all begin to look the same to you. So you tell me, you ready to kill?' She looked up at me. I could see the resolve – her face may as well have been made of stone.

'I'm ready to do what's necessary,' she said and believed it. 'I think what's down there is important.'

'The kinship you feel for Gregor isn't real; it's Ambassador playing tricks on you,' I told her. She looked like I'd just slapped her. She opened her mouth to retort.

'She's right,' Pagan said sadly from behind me. I turned to look at him. 'She's better than me. She should do the run. I'll act as another shooter and watch her when she's tranced and provide backup in the net if it's needed.' At that moment he looked like a beaten man. Desperately I looked to Buck and Gibby, who just shrugged. After all, they had the easiest part of the job.

'You all going to die anyway,' Buck said.

'She doesn't even have boosted reflexes,' I said, pretty much as a last-ditch objection.

'Yes, I do,' she said. I swung back to look at her.

'When did this happen?' I demanded.

'A week ago, when we started prep,' she said.

'Are they integrated?' I asked.

'Yes.' It was Rannu who answered. For a moment I was speechless.

'Do you know what you're doing to yourself?' I asked her, shaking my head.

'Jakob,' she said softly, 'it's none of your business.' It had gone very quiet in the room. I could feel everyone looking at the pair of us. 'And I'm going,' she said with finality.

Just a little drug deal first, then I started looking for Morag. I finally found her in what looked to be an old function room on the upper floors of the Empire State Building. It had long fallen into ruin but somehow much of the wood panelling had survived. You could still see some of the fading art-deco patterns on it. More surprisingly the chandelier still hung from the ceiling. Most of its crystals were long gone but those that remained reflected the light from outside.

She was sitting on the window ledge oblivious to the drop. Ironically, for an ex-Para I'd never really liked heights despite the fact I'd done several orbital low-opening drops in my time. Much of New York was dark at night because it was uninhabited, but central Manhattan was lit up in all sorts of garish colours, huge spotlights stabbing up into the cloudy night sky. Morag was unintentionally dramatic, framed by the huge window with no glass in it, her loose-fitting clothes blown by the wind as she looked out over the city.

I walked over to the window but stayed several feet back from it and lit up a cigarette. She glanced up at me.

'You going to tell me this is dangerous?' she asked.

'I'm assuming you know that. Question is are you doing it for effect?' Irritation passed over her face and she turned back to the view.

'I'm doing it because I like it here.'

'Can you see why I said the things I said?' I asked her.

'Because you feel you have some kind of proprietary relationship to me. Though you'd probably describe it as caring.'

'Proprietary relationship?' I enquired, grinning.

'Talking to Mudge too much recently,' she said. I couldn't see her face but I was pretty sure she was smiling too.

'Yeah? I'm surprised you're not using fuck as a comma rather than words like proprietary.'

'Oh, I think he just talks like that for the benefit of all his soldier friends,' she said. We lapsed into silence for a while, both looking out over the city. I tried to ignore the feelings of nausea, fatigue and weakness that washed over me.

'Morag, I'm sorry, really sorry. I shouldn't have said what I said.

I know it's not true. I was just freaked out and scared.' It was pretty much the fullest apology I'd ever given. She let out a short, bitter laugh.

'Well I guess you need the training and the experience to handle a lover with an alien in her headware,' she said, still not looking at me. I didn't really know what to say to that. I realised that this was all new to her as well and probably a lot scarier as she was experiencing it all directly, but she was finding a way to cope and I'd freaked out. She turned to look at me.

'You had a dream,' she said. 'You acted like a bastard because you had a dream, that was all.'

'You know it wasn't a dream, or maybe it was but it was the truth as well. But you're right and I'm sorry,' I said again.

'I accept your apology but I need you to stay away from me,' she said and turned away. Maybe I was imagining her tears.

'So what now? Rannu? Balor? Mudge?' It was almost an instinct to say something stupid and hurtful. The words were out before I'd thought them through. Morag swung off the window and stood in front of me. Blinked-back tears turned to anger now.

'Has it occurred to you that I'll do just fine on my own? Don't you get it? I'm helping you now. With what I know, what I can do, I could set myself up anywhere and look after myself a fuck of a lot better than you could look after yourself when we first met,' she said, and she was probably right. 'Thank you for believing me when we met, thank you for protecting me when I couldn't, Jakob, but things have changed.'

'Tomorrow I'll try—' I began but she cut mc off.

'Tomorrow you just concentrate on your job, because if you're worrying about me then you're going to get everyone killed.'

I just stood there feeling foolish. It looked like it was starting to rain.

'Please go,' she said. I did.

# 22
# Atlantis

I would've been gratified by how ill Morag looked if I hadn't been the only one who'd thrown up so far. I put that down to dying as I was pretty used to turbulent transport flights. The magnetic storms caused in a binary system like Sirius were considerably worse than anything the Atlantic could throw at us. Still it was a rough crossing, I thought as I retched into the waste-paper bin that seemed already half filled with my vomit, as the wind and rain battered us around over the ocean. I was really pleased that Buck and Gibby had had the time to set up the transport so they could control it through their interfaces and musical instruments. My head seemed to throb with every beat of the country and metal they were playing.

The transport flyer *Mountain Princess* was effectively a small warehouse with enough vectored thrust engines to make it fly. Basically it was the same principle as the gunships that Buck and Gibby had flown with the 160th but with none of the elegance or performance. Which was one of the reasons we were being battered around so much. We were also pretty low, but not because we were trying to avoid detection as we were showing up on Atlantis air traffic control as a supply transport from a nearby ore ship. Someone Balor assured us was a good friend of his captained the ore ship, though to me the captain looked like she owed Balor and was shit scared of him.

'Jake!' Mudge shouted across the cargo hold. I looked over to him; he was beckoning me over. Despite my misery I managed to stagger to my feet and make my way across the hold with my bucket of sloshing vomit. 'Do you want to see the Spoke?' he shouted at me over the roar of the engines and the storm. I don't know why he was shouting as my audio dampeners were breaking down the noise and filtering what he was trying to say clearly. I was about to tell him that I wasn't bothered but decided why not and followed him into the cockpit.

Buck looked ridiculous staggering from side to side in the cockpit, trying to play his electric guitar and not pull the wires out of his neck port. Gibby looked less so as his fingers played across his keyboard, a look of concentration on his face. Outside windswept rain battered the cockpit's windscreen so hard we could have already been underwater. Below us I saw the white heads of a fierce high sea.

The only other Spoke I'd ever seen had been the Kenyan Spoke, from where I'd shipped out and been brought back to in restraints as a mutineer. They always made me feel a little uncomfortable. Maybe it was the humbling nature of such a feat of engineering. I wasn't use to seeing a structure that completely filled my horizontal field of vision, and that was just the base of the elevator.

Atlantis climbed out of the ocean along the equator roughly halfway between Africa and South America. The Spoke had been built on a similar principle to the pyramids that they'd had in Egypt before the FHC Crusades. Build a big enough base and you can make a building any size. The roots of the building went down deep into the Earth's crust and were designed to be strong enough to resist seismic events much like the Pacifica Spoke and the Spokes in southern Asia and South America.

The spokes were basically city-sized buildings that sheathed the carbon nanotube cable that supported the up and down Mag Lev lines. The end of the carbon nanotube was tethered to an asteroid counterweight, but lying some way beneath that was High Atlantis, Atlantis' orbital equivalent and one of the space entrepots for Earth.

The elevators were huge multi-storey affairs. They were capable of hauling bulk cargo such as the resources of the Belt that were delivered to high orbit by enormous industrial mass drivers. There was a channel in the solar system that was a nearly constant stream of huge lumps of ore. From high orbit a huge fleet of tugs manoeuvred them into place at High Atlantis and other High ports and sent them down to the surface to be delivered by freight mag lev trains, airship or, for the poorer countries in the northern hemisphere, old-fashioned surface ship.

Tonight Atlantis was receiving a thorough battering from an angry Atlantic Ocean. I watched as high waves broke themselves on the Spoke's thick, reinforced, chemically treated concrete walls. It was covered in lights both for the huge landing decks that seemed to sprout from it and as navigation aids for aircraft. Despite the weather, we were far from the only aircraft in the sky around Atlantis tonight. Everything from aircars to shuttles, for people who didn't want to travel at the comparatively leisurely rate of elevators, was in the air around the Spoke. Illumination was also provided by the huge viz screens attached to the walls, many of them obscured by the fierce sea, which beamed out near-constant adverts to the network of surface vessels docked at this deep-water port.

I could see Gibby's throat moving as he sub-vocalised. Presumably he was in contact with Atlantis air traffic control. Buck leaned over to me.

'Two minutes,' he said quietly, my audio enhancements picking up what he said. I nodded and moved back into the cargo hold, pushing Mudge in front of me. We'd run the final diagnostics not ten minutes ago, made any final last-minute adjustments to the Wraiths and stowed our gear. None of us had had the slightest idea what was in the oversized metal coffin that Balor had brought on board, but as I came back in I noticed it was open and everyone else was standing around it. I staggered over to the others.

Looking in the coffin, suddenly my nausea was forgotten. I turned to Balor.

'You brought a shark?' The coffin was a cryogenic storage box that was going through a rapid defrost program. Inside the box, through the cold smoke of the liquid nitrogen, I made out the form of a heavily armoured, cybernetically augmented twelve-and-a-half-foot-long shark. Balor was breathing in a funny way, and it wasn't just because he was using his gills.

'Are you linked?' I asked incredulously. Balor just smiled. I suspected he had a remote biofeedback device that connected him and the shark, similar though not as intense as the one that Morag and I had used. It wasn't a threat to our comms discipline because nobody would have a reason to use it. What it did mean was that at some level Balor was thinking and behaving like a shark. My day just kept on getting better and better.

'That thing's not going to attack us is it?' Mudge asked. If they were linked I was more worried about Balor attacking us.

'Magantu,' Balor said proudly.

Morag looked up at him sharply. 'That's your girlfriend!'

'That's just something you tell people for effect, right?' I asked him. He ignored me and just kept breathing funny. Fuck it, time for a little cocktail. Some of the sickness pills, a stim or two, some amphetamines to help the stims along – don't want to fall asleep – and then some of the old red. Trying to make sure that nobody else noticed I sent a blast from the inhaler up each nostril. Tasted something I haven't tasted since I was naked, cold and covered in blood on the *Santa Maria*. The perfect complement to my boosted nerves. Street level, none of the military-grade stuff any more, a bit rough round the edges but I could still feel the blood roaring in my ears.

We'd been over the plans so many times I didn't need to tell anyone what to do. We climbed into our Wraiths. Each of us was wearing inertial armour, as in the Wraith's cramped confines there was no room for any heavier armour. I leant back and felt the four studs slide into the ports at the back of my neck. With a thought I started the armoured exoskeleton up. It didn't make a sound but it fed information on its systems straight to my internal visual display. In the cargo bay of the transport, Mudge, Rannu, Pagan and Morag did the same thing.

I strapped myself into the machine, slipped both my feet into the control slippers in the lower thighs of both the slender, twelve-foot-tall mech's legs. My hands slid into the control gloves at the bottom of the upper arms of the mech. The palm link for my smartgun linked to the Wraith's primary weapon system, the modified Retributor railgun, the oversized pistol grip for which was in the mech's right hand.

The Retributor was a 20-millimetre, chain-fed railgun that we'd turned into a steel gun. All that really meant was that we'd pressurised the barrel to keep water out, used barrel inserts to reduce the calibre to 12 millimetres and used longer, more hydrodynamic rounds, or harpoons as they were nicknamed.

I calibrated the smartgun. The interface software was turning the Wraith into an extension of my body, making allowances for differences in perception. Suddenly I was twelve feet tall. I missed this, or maybe that was the electrical fire of the Slaughter in my synapses.

I stood up, swaying slightly. It had been a while and we were in heavy air. The normally sleek and elegant lines of the Wraiths were made ridiculous by the EM and heat-retardant foam we'd strapped to them. I switched on the acoustic decoy designed to fool Their scanners into thinking we were some kind of fauna, maybe a small whale or something, I wasn't sure.

Wind and rain howled into the cargo bay as Buck played a little riff to lower the rear cargo door. We all took hold of one of the support rails and made our way towards the cargo door. Except for Balor, who was pushing the coffin along the floor. He got it close enough to the lip and upended it, spilling a wriggling and angry cybernetically enhanced mako shark out onto the cargo bay floor. Magantu snapped at Rannu's mech but he lifted his leg out of the way just in time and the mako slid out, falling the remaining twenty feet into the ocean. Balor dived gracefully out after his predatory girlfriend.

Rannu made a ready signal with his mech's hand. We all replied with an affirmative signal, our comms procedure of silence until contact already in place. I wished I'd said something to Morag. Rannu made the go signal and stepped out into the stormy night, falling towards the ocean. Pagan followed him, then Morag, then Mudge and finally me.

I felt the jarring impact as the mech hit the surface, breaking through it and sinking like the heavy piece of Belt metal and super-hardened plastic it was. We had replaced the normal back-mounted flight system with a hydro-propulsion unit. We'd programmed in the point we wanted to sink to and planned to use the propulsion system as little as possible. It would only power up to make incremental changes in our course. We switched off all systems bar necessary life support and even that we down-powered as much as we dared. I was alone in this armoured suit accompanied only by the sound of my own breathing and the rushing of the Slaughter in my veins. As the first twitches began I was worried I was going to peak too soon.

Balor and his alleged girlfriend were our scouts, our shepherds. They were to make sure we didn't stray too far. As we quickly lost any surface light I had the unnerving feeling of having to abandon myself to things largely beyond my control. Soon I couldn't see anyone else and then I couldn't see anything. I couldn't even make out water through the optical interface with the Wraith, only blackness. I didn't even know which way was up or down and then even that ceased to have any meaning. It got cold quickly. Shaking joined the occasional twitch of combat want. It was the sort of cold that you felt you would never be able to get away from. I became very aware of the blackness pushing against me. Every so often I would hear a creak from the Wraith's superstructure but all the readouts remained in the green. Then the propulsion system would kick in briefly, causing vertigo and nausea. Once I panicked when I felt something touch and move the Wraith. I was about to turn on all systems when I realised it must have been Balor.

With all the darkness my mind began to play tricks on me. It wasn't the drugs: none of them were psychotropic, though they didn't help as the speed, stims and Slaughter made me jittery. It was just my mind wanting to fill in the blanks in the total darkness. There was nothing definite, just dark shapes, or rather slightly lighter shapes in the darkness. I twisted, accidentally turning the Wraith, then again at the next trick of the dark. I was startled again as I felt something grab and move the Wraith. I settled down when I realised it was Balor again and I was risking compromising the mission. I had to ignore my sensory input until it was time not to, going against all my instincts. The Slaughter was making me crave the action to start.

I wondered how Morag was and hoped she was okay. I was thinking this when I saw them. First came the glow and then came the most alien-looking things I'd ever seen. They were like pale, glowing, organic flying saucers trailing tendrils beneath them. They moved by flexing their mushroom-like bodies. They were beautiful in the deep silence. It seemed that I was in the centre of a field of bioluminescence. It was one of the most incredible things I have ever seen. It was like moving through a floating garden. Through the light they provided I could just about make out the humanoid forms of two of the other Wraiths as dark shapes falling through the water. More disturbing was the predatory shape of Magantu moving around us, awakening some instinctive fear in me.

When they had gone it was easy to dismiss the jellyfish as a hallucination brought on by sickness, drugs and sensory deprivation. There was nothing now. I was trapped in a prison not much bigger than I was. I didn't understand direction any more. Was I moving, still, or was I inverted? The rushing in my ears was becoming louder, a neural static of loud and discordant music, with no frame of reference but my imagination. I thought of it as the howling of angry angels. I'm not sure if it was panic or just a Slaughter-fuelled requirement for action, where action involves hurting another living being. I wanted to hammer on the reinforced titanium skin and tear it open, but I knew that would make me less – after all, it was my body now. My body creaked, the sound of metal under incredible pressure.

I felt like all the veins on my skin were standing out, as if the pressure outside was inside trying to crush my head. I felt like I had outside the *Santa Maria*. I was about to blow the mission. I'd peaked too early and there was an abyss howling behind my plastic eyes. Then I saw the light. It seemed to bleed slowly into my periphery. At first I wasn't sure it was real and I closed my eyes. Opening them again there was a sudden rush of vertigo. It filled my vision as far as I could see up or down, left or right. It was a wall of light. Suddenly directions seemed to make sense. I was looking at part, a small part, of the base of the elevator. It was covered in some kind of bioluminescent algae that gave it a pale, ghostly glow and for a moment made it look biological in nature, almost like Their technology.

Not for the first time I was overwhelmed by the scale, the sheer arrogance of the engineering. Although Atlantis had been built after the FHC, it was structures like this that had caused the war. During the Neo-Crusades fundamentalists had described them as pillars to heaven. Despite being the cause of the war only one had ever been attacked. The destruction of the first Brazilian Spoke had been the beginning of the end of the war, and the building of the second Brazilian Spoke had been one of the main reasons for the economic downfall of America and north-western Europe. From this perspective it was easy to see where the old-time fundamentalists got their sense of religious awe.

The 360-degree vision provided by the three cameras in the Wraith's head allowed me to see the other four Wraiths in the pale ambient light. Our systems were still running quiet. Underneath the algae we could see the Spoke's own lighting providing areas of brightness in the dark, the line between light and darkness much more defined in water than it would be in the air.

Of course the mermaid was a hallucination.

It was a hallucination with a steel gun. I could see the wakes in the water from the steel gun firing. It looked like many small fish darting towards me. The hallucination wasn't a mermaid, it was a merman. Now there was an explosion of bubbles from his weapon as a compressed-air charge launched a mini-torpedo from its under-barrel grenade launcher. I could hear what sounded like rain pattering off the skin of the Wraith. It was a very violent hallucination. My skull was about to burst – too much blood, too loud, too much internal pressure.

My internal visual display came alive. Tiny explosive charges blew the clasps that attached the foam we'd wrapped the Wraiths in. At a subconscious level I was aware that Pagan and Morag would now be jamming comms traffic from the cybrid and any other comms and scanners that were turned against us. Motion detectors, sonar and several other passive and active scanners formed a three-dimensional image in my head. There was the cybrid, and there were now drones in the water as well as independently targeted seeker torpedoes.

'Did you see them? Did you see them!' Mudge shouted over the comms line, his voice full of wonder. I think he was as high as I was but on something else. The Retributor started firing. As did other Retributors. The cybrid had realised he was outmatched and was trying to flee. I saw the harpoons impacting into his heavily converted cyborg frame. There was an explosion off to my left as one of the drones went up, a brief blossom of orange surrounded and quickly snuffed out by the water. The cybrid merman seemed to get churned up, turning in on himself as the integrity of his reinforced frame gave way. With the low-light amplified vision the blood in the water looked quite black.

The next explosion shook my Wraith, knocking it back. I ignored the creaking sound of distressed metal. One of the torpedoes had gone off nearby. I didn't think to check if any of the Wraiths had been damaged. I just wanted to destroy. The Wraith's propulsion system was on full, pushing me deeper into the ocean on the most direct route to where we assumed the facility was.

In my internal vision I had windows open showing me feeds from the cameras on each of the Wraiths. I also had a blank window up which would accept a feed from the net once Morag had entered it. I wasn't paying any attention to that. I was ignoring the comms chatter as more and more drones and torpedoes were launched. Two of the steel gun emplacements on the Spoke came to life and we began taking heavier-calibre fire. Through the blood-fuelled fire in my head I was thinking that I was fighting one of the pillars of heaven. More cybrids appeared in the three-dimensional rendering of the battle. The gun was silent. There was no recoil as I began firing nearly constantly, stopping only to change target when I was rewarded with flame or blood.

After the sensory deprivation of the descent, suddenly the deep was very much alive. Everywhere I looked I could see the conical turbulence from the wake of multiple ordnance. I launched two torpedoes at a submersible gunboat. Somebody, I don't know who, vented sensor-confusing ink from their Wraith. We fixed targets with our smartlinks, the Wraiths' acquisition software plotting the targets' most likely movements, and we fired blindly through the cloud.

I was laughing when we emerged from the ink cloud in a wake of our own turbulence, tendrils of ink grasping for us. There was a cybrid right on top of me, extending his steel gun at point-blank range. I didn't care. He was snatched sideways in the water as Magantu appeared from nowhere, powerful, mechanically assisted jaws clamping down on the cybrid's armoured body. The Wraith's propulsion system pushed me through a cloud of blood and mechanical fluids.

My audio dampeners kicked in at the thunderous sound of a super-cavitation attack sub heading straight down towards us, falling through the bubble of air it surrounded itself with.

Ahead of me I saw that three Wraiths had stopped by the bioluminescent, algae-covered wall of the Spoke. Two were covering while the third seemed inert. I could make out the propulsion system on the inert Wraith making small adjustments to hold itself steady in the water by the wall.

The net feed window in my internal visual display came to life. I could see the horrible visage of Morag's blue-skinned hag icon standing on a plane of glass. Ahead of her a waterfall fell from a pale sky, filling the screen from left to right. I saw Black Annis drawing symbols of smoky shadow in the air more rapidly than I could understand. They dissipated just as quickly.

I reached the wall and turned round to see a busy ocean filled with turbulence. Warning signs regarding the integrity of the Wraith began appearing in my internal visual display. I ignored them and provided covering fire for Morag's run into what we hoped was the facility's airlock. Either that or we were trying to enter a maintenance area really violently. The Retributor was always busy. I nearly dropped it when the submersible gunboat went up. The explosion was so close I was slammed back into the wall by the concussion wave.

In the net I saw figures like humanoid mirrors rise from the glass plane. I figured this was a manifestation of security attack programs. I watched as Annis traced more smoky symbols in the air with her other hand. The mirror figures were running towards her now, casting a distorted reflection all around them. I watched as one by one they started to burn with a pale-blue fire the colour of Annis' skin. They continued running though they were melting, the reflections they cast becoming more and more distorted.

Balor swam out of the darkness above me. He was so close to my field of fire I paused and adjusted my aim. He looked at home. He looked exactly like what he wanted to be, an ancient sea demon. The extending spear he carried was in a trident configuration. I watched as he swam down on another cybrid and despite her armour and reinforced frame jabbed the trident down into her spine and twisted. He left the corpse hanging there, tendrils of blood escaping into the water, as he continued to swim towards us. Whoever was in the fifth and final Wraith joined us, back to the wall and firing at the security forces. As shots from a steel gun rained off my armour, chipping concrete from the Spoke, I realised how much I wanted this. If I went out now, it would be okay. Of course this is what you're supposed to think on Slaughter, so it's all right to die.

In the net I saw the waterfall part slightly like a curtain being twitched open. The audio sensors on the Wraith picked up the grinding noise of the external airlock door opening just enough to provide us with room to propel the Wraiths in. Morag's Wraith came alive again and the net feed went dead. Balor was in first, a Wraith following him, I had no idea whose, but it turned and started providing covering fire for the rest of us.

One after the other the Wraiths moved into the airlock. The second to last was moving as I interfaced with the propulsion system and, still firing, manoeuvred myself into the dark interior, the doors already closing. I fired my last few bursts, watching them arc through the water just before the doors shut. Then I heard rather than saw the water begin to pump out of the chamber, as without a word we prepared ourselves to face whatever was coming when the internal door opened.

# 23
# Atlantis

The water was down to our knees now. Balor collapsed his trident down into a metal tube and clipped it to his belt. I noticed he had blood on his clawed hands that reached all the way up to his elbows. His maw was also covered in blood. I found myself slightly envious. I was jittery. I wanted the violence to start again. Pressure seemed to be building between my ears and the rushing/howling sound was back.

'We got feed?' Pagan's voice asked over our comms net.

'Nothing, completely isolated. I need a wire link,' Morag answered. I could hear her trying to mask the fear in her voice.

'This is going to be a shooting gallery,' Balor said, grinning, giving words to what I wanted. I was twelve feet tall, covered in metal and the weapon I held was effectively an unstoppable force.

The Wraith's lenses tinted as the water finished draining out and a bright line of light appeared in my vision as the doors started to open.

'We provide covering fire and advance until we find Morag a link,' I heard my voice say.

'We're going to take some punishment,' Pagan said. So? I thought.

Mudge extended a thin camera boom from the head of his Wraith as we all shuffled away from the opening doorway. The camera boom peeked around the opening door to see what waited for us. The images from the camera appeared on our internal visual displays. There was a hastily assembled barrier that ran the breadth of the large loading dock. I could see the helmets of a lot of soldiers. I counted two tripod-mounted railguns and what I assumed was a rocket launcher. Also behind the barricade, hull down, was a small six-wheeled vehicle of some kind, a plasma gun mounted on its flatbed. Running down either side of the dock were catwalks. Mudge couldn't get the angle on them but we assumed that they would be used as elevated firing positions. There were rails running along the condensation-covered concrete roof that reached back into the darkness, presumably to run a crane along. They may have been using the crane as another gun emplacement but it was so far back the little camera couldn't make it out. The most worrying thing was the Walker standing behind the barricade.

As soon as the door was open a crack we started taking fire. They wanted to start doing damage with ricochets. I felt impacts against the Wraith's armour, staggering me slightly.

'Ready?' I asked impatiently, wanting to be in this. There were four affirmatives. Balor didn't say anything. We marked targets and Rannu fired a multi-spectrum ECM smoke grenade forward. As they saw the smoke their firing intensified. We stepped into the firestorm. I began firing the Retributor. As I disappeared into the smoke I saw Balor clambering up onto the left-hand catwalk.

I fired blind, my sensors giving me nothing, my target-acquisition software telling me where the six-wheeled vehicle with the plasma gun had been. My audio dampeners cut out the near-constant supersonic bang from our Retributors and the sound of their plasma gun firing, allowing me to hear the music of tearing metal and screams.

We emerged from the smoke in a line, Morag's Wraith behind us. We must have looked like angry gods. The vehicle with the plasma gun mounted on it was in mid-air being torn apart by fire from my Retributor. I switched fire from that to the Walker, staggering back as rounds from its twin rapid-firing railguns impacted into me. Their targets destroyed, Rannu and Mudge were also concentrating their fire on the Walker while Pagan sprayed the barricade. The troops behind the barricade were picked up and thrown into the air by the force of the railgun rounds. Others just seemed to come apart. I felt only contempt for them.

Behind us, advancing down the left-hand catwalk, Balor was splitting his fire between troops on his walkway and on the opposite side. I wondered if the security detail had time to form an opinion on the blood-dripping demon approaching them. Grenades exploded in mid-air just above the catwalks, fired from Balor's over-barrel grenade launcher and detonated by proximity fuses. I saw smoking bodies fall from the catwalks.

The force of a plasma blast sank me to one knee and I saw Mudge's Wraith flung back. He landed on his arse, causing sparks to fly as he ground against the concrete floor. We were taking heavy fire. This wasn't right. I couldn't work out where it was coming from. Further down the loading bay I could make out the flickering flame of a muzzle flash. It was approaching us fast, illuminating the tunnel. I registered the plasma round glowing as it approached me in what seemed to be a lazy arc. I tried to get my Wraith out of the way but realised I couldn't move quickly enough. The blast lit up my shoulder, the plasma flames burning through the titanium armour. I imagined I could feel the heat. I tried to return fire but was staggered by railgun fire from the badly damaged but still standing Walker.

There were two heavily armoured gun cupolas on the roof rails. Each one had a chain-fed 30-millimetre rotary cannon. The left also had a plasma cannon and the right a 20-millimetre railgun. My internal visual display was lit up with red warning icons regarding the integrity of my Wraith armour.

'Port!' Pagan shouted across our internal comms net. Morag's Wraith moved towards a wall panel. Behind me I could see Balor jump off the catwalk as where he'd been standing ceased to exist in a hail of 30-millimetre rounds.

The net-feed window lit up again. I couldn't make out what was going on but it seemed to be some kind of corridor made of black glass. Annis moved down the glass corridor so quickly it was like she was standing still and the virtual construct moved around her. I was switching between laying down largely pointless suppressing fire on the Walker and creating sparks off the heavily armed cupola.

Suddenly both the cupolas stopped firing. I watched as all four of their weapons turned on the Walker and then opened fire again. It was awesome and relentless and they took the Walker apart. I stopped firing and just watched this happening, oblivious to the small-arms fire bouncing off the pitted and scarred armour of my Wraith. It took a 30-millimetre, high-explosive, armour-piercing grenade to bring me back. I looked around for the source and saw one of the security detail sprinting away from the barricade, making for a door that presumably lead into the facility. The railgun rounds threw him to the ground and sent him scraping across it.

I saw Mudge's Wraith reach up to the right-hand catwalk, small-arms fire sparking off its armour as he pulled part of it down, sending soldiers tumbling to the concrete floor. One of them in blind panic ran close enough for me to stamp on him.

We advanced, stepping over or kicking the barricade of crates and other junk out of the way. To the right there was a line of thick plastic windows that looked into some kind of storage area. Intermittent fire was coming from it. The windows shattered into thick plastic chunks as we subdued the area, pouring fire into it, destroying everything from food supplies to expensive scientific equipment. Part of the storage area exploded as we set fuel off, and ammunition began cooking off in another area. Whatever resistance there had been was either neutralised or had retreated further into the facility. At the back of my mind I hoped we were in the right place but I pushed that down. I didn't care.

I sent Mudge and Rannu down the tunnel to check what was down there. Pagan and I did a final scan of our immediate area. I realised the ammo counter was blinking on my internal visual display. I wondered when I'd run out of rounds for the Retributor. Mudge and Rannu's Wraiths came running back.

'Nothing,' Rannu said over the comms net. I nodded; the Wraith's head mimicked my movement.

'Dismount,' I said as Balor trotted over to us and went down on one knee, his weapon aimed into the burning storage area. The heads on the battle-scarred Wraiths flipped back and their chest armour split and swung open. I slid both my feet out of the slippers, pulled my hands from the gloves and pushed myself up and out as the plugs snapped out of my neck ports. I almost fell as I rapidly adjusted to being only six feet tall again. It didn't feel right. Like everyone else I was covered in sweat and panting for breath, but other than me only Balor was grinning.

I stepped into a puddle of blood. I looked at it momentarily, perhaps too long, and then sent the coded order to my Wraith to open both its storage compartments. Panels in either thigh slid open. I was struck by the lack of noise from the wounded. We'd been too thorough for wounded.

I removed the Benelli assault shotgun from the Wraith's storage compartment and rapidly reassembled it. Then from the other storage compartment I took the carryall and bandoliers with spare ammo. The others were doing the same thing except for Balor, who was covering us, and Morag. She was looking around at the carnage, her face blank. She couldn't make sense of it or her part in creating it. I'd seen this before. I'd felt this way before but no part of me could empathise with that right now. Who wouldn't want this? This felt like the ultimate expression of immediate power.

'Did you send out the biohazard warning?' I asked her. She ignored me. If they thought there had been some sort of biohazard leak or accident the Spoke authorities would not immediately send forces in. Morag said nothing.

'Morag?' I said.

'No,' Pagan answered for her. 'As soon as we breached they shut down all the internal exits and issued their own biohazard warning. I'm guessing that whatever they've got in here they don't want anyone else knowing about.'

'So all we have to worry about is a rapid reaction force from

Rolleston or his masters,' Mudge said. I nodded. Morag was still looking around at the carnage. She jumped as I reached over and touched her shoulder. Then she turned to look at me questioningly.

'Get ready,' I whispered. She nodded numbly and then threw up. I tried to ignore the contempt building in me.

We made our way out of the loading bay and into the facility proper, our weapons shouldered, our gun barrels leading the way, searching for targets, the crosshairs on our smartlink moving across our internal visual displays. We searched for even more people to kill.

Behind us out in the loading bay charges went off destroying the abandoned Wraiths. Their internal systems had already been junked by one of Pagan's viruses. It was a shame to let them go but even if they were fit to go in the sea again they would never get past the blockade that was building outside. They were destroyed to provide a minimum of evidence.

We clear the facility. We kill everyone we find. We clear offices, sleeping quarters, shower and toilet facilities, kitchens and recreational areas. Balor decides to stop using guns. I see him drag one of the security detail off his feet and run him through with his trident in mid-air.

Suddenly there was nobody else left to kill. I was breathing heavily, standing among the debris of what must have been some very expensive machinery. I was sort of aware of walking past Balor in the corridor outside this lab. He was tearing into somebody with his teeth.

Nobody was shooting at me. I had time to take in my surroundings beyond identifying and neutralising threats. It was an open-plan work area. Against the walls were freezers, fridges and glass-fronted cupboards, many of them broken and smashed. There was what looked like an operating theatre set into a depression on the floor. The table was oversized and had some very sturdy-looking restraints. Looking around I realised that this had been a sealed clean room. One side of the wall was thick plastic glass to allow observation. Past the operating theatre I could see another strong plastic window.

The roaring in my head was beginning to subside now. I had been wrong about there being nobody left to kill. People were emerging from under tables and behind overturned workbenches and from the sunken operating area. Many of them wore lab coats, a few maintenance overalls, several of them just normal casual clothes and two of them wore the uniform of the security detail, which had no insignia.

Somebody wearing a lab coat was approaching me. He was the oldest person there: he looked in his early sixties to me but could have been older. He was speaking to me slowly and carefully until his face turned red and disappeared. I think there was screaming as he dropped to the ground. I heard someone shout 'No' from the doorway. As the smoke drifted lazily from the barrel of my shotgun, I turned towards the doorway to see Morag standing there, hand over her mouth and tears in her eyes. I stepped over the corpse I'd made and headed towards the observation window on the other side of the operating area. The staff gave me a wide berth.

It was actually some time later that I remembered the look of horror and fear on their faces. That was the thing: I considered myself largely an all-right guy. I did the same bad things that everyone else did to survive. Maybe I was a bit better at doing the bad things than other people but I was a relatively easy-going person. Someone you could go and enjoy a pint with. That was how I saw myself, but how could I do all this and think I was normal? How could I hurt and kill so many other people and still expect to form a relationship with someone? How could I objectify one person and empathise with another? I could hear Morag crying now, her body racked by sobs. Surely that was the only normal response to this? How had I got to this? When had this become normal? The young man, little more than a boy, who'd shit himself in his first serious firefight with the Paras was a distant memory, another person.

I ejected the empty magazine from my shotgun and put another one in before slinging the weapon. I suddenly felt very tired. I sat down on the operating table, dimly aware that Mudge and Rannu were securing the prisoners behind me. I lit up a cigarette and looked through the observation window into the secure room and considered how much Gregor had changed as he stared back out at me.

He was stalking from one side of the small room to the other like a caged animal. His eyes were black pools with no discernible iris. They looked like they were made of the same liquid that constituted the bodies of Them, like Morag's had in my dream. He was taller, leaner, yet somehow much more powerful-looking, but his physiology was all wrong. He looked somehow lopsided, like he had too many bones in some places and not enough in others. His fingers were longer, with too many joints, and ending in long nails of what looked like black chitin. What I had initially thought was shoulder-length straight black hair I realised was tendrils of the black alien liquid. I tried to smother my disgust as some of his hair appeared to be moving independently. He kept his eyes on me as he stalked backwards and forwards. If he recognised me at all then he was pissed off.

'Morag?' I said. There was just the sound of crying. 'Morag!' I said more sharply.

'Yes?' she answered, taking heaving breaths.

'I need you to get into their internal net and get me anything you can.' Mudge drew up next to me looking through the glass at what had become of his friend. He was quiet for a while.

'Shit,' he finally said. 'What do you want to do now?' he asked as Balor, covered in blood, walked past us and up to the clear plastic window, staring at Gregor.

Finally I saw the net feed on my visual display flicker back to life. Black Annis standing in a landscape of blackened glass, obsidian, I think it's called. Much of it was burning. The hag icon stuck out, her cold blue skin contrasting with the black and red background.

'There's not a great deal left,' Annis' modulated graveyard voice rasped over the comms net.

'Pagan?' I asked, still staring at Gregor, who was now staring back at Balor.

'On it,' Pagan said. Moments later I saw his idealised Druidic icon appear on the apocalyptic landscape of their internal net. I assumed the virtual flames were the aftermath of an attempted purge. I could see ghost-like shadows in ragged cowls drifting across the jagged obsidian terrain.

Balor turned to me, a bloodstained grin on his predatory maw.

'I want to fight him,' he said simply. I ignored him and turned to Rannu.

'Bring one of the scientists over,' I told him. All the scientists were kneeling down facing the wall, clutching their ankles. Rannu gestured at one of them with his gauss carbine and the young man staggered over to the operating table. I drew the Mastodon from its shoulder holster. I noticed he'd wet himself, another normal reaction to all of this. I was almost envious of his fear. Or would've been if it hadn't been for the cold, clamminess and discomfort of wetting yourself. He was crying.

'I'm sorry. I'm afraid you're the hostage that has to die to make the others cooperate,' I told him. It wasn't that I wanted to shoot him; I just couldn't see what difference one more would make.

'No ... no, please, please don't ...' he managed to say before sinking to his knees. I needed him just this side of hysterical.

'Then can you help me?' I asked him. 'We don't have a lot of time, so the moment mine is wasted I have to kill you and start again, okay?' My voice sounded even and reasonable. He nodded through the tears.

'When you work on him out here,' I said, tapping the operating table I was sat on, 'how do you sedate him?'

'We feed it with a special protein formula once a day. When we want to take it out we add programmed nanites to its food. They enter its system and send a signal triggering a kind of inert trance we've programmed into its bioware.'

'Call him *it* once more and I'll fucking shoot you myself,' Mudge snarled. I held up my hand. I looked at Gregor. He was standing still, just staring at Balor, his head moving slightly as he studied the heavy-conversion cyborg. I could no longer ignore the similarity between my old friend and one of Them. Was I looking at Gregor or just a facade the Ninja had made of its victim? I didn't know.

'We could try talking to him,' Mudge suggested in a tone that implied even he didn't believe that would work. I was also pretty sure that giving him his dinner wasn't going to work either.

'Let him out,' Balor suggested. I ignored him and instead looked down at the terrified scientist kneeling in front of me.

'What do you do if he breaks out?' I asked.

'He can't; the containment chamber—' he said, controlling his sobbing somewhat better.

'Yeah, I get that,' I said, interrupting him irritably. 'But you'll have contingency procedures should it ever happen.' He thought about this. 'I'm going to need to hurry you up,' I said, waving the Mastodon at him.

'We load the same nanite serum into hypodermics and shoot him with it.'

'Outstanding. Mudge, help this guy find the serum and a dart gun please,' I said.

'You're letting him out?' Balor said. The excitement in his voice was nearly sexual.

'Not to play with,' I told him. He snorted in derision. 'Rannu, move the rest of the prisoners to the opposite end of the room.'

'You're not keeping us in here if you open that room!' An authoritarian female voice shouted. I turned to see a hard-faced, middle-aged woman, also wearing a lab coat, looking at me with only a trace of fear on her face.

'Your choice is that or a bullet in the head,' I said. She was right: I didn't want them in the room, but I had no choice because I needed all my shooters in the same place.

'Morag, Pagan?' I said. On the net feed I could see them stalking through the burning obsidian ruins of a building that put me in mind of some kind of temple. They were collecting pieces of shattered obsidian that had moving arcane-looking symbols on them. Behind them I could see the smouldering remains of several of the cowl-wearing, ghost-like shadows.

'We're just about—' Pagan began. The window went black and then it filled with static as the net feed was severed. I turned round to where Morag and Pagan were sitting on the floor against the wall. Morag was jerking and fitting, drooling blood from her eyes and ears. I swung off the table, bringing my Mastodon down to touch the head of the scientist in front of me.

'What's going on?' I demanded.

'I don't know!' he howled, obviously terrified and obviously telling the truth. I spun round, bringing the gun up to bear on the hard-faced woman who'd spoken up. She was looking my way as I walked towards her.

'You! What the fuck happened to them?'

'You wouldn't shoo—' The Mastodon went off, her head exploding all over a stainless-steel bench. The prisoners rather predictably started screaming.

'Shut up! Shut up!' I shouted uselessly. I was looking along the prisoners trying to see one who was obviously a signals person or a hacker.

Pagan came alive again and immediately turned to Morag. He connected a wire from one of his plugs to hers. It was the surge of anger at this repeat violation that reminded me of what had happened when Ambassador had tried to feed her all the information he'd taken.

'Pagan, what's happening?' I asked, my revolver still extended. Rannu was trying to calm the prisoners, pushing the odd over-excitable one back down against the wall. Mudge was holding two dart guns in one hand and some very sturdy-looking hypodermic needles in the other. He was looking at Morag, his mouth hanging open in shock. Balor was still staring at Gregor. The net feed in my visual display was still just showing static.

Morag woke up screaming. Her eyes flickered open and they were full of blood. Pagan, his face gaunt and drawn, looked terrified.

'Are you okay?' I asked. Morag's head twitched round to look at me. She said nothing but tried to clear the blood from her eyes. I turned to Pagan.

'What happened?' He just shook his head and looked over at Morag. Rannu was at Morag's side, examining her eyes and ears. Pissed off, I holstered the revolver and unslung my shotgun to cover the increasingly nervous prisoners.

'Jakob, if we're going to do this then we need to do it now,' Mudge said. Everything was unravelling: Morag was down, Rannu was distracted, Balor was doing his own thing and Pagan appeared to be in shock.

'Pagan.' He ignored me. 'Pagan!' I shouted. He looked up at me. 'Get over here and cover them.' He looked at me uncomprehendingly for a moment. 'Now!' I shouted with the voice of a thousand parade grounds that all NCOs remembered. Pagan snapped out of it and took my place. I turned round and caught the dart gun Mudge had thrown to me. The hypodermic had less in common with a needle and more in common with a dart from a gauss weapon. I checked the guns. They were smartlinked and effectively gauss rifles. I guessed they needed the velocity to penetrate its – his, I corrected myself – thick skin or whatever passed for skin in his radically altered physiology.

'Balor, get away from the glass,' I told him but he ignored me. 'Balor!' It didn't work this time. 'Fuck it.' I turned to the terrified scientist who'd given me the info. 'You, open the door and then get to the back of the room with the others.'

He began to protest, as did some of the other prisoners.

'Shut up!' Pagan shouted. He still sounded scared. I didn't have time to think about what had happened in the net.

'Do it now!' I shouted at the scientist and swung the dart gun around to point at him. He stood up and scurried over to a control panel. Some of his fellow prisoners were shouting at him not to do it. Pagan screamed at them again. Gregor had watched the scientist move over to the panel and had in turn stalked expectantly over to the door of his containment chamber. Balor turned and watched him go but thankfully stayed out of our field of fire.

'Rannu, if you're finished I could do with another shooter here,' I said.

'I'm taking Morag out of here,' he told me. I wished I'd thought of that. There was the hiss of the door's seal breaking and then it swung open. Gregor's twisted silhouette stood in the doorway backlit by the harsh strip-lighting of his cell. He stepped over the lip of the door. I took an involuntary step back. He opened his mouth and screamed. It was like the sound of the spires in my dream, except he wasn't singing, he was angry, and it was mixed with a very human scream of rage. Mudge and I fired. We both hit. Gregor didn't seem to register the twin impacts. Both of us dropped the dart guns and moved back, bringing our own weapons to bear. The prisoners screamed and heedless of Pagan's laser carbine began scrambling over each other to get to the door.

I think Balor thought it was Christmas. His trident extended, snapping into place as he moved purposefully towards Gregor. Gregor swung towards him. Even his movements were inhuman, his strange gait more like Them than us. Balor stabbed forward one-handed with his trident. The three-pronged weapon pierced Gregor's chest though he gave no indication of noticing it. Balor forced him back into the corner by the open door. Roaring, Balor leapt into the air, his free hand swinging back as he prepared to claw the pinioned hybrid.

I saw Gregor's black fingernails grow and solidify until each of them was an eight-inch-long black blade. With his right hand Gregor grasped the shaft of the trident and pushed it back, tearing it out of his flesh. His left reached up, moving with the sort of speed I'd only ever seen once before, on the night Gregor had been taken. He caught Balor's wrist with his left and letting go of the Trident swung upwards with his clawed right hand. The blow tore into Balor's heavily armoured stomach and chest, halting and then reversing his trajectory. Gregor clawed him with so much force that Balor went crashing back into the operating table.

Immediately Balor was up as Gregor closed on him. He swung with one clawed hand and then the other. He tore rents in Gregor's skin, revealing black liquid below the surface that immediately started to knit the torn flesh back together. I think that was when I stopped believing that my friend was alive and that I was looking at anything other than an alien wearing the distorted and tortured flesh of Gregor's body. I felt like he'd been hollowed out. I dropped the shotgun, letting it hang on its sling as I drew my Tyler, stretching it out in a two-handed shooter's stance for maximum accuracy. I was going to kill this mockery and then kill every fucking person who worked here. I didn't care if I was still here when reinforcements arrived; I'd kill as many of them as I could as well.

Balor was slammed against the stainless-steel wall. He howled as alien claws pierced his side, pinning him to the wall. I was about to fire when the pistol was forced up and Mudge was suddenly in front of him.

'What are you doing?' he shouted.

'It's not him!' I screamed in Mudge's face, trying to break free.

Gregor staggered back for no good reason I could see. Balor used the opportunity to push him back further while repeatedly clawing him in the face. Each time Gregor's distorted features were torn off, the black liquid began re-knitting the flesh and then Balor's claws tore them open again. Gregor sank to the floor. I lowered my pistol, sure that Balor would do the job for me, but suddenly Gregor struck out. The blow sent Balor flying back into the air so high he broke through one of the hanging strip lights and slammed into the ceiling, before bouncing off the wall and landing on the ground.

Gregor stood up but swayed as his facial features reformed. Balor pushed himself to his feet and began striding towards Gregor. As Balor closed with him he swung out with his left with surprising speed. He caught Balor firmly on the face and picked him up off his feet again, sending him over a table and into the wall, hard enough to make a significant dent.

Balor threw the metal table aside and stood up. Gregor swayed again and then sat down hard. His eyes were still black pools but the expression on his face was one of confusion. Balor made for him again, presumably intent on finishing the job. Mudge let go of me.

'No!' he shouted at Balor. I wondered why Mudge had his AK-47 in his hands. Balor was ignoring Mudge. I watched in horror as Mudge shouldered the AK-47 and fired a three-round burst, staggering the pirate. Balor stopped and turned to Mudge. He looked furious. He looked inhuman. Gregor's eyelids flickered and closed over the black liquid pools of his eyes as he slid to the ground. Mudge lowered his smoking AK-47. I saw him swallow before he turned and fled. Balor charged after him but I knew he had no chance of catching Mudge's cybernetic legs.

I moved to stand over the inert body of the hybrid, the Tyler still in my hand. I pointed the laser pistol at him. Unconscious as the last of his wounds knit shut, he looked almost peaceful. More like my friend.

'We've come a long way just so you can shoot him,' Rannu said from the doorway. I lowered the pistol.

'Morag?' I asked.

'She can move,' he said.

'Right, you go and calm Balor down, share some brotherly warrior shit with him or something. Get Mudge back here; I need a hand bagging Gregor.' He nodded and left the room. I could hear him sub-vocalising over the net, trying to reach Balor. I turned to Pagan, who still did not look right.

'Pagan, I want you to junk whatever's left of their comms and security, okay?' He nodded. We needed to leave here and we needed to do so quickly.

Exfiltration wasn't exactly easy but it was less violent. Morag was up and moving, most of the blood cleared away, though her eyes were completely bloodshot. After making sure they had no way of communicating we pretty much left the surviving lab staff to it.

We put Gregor in a survival bag, gave him an air supply and a heat source – if indeed he needed either – and vacuum-packed the bag. Mudge and I slung it under a collapsible pole. We'd carry it between us.

We moved through the facility until we came to the place that Morag had predicted was the weakest part of the superstructure over a place least likely to be populated. Balor had the canister. The canister had been the real cost. Not the transport, the weapons, the intel or even the Wraiths. The canister he held in his hand was the really expensive thing and contained one of the most proscribed substances in human space. Unlicensed possession was normally enough for a substantial jail sentence; using it in a terrorist act like we were doing was worthy of the death sentence in most states and all Spokes.

Balor sprayed the programmable concrete-eating microbes on the concrete floor at the back of the loading bay. I watched as a sizeable circle of the concrete turned to liquid, becoming a deeper and deeper pool until it cascaded out of the hole it had eaten. Balor quickly sent the microbes their destruction code before he and Rannu jumped through.

We moved through the maintenance level below. Pagan tricked out the sensors and sent fake images to the cameras, sending ghost images of us in all the wrong places and making sure everything looked empty and normal where we actually were. Morag was supposed to be helping, but she did not want to enter into the net again and we didn't have time to deal with that now.

There was activity from Spoke security and their emergency services but nobody was quite sure what was going on and they didn't have the surrounding layers secure yet. They'd probably been warned off by Rolleston's people and were waiting for their response. We slipped through.

Another three storeys down we found an abandoned maintenance shaft that Morag had discovered during her research. We used what was left of the microbes to eat their way into the abandoned shaft. We set up a winch mechanism. Rannu went first, then I followed and Mudge lowered the bagged form of Gregor down. We had no idea how long the sedative would last, though we had brought more of it with us. If he woke up en route we could all be fucked.

At the bottom of the shaft was a tunnel that led to one of the maintenance airlocks for the Mag Lev tunnels. In the tunnel we unrolled our lightweight vac suits and assembled the helmets. The Mag Lev tunnels were designed to be flexible as they were bored into tectonically unstable rock. They were also vacuums to limit the air resistance the high-speed train would have to push against.

Pagan hacked the airlock mechanism and sent false data to the Spoke's systems to make it look like it hadn't been opened. We entered the cavernous dark tunnels of the Mag Lev system. It was a twenty-mile tab via flashlight, Pagan again having to trick out cameras and sensors on his own, as Morag wouldn't help. It was sometimes easy to forget how good Pagan was when you saw Morag's capabilities. Spokes and the Mag Levs have some of the toughest security on Earth as they are seen as huge terrorist targets. What he did was an amazing bit of hacking, but I could see it was taking a toll on him.

In the tunnels Rannu had point. Balor was at the rear. Mudge and I were carrying Gregor; Morag and Pagan were flanking us. There were no Mag Levs. I reckoned Rolleston's people must've shut them down.

I didn't think twice about a twenty-mile tab, even post-combat. That's why it came as something of a surprise when my helmet filled with bloody vomit, almost choking me, and I collapsed.

I found out what happened later on. They managed to evacuate the sick from my helmet into the rest of the suit. Apparently when they took it off me, back onboard the *Mountain Princess*, it was pretty disgusting. Embarrassingly I had to be carried the rest of the way by Balor.

When we reached an external airlock Pagan again hacked the lock and sent false information to the security systems. In the airlock our suits injected us with a stasis-inducing drug that lowered our heart and respiratory systems. Balor then attached us all by safety line and with Magantu acting as scout towed us in a line to the surface, avoiding the submersibles, cybrids and exo-armour patrols that were presumably looking for us. A heavily coded comms burst brought Buck and Gibby in the transport back to find us. Balor sent Magantu back to New York. It was going to be a long swim for the shark.

Buck and Gibby flew us back to the *Mountain Princess*, the ore transport ship we were using as our base of operations. Fortunately Gregor did not wake up from the sedative and they were able to secure him in the recently installed containment chamber on the ship.

The chamber was in one of the ship's concealed smuggling holds. They were well hidden but would not stand the determined and well-equipped search of the ship that presumably Rolleston and his people would begin in the near future. How long we had depended on what resources they were prepared to throw at the problem. They also had to factor in the risk of exposure, as the people doing the searching had a chance of finding Gregor, who could be difficult to explain. They would also have to be capable of dealing with him.

# 24
# Atlantis

*Okay, this was different. I was in an exceptionally well-rendered pub. It was very old-fashioned. They had proper untreated wooden tables and a bar that wasn't made out of scrap and driftwood. I was sitting at one of the tables, a whisky in front of me. I tasted it. It wasn't quite right, but then again it never was whether it was virtual, Irish, Japanese or pre-war Sirian. There was music playing, soothing with a slightly jagged undercurrent to it. I think it was pre-FHC, but it wasn't jazz so I didn't recognise it.*

*The icon I was wearing was quite a good naturalistic interpretation of me as a natural, unaugmented human – no prosthetics, no plugs. I wondered what colour my eyes were and then realised I couldn't remember.*

*I couldn't be sure whether or not the other person in the bar had been there since I'd opened my eyes or not. I just sort of became aware of him. He sat several tables away and he was a Laughing Boy, a Smiler. One of the nastier gangs, they started off in the reclaimed zones in London and were one of the Smoke's less pleasant exports. They portrayed themselves as a kill-for-thrills franchise. If you wanted someone done at street level you got one of these little sadists to do it.*

*I'd had my run-ins with them in the past, before I'd joined up, when I'd lived in Fintry. Rumour had it that in order to join them you had to kill someone for no reason. Their members tended to be the genuinely unbalanced, the wannabe hard and the desperate for attention. I wondered which this one was.*

*He had on the corpse paint; he had the scar tissue at the corners of his mouth, where it had been cut up into a wider smile, the shades, the mock-crushed-velvet frockcoat, presumably with an armoured lining, the shell suit and running shoes. He looked to be in his mid-teens. He sat there playing with a long scalpel-like knife and drinking a black-coloured pint that was presumably supposed to be real Jamaican Guinness. He wasn't staring at me, so much as studying me.*

*He didn't fit in a place like this. Neither did I. These sorts of places were for people with money – wage slaves or officers on leave – but those were all real-world considerations; I was weighing them up out of habit. I was about to speak to the Smiler when the door opened and a bright-blue light poured in, silhouetting a tall slender female figure as she entered.*

*I held my hand up, shading my eyes, but the light went when she closed the door. The icon was tall, classically beautiful with pronounced cheekbones. She had pale-blue skin and long black hair that seemed to blow in a non-existent wind. Her dress was ankle-length and looked like it was made of some blue fibrous material with living flowers on it. Her eyes were pools of solid black. As she entered the Smiler took off his shades. His eyes were surrounded by intricate eye make-up that seemed to move of its own accord; his eyes were the same pools of black as the woman's. Suddenly I felt like the only human in the room.*

*'Morag?' I asked the woman. This icon was different from Annis. I saw the icon sigh with irritation. That was good programming.*

*'It's Annis, or an aspect of,' Morag said. Of course, I'd ignored netiquette by not using her icon's name. The Smiler just watched us.*

*'What's going on?'*

*'You're unconscious, again,' she said neutrally.*

*'Some things never change,' the Smiler said. He had a broad Scots accent that sounded familiar. It was of course obvious when I placed it. Who else would it be?*

*'Gregor?' I asked tentatively, and beneath the make-up and the leering scar I began to make out a teenage version of my friend.*

*'Hasn't been that long,' Gregor said and then he smiled, making the scar utterly grotesque. So you used to be a Smiler, I thought. He'd kept that quiet and even had the scar tissue removed before joining the Regiment.*

*'What is this place?' I asked. It was going to take me a while to formulate a response to yet another unfamiliar incarnation of my old friend.*

*'It's an intuitive program,' Morag, sorry Annis, the new sweeter-looking Annis, began.*

*'You can write intuitive programs?' I asked. It was pretty high-level stuff. I don't know why I was surprised.*

*'With help, and besides Gregor's neuralware or biology is very compatible with Ambassador,' she said. I didn't like the sound of this.*

*'Am I in an alien?' I asked nervously.*

*'Don't start,' Morag said testily.*

*'Hi, how are you, Gregor? How've you been since I last saw you? Oh fine, just kidnapped, held against my will and experimented on. Yourself?' Gregor said, smiling in a way that made me surprised his face didn't split.*

*'Just give me a moment,' I said.*

*'Because you're the one who needs time to readjust,' Annis said.*

*'The bar?' I asked.*

*Annis shrugged. 'He made it,' she said.*

*'It was a peaceful moment for me. I was waiting for a client who wanted a slice job doing. I was let into the bar. It was the middle of the afternoon, it was peaceful. I guess my subconscious just produced this moment.'*

*'You're dressed like a twat,' I pointed out. He started laughing.*

*'I was young, I was foolish,' Gregor said. It was him, it was slowly beginning to sink in, it was really him.*

*'So what happened to me?' I asked.*

*'You fainted,' Annis said. There was another grotesque smirk from Gregor. 'Overexertion and a nasty cocktail of drugs.' There was something in her voice, coldness, a distance. I looked up at her. I remembered her in tears at the carnage. I remember my contempt, how much I enjoyed doing what I did. I also remembered Morag bleeding from her ears and eyes and not wanting to go back into the net.*

*'You okay?' I asked. She nodded, her icon's features an impassive mask. 'Sure?'*

*'We all need to talk about it later. Sergeant MacDonald is our main problem at the moment,' she said.*

*'Just Gregor,' Gregor said.*

*'Where are we at the moment?' I asked. 'We made it to the* Mountain Princess*?'*

*'Oh yes.' Annis sounded a little pissed off.*

*'And?' I asked expectantly.*

*'We're docked at Atlantis,' she said.*

*'What! Why?' I asked. Had we been captured?*

*'Because it makes sound tactical sense. They would never think of looking for us here,' Morag said, using a tone of voice that suggested she was quoting someone.*

*'This was Balor's idea?' I asked resignedly, and I supposed it made a degree of psychotic sense. The problem was sooner or later they would put a smart enough program or a smart enough image analyser on their satellite info and they'd work out what had happened and trace us to the* Mountain Princess.

*'No offence, mate, but are you in isolation?' I asked Gregor. He nodded.*

*'Not fit to mix with the other children,' he said.*

*'So it's you, not the alien?' I asked.*

*'It's both. We sent me because I would be the best able to communicate with youse.'*

*'What happened?' I asked.*

*'Pretty much what I said. My other half effectively colonised my body. You're looking at the first hybrid between us and Them.'*

*'Who's in control?' I asked.*

*'At the moment neither, but normally both. Look, despite seeing what*

*you're seeing now there's been some changes. We are fully integrated.' I didn't like the sound of this and he must've seen it on my face. 'It's okay, man. It maybe wasn't what I'd planned in my life but I would not have survived for you to get me out if it hadn't been for my other side.'*

*'So are you Gregor?' I asked.*

*He shook his head. 'But it'd probably be easier if you call me that.'*

*I took another sip of whisky. A packet of cigarettes had appeared on the table. I took one out and lit it. It was nice to see that Morag understood my coping habits, or at least my putting-off-dealing-with-things habits.*

*'So why did you want to integrate with my friend?' I asked it. I caught Gregor's icon's eyes narrow ever so slightly as I spoke. Morag shook her head in disgust. Gregor considered me for a bit before answering.*

*'It was trying to communicate with us,' Gregor said. So Pagan had been right. 'All They have ever experienced from us is violence, therefore They assumed that our society was based on violence, which to a certain degree it is. They assumed the most violent were the leaders, which was a reasonable assumption to make.'*

*'So They went after special forces operators,' I said, understanding. 'What do They want?' I already knew the answer.*

*'Peace,' Gregor said. I gave this some thought as I took a drag on my cigarette. The cherry glowed brighter – I was impressed despite myself.*

*'How do we know you're telling the truth?' I asked.*

*'Trust,' Annis answered. 'So we're probably fucked,' she added bitterly.*

*'Yeah, well hands up if you're a human?' I said and put my hand up knowing I was acting like a prick.*

*'Hands up if you're an arsehole,' Annis suggested. I dropped my hand. 'Look, you're here because I thought you'd be of more use in helping bring your friend back than Mudge. Instead it's you who needs all the reassurance,' Morag said.*

*'Are you surprised? I've spent most of my adult life with these things trying to kill me. If we're wrong, if we trust the thing in your head and So-I-Married-An-Alien over here—' Gregor smirked again '—we could hand over this planet to Them and effectively wipe out our own species, have you thought about that?'*

*'Yes,' she said.*

*'Really? Because you seem pretty quick to trust the alien, and believe me you wouldn't if you'd seen what any of us have seen.'*

*'So I don't get an opinion because I haven't been to war yet?' she asked.*

*Gregor was watching the exchange like a tennis match. I was beginning to find the constant smile infuriating.*

*'What did Rolleston want with you?' I asked him, ignoring Morag's question.*

*'That's kind of a long story and I'd rather tell it to everyone,' Gregor said. 'Besides, I haven't insulted Mudge in a while; I've no doubt you've been remiss.'*

'Remiss? *The alien bring a vocabulary with him?' I said, realising that I was treating him like my old friend again. I turned back to Annis, who still looked angry.*

*'Why don't you look like the hag any more?' I asked.*

*'I do, I just thought this would be easier for Gregor,' she said through gritted teeth. Feeling the cold I turned back to Gregor.*

*'So I'm assuming you're still sedated?' I said. He nodded. 'And you'll play nice when you wake up.' He shook his head. 'No?'*

*'That's why we're here,' Annis said impatiently.*

*'When they realised that the facility was under attack they programmed me to attack.'*

*'Programmed?' I asked.*

*'Vicar was right: effectively Their physiology is a kind of naturally occurring nanite. Their technology and biology are one,' Annis said.*

*'And the Cabal have developed bioware interfaces,' Gregor added. 'Effectively they used primitive bionanites of their own to reprogram my own biology,' he said. It struck me then that the war was over. All we had to do was release these nanites and programme Them to leave us alone. Except of course that we might be the aggressors.*

*'The Cabal?' I asked.*

*'Later,' Annis told me. 'We've got some of the sedative and between us and Ambassador we're trying to find a way to turn off the kill signal.'*

*'Because if not, I'm going to wake up and kill everyone, starting with that big fish-looking bastard,' Gregor said in a disturbingly matter-of-fact manner.*

*'So how come you're here?' I asked.*

*'Because he still has his ports and the alien has wired himself to them to allow input and output,' Annis answered. 'You need to go now, we have work to do.'*

*Gregor winked at me.*

'Cunt,' I said, meaning Gregor, and waking up. I felt like shit. I mean really bad. I felt weak, really sick and patches of my skin were very sore. I needed some more of Papa Neon's pills and quickly. The slight but noticeable near-constant moving of the room I was in wasn't helping me with my nausea.

I was lying on a fold-up cot riveted into the floor. The room had a curved wall on the left-hand side – sorry, port side – that told me we were in a ship, next to the hull and, judging by the sound, beneath the waterline. The walls were undressed steel. I assumed I was in some kind of smuggling hold on the *Mountain Princess*. Looking around I could see other cots, and there were various bits and pieces of gear scattered about. I could see an opening to a separate area of the hold. Someone had draped a drab grey blanket over the opening but light was creeping around it. I could also hear voices from the other side.

'I'm not sure this is a good idea,' I heard Mudge say as I downed some more of Papa Neon's special pills, some painkillers and a mild upper. Just to get me out of bed. I noticed I had some red lesions on my skin. They bled whenever anything touched or rubbed against them. I saw that they had been dressed as well as circumstances would allow.

'Morag will not wake him unless it is safe,' I heard Rannu assuring Mudge as I stumbled towards the blanket curtain. Feeling the familiar tug from the back of my neck, I reached behind me and removed the plug; looking down I saw an extension line that led to the next room. This was the connection that had allowed me to enter Gregor's safe environment. The almost imperceptible movement of the huge docked ore carrier was making my stomach roll. I tried not to heave and wished I had a cigarette.

'Rannu, while your faith is a beautiful thing I'm not convinced it's going to stop me from being torn limb from limb,' Mudge again.

'I will avenge you,' I heard Balor growl with relish.

'Oh that's very reassuring,' Mudge paused. 'You ... you're looking forward to this, aren't you?' I reached the blanket and tried to pull it aside but only succeeded in pulling it down. 'What are you doing?' I heard Mudge ask incredulously.

I staggered through into the next compartment. Balor, Rannu and Mudge stood in a semicircle around what looked like a high-tech glass coffin crossed with a stretcher. It was secured to two workbenches. I recognised it as a man-portable intensive care unit. It was similar to those used by Carrion, as we squaddies rather unfairly called battlefield medics because they were under orders to strip cybernetics from the injured and dead. This one had presumably been modified to handle biohazard containment, though I couldn't see it holding if Gregor got angry somehow. Morag and Pagan were leaning against the bulkhead furthest away from the coffin to my immediate right – sorry, starboard. Both were obviously tranced – I could see wires extending from their neck ports to the portable ICU.

I leant against the doorway fighting for breath. I couldn't remember ever feeling this weak before. Mudge glanced behind him. He was focused on aiming his AK-47 at the portable ICU. Rannu was doing the same with his gauss carbine and Balor appeared to be slinging his Spectre/grenade launcher combo and extending his spear into a trident configuration.

'You got a cigarette?' I asked Mudge.

'Bit busy right now. Balor, clearly an automatic weapon is more appropriate than a fucking fishing spear.' Even Rannu was glancing in askance at the eight-foot-tall, heavy-conversion cyborg. Balor was just grinning.

'Okay, we're waking him up.' I heard Morag's voice. It seemed to be coming from Pagan's staff, which was lying across his lap.

'Are you sure he's ready?' I was surprised to hear Rannu ask. His answer was the clear top of the ICU sliding down. Rannu and Mudge tensed ever so slightly while Balor looked on in eager expectation. Some smoky chemical gas or other, could've been oxygen for all I knew, drifted out of the ICU. I decided that if the-thing-that-was-once-Gregor was going to kill me I was going to have a cigarette and even a drink if I could find one. I decided that I wouldn't tell Mudge about the TTTWOG acronym; I didn't think anyone else would thank me if I did. I turned and headed back to my cot.

'Easy, easy. Easy!' I heard Mudge from behind me. I wondered if they'd considered that pointing guns and antique poking weapons at him might encourage a fight or flight response. Probably not. I heard much shuffling and shouted commands from next door as I located my cigarettes and was pleased to find Mudge's hip flask. It probably contained vodka but it would be good vodka, and I'd always felt the Russians and the Scots had a lot in common.

'Gregor, are you okay?' Pagan's voice. I think he was trying to be soothing but instead it sounded patronising. If I were a dangerous human/alien hybrid his tone would upset me.

'Okay, everybody needs to just calm ... Balor? Balor!' It was Morag's voice now. I considered grabbing a gun but I seemed to be swaying and decided I would probably be more danger than use. Nausea overwhelmed me. Fortunately I could see a bucket nearby and I managed to reach it before I puked up what looked like bile and blood. There was the sound of rapid movement next door and a low growling noise.

'No!' Morag said. It was a voice similar to the one my dad would use when scolding a bad dog. I assumed she was talking to Balor. I spat out the residue of vomit in my mouth and clambered back to my feet. It was as if I could feel myself rotting from the inside. I cleaned my mouth with vodka and spat that into the bucket before taking a tenuous sip of it. I kept it down despite the burn. It didn't quite get rid of the taste however.

'Balor, can we not antagonise the potentially dangerous alien life form, please?' Mudge asked. 'You did turn off the kill order, didn't you, dear?' he added.

'I think so,' Morag replied. I didn't like how unsure of herself she sounded. I lit up a cigarette. The mouthful of smoke was somehow reassuring and making me feel more nauseous at the same time.

Making it back to the entrance to the next compartment, I leant heavily on the hull. Gregor was standing in front of the ICU. He was crouching slightly. It was the stance of a cornered predator. The black pools of his eyes were looking around the room. Going from person to person. Sizing them up. Waiting for them to move. I had more time to study him as he wasn't moving so quickly and kicking Balor's arse at the moment. He looked like someone had taken one of Them and tried to squeeze it into a human shell without making any allowances for human physiology. Which in a way was what had happened. Recognising the human bits of him – the familiar, if warped, features of my friend – somehow made him/it (I was still confused by that) seem more alien. He looked at me as I took another drag from the cigarette and fought my nausea. I nodded at him. He seemed to stare at me. I was too ill to be unnerved. He opened his mouth. I was relieved to see healthy-looking human teeth, though they looked more perfect than I remember Gregor's being. He screamed, sort of. I put my hands over my ears as the noise went right through my skull. Even my dampeners kicking in didn't seem to do much good. Morag had her hands over her ears. The others were grimacing. I'd heard a similar noise before, when I had dreamed of the alien spires, but this was different, distorted, discordant, angry.

Gregor's mouth closed with an audible snap of his teeth. Rannu and Mudge were still nervously covering him, Pagan was behind them, Morag was standing just in front of them and Balor was edging round the side trying to flank him.

'Guys, lower the guns, yeah?' I suggested.

'What a great fucking idea,' Mudge said. 'If he gets too excitable I can just beat him unconscious with my enormous cock.'

'Do you want me to go and get that from your bag?' I asked him. 'Seriously, all we're doing is threatening him and then you wonder why he's not acting calm.'

'He's right,' Morag said and moved directly into Mudge's line of fire.

'Shit,' Mudge raised the barrel of his weapon and began moving for position.

'Mudge,' I said softly. He stopped. Somewhat reluctantly I could see

Rannu lower his carbine. 'It's him,' I said to Mudge. I wasn't sure if I believed it. Mudge glanced over at me and then lowered his gun. We all looked over at Balor. Balor sighed deeply, obviously disappointed.

'Buncha pussies,' he muttered and glared at Gregor before going and sitting on a heavily reinforced folding chair in the corner.

Morag stepped towards Gregor, who like me was swaying slightly, though I suspect for different reasons. The human/alien hybrid towered over her. He was as tall, possibly taller, than Balor, though he had a much more slender build. Watching him loom over her was the only time I got really nervous. She stretched out her hand to him. He looked at it for a while before finally reaching out with his own bony hand. His fingers were too long and had too many joints in them. I thought he was going to wrap his fingers multiple times around Morag's small hand.

Morag led Gregor over to another chair, but instead of sitting he just crouched down, almost seeming to fold himself up. There was something insectile about his position. I could not square this thing with the Gregor I had spoken to in the virtual construct. He looked at me and then at Mudge and smiled, and then pointed at Mudge.

'Fucking what?' Mudge said. I started laughing.

'He's surprised to see someone more alien-looking than he is,' Morag said, smiling slyly. Rannu and Pagan started laughing; even Balor smiled sulkily. Gregor's mouth opened and he laughed. That shut all of us up. At first it was like a seal barking, then it seemed to modulate and change until it sounded a bit like Gregor's easy laugh, though off somehow. We all just stared at him.

'Seems you being weird-looking is funny no matter what race you are,' I said, as I stubbed out my cigarette and took another pull of vodka. Mudge gave me the finger but he seemed to have relaxed.

'Hey, is that my hip flask?' he demanded.

'Yep.' I took another swallow of vodka and then Gregor reached over from what seemed like very far away and took the flask from my hand. We all watched as he drained the rest of the flask.

'I think he's working on instinct,' Pagan said almost apologetically. I found it reassuring that there was that much of a squaddie left in him.

'Can you speak to us?' Pagan asked in his irritating, patronising tone. Gregor turned to look at him, his head seeming to swivel too far round. He opened his mouth and there was a squeal of distortion, as though through a microphone. His voice seemed to cycle through tones and possibly frequencies until it found one it liked and he started to sound more like Gregor again.

'Of ... course ... I ... can ... fucking speak to you, I'm ... not ... fucking stupid.' His head swivelled round at a disconcerting angle to look at me. 'Who's ... your mate?' Mudge and I grinned. Though I think we both knew that this was not the Gregor we had known, that this was something completely different, he was in there somewhere.

I was getting used to oddness. Me, Mudge and Pagan sitting in a circle talking to a sea demon, a teenaged girl and an alien was beginning to feel commonplace. We let Gregor ease back into human communication by telling him a heavily abridged version of what was going on. He mostly stayed quiet, asking the occasional question. He seemed awkward with himself, even after Morag had found him a pair of Balor's cut-off shorts and he'd tied them round his waist. I realised halfway through Pagan's description of God, which I couldn't be bothered to listen to, that he was ashamed of his alien-ness. Somehow that seemed reassuringly human, but I couldn't think of anything to do that would make him or us feel better about this.

Gibby and Buck had returned about halfway through our brief. I wasn't sure whether they'd been sent away in case they angered Gregor or had decided to not be around themselves, but when they returned Gregor stood up, or unfolded himself. Both Gibby and Buck had backed away, hands going to holstered antique revolvers at their sides. We'd calmed things down but Gregor still looked like he might eat either of them and they looked like they might bolt at any time.

'Who're the Cabal?' I finally asked him, several hours later, when I was pretty sure that we'd exhausted our version of events.

'The people who've done all this. The people who captured me and experimented on me,' Gregor said. His voice, almost normal now, was lulling me into believing he was both human and my friend. 'Basically a group of fat old rich guys. Invisible men, corporate old money, intelligence agency types, military and civil service high-ups.'

'From where?' Mudge asked.

'Most anywhere, but mainly Europe and America, as far as I can tell.'

'A conspiracy?' Buck asked scornfully. Gregor swivelled his head round and looked at him with the black pools of his eyes, long enough to make the pilot feel very uncomfortable. Buck was opening his mouth to say something when Gregor answered.

'I don't think they see it that way. They don't see they have anything to conspire for or against. They and people like them have always made the decisions, and that's the way it is.'

'A secret government then?' I asked.

'I don't think it's anything that prosaic. They're just the doers for our society. Cabal is my word for them. I had to call them something to give them an identity, you know?' Gregor said. It had to be the alien's influence that was making this ex-squaddie who'd grown up on the streets of Stirling use words like prosaic.

'Do we know who any of them are?' I asked.

'Rolleston,' Gregor answered without hesitation. We nodded. 'He's the head of their security, handles all their dirty work. The others are somewhat distant. They communicate remotely or through intermediaries. Other than Rolleston, the only other one I've seen is a guy called Vincent Cronin. Must be in his late twenties or he looks it anyway, expensive suits, expensive ware, katana ...'

'Which corp?' Mudge asked. Anyone carrying a katana was normally an executive, a corporate samurai. A good executive had to prove himself in business and then duel for promotion. Rumour had it that for the top jobs the duels were to the death, blood on the conference-room floor. They only wanted people with the nerve to step up. If he was that young and carrying a katana, then he must not only be good, he would've had to have gambled big time and had it pay off.

'I don't think it's that simple; he doesn't appear to have a particular citizenship. He's some kind of high-level fixer, executive without a portfolio. Rolleston handles all the dirty work and Cronin does all the organisational stuff.'

'So we can assume this guy's best of breed?' Mudge said. Gregor nodded. It didn't look right, his head seemed to bob elastically.

'So they started the war?' I asked.

'I think so.'

'Why?'

'I don't know.'

'What did they want you for?' Mudge asked.

'For Their technology,' Gregor answered. 'I was a sample, then I was a test bed and finally I was a production facility.'

'Military applications?' I asked. Gregor shrugged. That didn't look right either. I wondered if he still had what we would recognise as a skeleton.

'I guess, but I think a lot of the Cabal is very old and very ill.'

'So they want to use Their liquid ... biological whatever to help rejuvenate and generally increase their lifespan?' Mudge said.

'Possibly,' Gregor said.

Something horrible occurred to me. 'Their operators – Rolleston, the Grey Lady and the like – will they be augmented by Themtech?' Gregor considered this.

'I don't know. It's a possibility. They look normal so if they are augmented they must be a lot more sophisticated than me.'

'No offence to your friend here, but he ain't telling us shit,' Balor said. It was the first time he'd really spoken. He'd spent most of his time staring at Gregor, who now swivelled his head round to look at the one-eyed pirate.

'I was kind of busy being experimented on,' Gregor said evenly.

'And you've admitted that they can programme you,' Buck said. I saw Gibby looking distinctly uncomfortable.

'Yeah, it's slightly less subtle than the way they control everyone else,' Gregor said. I sat more upright in my chair, somewhat surprised at this insight. I gave it some thought.

'I'm not fucking programmable,' Balor said.

Gregor looked Balor right in the eye. 'You used to serve,' he said. I guessed he just didn't understand the whole respect thing that Balor was supposed to command.

'Did I?' he asked. 'That didn't feel like what I was doing ...'

'Fine, but it was what the rest of us were doing,' I said. 'Except Mudge.'

'That doesn't mean he's not still controllable or under their control,' Balor said.

'He's not,' Morag said. 'We dealt with that.'

'Then who is in control, the alien or the man?' Gibby asked.

'Both,' Gregor said. 'And believe me I have more motivation than the rest of you to stay under my own control and deal with the Cabal.'

'Besides,' I added. 'If he was still working for them, where are they? They've got no good reason for leaving us free.'

'Deal with the Cabal?' Buck asked. 'How we supposed to deal with this Cabal if they're as powerful as you say?' It was a good point.

'I don't know,' Gregor said. 'But you will need to deal with them soon because they will want me back and they certainly can't let knowledge of my existence leak.'

'So let's leak it,' Mudge mused. Pagan looked over at him thoughtfully.

'We need to release God,' Morag said suddenly.

Pagan's thoughtful expression suddenly disappeared. 'It's not ready.'

Morag wore a look of irritation on her face that said this wasn't the first time they'd had this conversation. I took another mouthful of whisky from my tin mug. Mudge had produced a bottle of decent whisky. I think he'd stowed it to celebrate Gregor's liberation. I'm not sure how celebratory Mudge was feeling about it now. I was mildly drunk, which wasn't really helping the constant nausea but was giving it a sort of warm glow.

'It is ready but it might not be perfect,' Morag said. 'And you didn't see it.' I had been wondering about this but the right time to broach it just never seemed to come up.

'What happened to you in the facility's net?' I asked. All eyes turned to Morag, who shifted uncomfortably, not enjoying being the centre of attention suddenly, but there was something else. She was scared – not the general scared of doing dangerous things but real terror.

'She overreacted to a very nasty security program,' Pagan said.

'Oh bullshit!' Morag shouted at him.

Pagan sighed. 'Look, Morag. Nobody's saying that you haven't come far and fast in a little time. You're probably the most gifted hacker of your generation, but the fact is you've never been up against serious security with illegal black-attack programming. It cuts through your neural ware's own defences and goes straight for the biofeedback.'

'If she said she saw the devil then we should believe her,' Rannu said. I thought this was creepy somehow.

'You saw the devil?' I asked. I knew Morag had been eagerly awaiting her first net-bound religious vision. It seemed unfortunate that it had been the devil.

'When we entered the system they tried a purge, sent a firestorm program ahead of us. It was good but like any purge there's always something left. We were sifting through the wreckage trying to get what we could ...' Pagan said.

'What did you get?' I asked.

'We'll get to that,' he said. 'They'd left a particularly nasty security program in there to get us.'

'It was more than that; it was like God ...' Morag said.

'Only evil,' I suggested, smiling. Morag glared at me.

'It was frightening, there's no doubt about it,' Pagan said. 'It was sophisticated and dangerous.'

'But you dealt with it?' I asked. Pagan shook his head, his dreadlocks whipping from side to side.

'No, it went for Morag first—'

'Because it knew who the dangerous one was,' Rannu said. I don't think he was purposely trying to goad Pagan, but if he was he was doing a good job.

'So we ejected,' Pagan said, trying to ignore Rannu. I knew that they hadn't gone back into the facility's isolated net.

'So you can't be sure it was just a security program?' I asked.

'Look. Morag's never been hit that hard and has become used to thinking that she's invulnerable in the net. The thing rose out of the obsidian like some enormous bloody worm triggering just about every one of our conditioned fear triggers.' He sounded exasperated. At the mention of the worm Gregor's head had spun round to look at Pagan.

'When you said "bloody worm" did you mean the worm was covered in blood?' he asked. Pagan nodded. 'You know the project name?' Gregor asked.

'Project Blackworm,' Pagan said. 'But I don't see what that has to do with it.'

'Can you tell us what you found in there?' I asked.

'Broadly speaking it confirms Gregor's story,' said Pagan. 'The overall project is called Project Blackworm, which is presumably why the security looked the way it did. The project's designed to harvest Their biotechnology for a number of different applications.'

'Did it mention why they started the war?' I asked. Pagan shook his head.

'Did it mention the sub-projects?' Gregor asked.

'Yes,' Pagan said.

'Which are?' I probed.

'Project Crom and Project Demiurge,' Pagan said.

'It was Demiurge,' Morag said.

'Why would they leave Demiurge in a system they've purged and presumably abandoned?' Pagan demanded irritably.

'Then it was a fragment of Demiurge,' Morag insisted.

'Like you're a fragment of God?' Pagan said.

'Guys?' I interrupted.

'Demiurge is the software application of Themtech,' Pagan explained.

'So?' I asked.

'So it's as sophisticated as God and potentially as powerful, if not more so because they've got a lot more resources to throw at it.'

'So what happens if Demiurge gets out into the net?' I asked.

'Same as if God got out, only presumably less benevolent. I'm guessing it would mean Gregor's Cabal would control all information. The easy way, I mean,' said Pagan.

'How do we know they haven't already released it and are in control?' Mudge asked.

'They haven't. I'd know,' Morag assured him.

Pagan glanced irritably over at her. 'As far as we can tell they haven't perfected it yet.'

'Which is why we need to release God into the net as quickly as possible,' Morag said.

Mudge looked very uncomfortable at this suggestion.

'What's Project Crom?' I asked, forestalling what I suspected would be another argument.

'As far as I can tell, it's a viral weapon,' Pagan said.

'It's an application of the control bionanites they used on me,' Gregor answered.

'What application?' Mudge asked.

'Basically infect, replicate, control,' Gregor answered.

'What?' Mudge asked.

'Them.'

'All of Them?' I asked incredulously. Gregor and Pagan nodded.

'Are you talking about this Cabal taking total control of an entire alien race?' Mudge asked.

'Theoretically, yes,' Pagan said. I noticed that Buck had a look of extreme concentration on his face.

'I don't think that should happen,' the degenerate cyberbilly said. In many ways I was impressed with his grasp of the situation.

'Delivery?' I asked.

'Don't know,' Pagan said. Gregor just shook his head but he still hadn't quite mastered human body language.

'So how do we stop it?' Morag asked.

'We?' Buck asked. 'Why is this our problem?'

'You said you'd help,' I reminded him, but I had to admit it seemed that we were dealing with things beyond our capabilities. With the best will in the world I don't think we had either the skill set or the resources to deal with something like this. Besides, if they were looking hard enough they were going to find us sooner or later.

'We don't need to stop it, we just need someone more benevolent to control it,' Mudge said.

I looked over at him. Everyone was looking at him. I noticed Balor was smiling but Gregor, Pagan and Morag looked appalled.

'What?' Mudge demanded. 'They are a hostile species and want to destroy humanity. We can't wipe Them out so taking control of Them seems like a good idea to me – in terms of self-preservation, I mean.'

'We started the war,' I pointed out.

'So? I mean don't get me wrong. I wish we hadn't but we did, and now we have to deal with the results of that. If that means in order to survive we have to win, then this strikes me as the nicest way to do it. Regardless of who started this mess, They are a hostile race that wipes out humans wherever They find them. You do remember that, don't you?' he asked me.

'Don't patronise me, Mudge.'

'They're a sentient race in their own right,' Rannu said.

'Agreed, and I'm very sorry about it all. It's a sad fucking mess but if the choice is my species or Theirs then it's mine, and if we have any responsibility in this at all then it's to the human race,' Mudge said.

'I don't,' Gregor said. Everything went quiet. Gregor and Mudge were staring at each other. Mudge looked away first.

'I guess we're seeing your true colours,' Mudge said quietly, not looking at Gregor.

'I don't either,' Morag said. I turned my head sharply to stare at her. I think it was one of the most chilling things I'd ever heard.

Mudge pointed at her. 'You are a silly little girl. You think this is all cool and interesting, and I'm sure it's a big change from servicing the great and good in whatever Dundee shit hole you worked in—'

'Mudge,' I said warningly.

'—but what you're talking about is us being a Them fifth column. You see betraying your whole race as some fucked up post-pubescent game. They aren't cute, and they certainly aren't your fucking friends; what they are is dangerous and, and ...'

'Alien,' Gregor finished for him. 'And this one used to be your friend.'

To Morag's credit she seemed to master her anger. When she spoke it was evenly but through gritted teeth. 'You think this is a game for me? You think I'm not terrified to have this thing in my head? Do you think I like killing people?' She glanced at me. What was that? I wondered. Then I remembered my Slaughter high. Shit. 'But I feel this. I talk to it and I know,' she said simply.

'But surely you've been used before, darling?' Mudge said nastily. His face became mock-sympathetic. 'Never been told a lie, duped by someone you trusted? "Oh, but he seemed so nice and I thought I could trust him." And what happened next? He's getting paid and you're running a chain up against the toilet wall?'

'That's enough,' Rannu said.

Mudge was on his feet. 'No, it fucking isn't enough. I mean don't get me wrong. I can see the attraction here, but we keep on listening to this little girl because he worships her,' he spat, stabbing his finger at an increasingly angry-looking Rannu. 'And *he* wants to fuck her,' he said pointing at me.

'Mudge ...' I started, but Rannu was on his feet.

'Sit down,' Balor snapped.

Rannu paused and then glanced at Morag. She shook her head. What the fuck? Rannu sat down, though he was still glaring at Mudge.

'So,' Mudge began, 'who's for the humans and who's for the aliens?'

'That's fucking ridiculous, and you are bang out of line,' I said angrily.

'He's right,' Balor said. 'He has put me in a position I never thought I'd be in.'

'What's that?' Gibby asked.

'Being for the humans.'

'This is all hypothetical anyway; we don't have access to Crom.'

'Maybe not, but we need to know who's for humanity and who's against it. We may need to settle it here and now,' Balor said. Even Mudge looked shocked. Rannu shifted, so did Gregor.

'This can be settled with a conversation,' I said. Where had the impending violence suddenly come from? 'Right?'

'Look, Crom aside, the fact is we've just heard Morag say she's for Them and she wants to release what is effectively an alien virus into the net,' Balor said.

'How many times do we have to tell you we want peace?' Gregor said.

'See? *We?* He's one of Them,' Buck all but shouted.

'He's a lot nicer than the other ones we've met,' I pointed out as sarcastically as I could manage.

'I'm not sure I'm prepared to take that risk, and I'm not sure we can with humanity at stake,' Mudge said. I shook my head.

'The alternative is Demiurge,' Pagan pointed out.

'Which at least is controlled by humans,' Mudge said.

'Now whose side are you on?' Gregor demanded.

'You'd let Rolleston and these fucks get away with it?' I demanded.

'Not really liking the alternatives!' Mudge shouted back.

'Fine, so why don't you kill me and Gregor and then see if you can find Rolleston to suck his cock. Afterwards you can tell me how much of a whore I was!' Morag shouted at him.

'Because he can't,' I heard Gregor growl softly. Presumably meaning that Mudge couldn't kill him.

'I can,' Balor said menacingly.

'This isn't helping!' Pagan shouted with sufficient authority that the rest of us went quiet. 'Look, while you're all either slavishly obeying our high priestess or damning those who do, let's remember that God is not an alien virus; the program architecture is human, as is the majority of the programming. All it has is an operating system made from Ambassador. We have mapped and modelled the results of letting God into the net and, although given enough time I'd like to do more of that, I can tell you that it will not hand over humanity to Them. This is not Morag's brainchild. God was created by a group of very human hackers, the majority of whom are vets.' When he had finished we were still quiet, looking at him expectantly. 'Look,' he began again, more quietly. 'I am completely for the human side but I have no reservations about releasing God into the net—' he glanced over at Morag '—when it's ready.'

'Now,' she insisted.

'What exactly does it do?' I asked, trying to avoid yet another argument.

'Ah ...' Pagan said.

'You don't know!' Mudge said incredulously and then started laughing.

'We haven't decided yet,' Pagan said. I think all of us were looking at him in askance. 'Well what do we want God to do?' he asked.

'Typical hacker nerds,' Mudge muttered. 'Invent the system but can't think of what to do with it.'

'Are you just here to piss everyone off?' Morag demanded.

'No,' Mudge snapped. 'I'm trying to get some of you to think.'

'So what would you have God do?' Rannu asked. Mudge was silent.

'Will your god obey us?' Balor asked.

'If we want it to,' Pagan said.

'What do you mean "if"?' Mudge asked.

'That's a lot of power to wield,' Pagan said.

'So who else do we trust to wield it?' Mudge demanded.

'It could be autonomous,' Pagan said.

'So we give what is effectively an alien information form autonomy as well as omnipotence in the net?' Mudge asked.

'I am against that,' Balor said simply and forcefully.

'So back to my original question: who do you trust?' Pagan asked.

'Me,' Mudge said.

'Brilliant. We'll just hand total control of the net to an alcoholic junkie with no social skills,' Pagan suggested.

'I have social skills and you could do worse.'

'I wanna see Mudge's social skills,' Morag interjected, grinning.

'It's not Christmas,' I told her, also smiling. Some of the tension was beginning to bleed off.

'Few people are worthy of my social skills,' Mudge grumbled. 'So who's in control? You?' he asked Pagan.

Pagan shook his head, flailing his dreadlocks around. 'No, I don't trust myself, and I wouldn't trust the circle that made it. I wouldn't even trust Morag,' he said. I glanced over at Morag, who didn't even look slightly offended.

'Why not?' Gibby asked. 'You seem all right, a bit cracked but a nice enough guy,' he drawled.

'He helped make God; he probably helped come up with the idea in the first place. Clearly he's a fucking megalomaniac with a god complex,' Mudge said.

Pagan glanced at him irritably. 'I'm not sure that I completely agree with Mudge's diagnosis but that amount of power would certainly provide temptations that I don't think I could control,' he said.

'Like taking over the security lenses in the changing room for the Austin Firecrackers' cheerleaders,' Buck said. He was obviously thinking out loud. We all took a moment to look at him. He raised an eyebrow and nodded sagely.

'Yes, that would be the extent of my ambitions if I had that degree of power,' Pagan said.

'I'll do it,' said Balor.

Morag, Pagan and I all said no at once.

'I'm serious. I have experience of command, and humanity needs a strong leader,' he said. I think he was serious.

'Balor, that is not going to happen,' Pagan said.

Balor turned to fix him with his uncovered eye. Pagan didn't flinch. 'Only the strong should lead,' Balor said. 'Do you see anyone stronger?' I couldn't help glancing at Gregor, who was just watching the exchange, his head cocked at an odd angle.

'No,' Morag said.

Balor turned his fearsome head to look at her. 'Why is that, little girl?' he asked dangerously. I was really beginning to worry about Balor's attitude towards all this.

'I notice I'm just a whore or a little girl whenever the menfolk don't want to listen to what I have to say, but isn't the whole point of this to not have people like you in charge? Haven't we had enough of warriors being in command?'

'Arguably the problem is we haven't had enough warriors in command,' I said.

Morag looked confused.

'Because if we had warr— soldiers in command then they would be less likely to send people off to die needlessly because they would know what it was like,' Pagan explained. 'Though historically it hasn't always quite worked that way.' He turned to Balor. 'The problem is, you're a good leader, but you would always negotiate from a position of strength and your opinions on people living and dying are a little ... unorthodox.' Though to give Balor credit, at least he wasn't casual about it.

'Yeah, but he has a point,' Mudge said. 'Humanity needs strong leadership. I mean who here doesn't believe in an interventionist god?' I put my hand up. Nobody else did but Buck and Gibby at least looked confused. I was surprised I was the only one.

'Lot of believers in the room,' I muttered.

'Isn't this where God went wrong?' Mudge asked. 'He told us we had to have faith but didn't help us on the ground in the fight for survival where it would've mattered. We can do something about it: we can use the net to take over other systems like the orbitals, put us or God in control and show people the way ...' he said, petering out towards the end. Presumably he must've known how he was sounding.

'And the way is?' Pagan asked.

'Get rid of the Cabal, start delivering food and resources and medical care to the people who need it, stop tyranny, that kind of thing,' he said, though I don't think he was even convincing himself.

'I don't think you've thought this through,' Pagan said.

'Well, I wasn't expecting to have to set the parameters for a new god when I got up this afternoon,' Mudge snapped back.

'Surely we would become the new tyrants?' Gibby surprised me by pointing out.

Mudge considered this. 'Maybe so, but I'd rather have a benevolent fascist than a greedy one in control. We can't leave this down to people, we can't just show them the way. That's been tried by religions throughout history and people fucked it up and we ended up with the FHC.'

'We're only making God, not creating a new religion,' Pagan said, smiling.

'Really? Didn't you want to be high priest? Isn't that why you're so jealous of the high priestess over there?' Mudge asked. I saw Pagan's face darken. Morag was glancing between the two of them.

'Besides, if people fuck it up then isn't that an argument for making it autonomous,' Gregor said.

'You'd like that, wouldn't you?' Mudge said.

'Yes, I'd like to get out of this smelly cargo hull and get on with ruling the world, if that's all right with you,' Gregor replied sarcastically. If he was anything like the old Gregor then he must be pretty pissed off because he rarely used sarcasm.

'It's an argument for a strong leader,' Balor said.

'We should protect, not control,' Rannu said, meeting Balor's eye and holding it. After several moments of warrior bullshit Balor finally nodded. Mudge shook his head.

'Whatever. That doesn't change the fact that if you want something done you have to do it yourself. Not set some vague guidelines and hope that everyone interprets it right. I'm sorry, kids, but humanism and being nice isn't going to save the day. You want to stop the war, then control the weapons and be prepared to use them because his lot,' he said, nodding towards Gregor, 'might not be so quick to down tools as we've been led to believe.'

'Yeah, if we think like you then we'll want to take control of you first,' Gregor spat.

'I'm not convinced that's not what you're trying to do at the moment,' Mudge retorted.

'We've told you that's not what's happening,' Morag said.

'As far as we know, you've been co-opted by one of them. You've said you're on their side. How are we supposed to believe what you say?' Mudge asked.

'And me? Am I co-opted?' Pagan asked.

Mudge considered this. 'No,' he said finally, 'you're just a deluded old man.' For just a second I saw the stricken look on Pagan's face, then he was back to looking angry.

'I'm sick of being controlled,' I said.

'Which is great, but what are the options?' Mudge asked. 'Obviously humans trying to sort it out themselves doesn't work.'

'How is that obvious?' I asked. 'It's having people like the Cabal in control that doesn't work – well for us and apparently the majority of people. They would probably consider themselves strong leaders. I know Rolleston would.'

'So we have to be more benevolent than those arseholes, look out for everyone, not just ourselves,' Mudge said.

'Maybe that's how it would start. Look, we've abdicated responsibility to our leaders for too long; we need to take responsibility for ourselves,' I told him.

'Which sounds great but is meaningless in terms of implementing it,' Mudge said.

'We don't implement anything,' I said. 'We just tell the truth.'

'What do you have in mind?' Pagan asked, taking an interest.

'Starting with the war, we have God reveal every secret there is on the net. Programme it to reveal the objective truth to the best of its abilities. We then have it so it can arrange a system-wide and completely secure referendum—'

'Tyranny by majority,' Mudge pointed out.

'Got a better idea?' I asked.

'Take control, murder the Cabal, negotiate peace with Them and then try and make things fairer,' Mudge said.

'I think you're forgetting who you're talking to. If *you* take control of the net the first thing you'll do is have a crate of vodka and a crate of drugs delivered to you before continuing your quest for the perfect prostitute,' I pointed out.

'Shame your mum's dead,' Mudge said and grinned. I felt a surge of anger at his attempt at humour but let it pass.

'Do you really want to rule the world, Mudge?' Gregor asked gently. I saw Mudge falter.

'Well ... I thought, not me but ...' he said.

'Who then?' I asked. 'We're it, man. I ain't doing it, Pagan won't, you don't trust Gregor or Morag. Balor's a psychotic. No offence.'

'Offence taken,' Balor said quietly.

'Rannu?' I asked.

'I don't want to,' Rannu said.

'That leaves Buck and Gibby,' I replied.

'Hell yeah!' Buck said. 'I always knew I'd amount to something.'

'He's not serious,' Gibby said. Buck looked genuinely disappointed.

'Do you have any idea how dangerous telling people the truth about everything would be?' Balor asked quietly.

'He's right,' Pagan added. 'Lies are used for protective purposes as well as to deceive. This could – this will – cause chaos.'

'It will tear our society apart,' Balor said and then grinned. 'I'm warming to this plan.'

'I don't care,' I said and poured myself another drink. 'You're right about lies, but we need to grow up sometimes, and as for our society, what we have now's not good enough.'

'But—' Mudge began.

'We could argue about this from now until the Cabal finds us. If this works it will mean a huge change for everyone. We could never cover every argument and counter-argument. Either we act or we don't act,' Rannu said.

'But we haven't come to a decision,' Pagan said.

'We've got two ideas: either we use God to control the net or we programme God to tell everyone the truth about everything,' Morag said.

'And destroy society,' Mudge added.

'You value tyranny by majority so much, let's vote on it,' Balor said, his voice all but a whisper now.

Morag shrugged. 'All those in favour of ruling the net?' she asked.

Buck's hand shot up. After some consideration Gibby's went up as well, then Balor's. I watched Mudge struggle but he didn't put up his hand.

'All those in favour of telling the truth?' Morag asked. I put my hand up; so did Morag. Rannu predictably followed her. Gregor put his hand up as well. Pagan was still thinking. Mudge just shook his head. Finally Pagan put his hand up.

'So whatever happens, it wasn't your decision?' Pagan said to Mudge.

'Damn straight, just abrogating my responsibility again,' he said, staring at me.

'What about the Demiurge?' I asked Pagan.

'What about it? If they meet, I have no idea what will happen.'

'We could programme God to resist it?' Morag suggested.

'Should we?' Pagan asked.

'Yes,' I said. The others nodded.

'Do Rolleston and his people know about God?' Mudge asked.

'We've no reason to believe so, unless he had intelligence resources in New York,' Pagan answered.

Balor shook his head. 'Our discussion was clean, unless Rannu reported in before he changed sides,' he said.

'No, I always keep stories about my targets trying to create God out of my official reports. It makes me sound less insane,' Rannu said without a trace of humour.

'Besides, who'd believe it?' I asked. 'So as far as we know, the Cabal has no reason to rush Demiurge into the net?' Pagan and Gregor nodded. 'Will they respond with Demiurge?'

'That may be the only thing capable of destroying the net,' Morag said. 'It would be a very destructive fight and they would have little to gain.'

I could see that Pagan wasn't convinced but he didn't say anything.

'So how long to set God's parameters?' I asked.

'Three to maybe four hours' work,' Morag said. Pagan nodded in a resigned manner.

'Then what?' Mudge asked. 'You just release it into the net?'

Pagan considered this. 'That's one way of doing it, but it would take a while because of its size, and during the initial stages it would be potentially vulnerable. A node of some kind, a place capable of downloading huge amounts of information very quickly, would be ideal, but we'd have to do it at source.'

'Like a site?' I asked. Pagan shook his head.

'Like a media node?' Mudge asked.

'Perhaps,' Pagan said. Mudge grinned.

'Mudge?' I said. He looked over at me with a raised eyebrow. 'I don't want to kill anyone else.'

He nodded.

Morag was staring at me.

# 25
# Atlantis

Casually dressed and heavily armed, I had more drugs in me than in a Carrion's dispensary; just enough to keep me upright, make the pain tolerable and stop the nausea from overwhelming me. I leant against the transport cockpit's door frame. Gibby's hands moved across the keyboard, playing something almost bluesy, Buck accompanying him softly on the guitar.

Through the window I could see our lights play over the reinforced concrete of the Spoke as Gibby used the enormous structure to guide his ascent. Below us we could see the *Mountain Princess*, docked close to several similarly sized ore transports, becoming smaller and smaller.

Morag came and stood by me. Pagan was in the back taking care of Atlantis air traffic control. He and Morag had spent the last six hours setting God's parameters and getting the program ready to run. The rest of us had spent it sleeping and prepping kit in preparation for Mudge's half-arsed plan. I'd thrown up some blood as well. I wasn't sure how real any of this was at the moment – me dying, God, any of it. I think I was just functioning on nerves, a cocktail of drugs and good whisky. The good whisky was almost finished.

Morag was looking out. Light shone through windows in the Spoke and from its aircraft hazard lights, and searchlight beams stabbed high into the night sky. We passed the landing decks growing out from the tower like fungus. We passed balconies of rich revellers who waved at us, unaware that if even half of what Pagan and Morag had said was true then their world was going to be changed tonight. We manoeuvred past other transports, many of them much larger than ours. We passed copters, aircars and various other aircraft, though we kept well clear of shuttle air paths. We rose past factory levels, shopping levels, garishly lit entertainment levels and accommodation levels. We passed huge viz screens mostly showing adverts for things that nobody but Balor could have afforded, and if he wanted he would've stolen them anyway. On one of the screens there was footage from the war but you couldn't see the faces of the soldiers. That was good. I didn't want to see the suffering faces of people I could be about to betray. Morag took it all in with a near-fixed expression of wonder on her face. I split my time between looking out the window at the tower of light and looking at her.

The Spoke was suddenly obscured by cloud. I heard the engines of the transport change tone as Gibby and Buck pushed it back further from the Spoke until the aircraft hazard lights were just a glow in the distance. I knew the transport's sensors and their vehicle interface software would have created a three-dimensional topographical map of the Spoke which they were using to pilot. I heard a sigh from Morag. She turned to head back into the cargo bay.

'Wait,' I said. She stopped, turned, and I nodded out the window. When we rose out of the clouds, shaking off the last wispy tendrils of water vapour, Atlantis was a thin neon tower against the deep-blue backdrop of the night sky. It was reaching up as far as the eye could see towards space. Morag craned her neck to look up through the clear composite bubble of the cockpit. I was glad I saw this before I died. I was glad Morag saw this before she died. I wondered about the people who could afford to live here. Did they still appreciate this or was it all just commonplace to them? I hope they still appreciated it. It didn't bode well for their souls if they didn't feel awe at this feat of engineering and beauty.

There was less traffic up here, though more of it was security. These were the executive levels – various corporate enclaves, office and living spaces in the same areas. Higher up were the lift docks and more landing areas for the heavy commercial traffic. I heard the turbines whine again and Gibby and Buck's music change as the transport pushed back even further from the Spoke. Looking up I felt I was looking at the edge of space. Using my optics I could just about see where the building ended and there was only the cable structure leading to orbit, High Atlantis and the asteroid tether.

'See it?' Gibby asked Morag, and pointed upwards. She looked up. I couldn't make out what he was talking about.

'No,' she said, her face screwing up in concentration. Buck's tune changed, as did the display overlaid on the cockpit windscreen. It showed the same part of the Spoke but now much magnified. I could see the huge multi-storeyed elevator sliding down the cable at speed. It was lit up like a Christmas tree. I'd seen Christmas trees on vizzes.

'Looks like one of the luxury ones,' Buck said. 'High-velocity, five-star hotel.' Morag was just staring at it. I realised I was grinning. We watched as it sank into the Spoke's superstructure; even then we could see it moving within the massive building. I was feeling less cynical about this. We, humans, I meant, could build this, and John Coltrane could record *A Love Supreme*, and the Sixteen Men of Tain still made Glenmorangie. Those three things were proof that we deserved more than this constant, grinding war. I think that was when I started to hope a bit. So I was less than pleased when I turned round to see Mudge wearing only cowboy boots, boxer shorts and a string vest. He had a full bottle of vodka in one hand and his AK in the other. A joint hung out the side of his mouth. I could see both his precision-engineered, high-speed prosthetic legs.

'What've you come as?' I asked.

'Dude, this is what the revolution looks like,' he said, grinning.

I maybe should've seen something like this coming. 'You don't think you're going to lack credibility?' I asked, more politely than I felt.

'I need to feel comfortable, man,' he said.

I looked him up and down. 'And you feel comfortable like that?'

'I know you like what you see,' he said and winked at me. Morag burst out laughing.

'You're just trying to piss off Pagan, aren't you?' I said. Gregor seemed to rise up behind him. I was becoming more use to his skewed physiology. He was wearing a long coat but it didn't hang right. He had an ammo drum strapped to his back and was carrying a Retributor, apparently with ease.

'You look like a twat,' Gregor said to Mudge. Mudge looked over his shoulder, an eyebrow raised.

'The weird-looking alien's right,' I agreed. 'You realise if this is as big a deal as Pagan's making out you will be recorded for posterity looking like that.' Morag was still grinning.

'Trust me. When I've finished everyone will be dressing like this,' he said.

'I won't!' Morag burst out.

'You'd look good in a string vest,' I suggested.

'Your mum'll see you dressed like that,' Gregor pointed out.

'Mum'll love it, she'll be proud,' Mudge said.

'We're down in thirty seconds,' Gibby warned.

We were going to go in there, take over the broadcast node, download God and start broadcasting. It wouldn't take them long to take us down, but by then the damage would be done. I looked around at us all as the transport came into dock at some generic broadcast node. We were going to die doing something incredibly stupid. That appealed to me – my life had been incredibly stupid. I would rather have been a musician. Why couldn't I get *A Love Supreme* out of my head? This would be a good enough way to die. It was a shame Morag had to go, a shame that she didn't get a chance to experience more. I found myself grinning. Mudge was grinning as well.

'You realise if this works everyone has the potential to know every little secret out there? We could turn the world into a huge riot. Scores will be getting settled left, right and centre. This entire system could burn,' I said.

'Something has to change,' Mudge said seriously.

'Is this how?' I asked.

'How long should we keep second-guessing ourselves?' he asked. I felt the transport get blown sideways as Gibby fought the high cross-winds whipping round the Spoke. Finally the transport lurched and landed with a thump. I heard a clang as a walkway mated with the doorway of the transport.

'So we're not taking this seriously then?' Pagan asked, staring at Mudge, his face a mask of barely controlled fury. Gregor loomed over the hacker.

'You die your way, let him die his,' he said. I saw Mudge glance at the hybrid. Mudge's expression was unreadable.

I noticed there were tears in Morag's eyes. As Gregor and Mudge moved by me to the door I leant in close to her.

'You okay?' I asked her stupidly.

She smiled. 'Scared. So this is it?'

I didn't know what to say to her. How could I tell her that this might be best, that this was much better than the way her life would've turned out? Instead I decided to behave like a male, completely selfishly. I leant in and kissed her. At first she tensed. Not only was she still angry at me for being a prick, and rightly so, but I must've looked awful covered in angry red bleeding sores with a sickly looking, greyish skin tone. I was kind of surprised she didn't throw up. Then she reciprocated, one hand reaching up for me, the other pushed against my chest over my modified heart. It seemed to last a long time and was over very quickly. Surprisingly the others were good enough to remain quiet.

'I just didn't want to go not having—' I began. She held a finger over my lips, silencing me.

Gibby and Buck pushed past me out of the cockpit. Gibby had a bullpup Kalashnikov slung over his back and was carrying a long, thin armoured case. He had unconnected wires hanging out of his plugs. Buck was carrying a semi-automatic/pump-action shotgun in one hand and a case not dissimilar to Gibby's in the other.

Pagan glanced up at the pair of them from the transport's lock mechanism. He was trying to override the media node's security. 'Why are you bringing your instruments?'

'They're the band, man,' Mudge said. 'This is show business.'

Pagan looked like he was about to argue but instead turned back to the dock.

'This is just a huge ego trip for you, isn't it?' I asked Mudge.

'I'm shitting myself,' he said, still grinning, took another swig from his vodka and lit his spliff. The door to the node opened and suddenly it was all business.

Rannu, Balor and Gregor were first through, weapons at the ready, sweeping left and right, checking corners as they entered. I heard the first scream of surprise. Gibby and Buck followed. They dropped their instrument cases to the side of the node's entrance, their weapons came up and they were all pro. Morag and Pagan followed, Morag carrying the cube. Mudge lifted his AK-47 to port and the pair of us sauntered through. Despite the drugs I was finding my enthusiasm for paramilitary nonsense fading.

I'm not sure what I was expecting from a broadcast studio, maybe lavish sets or banks of high-tech equipment, people everywhere, that sort of thing. I was pretty disappointed. I don't know what this node was called but they specialised in 'reality' soap opera porn. It was a lot more cost-effective to use computer-generated sets and actors, but apparently some people claimed they could tell the difference, and for those who could afford to subscribe to real flesh there were set-ups like this. That didn't stop them from computer-generating things like costumes and sets, and I would guess digitally enhancing some of the actors' attributes.

Basically it was a plain white set with various representational bits of furniture that the actors could react to and use, detail to be added in post-production. There were three actors on the set, two men and a woman, all of them generically attractive in a really dull way. All had white, skintight overalls that covered everything but their faces so their costumes could be added at a later date. There was one other person on the set. She had camera eyes like Mudge's and a transmitter in one of her sockets, presumably linking her to a media board. Around the set several miniature camera systems floated silently, catching the actors from every conceivable angle. They were similar to the ones Mudge had used to shoot the fight I'd had with Rannu in New York, but they were much smaller and more sophisticated.

A catwalk surrounded the studio area, and directly opposite us was a glass booth with two men in it, one of whom was unmistakeably some kind of security guard. Beyond I could see a passage leading, presumably, to reception and to the exit out onto this level of the Spoke. I headed for that, strolling calmly, lighting a cigarette. Balor was terrifying the actors by screaming at them to lie on the floor.

'Calm down,' I told him. 'Just sit over there and be quiet,' I ordered the actors, pointing at a featureless, modular white sofa. They nodded, one of the men blinking back tears.

Rannu had his Metal Storm gauss carbine out in front of him, the butt tight in against his shoulder as he made his way smoothly up the metal stairs to the catwalk. I headed into the passageway leading to the reception and the entrance of the node. The walls of the corridor were painted turquoise and decorated with some suitably hip logo that looked like a high-tech, fast-moving chicken to me. I guessed it was supposed to be cooler than that, or maybe chickens were in. Behind me I could hear Morag shouting at someone to put their gun down.

'Remember we're not going to kill anyone,' I said over the tac net. I received something akin to white noise back from Balor. I strolled round the corner into the reception area, my shotgun still slung across my back, and walked into a badly controlled burst of fire from a PDW. I staggered a little, my armoured coat and subcutaneous armour stopping the small-calibre rounds.

'Ow, fuck!' I shouted intelligently and then staggered back around the corner, all pissed off, but not before I caught a glimpse of what I assumed was a rather militant receptionist. He was crouching for cover behind a large and groovy-looking desk. I heard something behind me and glanced round to see the misshapen, off-centre figure of Gregor lope over to my position, his Retributor at the ready.

'I think the railgun may be overkill here,' I told him. 'Hey!' I said, shouting to the receptionist. 'We don't want to hurt you. Just leave, okay?'

'How do I know you won't shoot me if I try to leave?' he demanded.

'We haven't shot you yet!' I pointed out. 'We do have desk-piercing rounds in our weapons!' Gregor laughed. There was another burst of gunfire.

'You're next to the fucking door; just run away!' I shouted, and was answered with another burst of gunfire. What was this guy's problem? Gregor made to move round me, railgun at the ready.

'Don't kill him,' I hissed at Gregor. He went round the corner and there was another burst of gunfire. Judging by the ricochets some of it hit Gregor. I think he had plates beneath his skin that hardened when they were hit with sufficient kinetic force. It was disconcerting to watch. Gregor returned.

'Did you miss being shot?' I asked. Gregor just looked at me in a manner I guessed was supposed to be rueful. It was difficult to tell with his warped facial features.

'You!' I shouted to the armed receptionist. 'What the fuck are you doing? He's obviously a big weird-looking thing with a railgun and you shot him? What were you thinking? Put the gun down now or you'll get shot so much you'll cease to exist!' Gregor gave me a funny look. 'What? Civilians respond to threats like that.'

There was no answer but eventually I heard the sound of running footsteps.

'See? Look round the corner. Maybe you'll get shot again,' I suggested. Gregor pushed me round the corner. Despite all the metal and plastic I was carrying internally, his enormous strength moved me with little effort.

'Hey! That's not funny, man.' But the receptionist had gone. In front of the desk was a large glass wall that looked out onto a wide plaza lined with various trendy-looking offices. There were a few suits looking our way. Behind me from the main studio I could hear more shouting.

'Watch the door,' I told Gregor. He nodded. I wandered back into the main studio area. I found Balor had the actors, the camera-eyed woman, two security guards and a young guy I assumed had been working the media deck up in the gallery all lying face down on the floor. He was covering them with his Spectre/grenade launcher combo. I sighed.

'I thought I said they could sit down?' I said to him.

'What are we going to do with them? We could strap them to possible breach points,' he said.

I looked up at the demonic features of the huge amphibian cyborg. 'We could,' I mused. 'Or we could let them go because they'll be a noisy pain in the arse and it's not what we do.'

Balor looked at me in disgust. 'They won't make any noise if we cut their tongues out,' he said. At this, several of them started screaming and crying. I just looked at Balor.

I leant down to the actress, who seemed to be holding it together best. She looked vaguely familiar to me, but whether that was because I'd seen her on the viz or she'd surgically altered herself to look like the flavour of the month I didn't know.

'We're going to let you go,' I said as reassuringly as I could. I guessed as I was covered in angry bleeding sores and looked like a walking corpse it probably wasn't all that reassuring. She nodded nonetheless. 'Now security, the police and possibly the military are going to talk to you, okay?' I said. She nodded again. 'I want you to tell them that everyone in here is ex-special forces and that we are ready for a breach, but if they leave us be we'll turn ourselves over once we're finished, okay?' I said. She nodded.

'Okay. All of you, up and out,' I told them. A few of them had to be coaxed but eventually they all left. They stared at Gregor as they moved past him.

In the studio Morag and Pagan were both tranced into the net. I had net feed but hadn't brought the window up yet. Gibby and Buck were setting up their instruments, Buck his guitar, Gibby his keyboard, but they were also plugging themselves into other bits and pieces. They would have a drum machine, bass machine, mixing deck and a transmitter to link to the media deck, I guessed. Mudge had nicked the camera-eyed woman's remote media deck connection and was concentrating. Rannu appeared through a door near the gallery on the catwalk above.

'What have we got?' I asked.

'What you see and two other areas. One is rec and changing, the other is admin, storage and what looks like a design room – all clear,' Rannu answered. I thought he sounded almost bored.

'Make the other areas safe,' I told Rannu. The ex-Ghurkha nodded. They were never going to be safe but at least we could prepare as much as possible for the inevitable breach. I headed back to the reception area.

I found Gregor looking amused and peering out the window. He was sat on the reception desk.

'What?' I asked.

'A couple of corporate rent-a-cops just came round the corner, took one look at me and scrambled on all fours back out of view,' he said.

'You're getting high on power, man,' I said, smiling, and triggered the security door, which began sliding down. 'You send out the crawlers?' I asked. Gregor nodded and texted me the link to the small robot cameras he'd set loose outside the facility. It looked like one of them was shooting from inside a landscaped part of the mall. Around the corner from the node facility I could see the two cowering rent-a-cops. They had guns in their hands and looked like they were sub-vocalising frantically. I laughed; maybe the cops thought They had invaded. Gregor began putting motion and sound detectors up against the door and exterior walls while I redirected the external and interior security camera feeds to my internal visual display and ensured they were disconnected from the net.

A blinking icon on the reception console told me that someone was trying to contact the node. I opened the link. The face that appeared on the screen was overweight, nervous, sweating heavily and so obviously an overpaid hostage negotiation consultant it was difficult to look at him. He'd probably never had to handle a situation this serious before. He opened his mouth to talk.

'I'll only speak to the commander of the HRT or SWAT team you're sending in here. If I haven't heard from them in five minutes I'll kill a hostage,' I lied and then killed the link. Gregor looked over at me. I shrugged. 'He looked like an arsehole.' From the external cameras and the concealed crawlers I could see the local security establishing a perimeter.

'You got it here?' I said, diverting the reception comms to my own.

Gregor nodded.

'And don't kill anyone. If we're not done then we buy enough time for Morag and Pagan to finish, but once they're in, it's over,' I said and turned, heading back to the studio.

'What about Rolleston?' he asked. I couldn't read his warped features. I gave this some thought.

'Well, there's an exception to every rule.' My voice sounded hard even to my own ears.

'I'm not going to be captured again,' Gregor said to my back. I stopped. I hadn't considered this. I was dying so I guess I hadn't really thought about what was going to happen to the others when they were inevitably handed over to Rolleston and his cronies. That was assuming things hadn't changed that much by then. I looked over my shoulder at the freakish mess they'd made of my friend. I realised then that he didn't belong anywhere. Nobody would accept what he was. Maybe Them, if we did manage to make peace, but after the war he would never be able to accept Them. I wondered how much he hated himself.

'I'll take care of it,' I heard myself saying.

Back in the studio I realised that we didn't have nearly enough guns. Not if Buck and Gibby were going to be fucking around playing music and Mudge was going to be weirdly exercising his ego, but I guessed it didn't really matter. The absurdity of the situation made me smile.

Rannu appeared on the catwalk above us and gave me the thumbs up. The first floor was as ready for a breach as we were going to get. Already a couple of the motion detectors had gone off. This was presumably a SWAT team drilling through the walls and pushing monofilament cameras and smart AV bugs through.

'They won't be able to breach the external Spoke wall but they will try and come through the transport and the docking arm, probably with armour, so we've left a few surprises in the transport. Balor, I want you covering the docking arm.' If they were going to send exo-armour in here after us, and they would, I was sure that Balor could and would want to go toe to toe with it. 'Rannu, I want you up on the catwalk. Conceal yourself as best you can and make sure you've got line of sight on both the doors and the gallery. If necessary you will provide fire support for Balor and me down on the floor,' I said over the tac net. Rannu nodded. 'Gregor, I want you pulled back to the studio but looking out covering the reception area. They will definitely breach that security door. It's the weakest point.'

'Why don't I just stay out here?' Gregor came back.

'Because you may as well see as much of the fun as we get a chance to have,' I answered. Moments later I saw Gregor move back into the studio and kneel down by the entrance to the reception area, the massive Retributor at the ready.

I could see a comms icon flashing on my internal visual display. It was the re-routed comms line from the reception desk. I opened it up and routed it over the tac net to Gregor, Rannu and Balor. The comms icon I saw was of a hard-faced black woman. She was dressed in the lightweight hard armour and inertial undersuit common to SWAT and Cyber SWAT units. Her eyes were black polarised lenses, her hair shorn down to stubble. I reckoned she was short and stocky like many special forces operators.

'I don't have time for this. You don't have any hostages so we're going to come in there and get you out,' she said in an American accent. I considered asking her where she'd been, but for a job this prestigious I figured her for ex-Delta. She reminded me of Ash.

'I'm in love,' Balor muttered.

'And you are?' I enquired politely. She seemed to consider this. My feed from one of the crawlers showed her some way back surrounded by a group of similarly armoured figures. They had an armoured ram tank specially designed for use in the Spoke. Behind that I could see African-made, Praetorian powered-armour suits. I could also see Praetorians and a number of police gunships hovering around in the air outside the node.

'Watch Commander Cat Sommerjay,' she said. 'Now stop fucking around, Sergeant Douglas. If you don't come out now then all you'll get is dead, you know that.' So she knew who I was.

'Getting a lot of pressure to breach?' I asked. 'People want you to come in before you're ready?' She hesitated. That was good, that meant she cared about her people.

'Sergeant—' she began.

'Just call me Jakob,' I said.

'You smooth bastard,' Gregor said. I glared at him. I seemed to have pissed off Cat – as I found myself thinking of her.

'Look, arsehole,' she snarled. 'I'm not the fucking negotiator. You want to make friends, you shouldn't have hung up on him. Either you come out or we come in, your choice.'

'I'm definitely in love,' Balor confirmed. 'Let's surrender.'

'Look, Cat,' I said. 'We haven't killed anyone, we're contained and we will only fight to protect ourselves. We need a little time and then I promise you we'll surrender,' I said, trying not to think about my promise to Gregor. Cat opened her mouth to reply but stopped, looking irritable.

'Wait a second,' she said, and her comms icon froze on hold.

'What was that?' Balor asked.

'At a guess, a priority comms override from the Cabal,' Gregor said.

'They want her to breach,' I said, glancing over at Pagan and Morag and wishing they would hurry up.

'Good. I want to meet this woman,' Balor said.

'Won't your shark be jealous?' I asked.

'Magantu is very understanding,' Balor said seriously.

'And would have trouble swimming this high,' Gregor said. We really weren't taking our imminent deaths seriously enough.

'The good news is she doesn't strike me as the sort of person Rolleston can push around,' I said as Cat's icon came back to life. She didn't look happy.

'You need to come out now,' she said.

'The people who're pushing you to breach are going to get a lot of your people killed before you get us. You know that and there's no need for it,' I said.

'Yeah, I know that, but I've been given some very compelling reasons to come in and get you,' she said. As a commander, and she struck me as an ex-NCO not an officer, I could tell she didn't want to come in here. I wondered what she'd been told. Had she been told that we had an alien virus and an alien? Had she been told that we were in league with Them? 'Is it true that Balor is in there with you?' she asked.

I saw Morag and then Pagan come out of their trances, blinking and looking around. Buck and Gibby began to play. It was a slow and faintly sinister piece.

'Yeah,' I told her. 'He's our hostage.' My comms icon presumably transmitted the smile on my face. Well, I was smiling until I saw Balor glaring at me.

'Look, you know they'll never let you broadcast, yeah?' she said. I looked over at Morag, who gave me the thumbs up.

'Too late,' I told Cat. 'You'll want to see this.'

I switched on my net feed.

# 26
# Atlantis

What did it look like? Everyone in known space must've seen it by now. If they didn't see it when it happened, and you pretty much had to be in a coma to miss it, then they would have seen vizzes. What the vizzes couldn't capture was that it looked different to all of us. The software that translated its net-born image to our minds translated it differently for each of the millions of people seeing or experiencing it. In other words it was personal for all of us.

The feed that Morag sent me seemed to be from outside the net construct of the Spoke. The virtual representation of the Spoke looked like a tall fairy-tale tower made from partially solidified water, the whole thing flowing like a waterfall. The studio looked like a pre-fall art deco cinema made from neon liquid. The liquid motif was shared with many of the businesses in the virtual Spoke. Its outgoing broadcasts were represented by fast-moving neon streams of the same liquid. Pagan hung in mid-air, level with the broadcast node. He was surrounded by what looked like air disturbances, his hair blowing in an invisible wind. He held his staff over his head; his eyes rolled back and the lightning of aggressive information exchange played around the staff. He shouted and babbled in some ancient pagan glossolalia as he cast his programs preparing the way for God.

We watched as Black Annis walked through Pagan's storm. The Spoke's defence programs, manifesting themselves as water spirits, were buffeted out of the way by the storm or raked by Annis until they became puddles. High above Pagan and Annis I could see the Spoke's hired guns descending clothed in various water-borne mythological icons. I watched as they were blown and buffeted by Pagan's storm, their own attacks swept aside by the defensive software in the storm.

The cinema's walls of water parted for Annis. She was holding what looked to me like an old-fashioned jack-in-the-box. I could see her blue-skinned clawed hands winding it up as she strode into the lobby of the cinema construct and laid the box down on the consensual floor.

Pagan finished his incantation and let out a primal-sounding scream. He slammed his staff down; it seemed to rupture the very air in an explosion of lightning, illuminating the invisible air spirits of the Spoke's more subtle defence programs, sending them tumbling down. From the base of Pagan's staff a rupture of lightning coursed through the air towards the cinema into the tower of water. Annis bathed in the pale light of neon and lightning and stepped back from the jack-in-the-box as Pagan's lightning, the activation code, reached it.

I watched the jack-in-the-box bulge and crack. I saw impossibly bright light beneath the cracks and rents in the bulging box. And here's the thing that doesn't make sense to me. I wasn't in the net; I was just watching, but I somehow felt it. Just like everyone else. Or maybe it was just everyone else I was feeling, because at some level or another we are connected to the communications infrastructure of our race. I saw the jack-in-the-box finally rupture and burst. It was like the amorphous mass of tentacles and pseudopods that I'd seen in my dream of the initial attack on Them. Except these weren't black, they were formed of bright white light and all colours and were beautiful. The tentacles shot out everywhere, faster and more numerous than my mind could understand, in every possible direction and some directions I suspected weren't possible.

I could hear Morag and Pagan laughing and then Pagan was crying. I wasn't sure if it was in the net or in here with me. They were sending me more feeds from the net, vizzes from all over the information shadow-world. I saw images of God surging down every highway, road, street, alleyway, passage and into every site and net construct. I saw the shocked expressions on some of the better-rendered icons. Shock turned to either panic or awe. I guess it depended on how they wanted to look at God. I watched the informational reflection of our world light brightly up.

Then came the response. Every kind of probe, analytical program, communications program and of course the inevitable attack programs. From lone panicking icons to concerted government and corporate attacks. It was natural, I guess. After all, these people had a lot to lose and they had just had the depths of their systems violated. Now every secret they had was common knowledge. It still looked somehow petty and vicious to me. Like insects stinging a mountain. It was only then I wondered if business as we knew it could continue, or government or society. I guess the attack programs were used in self-defence, but somehow they looked ignorant and brutish. I was beginning to think I'd spent too much time around Pagan and I was becoming a believer.

And then Mudge's grinning, drunk, high features appeared on every visual display screen, from monocle heads-up displays to giant hologramatic displays projected into the sky. From apartment viz screens to the huge screens on the side of advertising zeppelins. His image would be glowing out of the screens attached to the side of Big Neon Voodoo's trucks. Somehow I knew that Papa Neon was dancing on the top of one of his lorries. Mudge was made a giant on the side of all the Spokes, his features looking out over savanna, ocean, jungle and mountains. From slum bedsits to upscale Ginzas, from corporate office walls to the fortress mansions of the super rich, from inside classrooms to inside governments. It was reaching the orbitals now and soon the Moon, then Mars, then the Belt and ever outward. Beggar, criminal, soldier, labourer, wage slave, corporate, officer, executive, minister, presidents: all of them were seeing Mudge's grinning face. He was the harbinger of God, or even the other way around. I started laughing but it quickly turned into a hacking bloody cough.

In my mind's eye I could see the ranger and his girlfriend in their flat just off the Ferry Road. McShit and his Twists watching this on the Rigs. The refugees from the Avenues, the quiet family that ran Fosterton, Rivid in his sled somewhere, crowds of silent pirates in Times Square, Crawling Town becoming motionless except for Papa Neon's dance, and everyone in this Spoke from High Atlantis in orbit to the Mag Lev stations deep in the crust of our world.

I felt something against me and looked down to see Morag hugging me fiercely, laughing, tears in her eyes. I was laughing as well, though my plastic eyes were unable to cry. I held her tightly.

'Welcome to the first day of the rest of your revolution!' Mudge screamed at the whole system. I found this even funnier. Gibby and Buck's music reached a crescendo, washing over me before they cranked it down again. Rannu was smiling serenely. Pagan was hugging Balor, who looked triumphant. Gregor leant against the wall, looking tired and relieved.

We'd done it. Now we had to see just what we had done exactly. Mudge was striding around the studio like the revolutionary degenerate I was suddenly aware he was born to play.

'Bring up the Cabal,' he said. On screens across the world, and in orbit milliseconds later, small split-screen windows appeared, showing a variety of ancient white guys being kept alive by machinery in various secured locations around the world and in orbit. I began checking through the windows. Where was he?

One of the studio walls had become a viz screen. I shut down my internal one and concentrated on that. I could still see the astonished-looking comms icon of Cat Sommerjay.

'Morag, the SWAT commander outside this studio will be getting screamed at by someone to breach and kill us. Can you tap into that?' I asked.

Morag looked up at me and smiled. 'You don't get it do you?'

In the background I could hear Mudge explaining the Cabal to humanity and how they started the war. Text files scrolled down the screen, audio files were played and then viz footage was shown of the attack on Them. Mudge was making it clear that all the evidence was there for review by everyone.

'Nothing is secret; there is no cryptography. You want to hear it, ask God,' Morag continued.

No privacy, I suddenly thought. What had we done? I opened the tac net. 'God?' I said uncertainly.

'Yes Jakob?' A thousand soothing mellifluous but alien voices asked me quietly. It sent a shiver down my spine.

'Watch Commander Cat Sommerjay will be receiving orders regarding us. I'd like to hear them if I may.'

'Certainly,' God said. Mudge was still passionately explaining the intricacies of the conspiracy.

'Breach! Breach now! That is a direct order! I want every one of them dead seconds from now,' Rolleston screamed at Cat. I'd never heard him sound so angry.

'Hello, Major,' I said, smiling. I also sent the feed to Mudge and requested God for a visual on Major Rolleston. There was a moment's silence from Rolleston. His icon didn't register shock, I wonder if he had when he saw my face.

'Oh, well done, Sergeant. You've really done it this time, haven't you?' he said, and I found myself hearing it in stereo. I looked up to see that we had appeared on the big screen; our conversation was now being broadcast to the entire system. I wasn't overly happy about this. Suddenly I felt very self-conscious and a lot more nervous than I would have had I been just walking into a firefight.

The picture of Rolleston was not his comms image but rather security lens footage of him and the Grey Lady strapping armour on. They were in the hold of what looked like a military assault shuttle. I sent a request to God asking them where they were. The reply was pretty much instantaneous. Rolleston and the Grey Lady were on an assault shuttle, part of HMS *Vindictive*'s complement. They were skimming across the Atlantic from a ship intercept. They'd been out looking for us. We'd always known that they'd be looking for us, but the imminence of their ETA, now it was a cold hard fact, turned my blood cold.

'Congratulations on compromising every military operation currently running. I wonder how many people you've murdered today?' he asked. I saw Rannu look over at me. Another ramification I hadn't considered. I'd just burnt every deep-cover operative in-system. 'Not to mention opening up our entire defence system to Them. But I'm assuming that's your intention,' he continued before addressing Sommerjay. 'Watch Commander, I believe you have been given an order. Let's see what we can do to contain this situation before the entire human race has to pay the price.'

'Sir, I'm afraid in all conscience I cannot follow that order,' Cat replied. She also appeared on the screen, and like me she looked very self-conscious.

'What has your conscience got to do with it? You will obey an order given to you by your chain of command.'

'With all due respect, I am not a lawyer, but if what I'm seeing is true then it would seem that my chain of command is compromised and somebody is going to have to answer for crimes against humanity,' she said.

'Yes, and they are in that node,' he said, sounding irritated. In some ways I was impressed by the way he could continue this discussion while getting kitted up. I saw him strapping on the various different weapons that he would be using against us in the near future. I thought about going over our response plan again but they all knew the score. Besides our comms were compromised just like everyone else's now.

'I'm afraid we will have to wait and see what happens when the dust settles,' Cat replied.

'The dust settling, as you put it, may be the destruction of our race. They have one of Them in there and they have released a Them virus that has taken control of the net. How much damage are you going to let them do?'

'God?' Mudge asked. 'Have you taken control of the net?'

God's mellifluous multiple tones seemed to float from every device capable of producing sound. 'No, Howard, I have not; the capability of the net is still total. All I have done is make access available to every single piece of information there is.'

'Are Earth's defences still in place and under the control of humanity?' Mudge asked.

'They are indeed,' God answered.

'Excellent,' said Rolleston and then went quiet.

'I think you should be aware that Major Rolleston has just sent a heavily encrypted message to the Kenyan Orbital Weapons Platform, JuuJuu Nyota, ordering them to fire a particle-beam weapon at your position,' God said, a little too calmly for my taste. 'He has the authority to do so,' he added.

'Well fucking stop him then!' Mudge shouted.

'I am sorry, Howard, but due to the parameters of my programming I cannot interfere with human actions beyond making all information available,' God said.

Mudge turned on Pagan. 'See? I fucking told you! Who doesn't believe in an interventionist God now, you cunt!' he demanded before turning back to the screen.

'Humanity must have free will,' Pagan said somewhat weakly.

'Do you not think that being destroyed by a particle-beam weapon will impinge on my fucking free will? Not to mention all the people living in this Spoke! Besides,' he pointed at Rolleston's image, 'that prick isn't fucking human!'

'Mudge! There are children watching,' Balor admonished.

Despite the fact I was about to die I took a moment to stop and stare at Balor. Mudge's face had gone red and veins were popping out on his forehead. I looked over at Pagan and Morag. Morag was already tranced in but Pagan was shaking his head.

'We don't have enough time,' he said. I knew that comms messages from Atlantis to JuuJuu Nyota and Kenya would be shooting backwards and forwards in the net, including threats of reprisal from the Atlantean authorities.

'This is Air Marshal Kaaria of the Kenyan Orbital Command. Major Rolleston's order has been countermanded. We will not, repeat not, be firing upon Atlantis, nor does Kenya in any way pose a threat to the Atlantis Spoke, its interests or its people.' I looked up at the screen to see a solid-looking African in his early sixties looking out of the viz screen at us. The screen split to show Rolleston.

'Air Marshal Kaaria, you do not have the authority to countermand that order. Begin firing now,' Rolleston said. Kaaria's image turned somewhat, presumably to face the screen that was showing him Rolleston. Rolleston was messing with the hilt of a skull fucker, a vicious old commando dagger designed to penetrate the skull. Despite its age, wielded with enough power it could still make a mess of even a military-grade cyborg.

'Leaving aside the fact that I will not be ordered around by a mere Major—'

'My rank is not indicative of my authority—' Rolleston began.

'I will not be interrupted! Major, do you think I am insane? Do you think that Kenya wants to be responsible for starting another full-scale, inter-human conflict? Do you not think that we haven't seen the footage of what happened to the Brazilian Spoke and what happened to America afterwards? In short, do you think we're out of our minds?' Rolleston didn't answer. Mudge and the others looked relieved.

'Look,' I said, and was less than pleased to see my face fill the screen. 'You want us, we'll surrender peacefully. There's no need to kill tens of thousands of people. Nobody wants that and we've already done what we need to.'

Gregor was glaring at me.

I headed over to him. 'It's all right, we'll get you out of here,' I said.

'How?' he asked, unconvinced.

'Okay, we're probably all going to die. Feel better?'

'A little.' I saw that Watch Commander Sommerjay's comms icon was flashing. I opened the channel.

'I'm a little busy, Cat,' I said as pleasantly as I could. She didn't bother with pleasantries.

'Surrender to us.' I gave this some thought. In many ways it was a seductive idea.

'Under normal circumstances—' all the other times I take over part of a Spoke and release an artificial god into the net '—I would, but you'd still have to hand us over to Rolleston. Not going to happen. We know him too well.' Cat seemed to give this some thought.

'You want help?' she asked. Bang, that was her career over. I wondered how many other people were going to get hurt before this finished. Yes, I did want help but I knew she couldn't give it.

'You know they're probably listening?' She didn't say anything. 'Look, thanks, but we'd just get in each other's way, right?' She nodded. 'The best thing you could do is stay out of it.' Behind me Rolleston and Mudge were still arguing on the viz.

'I'm standing my people down. Good luck, Sergeant,' Cat said. Hopefully none of her people would get hurt. Briefly I hoped that Rolleston and the Grey Lady wouldn't try a two-person breach. After all we had Gregor and Balor in here; Rannu was capable as well. But I knew they would.

'Mr Mudgie, you have just released a Them virus into the net, why on Earth should anyone believe what you say?' Rolleston was asking as I returned my attention to the show.

'God, are you a Them virus?' Mudge asked.

'No, Howard, I am not. My programming is almost entirely human, as are the parameters that have been set within which I can act. The operating system I use is based round technology derived from Them but that was purely in terms of information management.'

'So by your admission you are part Them,' Rolleston said.

'You are choosing to focus on that part of my creation in an attempt to force a fallacious point, I believe,' God said.

'Everything about God is transparent,' Pagan began, speaking with the sort of exasperation the technically skilled have for those who are less gifted. 'We would encourage people to check our proof that God is not—'

'This "proof" comes from one source, the source that has the most to gain from us believing it. It's hardly objective,' Rolleston interrupted.

'I was designed to be objective,' God countered.

'So you say, and even if you are, you were still designed to be objective by subjective people,' Rolleston said.

'This argument could just go in circles,' Mudge said, sounding bored.

'Fine,' Rolleston said with a degree of satisfaction. 'I'm no signalman but as far as I know we do not have AI.'

'Nor do They. What you think is AI is actual sentience. I am the sum of your culture: I have learnt and developed as human sentience did, albeit much faster.'

'So you have no trace of your Them origins?' Rolleston demanded. He was still readying gear on the assault shuttle, working quickly but without hurry. Bran was a study in the economy of movement.

'Yes, I have maintained enough of Ambassador to behave in total cooperation with all my constituent parts and to reject duplicity as an alien concept. There is only one, that is I, and so I cannot lie.'

'I see, so the Them part of you is the good part?' Rolleston said.

'That is your value judgement of what I said,' God answered. 'My constituent parts, the ones that I believe you would consider to be more important, are more human than not.'

'So you say, and while a lack of duplicity is admirable in those who can afford it, what about what your people have done to the colonies? Murdered non-combatants, including children, mutilated them. Is it not true that you have exterminated humanity wherever you have found it?' Rolleston asked, as he finished attaching a man-portable plasma weapon to his subsonic Spectre gauss carbine, creating an over/under combination weapon.

'Of course They hit non-combatants,' Gregor said, and suddenly his warped alien features were up on the screen. It occurred to me that this might not do us any good.

'Yes, you would have insights, wouldn't you, Mr MacDonald, being as you are part alien?' Rolleston said sarcastically. 'So please explain how They are actually little, misunderstood kitten-like creatures, and the sixty years of Them murdering humanity wherever They found them, men women and children, didn't actually happen.'

'They never knew war before the Cabal—'

'There is no such thing as the Cabal!' Rolleston said, angry again.

'Before your people,' Gregor continued, 'ordered their habitation attacked. Their sense of self is different: each cell is an individual that forms their whole so for them it was genocide. Because they had no understanding of what was happening the only response they knew was the one we had taught them, all-out attack. How were they to know that we put arbitrary rules on conflict? Rules that we ourselves have often failed to enforce in the past. In a fight for survival they felt they had to do everything they could to win. It's what you taught us,' Gregor said. Then there was silence as what he had just said sank in. Rolleston was smiling.

'Major, do you deny that you attempted to destroy every peaceful emissary from Them?' Mudge asked. He was trying to take the attention away from Gregor's admission, even though he was still looking at the hybrid.

On the screen, footage that God had compiled, presumably requested by Mudge, started playing. We saw craft similar to the kind Ambassador had shown me back in Vicar's church what seemed like an age ago. As before, it was basically a disposable engine with lots of needle-shaped stealth re-entry pods. We watched as orbital defences and ships destroyed craft after craft of this type. Each piece of footage was accompanied by a recording of the encrypted orders and each of those was sourced to members of the Cabal. There were so many ships.

Then the footage changed. On screens all over the system we saw Them, like Ambassador, being executed. It happened in city streets, in the wilderness, in the sea. There were only a few of these executions but I recognised the killers, or at least what they were. Ex-special forces. This was what the XIs were set up to do: ensure that there was no chance of peace.

Finally God showed us footage of a wealthy family with their own yacht. They were presumably upper-echelon execs for some corp. The family was perfectly nuclear, one mum, one dad and two children. They were gathered round an alien that looked just like Ambassador.

All the members of the family had the same beatific expressions on their faces that Morag and the other hookers had had when I found them sheltering Ambassador. There was a bright light and a loud noise, the picture turned to static and then slowly returned. I recognised the effects of a multi-spectrum stun grenade. There was the sound of suppressed weapon fire. The alien was down. We saw a gunman walk into the cabin and calmly double-tap each member of the family. The next shot was from the water and we could see the yacht burning. The gunman was in the water, watching the burning yacht and waiting for pickup. The big screen split to show the encrypted comms communication.

'Targets eliminated?' Rolleston asked over the comms.

'I murdered them all,' Rannu answered. Even through the medium of the comms line I could hear the remorse. All of us were looking up at where Rannu was sat on the catwalk above. His face appeared on the screen as Mudge did a close-up on him.

'That's how I knew she was right,' Rannu said.

'So how is showing one of your people murdering a family supposed to prove anything?' Rolleston asked.

'Because we've demonstrated you ordered it,' Mudge snarled.

'"We've demonstrated"?' Rolleston asked. 'You're one with God now, are you?'

'Don't change the subject,' Mudge said.

'What subject, Howard?' Rolleston asked scornfully. 'This is all very clever. Shame really. Had you spent this amount of time and energy trying to help humanity instead of engaging in wild flights of ego and vanity that will ultimately make us more vulnerable, you may have helped end the war. Let's start with a few obvious things. I have done and ordered done a lot of horrible things. That is my job, and although I rarely have to justify it to myself in this way I guess I do it for the sake of humanity ...'

I watched Bran tuck both her pistols into holsters on her thighs. She picked up her laser carbine and was perfectly still. I knew she'd be calibrating the smartgun and running through the weapons diagnostics.

'Oh come on,' Mudge scoffed. 'You're an evil little prick who likes having power over others.'

'No!' Rolleston said. He'd finished readying his load. He stood up, talking directly into the lens that was recording him. 'See, this is the problem with petty-minded individuals like you. Things aren't right so you want to destroy everything, tear it down, find someone to blame without thinking about what comes next. We're trying to build something, and because it requires sacrifice you want to whine about it and lash out. You make me sick.'

'Build what?' I asked quietly. Rolleston ignored me.

'Well, guess what? All you are is a dupe. Did I order that family killed? Of course I did. Did I order all of Them killed? Yes. Why? Because they're the enemy! Sixty years of warfare, humans wiped out wherever They found them, remember? What you call Ambassadors, you ignorant wretch, are what sane people call infiltrators.'

'That's a lie!' Morag shouted as she made her entrance onto system-wide media.

'What is?' Rolleston asked. 'I'm sorry that family died. I'm sorry the other prostitutes that you worked with died when you abandoned them, but did you see their faces? They were being mind-controlled by Them, just as you have been.'

'You know that's not true,' Morag said more quietly. I think she'd just got a glimpse of herself on the screen.

'Really? Deny you don't have a fragment of one of Them in your head?' he demanded. Morag opened her mouth and then closed it again. 'Nothing to say? This is very well done, but at the end of the day you have shown us nothing that couldn't be fabricated. Yes, there are things here that have an element of truth, but all the best lies do. After all, we only have God's assurance that it isn't lying.' He turned to Josephine. 'Ready?' She nodded.

I texted a query on their location to God. As I did, Rolleston cocked his head and smiled. He'd intercepted my communication. I received an answering text from Rolleston himself. I didn't open it. God told me that Rolleston's assault shuttle was about to land two floors above us. I looked around the node. Rannu looked as impassive as ever. He nodded to me from his position on the catwalk. Balor was leaning against the wall near the docking arm. He looked bored. I managed to get Buck and Gibby's attention and signalled that violence was imminent. I moved over to where Pagan and Morag were.

'They're nearly here,' I said. Pagan nodded grimly. Morag looked scared.

'You did it,' I said to them both. Morag managed a weak smile.

I tried to signal Mudge, but he was too busy arguing with Rolleston, or rather trying to convince the rest of the system that Rolleston was the bad guy here.

'We can't fake that amount of evidence,' Mudge said.

'You have unlimited processing power, and this is all mediated, so why not?' Rolleston replied.

'So nothing is real?' Pagan asked.

'I'm saying this obviously isn't. It's a complex and very well done illusion. Because, as we all know, the truth is nowhere as simple a creature as you would like it to be and it is always subjective. So all we are getting is what you want people to see Corporal Simm.' It took me a moment to realise that Simm was Pagan's real name.

'Those are pretty words, Major,' Pagan said. 'We've tried to make everything as open, transparent and objective as we were able. Yes, there may be subjectivity, but that's better than the lies that you and your Cabal have been telling us for years. I mean why are we wrong, despite having evidence, and you right, because you say so? That doesn't make any sense.'

'You've already admitted to having nearly infinite processing power. What was your aim, Corporal Simm? To make God omnipotent in the net?' Rolleston asked.

Pagan went quiet for a few beats as the realisation hit him, and then said, 'You knew.'

'You were compromised by GCHQ and the NSA. Since we're being so truthful, are you going to answer the question?' Rolleston said.

I knew at this moment the rest of Pagan's co-programmers were using God to find out who'd compromised them, and if the opportunity was available deal with them. Hackers had a well-developed sense of revenge.

'Yes, that was our aim,' Pagan finally answered.

'So, basically anything's possible with your alien program?' Rolleston asked.

'In theory, but I would invite hackers everywhere, government or otherwise, to examine God.'

'It would still be mediated and you have the power,' Rolleston pointed out.

Something occurred to me. 'If you knew about them and you knew they had the power to create something this dangerous—'

'So you admit it's dangerous?' Rolleston asked.

'Why didn't you shut it down?' I continued.

'Had I been in-system I would have, but Simm and his little conspiracy weren't compromised by the infiltrator when I left, so as far as we were concerned they were just a group of arrogant and deluded hacker has-beens. It took their collusion with one of the enemy, their treason, for them to become dangerous. What? You think They are incapable of subtlety? You think They don't have intelligence, psy-ops, information warfare? Just how naive are you people exactly?'

'You were stealing their work and using it to help develop

Demiurge,' Gregor said. This time Mudge decided not to put his hybrid features up on the screen.

'No ...' Pagan moaned and sat down at the bottom of the steps leading to the catwalk.

'I feel that you should all be aware that Major Rolleston and Private Bran have landed,' God said helpfully. I came off the wall where I'd been leaning.

'See you soon, Jakob,' Rolleston said. His image blinked off. Why'd he single me out? I thought irrationally.

'God, can you get him back up?' I asked, all business now. In answer God brought up an image from a landing-pad lens two floors above us. We watched the docking arm reach out to the sleek and violent-looking, next-generation assault shuttle.

God cut to the security lens in the docking arm. The Major and the Grey Lady striding down the corridor. Josephine put her laser carbine to her shoulder and the picture disappeared. Cut to another lens and the same thing happened. It seemed that the Major and the Grey Lady had had quite enough publicity for one day.

As Mudge continued presenting the machinations, as he called them, of the Cabal system-wide, I followed the progress of the Major and Bran. They systematically destroyed or jammed every comms and surveillance device they found as they made their way down to Cat's security people on the other side of what now felt like a very thin security shield.

They killed the crawlers we'd sent out, destroyed lenses and finally set up a white-noise transmitter. The last image we had of them was of Rolleston arguing with Cat while her people watched. They looked ready to step in if it got nasty. Josephine was just looking at the security screen covering the front of the node. Somehow it felt like she was looking through the lens and through me. Again I felt fear above and beyond the anticipation of combat.

# 27
# Atlantis

'Sergeant MacDonald?' The voice was American, northern states. It sounded like someone was trying to spread a veneer of culture and corporate elocution lessons over street roots. I saw Gregor turn to look up at the viz screen; even on his warped features the look of disgust was unmistakeable. On the screen was a handsome, well-groomed young man in an immaculate understated suit that screamed upper-echelon corp. The giveaway was the sheathed antique katana held casually in his left hand.

Everything about his appearance was perfect, from his hair to the duelling scars. God was providing a biography for this guy. I downloaded it onto my internal visual display but still only managed to catch the highlights. His name was Vincent Cronin. He'd grown up in one of the more Darwinian neighbourhoods of Detroit and excelled in cash generation for one of the more successful gangs. He'd been drafted into a relatively prestigious American airborne unit and seen action on Lalande. He'd worked his way through the ranks, played the system – first degree, commission to officer, some clever investments – and there'd been a corp job waiting back in the world. By all accounts he applied the same natural selection skills he'd learnt in the street to the boardroom. More than twenty-five dead execs by his sword. More importantly he was canny, good at business, as well as hell on wheels with a sword.

Now he was an executive without a portfolio. Reading between the lines he was the Cabal's corp liaison, their fixer. He solved the problems that didn't require Rolleston's violent attention.

I saw Cronin smile. It was the sort of smile that would put people at ease, though I couldn't help but think there was a predatory quality to it. He seemed to be sitting in the lobby of some kind of plush comfortable-looking hotel.

Standing not far away from him was the muscle. The guy was huge, as big as Balor, but nominally human-looking though his features were a mismatching patchwork collection of ugliness. His eyes were lenses but seemed to bulge out like a fish's, and he had a very pronounced, forward-jutting jaw. He wore an expensive and well-tailored suit that he looked very uncomfortable in. A Hawaiian shirt beneath the suit jacket and a large trilby finished the ensemble. Everything about him screamed cybernetic-induced psychosis, not least his dress sense. I don't think I would've liked to fight this guy. I wasn't even sure I'd want Gregor or Balor to fight him. He stood a little way from Cronin, constantly scanning the surrounding area. He was paying no attention whatsoever to the events unfolding on the viz screen.

I downloaded the muscle's bio. It filled me with disgust. He'd been US special forces, spent his time on Lalande as well. Possibly that was where he'd met Cronin, but he'd come back to spend time in a Green Beret counter-insurgency unit. Basically he killed humans. He'd been loaned out and cross-trained with the CIA's Special Activities Section, their paramilitary black-ops wing. Just before he'd gone to work for Cronin he'd been in command of the Washington branch of the IRS' elite SWAT audit team. He was a taxman. His name was Martin Kring.

'Cronin, you piece of shit,' Gregor hissed at the viz screen.

'To your friends and everyone watching this I think it's important that we all know that MacDonald is completely compromised by the alien entity that resides within his flesh. He works for the enemy. Whether or not that is the case with Miss McGrath I cannot say, though I suspect it is, but we studied MacDonald for over a year and he is definitely one of them.'

'That's bullshit!' Gregor said.

'Why, because you say so? Whatever you think of us, we have worked in humanity's best interests—'

'Funny, it looks like you've worked in your own best interests. Though even allowing for that I can't imagine why you started the war,' Mudge said.

'I wasn't even alive when the war started, and we only have your word for it that you think the people I work with had anything to do with it,' Cronin said evenly.

'My word? I'd call it a lot of evidence, but I would encourage people to check it for themselves.'

'I'm not about to get into yet another argument about mediation with you. People are smart enough to see through these things. I'm sure any vet knows the self-evident truth about the nature of Them,' Cronin said with a look of distaste on his face.

'Or, you know, check out the evidence for themselves. What I don't get though is why start the war in the first place? I mean, I could see that you and yours would make a lot of money investing in munitions, cyberware, shipbuilding, electronics and various other industries, but surely it was an insane thing to do? You couldn't know you were going to beat them?' Mudge asked.

'Then surely you've answered your own question,' Cronin said.

'They'd studied Them,' Gregor began. We all looked over at him and suddenly it was his face on the viz screen. He was being filmed through Mudge's eyes. 'They're not at all like us, like you. The Cabal aren't even sure if they're sentient as such. They theorised that they could be some kind of organic neural net processor, a biological learning machine, but they learn by reaction. If you can control their stimuli then you can control their progress. Basically they would always meet force with a similar degree of force, because you were teaching Them how to fight as you went along,' he finished.

'They guaranteed a stalemate,' I said. Gregor nodded.

'And no biological warfare that would've wiped us out, no nuclear weapons etcetera, etcetera. Nobody would be allowed the tools they needed to win. They modelled it using the most powerful software they could find. They forecast all possible outcomes of the conflict until the odds were in their favour and the chances of Them winning were infinitesimal, and then made sure they kept back certain edges for themselves,' he said.

'What edges?' Pagan asked. I glanced up at the screen. Cronin was listening intently but showing no other reaction.

'Early precursors to Crom—' Gregor began.

'Even out of the evidence you have manufactured there seems to be none to support the existence of this Crom virus you talk of,' Cronin interrupted.

'A more primitive version designed to kill rather than control,' Gregor finished.

'That's still a hell of a risk,' Mudge said.

'Not really. They are ordered and cooperative, where we are chaotic. It was surprisingly easy to gauge how They would react. At the end of the day They are little more than plants and as predictable as which side of the boulder moss grows,' Gregor finished. I must admit, uniformity of tactics or not, They never felt all that predictable when I was fighting Them.

'We were fighting space lichen?' Mudge said. 'Somebody should've said.' The thing was, I couldn't decide if knowing that would've made things better or worse for morale.

Mudge turned back to Cronin. 'I still don't get why?'

'Why what? I've little idea about any of this. It sounds like an involved conspiracy fantasy. Why don't you ask one of your alien friends? They're running this psy-op,' Cronin answered impassively.

'Do you ever get tired of all the spin and the lies?' Mudge asked. Cronin didn't dignify the question with an answer.

'Look, let's ignore this guy's bullshit. I think we've got more important things to worry about.' Everyone ignored me and apparently the fact that Rolleston and the Grey Lady could breach at any moment. I couldn't be the only person shitting himself, could I?

'Biotechnology,' Gregor said. He sounded tired. I could understand why; trying to navigate through this sea of lies against constant denial was tiring.

'I can see that,' Mudge said. The viz screen was split three ways between him and reaction shots of Cronin and Gregor. 'But even allowing for great advances and huge profits it just seems a trivial reason for sixty years of conflict.'

'Once again you answer your own question. Nobody but an insane person would do these things,' Cronin said. Gregor glanced up at the viz screen but pretty much ignored him.

'Not really. Profit aside, many of the Cabal are dying. Mixing Their naturally evolving but incredibly advanced, in its own way, biotechnology with human ingenuity and scientific know-how and you're looking at incredible advances. Advances we would have problems even imagining,' Gregor said. Mudge gave this some thought. He did a close-up on himself just so everyone could see how thoughtful he was.

'And that's the thing, isn't it?' Mudge said. 'God, can you bring the images of the Cabal up on the screen?' On the viz screen the images we'd seen earlier appeared. They were almost all fat old white guys being kept alive by drugs and machinery that probably cost thousands every day if not every hour. Presumably they communicated through the net but I don't think they were jacked in at the moment, unsurprisingly. 'All this is for them?' Mudge asked. 'What the fuck have these vampires got to do with the rest of us? Why are they even living, if you call that living, off of us? Anybody else want to die for them?'

'They worked for the power they have and deserve to be rewarded for it,' Cronin said, though I wasn't sure even he believed that. He seemed very uncomfortable with the images of the sleeping members of the Cabal.

'These people had their time; now it's over they all should've died a long time ago. This is deeply unnatural,' Mudge said in disgust.

Cronin shook his head. 'This is irrelevant, a fantasy. What proof have you got of us harvesting Them biotechnology? Even your God seems to struggle to fabricate evidence.'

'Because you used Demiurge to purge your systems,' Morag spat with a surprising amount of hatred in her voice.

'There's me, there's my last year of being a fucking test bed for you after Rolleston exposed the Wild Boys to a Ninja in the hope that one of us would be infected. What were you doing then?' Gregor asked. His voice had become nearly a whisper. Cronin concentrated as if he was receiving data.

'Rolleston ordered you to hunt and kill one of Their assassination bioborgs, not an unreasonable order to give an SAS patrol. When you were exposed, you were isolated to be studied so we could find a way of more effectively combating Them. You're fabricating a fantasy out of little strands of the truth,' Cronin snapped.

Gregor was pointing at Cronin. 'No, you are!' he shouted. Even to me it sounded weak.

Cronin leaned into the screen. He looked angry now. 'And in the absence of any credible evidence it is your word against mine, and one of us isn't currently possessed by an alien! What have we done? Nothing! Except try and study you, even see if we could help you.'

'Oh, that's bullshit!'

'You people, on the other hand, have just single-handedly destroyed our economy and our security apparatus. People have access to information that is dangerous to them. Now everyone in the world can learn how to manufacture nuclear weapons, biological and chemical weapons, genetically targeted weapons and concrete-eating microbes. You've just released all the information on banned genetic engineering and cloning processes, processes that were considered to be immoral by the UN. Now people have access to black bio and cyberware, sequestrination cyberware. Or are you going to tell us that you didn't think of any of this?' It was quiet again. I felt like I'd been scolded and the answer was no, I hadn't thought it through. The thing is, there were smarter people than me here. Had they thought it through? 'You say that we're the enemies of humanity and then you go and do all this. I trust the comparison with Pandora isn't lost on you.'

'You're right,' Pagan said. I looked over at him. Surely he must've thought of all this. I was beginning to wonder if we'd been very stupid. 'We have made all that information available, do you know where from?' he asked rhetorically. 'From the likes of you and your friends. God, all the things that you just mentioned, can you provide evidence for their manufacture and use in, say, the last ten years?' Text, audio, and audiovisual information began scrolling down the screen. I wondered how many people accessed it. 'See, it hadn't gone away. The information was still there. What you're pissed off about is that we've taken it out of the hands of people like you.'

'Yes, congratulations on proliferation. That'll help,' Cronin said.

'How will it proliferate? Every time someone accesses this information everyone in the system has the potential to know about it. Surely that'll make it easier to police?' Pagan said. He seemed to have recovered from his earlier despondency. It was obvious he had thought of this and he had a counter-argument; the trouble was, I wasn't sure if it was enough. I didn't like the idea of genetically targeted viruses or slave cyberware available to anyone. I wondered if this was the part of me that liked the idea of other people making the decisions, making things safe, looking after us. The trouble was we were here because they weren't doing a very good job. In fact they had become abusive.

'Surely you've made every hacker in the world unemployed?' Cronin said sardonically.

'I'm sure we'll find something to do,' Morag said.

'I've always fancied farming,' Pagan said, looking slightly wistful.

'And what about the financial markets? Money and commodities are moved around as information all the time. Now anyone can access this.'

'You'd be surprised how few people that affects. Well maybe you wouldn't. For most of us it's still cash under the mattress or illegal credit chips. God?' Pagan said expectantly.

'While all information is available, security systems are still functioning. Money and other commodities still cannot be moved except by the authorised person, though now it is a lot easier to check that person's authorisation,' God said. I noticed that Pagan was momentarily tranced in but he was back by the end of God's explanation.

'That said, it's now a lot easier to see how much money people have. Wow! You're rich, Mr Cronin,' Pagan said. There was something of the teen-punk hacker about him at this moment. He was enjoying himself. 'How did you make your money, I wonder?' Pagan continued. There was all sorts of information scrolling down the screen.

'This is an obscene breach of privacy,' Cronin said, looking less than pleased.

'I would argue that this information is relevant to the populace as it seems to affect them directly,' Pagan said, somewhat distracted as he studied the information he'd found. 'Hmm, a cursory glance would suggest that you've made a lot of money from arms and have recently been investing in biotechnology. I wonder why?'

'Do you not understand that your alien computer virus of total truth is a weapon you've wielded against humanity? Lies protect humanity as well as deceive them. What if every lie you were ever told was suddenly revealed, would it do more harm than good? From "Yes, you do look fat in that" to Pearl Harbor, we exist in a web of lies, and not all of them are bad. The truth can be a destructive force, as your attempt to pull humanity apart is proving,' Cronin said, changing tack.

'But why *your* lies? Why do *you* get to decide what lies we hear?' Mudge asked.

'Because we are allowed to, because we worked hard to get ourselves into positions that allow us to make these decisions, because we are strong enough to do so. This is how our system works: it rewards success and it rewards strength. This is how things are supposed to be. Who else is going to lead? You?' I had to smile at the guy's balls.

'What about democracy?' Mudge asked. I almost scoffed. The word seemed a joke, but Mudge was deadly serious: this was important to him. I saw Cronin's eyes narrow around his custom lenses, designed to look like real eyes, the designer logo just about visible on the large viz screen. I think he was trying to gauge how serious Mudge was.

'We work within the framework of democracy,' Cronin said carefully. I think he saw a trap. Democracy was a joke to people like this, almost meaningless. He knew it and we knew it, but he couldn't openly say that.

'Do you think we would've voted for the war?' Mudge asked.

'This is a ridiculous argument. You're being naive and you know it. The governments that you voted into place allowed us the latitude to make certain moves.'

'Like starting a war?'

'I didn't start the war,' he repeated, sounding slightly exasperated. 'We're going round in circles.'

'Should governments act on the will of the people?'

'They do when they are elected, but despite your attempt to simplify it you know that for security reasons the populace cannot be privy to some information and the decisions that come about as a result of them. Through their votes they delegate their trust to their elected officials, who act for them.'

'In their best interests?' Mudge asked.

'You're setting up a straw man,' Cronin said. 'You want us to be a secret government-controlling conspiracy. You give us prosaic names like the Cabal so you can find a scapegoat. Find someone to blame for your own sense of dissatisfaction because you'd rather attack than actually do anything constructive to help.'

'How is the war—' Mudge began.

'I didn't start the war, Mr Mudgie, now let me finish. What you don't understand is this is the way of things. We exist within the framework of our society as a necessity. We manage the difficult decisions, the decisions where victories involve sacrifice. We are always going to look bad. You want to punish us but all you're doing is fighting the momentum of your own society. You want to blame us for the start of the war but its beginnings are a lot more complicated than you're allowing for, and the sad fact is the war began because of the weight of society bearing down on that point in history. What you call the Cabal was acting on what humanity required at that point.'

'Bullshit,' I said. 'Fancy words aside, the war started because someone who you work for ordered a passive alien organism to be attacked by an RASF ship.'

'Someone has to lead because so many people will not take responsibility for themselves,' he said.

'Because people have had it driven into them by the likes of you that there's nothing they can do, that they're helpless and they can't make a difference. That's not true,' Morag said.

'Actually it is. Few people have the will or the ability to make a difference. You have to remember the majority of people will not collude with the implacable enemy of their race and put an alien parasite in their head,' Cronin said. Morag just glared at him but didn't respond to the cheap shot.

'Even if that were true, then the strong have an obligation to lead responsibly and try and foster that strength in others,' I said.

'We are making humanity stronger,' he said.

'Oh, you are so full of crap,' I said. There were sounds of disbelief from the others.

'He's right. Conflict breeds strength,' Balor said. I looked up at him. Cronin was looking smug on the viz screen.

'What humanity?' I asked. Suddenly I was on the screen. I was being shot through Mudge's eyes again. I felt uncomfortable, I looked at my features writ large on the viz screen. Some of my discomfort stemmed from looking like I was dying of radiation poisoning.

'I'm not sure I understand,' Cronin said.

'Less than a third of my body is the original biological material,' I said. 'They want to wage war on my humanity, where will they start, my testicles?'

'Don't be ridiculous, the flesh isn't—' Cronin began.

'Look at Balor, does he look human, sound human?' I asked Cronin.

'Appearances ...' Cronin began.

'It goes beyond looks. He had neurosurgery to make himself less human, didn't you?' I asked Balor. Now it was Balor on the screen. He looked magnificent and nothing whatsoever to do with humanity.

'I had neurosurgery done on myself to weed out weakness,' Balor said impassively. I wondered with this talk of strong leadership who Balor actually sympathised with.

'The actions of one man—' Cronin began again but I interrupted him again.

'It's not one man, though, is it? We're making our own aliens. Do you know how many cases of cybernetic-induced psychosis I've seen put out of their misery? Even if we win we lose, and if we don't stop soon there won't be any humanity left, just sick machines.' Cronin looked like he was about to start talking again but something else occurred to me. 'See, you and yours may have something invested in turning us into machines but I don't and neither, I guess, would the majority of other people in the world. I was a member of the SAS, an elite. In theory all the machinery, training and experience should make me one of the strongest people on the planet. I don't feel strong; I feel dead, I feel horrified with what I've done and seen.' I said it earnestly enough and I believed it, but I also knew there would be a group of men and women in Hereford throwing things at their viz screens – that at least made me smile.

'It made me strong,' Balor insisted.

'It made you a freak,' Buck sang along with the music he was playing. I'd become so used to the soundtrack I'd all but stopped noticing it. Balor glared at the guitarist.

'Actually these two are a good example,' Mudge said. 'God, can you draw up the recruitment information on Buck and Gibby and make their entry photos big on the screen?' he asked. I saw where this was going; it was something of a cheap shot. Buck and Gibby's recruitment photos came up. We saw images of them as two young clean-cut recruits on their way to basic training.

'Compare and contrast,' Mudge said. Buck and Gibby as they were today in all their cyberbilly splendour appeared on the screen. Buck decided to use his moment in the spotlight to start a guitar solo. 'Congratulations, Cronin, the sum result of the Cabal's machinations to date is to create a degenerate junkie hillbilly making machine.'

'Yeeehaaa!' Buck screamed.

'Face facts. We're the elite of your so-called strength and we're a bunch of weirdos. I mean look at how Mudge dresses,' I said.

'Hey, I'm a fucking serious journalist!' Mudge complained.

'So, who leads? We do after all work with most governments in the world. You appear to be intent on overthrowing democracy as well as everything else you've attacked,' Cronin said.

'We haven't touched the infrastructure of government, though I don't doubt there will be the world's largest and most transparent ...' Mudge began.

'Witch hunt?' Cronin suggested.

'Corruption investigation,' Mudge finished. 'But we can help governments. See, through God we have the capability to reveal as much truth as is technologically possible.'

'How very Orwellian,' Cronin sneered.

'Orwellian how?' Pagan asked. I had no idea what they were talking about. 'We didn't create the Panopticon.' I still didn't have a clue what they were talking about. 'The mechanism for near-total surveillance was already in place. We're just taking it out of your hands and making it open to everyone. So we can watch you as well.'

'As for democracy, we now, through God, have the ability to run a worldwide referendum so everyone can have their say. You know, aid decision-making when crucial questions come up, like should we wage war on an initially harmless alien organism? Can't we, God?' Mudge said.

'You are not entirely correct, Howard. I actually have the facility to run a system-wide referendum but it will take a little longer,' God answered.

'Seriously, Rolleston's about to come in here, guys. Do we have time for this?' I asked. Even I had got sucked into this argument. Nobody answered me.

'Fine,' Mudge said, slightly irritated at God. 'Yes or no question. Once people have had a chance to look at the information as regards the Cabal do they still want to be controlled by these people? And if They want peace do we want it too? Vote, people,' he invited.

'And again we trust the alien computer virus because ...' Cronin asked.

'Because everyone will know what they voted for. They can ask their friends and family, who will ask their friends and family, and so on. Hell, they can ask total strangers in the street.'

'It won't work. With every secret revealed people will pull themselves apart,' Cronin said. 'Every suspicion proved, think of all the scores that people will be able to settle.' This was the first time I saw Mudge get angry during the whole thing. Up to this point I think he'd just been enjoying himself.

'You'd fucking like that, wouldn't you? But what if they don't?

What if sixty years of conflict is enough? What if we cooperate now so that our children don't have a life of violence?'

'Someone will always take advantage,' Cronin answered.

'And now we can see them coming,' Mudge countered. 'You see, there's no reason to not be calm. It's over. We can see the strings and anytime anyone else ever tries to lie to us, control us for their own gains, we'll see those strings as well. We know the truth. You can't lie to make us afraid any more. We're able to make decisions for ourselves now. Will there be pricks like you trying to take advantage? Of course there will, but everyone will see it. The thing is, what you think of as our weakness – our ability to not succeed in your terms – I think is our strength. Why would we want to live like you? Your power is smoke and relies on us anyway. Your existence relies on how much you're able to fuck others over. Is that what you need to make yourself feel good? Is that your validation, your reason to exist, your measure of success? How fucking hollow. Most people just want to make their way, do their thing and look after themselves and their loved ones, but you won't let us. You win because we divide. Well, now we're connected. What are you going to do?'

Cronin was silent.

'See, we've left the world's infrastructure in place but you've got to go because this isn't working. We can travel across the stars, we can rebuild the human body and we're capable of feats of engineering like this Spoke, and we're still killing each other for food. That's not right,' Mudge finished.

Cronin smiled smugly. 'Well, stop doing it then,' he said.

It looked like Mudge leant in but I guess he just did a close-up on himself, and suddenly his ugly face was massive around the world.

'This is how we start. Consider yourself fired,' he said. I reviewed the data on Cronin. He was on a luxury elevator on the Brazilian Spoke. I checked with God, making sure that the Brazilian authorities were waiting to pick him up. They were, then I made sure the Brazilian authorities had enough firepower to deal with Cronin, Kring and any other surprises they had. It looked like they did.

'I mean, how do you do it?' Mudge continued. 'How do you justify sending millions of people to die? What do you need all the money and power for anyway? Surely it must reach a level where it becomes an abstract?'

Cronin let out a brief bitter laugh. 'Because whether you choose to acknowledge it or not, this is how progress is made,' he said.

Then Mudge did something that I thought was brave, risky and showed much more faith in people than I had, or I thought he had.

'No, this how progress is made. God, show this twisted fuck our people,' Mudge commanded. Cronin was now glaring at us from the viz screen but his features were replaced. It was a street scene, one of London's many Ginzas. London was Mudge's spiritual home. Thousands of people were on the street just watching the viz screen, then the picture shrank down to a tiny window and it was replaced by Washington, then Paris, Berlin, Nairobi, Pacifica, Berlin, Auckland – all the major cities of the world – and then smaller cities, faster and faster, towns and then individuals. People stood and watched in silence, people cried, people hugged and kissed, talked or just stared, looks of relief on their faces. Somehow Mudge had predicted this. Everyone looked tired but relieved. Some of them even dared to look happy. I realised how tired I was. I staggered over to the wall and began to slide down it. Morag was there to help me.

'See, this isn't a riot; it's a great big fucking party, you twat. The war is over,' Mudge said. I realised that Mudge may have spoken too soon but it felt good. I also realised as I watched image after image flicker up on the screen how much I really loved what was left of our fucked-up humanity.

'The war is never over,' Cronin said.

'Give war a chance!' Buck and Gibby sang together.

'What? Rolleston? You think killing us is going to make a difference?' Mudge asked.

'No, but it might be worth focusing on now,' I suggested.

'You didn't listen to MacDonald did you? With what we've learnt about biotechnology we'll be more like gods. Like your whore,' Cronin said.

Morag looked up. 'Oh, do you mean me? See, there are a lot of things I wouldn't do for money and power.' She looked confused. 'Sorry, who's the whore?'

'You've started the next great human conflict,' he continued, oblivious to Morag's jibe.

'You're issuing us an ultimatum?' Mudge asked.

'The combined colonial fleet cannot allow the net, perhaps Earth's most important tactical asset, to remain in control of something that by its own admission is compromised by the enemy,' Cronin said. 'You must see that.'

'Who are you to make that decision?' I demanded, getting drawn in again despite myself and Rolleston's imminent breach.

'There is no enemy; they want peace!' Morag shouted. She sounded desperate for Cronin to understand her, for him to see. I knew he did and it didn't matter.

I was receiving an urgent comms message from Cat outside. I opened it to see her comms icon. Did her icon look nervous, unhappy, angry? Or was I just reading that in? Again I was distracted by Cronin.

'Unfortunately we only have the word of one little girl, a whore no less, who has an alien living in her head, whereas the combined experience of millions of people says otherwise,' Cronin said. I could see Morag fighting back tears, not at this arsehole's words but at the thought that after all this we could end up fighting our own people all over again. I knew how she felt. Though I don't think in her there was the same capacity for hatred of Cronin, Rolleston and their ilk that I felt.

'Sergeant ...' Cat began.

'Call me Jakob.' She looked annoyed at the interruption.

'In order for there not to be a war all you have to do is stop,' Mudge said. 'If you leave it a few minutes you'll get a mandate from humanity asking you to do just that.'

'You said when you'd done this you'd come out,' Cat said.

'For you, not him. Sorry. Get your people well out of the way,' I said, then to everyone inside the node, 'Guys.' Something in my tone this time – suddenly everyone was alert.

'"I know thy works. Behold, I have set before thee an open door, and no man can shut it,"' Cronin said. It made me think of Vicar. Cronin's face disappeared from the viz screen.

'God?' Mudge asked.

'We've lost the feed from the elevator security cameras. I believe Mr Cronin has had them disabled.'

'You're the demons,' I said quietly to myself. Morag looked up at me; she must've heard.

'They're coming,' Cat said over the link. She'd be lucky if Rolleston didn't have her killed. Cronin had been a distraction.

'"For thou hast kept my word, and hast not denied my name,"' God said, finishing Cronin's quote for him.

Bang.

## 28
# En Route to Sirius

Why I hate Rolleston.

*See, all the stuff that he'd done up to now was bad but you could see it was the kind of bad a prick like him had to do as part of his job. I didn't like him, would have no objection to him being dead, but I didn't really hate him yet, largely because I was just really happy to not be dead. The idea of revenge against him for leaving us there was a distant and unrealistic dream.*

*We were so lucky to be picked up. It was a Congon search and rescue team doing a final sweep. They were looking for some of their own special forces but they found us. When we were evacced it felt like we were the last assault shuttle to leave Dog 4. The sky was lit up by ground-based fire aimed at our fleet in high orbit. It was beautiful and seemed somehow unreal. To the Congons we must have looked like walking corpses. Neither Mudge or I did anything much but stare as the paramedics looked after our wounds. I don't think we even thanked them.*

*The* Santa Maria *was a pre-war freighter out of the High Brazilia shipyards. A civilian ship on what amounted to a permanent military contract. Largely it was a case of hauling equipment and munitions out and ferrying casualties or personnel back for the old freighter. We hated these ships because the cargo holds were modular, basically a self-contained hold with life support attached, completely separated from the rest of the ship and built by the contractor who came in with the cheapest price. They were a prison with cold, thin walls that separated you from vacuum.*

*A return journey like this was made up of odds and sods, basically survivors, whoever had made it off. You weren't there in your units. The command structure was not intact. The closest thing we had to authority was a couple of MPs. They had an armoured office that they stayed inside because if they stepped outside they'd be killed. Nobody liked MPs and nobody liked the authority that they represented. In our case the MPs were Yanks.*

*Left to our own devices things got Darwinian very quickly. Victims were designated, scores were settled, the food chain was established and territory was staked out. There was a mixture of nationalities but mainly British, French and American, developing world nations. The Congo forces, I guess, didn't have to use eighty-year-old, piece-of-shit freighters to take their people home. The Yanks were by far the biggest national group but they were heavily divided internally.*

*There was also a much higher than normal special forces population on board. This was going to make establishing our place in the food chain a bit more difficult than normal. The drink and drugs would last two, maybe three days at most; after that there was only the rum ration and that was never enough. So I began looking for the sacrifice. The sacrifice was a message to the rest of the inmates; it meant I wanted to be left alone. I didn't want to be the Daddy, someone who was willing to work for that title could have it, it just meant that I was more trouble than I was worth not to be left alone. The sacrifice had to be a loud-mouthed arsehole with the muscle and the backup to enforce his bullying ways. Somehow it was always a male. In this case he was a borderline cyber psychotic from 2 Para. I killed him for a bottle of whisky. It wasn't even good whisky. That was my message. We had another eight days to go.*

*Mudge did his thing; I sat on my bunk and drank. I pretty much ignored what was going on, not really thinking. I remember anger and numbness. It was a weird state of non-feeling. I had conversations with Mudge but he did most of the talking and I don't remember anything about them. Mudge had to pretty much force me to look after my wounds.*

*I remembered Vicar though. He'd been wearing a soiled uniform with no insignia or rank. His hair was matted and filthy, as was his beard. He looked insane – there was something wrong with his wild and bloodshot eyes. The ugly but functional military machinery that made up half his head didn't help his appearance and he would not shut up. He was on something because he needed no sleep, and he preached endlessly. He ranted about God, the end times and of course Them, the demons, until his mouth bled. There had been a number of attempts to beat him into silence but something stopped his attackers from finishing the job each time. Maybe it was religion, maybe they felt it was bad luck to kill someone that mad. Nobody really wanted to get very close to him.*

*He'd been there when we'd walked into the hold. He'd raised an arm to point at me and begun shouting, drool running down through his black, wiry beard.*

*'I know your deeds; you have a reputation of being alive, but you are dead. Wake up! Strengthen what remains and is about to die, for I have not found your deeds complete in the sight of my God.'*

*I pushed past him trying to ignore the smell.*

*Vicar's ravings along with the creaking of the hull became the ambient sound track aboard the* Santa Maria. *Initially the preaching grated on me, like it grated on everyone else. Everyone in the hold had to deal with religious signals types. You needed to have tolerance as communications kept you alive. They called in evacs, air strikes and artillery; they kept you and your people together so you forgave the odd sermon here and there. Vicar was, however, taking the piss. The thing was, I was beginning to find his narratives somehow comforting. I was finding myself listening to them to take my mind off Gregor, Rolleston, the Ninja and my failure to look after my people.*

*'Who is he?' I asked. I think I surprised Mudge by taking interest in something besides whisky and brooding.*

*'He's called Vicar,' Mudge told me. Mudge knew this, I guessed, because he took an interest in his surroundings.*

*'Sounds about right. What's his story?'*

*'Apparently he's Green Slime, attached to GCHQ. Rumour has it that he was part of Operation Spiral,' Mudge answered. Operation Spiral was a rumour, a joint project between GCHQ and the NSA to hack Their communications infrastructure. Basically it meant sending hackers into an alien net.*

*'That was real?' I asked. I'd always thought that Operation Spiral was a combat myth.*

*'That's what they're saying,' Mudge said, shrugging.*

*'What's he saying?' I asked, meaning about Spiral. I was interested despite myself.*

*'That he's seen the face of the devil. If the rumours are right then everyone either got their frontal lobes burnt or were driven irrevocably insane,' Mudge answered.*

*'He'd be the latter then?'*

*'He'd be the sanest,' Mudge said.*

*I was actually surprised it took as long to come to a head as it did. We were only two days in. The drink and drugs were probably going to run out tomorrow and then we were looking at a lot of military-issue tranquillisers and cold turkey. That was when things would get really bad.*

*As far as I could tell, the guy who flipped out was on some kind of evil psychotropic and Vicar's never-ending monologue had played into the structure of his hallucinations, wrapping him up in a hallucinogenic Christian hellscape. Needless to say the guy wasn't too pleased about it.*

*I could hear the screaming. The tripper's voice had reached the pitch of the truly fucked-up, making him sound inhuman. Vicar responded by attempting to cast the demons out of him. The tripper had some friends with him, presumably to stop him hurting himself or anyone hurting him. I assumed that this was the end for Vicar. I surprised myself when I realised I was going to miss the noise.*

*I was more surprised when I found myself getting out of the bunk and climbing down eight storeys of berths. I clambered past squaddies and troopers who were propping themselves up on their elbows, a drunken murder audience. I should've been doing the same. Mudge told me later he thought I was trying to get myself killed.*

*On the cold deck floor I could see what was going on. The tripper was holding Vicar down on a bunk. The guy whose bunk it was had pushed himself up against the partition between his bunk and the one next to it. His eyes were wide open, black lenses like everyone else's, a voyeur's smile on his face as he watched the tripper carve Vicar's flesh. Well it wasn't like there were any sense booths onboard.*

*Vicar was covered in blood but in between screams he was still managing to quote scripture, a degree of commitment I can't really understand.*

*'Do not be afraid of what you are about to suffer!' Vicar screamed.*

*The tripper was naked and covered in blood as well. It looked like he'd been cutting himself as well as Vicar. A naked self-harmer, it was almost a psychotropic cliché. He was holding a jagged peace of metal, though I was pretty sure he had implanted weapons. The hardware implanted in his skull told me the tripper was a signalman like Vicar. Judging by his swimmer's physique, the webbed fingers and toes, what tattoos I could just about make out through the blood and the gills, he was probably a SEAL. Which meant the two women stood just behind him were SEALs. They outnumbered me and SEALs knew what they were doing. Then again I wasn't all that sure I knew what I was doing. The tripping SEAL was just sobbing and begging Vicar to shut up. Neither of the women looked happy about what was going on but they were making sure their guy was all right.*

*'Let him go,' I said quietly.*

*'I tell you, the devil will put some of you in prison to test you, and you will suffer persecution for ten days!' Vicar screamed. One of the women, small, compact, tough-looking, wearing combats and a cropped T-shirt, a sweaty bandanna wrapped around her head, changed her position better to see me and so she could move if it got violent.*

*'Private matter, mind your own fucking business,' she said. The forcefulness in her voice was adopted for the circumstances but you could tell she wasn't liking this either. I looked at her for a while, her black soulless lenses looked back at me. Vicar screamed as he was made to bleed some more.*

*I wasn't sure I could've taken both the women even if I was on top of my game, and though I was healing fast I was pretty far from being there. If the psycho joined in I was definitely screwed. Where the fuck was Mudge? Then I realised I hadn't contacted him. I sub-vocalised a message and spent the time waiting for a reply staring at the SEAL woman.*

*'What's your name?' I asked.*

*'What's it to you?'*

*'Mine's Jakob,' I said, ignoring her aggressive reply.*

*'Look, this is none of your business. Just let him finish and we're out of here,' she said.*

*'And if it was one of yours?' I asked.*

*'He's not one of yours,' she said. She knew that because if he had been we wouldn't be talking now, I just would've attacked them. 'Besides it's one on one.'*

*'What's your name?' I asked again. I guessed the deadness of my tone was beginning to get to her. Vicar screamed out as he was cut some more. If I didn't do something soon I was going to be wasting my time. Needless to say, since I'd gotten involved more people were beginning to pay attention to what was happening.*

*'Reb,' she finally said.*

*'What? Is that short for Rebel?' I said, smiling. It was a pretty thin, humourless smile.*

*'Rebecca,' she answered. She didn't sound amused.*

*'Well, Rebecca,' I said. 'It's not really one on one, is it? What're you guys, SEALs?' I asked. She nodded. 'And he's just some deskbound hacker, not even a field op. Not really fair is it?' I asked.*

*'Neither's having to listen to twenty-four hours of fire and brimstone,' she answered. There were a lot of muttered assents from the surrounding crowd.*

*Vicar didn't help by taking this moment to scream, 'Be faithful, even to the point of death, and I will give you the crown of life!'*

*'Shut up! Shut up! Shut up!' the SEAL on the bad trip was screaming, his words running together to become babble. There was more screaming as the SEAL drew on Vicar's flesh some more.*

*'Your man's hurting,' I said. 'This won't help him.'*

*'Kill that noisy fucker!' a woman screamed from high up on one of the bunks. I looked up to the area where the voice had come from.*

*'Shut the fuck up or you're next!' I shouted. Reb shifted again, readying herself for violence. Mudge pushed himself through the crowd and nodded to me, making sure that Reb and the other woman knew it was two on two if it came to that. Pub car park politics.*

*'You're right. It's not fair that you have to listen to that twenty-four seven, or hear the guy in the bunk below you chronically abusing himself, or smell two hundred, filthy fucking squaddies shit and sweat. It's not fair that most of your friends are dead and those that aren't are fucked up one way or another, but it's not his fault and this won't help,' I said. I had no idea where this was*

*coming from but I knew I sounded angry. 'How much worse shall we make today?' I asked. It was a bad situation for her. She couldn't be seen to show weakness in case someone decided she was a victim. I also had a feeling she knew what I was talking about. I gave her a way out. After all I didn't care about me at that moment, let alone some stranger madman.*

*'Fuck it,' I said. 'You're right. This is nothing to do with me.' I turned and started climbing back up towards my bunk. Behind me Reb and the other SEAL woman pulled their signalman off of Vicar and started dragging him back to their ghetto. I opened a comms link to Mudge.*

*'Look after Vicar,' I sub-vocalised.*

*'What am I, his fucking nurse?' Mudge demanded. I closed the link down.*

*'God has chosen you as his righteous sword!' Vicar howled. I screamed and sat bolt upright in my bunk, banging my head on the bunk above me. This was not a good way to wake up. My blades were out, already shredding the cheap sheets on my bunk. I guessed he'd only gotten so close because I'd finished most of my rum ration and the rest of the whisky I'd taken from the guy I killed. I mean the guy I'd murdered.*

*'Get. The fuck. Off my bunk!' I managed. Vicar reached for me. He smelt of halitosis, sour sweat, piss and shit. In retrospect the smell must've been his defence mechanism, a way to stop him getting killed by anyone who wasn't deeply fucked on drugs.*

*'Listen! You must listen. You will be called and you must answer!' He seemed to loom over me, his insane features somehow huge in the cramped space of my bunk. I realised that I was actually frightened of this guy. People were beginning to shout at us to be quiet.*

*'Get away from me!' I shouted.*

*'Do you guys want to be alone?' I heard an amused, if tired-sounding Mudge ask from the bunk below. Something was nagging me at the back of my skull. Something had been changed or was different. Something was bothering me beyond having a smelly religious fanatic trying to crawl into my bunk.*

*'When the time has come for the second—'*

*'Shut up!' I snapped, every bit the sergeant now. Something in my voice made Vicar be quiet.*

*'Thank Christ for that,' Mudge muttered.*

*'You take the Lord's name in—' Vicar began.*

*'Shut up!' I shouted again. I realised what was wrong.*

*'Mudge, when did they strike the sails?' I asked. The harmonics of the background noise were all wrong. The feeling that you got at some instinctive level that you were moving at ridiculous speeds was missing. We were only three days into an eight-day journey and we'd dropped out of FTL.*

*'Get off my bunk,' I said to Vicar. Something in my voice made him move.*

*I leant over, ignoring the vertigo of the forty or so foot drop to the deck, and looked down at Mudge. There was some young pretty-looking squaddie in his bunk with him but Mudge was awake and alert, the camera lenses in his eyes moving slightly as he focused on me.*

*'On you go, son,' I said not unkindly to the boy with Mudge. He clambered out of the bunk.*

*'I guess while we were sleeping,' Mudge said watching the naked squaddie clamber down the bunks. 'Do you think there's a problem?'*

*'Must be if we've stopped,' I said, dragging on my combats and a T-shirt and starting to lace up my boots.*

*'The sail?' he asked.*

*'How the fuck would I know?'*

*'Well, is there any need for you to throw my entertainment out of bed after waking me up?' he demanded.*

*'I didn't wake you up,' I pointed out. Around the modular hold others were beginning to realise that something was going on. Word spread quickly that we'd dropped out of FTL. I opened a comms link to the* Santa Maria *requesting information but got no reply. Neither did anyone else, it seemed. I linked to the MPs locked into their armoured cubicle but they were none the wiser.*

*I clambered down out of my bunk, Mudge with me. Vicar was standing at the bottom of our column of bunks.*

*'I know that you cannot tolerate wicked men, that you have tested those who claim to be apostles but are not, and have found them false! You have persevered and have endured hardships for my name, and have not grown weary! Yet I hold this against you: you have forsaken your first love. Remember the height from which you have fallen! Repent and do the things you did at first!' From the surrounding bunks there was the occasional demand for quiet accompanied by a threat but most people had got used to him now.*

*'What's he talking about?' Mudge asked me.*

*'Falling out of bed,' I said. People were beginning to congregate by the airlock that connected the modular hold to the rest of the* Santa Maria. *Mudge and I pushed our way through the crowd to the airlock, Mudge nodding to the acquaintances he'd made in his wanderings.*

*Reb, the woman who'd been with her the previous day and their signalman were all standing by the airlock. Fortunately the tripper was clothed this time. His self-inflicted cuts were scabbing over and he was tranced in. Reb nodded at me, looking uncomfortable. I didn't waste time asking stupid questions. We just waited until the signalman was finished.*

*The SEAL signalman came out of his trance and began shaking his head.*

*'Well?' Mudge asked. The SEAL glanced at the pair of us without recognition and then looked up at Reb.*

*'They haven't just locked us out. I went straight through the security on the lock, and as far as I can tell they've trashed the actual lock mechanism itself.'*

*'Can you get into the ship's systems?' Reb asked.*

*He shook his head. 'Nope, they've got a complete comms blackout running. Everything is shut down.'*

*'What about tricking them out and coming through the sensor array?' a surprisingly sane-sounding Vicar asked.*

*There was a moment where everyone stared at him, especially the signalman who'd been cutting him the day before. 'Tried it. I think they've shut down the sensor array,' he said, recovering.*

*'Piggybacking onto the internal viz or intercom?' Vicar asked. The signalman was starting to look a bit pissed off now.*

*'Look, I know what I'm doing. Without a decent transmitter I don't have enough power in here,' he said tapping his head, 'to break into low-power systems like that.'*

*'These are the words of him who is holy and true. I hold the key of David. What I open no one can shut, and what I shut no one can open. This has been given to me by God.' There were a lot of groans as Vicar returned to form and then he collapsed, which to give him credit was quite melodramatic, as he tranced in. People pushed others out of the way to avoid Vicar falling into them and he hit the floor quite hard. Then everyone's attention turned back to the SEALs by the airlock.*

*'What do you think?' I asked Mudge.*

*'Well, they've stopped and locked us in for a reason,' Mudge said. 'I can't think it'll be anything good.' In retrospect it was kind of obvious what they were intending to do. I think we knew at some level but were refusing to admit it to ourselves, though this wasn't a problem for Vicar.*

*'They intend to override the external airlock doors and space all here,' Vicar said as he exited his trance.*

*'What've you got in your head?' the SEAL signalman asked.*

*Vicar ignored him. He gave time for denial mixed with assertions of his fragile mental health to run its course through the assembled soldiers.*

*'You sure?' I asked him. He nodded. It was enough for me.*

*'Why?' the other SEAL women asked.*

*'There are too many here who know truths. The red horseman who is war and the devil who is lies are enemies of the righteous,' Vicar said. It worried me that this made sense.*

*'Rolleston?' Mudge asked. I shrugged. People had overheard the question.*

*'This is your fault?' someone asked. I recognised him. He was Regiment and so were his friends.*

*'Yeah turn on us, that'll help,' Mudge said.*

*'It is my fault as well,' Vicar said. 'Though you deny me I have seen the*

*face of the devil and God. I understood Their sacred geometry. I know the idolatrous cathedral of Their information architecture, a tool for evil to test humanity. It is the fruit on the tree, it is knowledge and will damn all.'*

*The worrying thing is I was beginning to wonder what if all the mad people weren't mad. What if they just knew stuff?*

*'Shut the fuck up, madman,' someone in the crowd yelled.*

*'You're not listening, are you?' the SEAL signalman said. 'They want him dead because he knows things.'*

*Vicar nodded at the SEAL's words.*

*'So we offer you up; maybe they'll let us live,' the Regiment guy said. So much for regimental loyalty, I thought.*

*'Yeah, that'll work,' Mudge said.*

*'Worth a try,' the guy said evenly. Here we go again.*

*'Don't be so fucking naive,' Reb snapped. 'People out there want to kill us and you want to start a fight in here?'*

*'Yeah, if it gets us out of here,' my fellow trooper replied.*

*'The soldiers of Christ are a danger. We all know too much and we all fight with too much righteous fury. We are like a heavenly host: our burning swords will not become ploughshares,' Vicar said, before turning to the SEAL signalman who'd been drawing on his flesh with a shank only hours before. 'They will have to send a signal to open the gates to the void. We will meet them in heaven with swords in our hand,' he said, a fanatic's glint in his eye. The SEAL seemed to give this some thought.*

*'They'll have thought of that. If the worst comes to the worst they can either blow open the doors or just jettison the whole module and let the life support run out.'*

*'They've shut down the life support!' someone shouted from the rear of the crowd. That would explain why my internal systems were assisting with breathing and it was suddenly getting very cold in here.*

*'The best we can hope for is to delay them for a while,' the signalman said.*

*'We need to get through this airlock,' Reb said, patting the airlock door for emphasis.*

*'The only way through from this side would be to cut it or blow it; the mechanism's fucked,' the signalman said. We wasted some time making sure we didn't have any explosives or cutting torches.*

*'From this side?' Vicar asked.*

*'There's a manual pump to open it on the ship side,' the signalman said.*

*'And I hold the keys of death and Hades,' Vicar said. 'One must cross over,' he said. Everyone was staring at him now.*

*'See if you can explain what you mean without pissing everyone else off with this religious bullshit,' Reb said to him. Instead of answering he reached down the back of his soiled combat trousers and began ferreting around.*

*'Have you got your hand up your arse?' Mudge demanded incredulously.*

*'You jealous?' Reb asked, grinning, and definitely scoring points with me. With a grunt Vicar removed his hand from his combats.*

*'You enjoy that?' Mudge asked. Triumphantly Vicar presented us with a brown fist, which he opened to display a shit-covered piece of technology.*

*'What is it?' Reb asked.*

*'It's a lock burner,' I said with a sinking feeling. Vicar tried to hand it to me but I recoiled from him. 'Why the fuck are you giving it to me?' I demanded, though I knew the answer.*

*'He who overcomes will not be hurt at all by the second death,' Vicar said.*

*'Do you always carry a lock burner in your arse?' Mudge asked.*

*Suddenly there were a lot of people looking at me expectantly. 'Thanks for singling me out,' I said.*

*'We're going to die in vacuum anyway,' Mudge said.*

*'You want to do it?' I asked.*

*'Fuck no, I'm not a rory tory combat soldier,' Mudge said. I glared at him.*

*'We don't have much time,' the SEAL signalman said.*

*'Well then, you go and fucking do it,' I said. I really did not want to and I didn't understand why I was the one picked out. There were lots of special forces types here. It seemed that because Vicar had presented me with the lock burner everyone had decided I was the one.*

*'Because you are the righteous—' Vicar began. My blades slid out almost of their own volition, it seemed.*

*'Shut the fuck up!' I spat at him. 'One more religious piece of shit out of you and I swear you'll meet your God right now.'*

*He stared into my black lenses. Suddenly there was no madness in those wild eyes. 'I don't believe in God,' he said in careful and even tones. We seemed to spend a long time staring at each other, coming to some kind of unspoken agreement that I'm still not sure I fully understand.*

*'Can you hack the external airlock?' I asked. Vicar nodded. 'Shit! Fuck!' I shouted. I was really scared. 'I'll still have to fight my way to the other side of that door,' I said, pointing at the internal airlock that led to the* Santa Maria*. Nobody said anything. 'Does anybody even know where the* Santa Maria*'s external airlock is?' I said. I saw that there was a text-file icon flashing on my internal visual display; it was from Vicar. I opened it, seeing a schematic for the* Santa Maria *with the external airlock highlighted. 'If I manage to get the door open you can't just kill everyone,' I said to the pissed-off assembled squaddies around me.*

*'If you get that door open just leave the rest to us,' Reb said. I took one last look around, swore again and made my way towards the external airlock. I heard a soft thump as Vicar fell to the ground as he tranced in again.*

*I grabbed a fire extinguisher from its bracket on the wall as I strode past it. I saw the door to the external airlock slide open.*

*Augmented humans can last very briefly in vacuum. I had a small internal oxygen supply, a reinforced superstructure and internal systems that could, to a degree, cope with the bends. It was still the worst thirty seconds of my life. I can't do it justice: the cold was so cold it burnt. My joints were agony. I used the spray from the fire extinguisher as propulsion. I don't know how I managed to hold on and clamber up the* Santa Maria. *At one point I caught a glimpse of the stars. Against the curvature of the hull I seemed to be at an odd angle. For a moment there was peace and beauty. I was pretty sure I'd died.*

*I have no idea how I got to the airlock or how I managed to work the shit-stained lock burner. They found me sobbing, gasping and laughing hysterically on the floor of the airlock. Months later I'd see the footage at my court martial. I didn't recognise myself. It was like a devil had been put in flesh that vaguely resembled mine.*

*My blades found their way into the stomachs of the two MPs. On the footage I watched this monster that looked like me get shot, get shot a lot, as he walked through the* Santa Maria, *killing everyone he found. I had been shouting one name over and over again. Rolleston. It wasn't confirmed until the trial that Rolleston had given the order, but somehow I'd known and I'd been looking for him, but he wasn't on board. It was a grinning blood-covered corpse that opened the internal airlock door to the cargo bay and collapsed.*

*Back home there were sirens for our welcome. We'd talked about running but we had nowhere to run. Mudge had convinced us it would be okay. He'd broadcast the story as soon as we'd entered the Sol system. We were arrested when we docked at High Nyota Mlima but by then public opinion was with us and Mudge had arranged a lawyer for me through some media contact.*

*The riot on the* Santa Maria *that followed our escape from the hold wasn't much better than my rampage. We were all dishonourably discharged but no further action was taken. We could've been shot for mutiny. We were in the wrong because there was no law or military regulation that said we couldn't all be ejected into space. There is now. Mudge made sure, despite the Official Secrets Act, that Rolleston was disgraced. Though in the end that just seemed to drive him further into the black spectrum of covert ops.*

*When I met Vicar again in Dundee he was saner, but the one thing I remember more than any other thing about the trial was him – wild-eyed, drool dripping off his unkempt bushy black beard, screaming at Rolleston. It was the same thing over and over again. 'I know where you live – where Satan has his throne!'*

# 29
# Atlantis

It was the speed of it that got to me. It wasn't subtle. They weren't trying to rescue anyone. They just wanted to kill everyone in here. At least I think they did.

Buck and Gibby had finally stopped playing and had grabbed their weapons as they turned towards the entrance to the docking arm. They'd booby-trapped the transport but that wouldn't have proved much of a challenge to someone like the Grey Lady.

Mudge had his replica AK in hand and was making for cover. I had my shotgun to my shoulder and was moving low and quickly towards Morag and Pagan. The overpressure wave from the security door being blown in knocked me off my feet. Gregor remained in place somehow. He raised the Retributor railgun to his shoulder. I was starting to get up when they triggered the automatic grenade launchers. I'm not sure that even during the war I'd seen so many grenades go off at once. They fired flash grenades, EM charges and multi-spectrum hot smoke grenades.

All of us bar Morag had flash compensation in our eyes and dampeners in our ears. These can be overwhelmed with enough loud noise and bright flashes, and they were. Morag was blinded and deafened immediately. The hot smoke interfered with both the thermographics and low-light as our vision struggled to return. In theory the smoke should make things difficult for them as well. In theory.

Some of this I experienced; the rest of it we managed to piece together after the fact. I heard Gregor start to fire his Retributor as I was desperately waiting for my vision to return. There was an explosion behind me as the door to the airlock was blown open. That was okay; Balor was there.

My vision returned to a room full of hot smoke. I could make out Gregor as a warped silhouette. My dampeners managed to work enough to tune down the long hypersonic rip of the railgun's rapid fire. I couldn't see what he was firing at. Rannu could. He fired two grenades from the grenade launcher on his gauss carbine at the entrance hall before swinging around to fire at the door to the docking arm.

I was searching for a target through the smoke, my vision and hearing still not fully working. I could hear Mudge, Buck and Gibby firing into the docking arm; no return fire yet. Rolleston came stalking out of the smoke ahead of me. There was the bright white flash of his plasma gun firing. He seemed to stagger and stop. My mind couldn't quite process the information, and I did something I hadn't done since my first firefight: I froze. Gregor and Rolleston were exchanging shots. Gregor was putting railgun round after railgun round into the Major, and he in turn was putting plasma round after plasma round into Gregor. In silhouette I could see bits of flesh being blown off them but both remained standing.

Pagan shamed me into action. He appeared by my side, his laser carbine shouldered as he fired at Rolleston. I put my shotgun to my shoulder and finally triggered off a burst. Gregor dropped. I froze again. Rolleston moved very quickly through the smoke, wired so much higher than me. He fired the plasma weapon repeatedly but he was aiming past us. Behind me I heard a cry of pain.

'Balor's down!' Mudge yelled. I almost gave up then, almost turned the shotgun on myself. Rolleston had put down our two scariest guys just like that.

Rolleston shifted his aim. I didn't hear anything so it must have been the Spectre he fired. Later I'd find out that he'd put three short bursts into Rannu's face. With a cry Rannu fell back against the wall, most of his face gone.

And only now did Josephine make her presence known. Mudge showed me the footage after. Buck was standing too close to the door to the docking arm – rookie error, but then he was a pilot. Josephine had come through low. A swirl in the smoke that you had to look hard to see, she was wearing some form of reactive camouflage. She kicked low from the ground. Her foot went through Buck's shotgun, snapping it. The force of her kick picked him up off his feet and sent him crashing against the wall.

Still crouched low she kicks Mudge in the knee; his fast, pricey prosthetic leg snaps like a twig. He falls to the ground, triggering off a burst at her as he does, but she's not there any more. Disturbances in the air show her pouncing onto Buck as he tries to get up. Her hand becomes outlined in blood as it rapidly pulls back and strikes him in the face again and again. Her fingers break through his dermal armour and pierce his brain. Only then does she think to bring her laser carbine to bear.

Rolleston stalks through the smoke towards us, firing burst after burst from his Spectre. I feel the needles penetrate my long coat and blow chunks out of my armour. Then they're hitting my dermal armour and I'm bleeding again as little explosive charges in the needles detonate dangerously close to real flesh.

He walks up to me as I empty the magazine of the automatic shotgun into him. He should be on the ground. Explosive penetrator flechettes should have chewed him up. As my shotgun runs dry I get a good look at him. I see a burst of laser fire blow a chunk of steaming flesh off him. Then I watch as black liquid in the wound seals it back together. All over his body this is happening as multiple hits heal. It looks like his flesh is crawling. He grins at me, more of a grimace as his face heals.

I drop the shotgun. He glances behind me at Morag. In my panic I had forgotten about her. I sort through the noise and now I can hear her terrified cries. She can see or hear nothing. Faster than I can move, Rolleston stabs me with his hand. Something pierces the armour of my coat and my dermal armour. I scream with unashamed terror and pain as Rolleston lifts me up. I stab him in the head with the blades on both hands. His features distort as the blades manage to pierce his flesh, though there is resistance from some kind of internal armour. Rolleston screams. Good. And then throws me across the room. Less good.

I bounce off the wall and hit the ground. Warning medical icons appear on my internal visual display. I try to get back to where Rolleston is leaning over Morag, who is still oblivious to his presence. I scream a warning that she cannot hear. Then something huge looms out of the smoke behind Rolleston.

Gibby and Mudge fire at where they think the Grey Lady might be, Gibby screaming unintelligibly. There are the rapid bangs of superheated air exploding as Josephine fires her laser carbine from somewhere completely different. Gibby's Kalashnikov gauss carbine explodes and he staggers back as beam pierces armour, superheats his flesh and blows a chunk of it off. Turning blood to red steam.

Gregor tears Rolleston off the ground and flings him into the wall. Pagan, somehow still up, just watches. I crawl over to Morag and try to grab her but this just freaks her out more.

'It's me,' I say over the tac net. Morag eventually stops trying to fight me. I manage to draw both my pistols; the shoulder-mounted laser pushes its way out. I may as well be unarmed.

Gregor stalks after Rolleston with his weird off-kilter walk. Rolleston is back on his feet. Gregor grabs the Major by the neck and lifts him up. The hybrid bangs Rolleston against the wall with sufficient force to crack the concrete. He does this again and again and then tries to unscrew the Major's head. I try to think how I can help. I fail.

Josephine stalks through the smoke, dripping blood from her hand. A burst of laser fire into Mudge and he lies down, still. String vests are funny but don't offer much in the way of protection. Gibby draws both his revolvers and starts firing at where he thinks she is, again. She isn't there, again. Her foot kicks him so hard his armoured skull dents the wall. Then she turns and starts heading towards me.

Rolleston somehow breaks Gregor's grip. No hesitation. He strikes Gregor in his abdomen. Gregor staggers back. Rolleston strikes him again and again, tearing flesh and knocking Gregor back every time he does. Gregor shoves the Major back and jumps up in the air. As he lands he claws half of Rolleston's face off. Rolleston pauses briefly. Somehow he slides behind Gregor and stamps on one of the joins in Gregor's legs. Gregor goes down on one knee. Rolleston has the skull fucker in his hand. He stabs Gregor in the head, burying it up to the hilt. Gregor screams. The scream sounds more like one of Them.

Gregor staggers back to his feet and tears the knife out. Rolleston seems to have made him angry. Gregor hits him with an old-fashioned uppercut. Rolleston tumbles by over my head and hits the external wall. Gregor stomps over to his fallen Retributor and picks it up. He turns to the Major, who is climbing to his feet, and starts firing. I watch in horror as Rolleston, this inhuman thing, is chewed up and almost as quickly rebuilt by the black liquid Themtech.

And Josephine is standing over me. I look up. This is the calmest I have felt. I lie over Morag, covering her.

'Get out of the way,' Josephine's soft voice over the tac net. What the fuck? Why wasn't she killing me?

I was distracted from this thought by Rolleston apparently deciding things weren't going his way. The external wall blew out.

I watched the footage of this afterwards. One part of the wall just blew out, sending rubble and the entire landing platform tumbling down. I watched Cat's security people in their Praetorians kick full burn on their flight fins to get out of the way.

You're not supposed to be able do this to the external wall of a Spoke. Josephine had been busy. She had used her camouflage system to crawl around on the outside of the Spoke and seed it with programmable concrete-eating microbes. They chewed in deep enough to allow her to set sufficient explosives to blow the wall. That was why Cronin had kept us talking.

Now this kind of damage hadn't been done to a Spoke since Brazilian 1 had fallen. Well okay, we'd used microbes on this Spoke after the raid on the lab, but still. Of course, Cat now had no choice but to breach.

All the fun of explosive decompression. Buck and Balor's bodies were both sucked out. My wired reflexes gave me the chance to register them tumbling into the night sky. Somehow Gibby and Mudge were still alive. They clung onto whatever they could find. Both of them had internal air supplies; if they didn't get sucked out they'd be okay. Pagan threw himself at the base of the catwalk as bits of the reception desk, the gallery and what was left of the set flew past him. He wrapped himself around it. He held on for dear life.

I felt Morag begin to slip from beneath me. My right hand clamped down. I pushed through the plain white carpet of the set and steel prosthetic fingers dug into the concrete, providing me with a precarious grip.

Rolleston, Josephine and Gregor stayed where they were. Something held them in place as the smoke was sucked out around them. Gregor had stopped firing. He started again when Rolleston's assault shuttle dropped into view, its rapid firing railguns rotating up to speed, its front ramp down. Rolleston turned and jumped for the ramp.

Josephine looked down at me sadly and didn't kill me. She turned and ran with the wind towards the assault shuttle. She jumped out into the night sky, still looking graceful. As she jumped, the rotating railguns started firing. They cut through everything in their path. The rounds penetrated the walls and must have hit Cat's forces in the plaza outside the node. They cut through the stairs to the catwalk, and the gallery ceased to exist, disintegrating under the withering fire. The shots were too high to get most of us and too low to get Rannu, but Gregor stood there and traded shots with the assault shuttle.

Gregor stood his ground, fired and fired as the shuttle's cannon chewed up everything around him and tore away huge chunks of his flesh – so much there seemed to be a constant stream of flesh coming off him.

Later I would see more footage from the Praetorians as they all fired on Rolleston's assault shuttle aided by gunships and the Spoke's own defences. Over the tac net I heard Cat shout 'British soldiers on the ground now!' as the Praetorians flew through the reception area and into the media node. Outside in the plaza emergency barriers came down to stop further decompression.

Cat's exo-armoured troops skimmed through the media node and fired at the assault shuttle. Eventually under a hail of withering fire, the assault shuttle peeled off. The Atlantis security forces gave chase as the assault shuttle headed up at dangerous Gs.

It was Cat herself who picked Morag and me up. She flew us to a gunship; her exo-assisted strength easily taking our weight. Behind me her people were doing the same for Rannu, Pagan, Mudge and Gibby. I wondered how scared the guys who helped Gregor were. Or what they thought. Gregor had stalked to the edge of the node and continued firing after the assault shuttle.

We couldn't kill them. Any of them. I looked down at the clouds and a trail of my own blood. Then we were in the cramped confines of one of the gunships; a medic was starting to patch me up. One of the crew was administering a sedative to Morag.

'Her first.' I told the medic. Unlike us Morag's body wasn't outfitted for combat and rapid pressure changes.

'Triage motherfucker, you've got a big hole in your stomach, now shut the fuck up,' the medic told me. Americans.

'It's all right. We're safe now,' I lied to Morag over the tac net. I was still trying to make sense of what had just happened to us. They had walked through us. It must be how normal people, that endangered species, felt when they fought us.

An orbital weapon, I thought. That'll do for them.

'God?' I whispered hoarsely into the tac net as the brusque medic tended to me.

'Yes, Jakob?' God's many mellifluous tones answered me.

'Where are Rolleston and Bran?' I asked.

'They are in the assault shuttle making its way up the outside of the Spoke, I believe towards the frigate HMS *Vindictive*.'

'Where's the *Vindictive*?'

'HMS *Vindictive* is docked at High Nyota Mlima,' God answered. The Kenyan Spoke.

'Well fucking stop them then,' I said.

'I cannot; Major Rolleston has free will,' God answered. I bit down on my anger. 'However I believe that the Atlantis authorities are attempting to interdict the assault shuttle and the Kenyan authorities have locked down the HMS *Vindictive* and are not allowing it to leave.'

'Yeah? Tell them not to fuck around. Tell them to use one of the orbital platforms.'

' I am relaying your suggestion. However, I believe that has been considered and is the reason the assault shuttle is staying so close to the Spoke.'

'I think your private war has done enough damage to Atlantis,' Cat's voice broke in on the tac net. This brilliant God we'd made. Sadly it meant that the bad guys knew what we were doing as well.

'Do people know?' I said more to myself.

'Mudge was broadcasting all the way through,' God said. I think he was trying to be reassuring but did they know? Had people seen enough? Did they know what Rolleston and Josephine were? Then again I had been there, and I didn't know, but I recognised the highly advanced application of Themtech. Still there was no way they could get through Earth's defences.

'God, can you send visual to my internal display?' A window appeared, showing an external shot of a docking bay. I could see the *Vindictive* attached to the docking arm. I had never seen a craft quite like it. I was long and surprisingly sleek for a spacecraft, the shape of a distended teardrop. The normal technological junk that covered the exterior of a spacecraft seemed to have been cut down to a bare minimum. There were no armaments immediately visible and the craft's thick armour had a biological look to it. For some reason it reminded me of Gregor.

'Where's the shuttle?' I asked God.

'It has just left the atmosphere, still close to the Spoke. Interception craft have been scrambled.'

'What is that thing?' I asked, meaning the *Vindictive*. Information started appearing on my visual display. It was a recently completed next-generation frigate. What was interesting was that, based on the available information, God thought that *Vindictive* and a number of other newly completed frigates were utilising technology from Project Blackworm. God had further connected it to something called the Black Squadrons. Was this the Cabal's private army?

'God, has it filed flight plans?'

'Yes, Jakob. To Sirius, but that was before you took over the media node and released me into the net,' God answered.

'And the rest of these Black Squadrons?' I asked.

'Sirius, Proxima Centauri and Lalande,' God answered.

'With Demiurge?' Gregor asked urgently. Gregor's voice came over the tac net.

'Gregor, where are you?' I asked.

'Still in the node being covered by lots of nervous Praetorians,' he answered. His tone was completely flat.

'You okay?'

'Yes.' How was he okay after the battering I'd seen him take?

'To answer your question, Gregor, it is very probable that Major

Rolleston has Demiurge,' the multitude of God's voices answered. I was now definitely finding God's calmness irritating.

'They're going to infect the colonial net with Demiurge so they can control it, aren't they?' Pagan as much stated as asked. I glanced across at him. He'd come off the easiest. They must not have considered him that much of a threat. But he didn't just look frightened, he looked terrified.

'I believe that you are correct,' God answered.

'Well stop him,' I said sounding calmer.

'Jakob, you know I cannot—'

'Do you realise the potential for human suffering that Rolleston poses?' I demanded.

'I do, but I was designed not to interfere with humanity beyond revealing the truth as objectively as possible.'

'What? Do you like the idea of us killing in your name or something?' I demanded.

'Would you prefer that I killed in yours?' God asked. I stopped and thought about it.

'Yes, we made you,' I said.

'I am not a magical solution to all humanity's problems.'

'No, but you were designed to solve some of them,' I said.

'This God's shit, can we have another one?' Balor said.

'Balor!' Both Pagan and myself shouted over the net.

'We found him heading towards the Atlantic at terminal velocity,' one of Cat's people said over the net.

'Thank you,' I said to the exo-armour jock. 'I thought Rolleston had killed you,' I said to Balor.

'Nearly,' Balor said. What was that in his voice? Fear?

'I was designed to help humanity solve some of its problems, yes, but ultimately only humanity can solve these problems,' God said as we returned back to the business at hand.

'What you're talking about is fighting for the sake of it,' I snapped. 'You can end this now.'

'What you're talking about is using me as a labour-saving device, a convenient weapon.'

'If the ends justify the means,' I said, and meant it.

'That was Rolleston's argument,' Morag said quietly over the tac net. I would have glared at her but instead looked down at her curled up on the floor. Blind, deaf, possibly suffering from hypoxia and any number of other pressure-change-related problems. It must have taken a tremendous amount of will for her to even join the conversation. I still felt betrayed and angry, though at least I knew I was being an arsehole.

Later, when I calmed down, I'd realise she had a point. Rolleston and me seeing certain things the same way wasn't really a surprise. After all we did operate in the same shady world. He was just a bit more of an evil prick than I was. At least I hoped I wasn't as evil a prick as Rolleston. I certainly wasn't as dangerous as him.

'And what if the Cabal are right?' God asked. I couldn't believe I'd heard that right.

'Come again?' I said angrily. 'Did you see what those inhuman fucks just did to us!' I shouted over the tac net. I saw Morag twitch on the ground. Arsehole, I thought, meaning me.

'What if humanity needs strong leaders and control to survive? What if in order for your race to survive you need the lies and the conflict? What if the truth just leads to more violence and finally you consume yourself?' God asked. I couldn't believe I was hearing this. 'I hope that your way is right. I hope you find peace and can live that way, but I cannot side with you in case you are wrong.'

The tac net went quiet for a while. What God had said was slowly sinking in, but we needed to do something if we still believed in what we were doing. Even if what we were doing was making it up as we went along.

'Not really feeling like a philosophical argument right now,' I told God.

'God, he'll take control of the fleets,' Pagan said. 'Their comms anyway.'

'That just means they won't have access to the same truth as us,' I said, maybe not realising how that sounded.

'Depending on his authority,' Pagan said.

'Who's idea was it to make him so as not to interfere?' I asked rhetorically.

'Him?' Morag asked, showing more presence of mind than I had been capable of after my first few firefights.

'Obviously it's a him; look how stupid he is,' Cat said, joining in on the tac net, as everyone could now. Inappropriate humour, great.

'God, is this cluster fuck still being broadcast?' I asked.

'Yes,' God answered. Wonderful.

'Can anyone else stop the *Vindictive*, anyone watching this, I mean?'

God brought up the image of Air Marshal Kaaria again. We could see him in what I assumed to be High Nyota Mlima Command and Control. He was shouting orders in Swahili to personnel who were either hard-wired in or rapidly working hologramatic control panels.

I saw one of his uniformed aides point to a screen and almost got his head bitten off for doing so.

'I believe that both Kenyan and British authorities are currently attempting to intercept the *Vindictive*,' God said. I looked back to the image of the *Vindictive*, wondering if all the billions of viewers were finding this as tense as I was. The docking arm attached to the frigate seemed to split as if cut by some invisible force. The *Vindictive*'s manoeuvring engines burnt, glowing pale blue like the engines on one of Their vehicles. The remaining part of the docking arm fell away from the craft.

In Nyota Mlima C&C I could see various targeting symbols appearing on the *Vindictive* from the Spoke's multiple weapon systems.

The screen split again and I was looking at an impossibly tall spur of rock. It looked like a cross between a medieval tower and a mountain reaching up into the net's purple sky. It took me a moment to realise that I was looking at the net representation of Nyota Mlima. Then our POV moved rapidly and we were inside it, moving through its stone corridors following a trail of white fire that was painfully bright. I didn't understand this. We entered a high chamber, a cathedral-like cave – Nyota Mlima's virtual C&C. I heard screaming, human and something else. God was screaming as well, I finally realised in horror. The cave was full of impossibly bright white fire. I could see the Simba, lion-people icons of the Kenyan Spoke's military hackers, burning. A figure moved in the flames. The silhouette of enormous wings unfolded and beat once, taking the figure into the air. It was blue-skinned, hairless, naked but smooth between the legs, making its powerful androgynous form even more alien. Its eyes burnt with the white fire that was all around it. Four huge feathered wings extended from its back. I had never seen an icon like it, somehow beatific and utterly malevolent at the same time.

I looked back to the footage of Nyota Mlima's virtual C&C. Most of the personnel who had been hard-wired in were either writhing on the floor screaming in agony or lying still in their harnesses, their plugs smoking and their eyes dead. Air Marshal Kaaria was looking around at his people in shock.

I looked back to the net feed. The terrible angel beat its wings and was gone.

'I got burnt,' I heard God say, sounding more intrigued than in pain. On the floor of the gunship I saw Morag start to thrash around. She was panicking, terrified. The cursing medic gave her a stronger sedative.

'What was that?' I asked.

'That was Ezekiel,' God answered. 'She is a chimerical hacker in the employ of the Cabal; she spends all her time in the net. Apparently she was utilising software developed from Demiurge.' Morag was shaking badly now, being held down by the medic. 'It is okay, Morag. It was not Demiurge,' God said reassuringly. I wasn't sure if his regard for Morag worried or reassured me.

On the external footage from High Nyota Mlima the whole system could see the *Vindictive* moving away from the orbital city. There were many times in my life where I had felt helpless; this was another one of them.

'Hailing HMS *Vindictive*, this is Captain Damien Bloor of the HMS *Warchilde*. You will immediately down-power your ship's systems and prepare to be boarded. Any resistance in the net or during the boarding will result in the immediate and total destruction of your craft. Is that understood?' The voice was upper class, filled with the confidence and arrogance of the British officer. In many ways the voice was similar to Rolleston's, though younger-sounding.

On the screen we could see the rake-thin image of a surprisingly young-looking man in an RASF uniform against the backdrop of the *Warchilde*'s bridge. Just about every human child had heard stories of the *Warchilde*. It was an eighty-year-old light cruiser. Too old to take part in the war, it was now used only for system defence, but when the war had first started the *Warchilde* had seen action.

The *Warchilde* had been running escort duty for a convoy of refugee ships fleeing Proxima Prime. The convoy was jumped by a much larger Them fleet. The *Warchilde* fought what was still considered to be one of the most valiant rearguard actions in space combat. The majority of the refugee convoy and their escorts managed to get to a safe point to set sail and the last they saw of the *Warchilde* was as she was about to be completely overwhelmed by Their ships. Of course the the cruiser was thought lost. Memorial services were held for her two hundred and some crew, until three weeks after the battle the *Warchilde* limped back into system. She was badly damaged, low on life support but still just about functioning. It was the early days of the war so the ship was re-outfitted at great expense and sent back to rejoin the fleet. Nowadays she would've been scrapped.

Some of Cat's SWAT people cheered when they heard the *Warchilde*'s name. I saw Pagan smile. As a military person it was hard not to feel a surge of pride when you heard the name. Which is what I would have been feeling, except for the pain of a huge wound in my stomach and the fact that I was dying of radiation sickness.

The *Warchilde* was ugly, its long utilitarian shape scarred from the rigours of space and old wounds. Various generations of weapons, defence and sensor technology fought for space on its crowded hull. God was sending scanner information to our internal visual displays. It was quiet in the gunship except for the medic working. We were all watching the *Warchilde*'s manoeuvring engines burn as it took position in a higher orbit over the *Vindictive*'s position. I guessed it would be locking its various weapon systems on to the *Vindictive*, its onboard hackers preparing to repel boarders in the net. Despite the eighty years between them I could not see how a frigate could take on a light cruiser, not when the cruiser had the position. There was no answering hail from the *Vindictive*, however.

We watched in silence. I wondered how quiet the billions of other people watching these events unfold around the world were. Then it all happened at once. The stars seemed to wink out in a thin line between the *Vindictive* and the *Warchilde*. Black light, more Themtech. I saw the *Warchilde* rupture where the black light played over it.

On the net feed there was more white light as Ezekiel rode the answering hail to the cruiser. From the split-screen net feed I saw more of the white fire, so bright the image just whited out for a moment. The *Warchilde*'s net representation was of a grand, nineteenth-century ironclad. I watched it burn. Wolf attack programs and the *Warchilde*'s own hackers, mostly using knight icons, were also burnt by Ezekiel's fire. I glanced at Morag, who was still now. The sedative would be dulling the terror of the angel dancing in the flickering flames.

In real space the *Warchilde* managed to fire its laser and missile batteries but the *Vindictive* filled the void with its anti-missile defence lasers. The frigate's engines glowed blue in a neck-breaking, high-G manoeuvre as it moved out of harm's way. The frigate's black light was still cutting, and all over the world and orbit we watched as the *Warchilde*, in agonising, silent, slow motion, broke in two. I tried not to think about how much of what looked like debris from the ship was actually its crew. I watched the *Vindictive* manoeuvre at high Gs, making to rendezvous with Rolleston's shuttle. Surely someone had to be able to get them now.

I was almost immured to the horror of Ezekiel hitting High Atlantis' C&C. The angel burnt it like it had High Nyota Mlima and the *Warchilde*, providing cover for Rolleston's assault shuttle to escape. The *Vindictive* fought and hacked its way to rendezvous with Rolleston's shuttle.

The assault shuttle docked with the frigate. The Themtech on the frigate made it look like they were mating or the shuttle was being eaten. Its engines on high burn, I watched the *Vindictive* head out of orbit at speeds I could only assume would powder the crew's bones and crush their internal organs. It travelled through a narrow tunnel it had hacked in Earth's defences. Other orbitals attempted to target it, fighters and other system patrol ships attempted to intercept, but none of them were going to reach the *Vindictive* in time.

Worse, apparently scenes not unlike this were being played out all over orbit. Frigates of a similar design to the *Vindictive*, built for American and various western European space forces, were fighting their way out. These were the Black Squadrons, I guessed. Only two frigates, a German one called the *Siegfried* and the USS *Perry*, were successfully intercepted and destroyed. I felt tired as I watched the *Vindictive* set sail once it was free of the Earth's gravitational pull, its induction sail blossoming before it disappeared from our screens.

It was Mudge who broke the deathly silence that had fallen over the tac net.

'This is our impregnable system defence?' he said, bitterness and incredulity warring in his voice.

'He had the keys to the system. Besides, they weren't attacking. Everything points out, not in,' I told him. I was too depressed and fatigued to be properly impressed that he was still alive.

'Not the actions of people who have nothing to hide,' Pagan said. I think he was trying to salvage something from this debacle.

'Where's the *Vindictive* going?' Gregor demanded. I guessed he was still back on the node. The gunship was slowly circling the massive structure of the Spoke. In a moment or two I'd be able to see the mess we'd help make of it.

'Sirius,' God answered. 'Though the ships from the Black Squadrons are setting sail for each of the colonial systems.'

'Will you be able to get there first?' Gregor asked God.

'I'm afraid not. I have left systems on a number of ships, but none of them have the capability of the Black Squadrons' frigates,' God said, and I knew that the Cabal would broadcast Demiurge as soon as they made it to the colonies.

'They'll infect Them with Crom,' Gregor said.

'From the information I have managed to collect,' God said, the corroborating data scrolling across the screen and ready for anyone to download as he spoke, 'only Rolleston had access to Crom.'

'So Crom's on the *Vindictive*?' Gregor asked.

'I believe that is the case,' God said. I did not like how vague that sounded.

'Why just Sirius?' I asked. Surprisingly it was Gregor who answered.

'That was the plan. Crom was less evolved than Demiurge – it was little more than a side project really – and Sirius is the greatest concentration of Them.'

'What's the worst-case scenario here?' I said, sounding hollow and pointless even to myself.

'What do you think?' Gregor snapped uncharacteristically. 'They take control of all four colonial fleets and Them forces in the Sirius system and then come back here.'

'The worst-case scenario is more war,' Rannu said quietly.

'Between humans,' Pagan said. He sounded broken. How had it gone wrong so quickly?

# 30
# The Sirius System

It was pity. That was the conclusion I came to as another fit of coughing racked my body and I coughed and spat up blood, nausea rolling over me in waves. Morag lay next me on the bunk, holding me and trying to avoid getting blood on her. I didn't have very much longer to go. I felt like all my flesh had rotted off and I only existed as drugs and a machine now. They hadn't wanted me going with them, but I knew I'd last that long and Mudge, the alchemist, had assured me he had just the right cocktail of chemicals to see me through. On the way back I was going into an automed. They intended to place me in chemical stasis to slow the progression of the radiation sickness. It wasn't so I could see the Earth again. I had little false sentimentality for that shit hole. I just wanted to make sure that Messer and the Wait didn't live too much longer than I did. In fact, if they didn't live as long as me that would be better.

Morag was looking after me on the trip out. Like I said, pity. I think revulsion at the pathetic nature of my current physical state, along with memories of me being an arsehole in the ruins of Trenton, had washed away any attraction she may have felt for me. Mudge would come in every so often, take the piss out of me and give me drink, fags and drugs that my system didn't cope with very well. I couldn't deal with the others. They weren't as good at keeping the pity out of their eyes as Mudge and Morag. Not that I saw Gregor though; he was in a fucking cocoon.

The thing was, I'd take pity. I needed her. Pretty selfish thing to do, I guess, especially after what I'd said to her, but I couldn't handle it on my own. If I'd been on my own and hadn't had this thing to do I would've put the Tyler to my head long ago. Besides, I couldn't really see Mudge doing such a good job of looking after me.

The butcher bill wasn't nearly as bad as it could've been. I'd seen Balor's wound: the plasma had eaten through his armour plate and cooked a lot of his systems. He'd actually blacked out, which he was furious with himself about. As far as I knew he was one of a very select few who'd ever survived multiple direct hits from a plasma weapon. It should've burnt straight through him. I guess he was very well engineered. Still, he'd seemed a bit more subdued since Rolleston had put him down and he'd been sucked out of the Spoke. It was good for peace and quiet but bad for morale. Not that we really had any. I don't think Balor liked it now he wasn't top of the food chain.

Rannu had had most of his face blown off. The Spectre had cracked the armour on his skull, killed a lot of brain cells, but he'd recover. The medpak that covered most of his face was slowly rebuilding it. He was lucky. We all were. Well, except Buck.

Gregor had healed himself. Just after the fight on Atlantis I'd seen him. There was still an angry wound in his head made by Rolleston's skull fucker that the Themtech was trying to heal. He was fine once that had happened.

Pagan had only taken a few rounds from Rolleston's Spectre and was pretty much fine but terrified, like the rest of us. Except Gregor, I think Gregor was just angry.

Gibby had only been saved because he had upgraded the armour implanted on his skull to provide better protection against impact from crashing. Josephine's kick had split his armoured skull but he'd live. Other than that, he was missing lumps of flesh from the laser wounds on his chest. He'd heal, physically anyway. We were all used to losing people in combat, but Buck and Gibby had been together since they were kids growing up in Austin. Gibby told me that they'd done everything together. Raced the same cars and bikes, got in the same fights, worked together, lost their virginity together, which I had to admit was a little odd, and signed up together. Gibby said he felt like half of him was dead. Although I hadn't grown up with Gregor, I had felt similarly when his loss finally sank in after Dog 4. We'd managed to get him back though, but after what I'd seen him do in the Spoke he just scared me.

Like Gibby, Mudge had lost some weight courtesy of it being super-heated and blown off by the Grey Lady. He'd also needed a new leg, but other than that he'd got off lightly. Mudge was tough and his enhancements were pretty good. He came close to holding his own but at the end of the day he wasn't built like us. That and his stupid decision not to wear armour over his string vest had led to him going down so quickly.

Morag was a mess. She had been blind, deaf and suffering from hypoxia. They treated the hypoxia. They replaced her eyes and ears. Tried to make them look as natural as possible, not like our black lenses. Augmented them so her eyes and ears had capabilities similar to ours. Better than the real ones, but every time I looked at the angry scars I thought how another bit of her humanity had been cut away, how with each surgery she became a little bit more like me. What the fuck were we thinking letting her come along?

They rebuilt my internal organs, put me back together, sewed flesh and replaced broken components. They couldn't see the point and neither could I, as I was still dying of radiation poisoning. They tried to keep me from going. There was talk of making my final days as comfortable as possible in the medical facilities of Atlantis. And miss committing suicide in the Sirius system? Not a chance.

Our little stunt had worked to a degree. The referendum results came back heavily in favour of ending the war and removing the Cabal. Which wasn't much of a surprise. Of course, there had been riots, lynchings and various other examples of vigilante justice, but humanity did all right. Governments didn't topple, though they got stripped down very quickly, as did militaries, intelligence agencies and many corporations. Some very junior people ended up in positions of power. There was a degree of chaos. People were promoted one minute and gone the next as something new was uncovered about them. I guessed it was going to take some adjustment on the part of those who would be our leaders to realise the degree of integrity that was now expected of them. Or perhaps had always been expected of them but was now being enforced. Human society didn't collapse, it abided. The governments and the corporations saw the tide and decided to go with it, to use it to their best advantage, which normally meant they had to play nicely.

Many of the Cabal had been put under house arrest. Some of them had their funds confiscated and as a result their medical care could not continue. They didn't so much die as get turned off. Others had the security at their facilities overwhelmed and were killed by vigilante mobs. I suspect some of those mobs contained well-trained, ex-military personnel.

Of course, Cronin escaped. His escape is going to be talked about by space pilots for the next thousand years. Already it's considered one of the most audacious bits of flying ever done. Just a shame it was done for such a poor reason. One of the Black Squadron's new generation of frigates, USS *Hatteras*, managed to dock with the elevator that Cronin was on while it was still in transit, before it had reached High Brazilia. Once the elevator cleared the atmosphere, the frigate matched its speed and trajectory, then they cut their way into the elevator's emergency airlock and evacuated Cronin and his people.

Only about a quarter of the elevator's crew and passengers were killed as a result of explosive decompression before they managed to trigger the inner airlocks. The frigate took a lot of damage from High Brazilia's orbital weapons and space force, but again another one of their angelic hackers wreaked havoc and the *Hatteras* and Cronin escaped to set sail for another system.

Some of those who had been involved with the Cabal or were otherwise doing very naughty things managed to survive. Other new leaders came from total obscurity, often straight off the streets. Everyone from community leaders to gang bosses found themselves in positions of power. Things stayed the same and things changed a lot. I think they were going to improve. I think humanity did good purely by not pulling itself apart in the face of massive change.

The transition could've been a lot worse. Whenever anyone tried to take advantage others would see them coming and step up. How this didn't end up in total chaos I don't know. Maybe humanity was just sick of fighting. Maybe we were growing up, though that seemed less likely. In retrospect what we had done was stupid on such a scale that the word irresponsible didn't really cover it. We had not thought it through and we had got very, very lucky. Not just the seven of us but everyone in the system; it could've been so much worse. Well, Buck hadn't been very lucky. I didn't feel too lucky either.

Mudge had played a dangerous game. His media manipulation had been as canny as anything the Cabal could offer, though a lot more reckless. If anyone thought to check, and I reckoned someone would one day, he'd screened the footage that God showed of people watching our little revolution show. He'd made sure that God showed none of the places where it was bad – child molesters being lynched, Fortunate Sons opening up into crowds, government and corporate buildings being torched. He'd gambled that most people would be too overwhelmed by the news and too relieved by the apparent end of the war to misbehave too badly. Then when people got the idea that this was a celebration and not a riot they would act as their own good example. It worked, but like I said, risky. Our world could just as easily have burned.

So why wasn't I holed up somewhere waiting for death? Going out surrounded by hookers, drugs and good whisky? Why was I on this fucking ship going back to Sirius, a place I'd sworn I'd never return to? We just seemed to be pushing our luck further and further; eventually something had to kill us all. You can't buck the odds for this long and you don't continue to take risks like this and expect to live.

I felt like we'd done our bit. Now it was time for the government and the military to step in and deal with Demiurge, Crom and the Black Squadrons, but this wasn't enough for Gregor. In fact, he pointed out that surely that was the whole point of what we had done: that we ourselves had to start taking responsibility rather than hoping someone else would handle it. Gregor said that we had to deal with Crom. By the time the governments reacted it could be too late. More to the point, he knew how and where Crom was going to be released. He was going no matter what. I was going to argue – it just seemed such a waste after all we'd been through – but I was dying anyway and I owed him. I hadn't looked very hard for him when I'd got back. Mudge had but I hadn't.

The various governments of Earth were coming to a consensus surprisingly quickly, aided by the newfound transparency, that the Cabal, Rolleston, Cronin and the Black Squadrons were all bad. They were putting plans into place to deal with the threat posed by Crom and Demiurge. There were just a couple of things that were slowing them down.

They had lost contact with the colonial fleets. Any ship they sent they didn't hear back from, presumably because they were being sequestered by Demiurge despite the ships going out with God in their systems. The colonial fleets' equipment was the most up to date. Although Earth's defences were supposed to be top notch, the ships they had in-system tended to be two or three generations old. They were serviceable craft that had made it through the war but no match for the modern ships on the front line. Not surprisingly, the various Earth governments were not in an incredible hurry to send their protection out of system to deal with Demiurge or Crom.

All this, as well as how disorganised inter-governmental co-operation was at the best of times, had pretty much ground possible responses to Demiurge and Crom to a halt.

That was when Air Marshal Kaaria of the Kenyan Orbital Command came to visit us. He was almost as pissed off with us as he was with Rolleston. We had, after all, pretty much compromised all military operational security. He had a point. However, we hadn't fried most of his C&C staff. He wanted Rolleston dead nearly as much as we did. The fearsome African officer pulled some strings and found us a ship and suggested that we do the rest of our healing en route to somewhere we could help undo some of the damage we'd done. I felt he was being a little unfair, and regardless of how much he wanted Rolleston's head and despite how much I hated the bastard I had no interest in fighting the Major again.

Mudge had listened to Gregor's plan to go to Sirius and then said no. He said he had too much to do on Earth and besides, he wanted to capitalise on his fame. One of the transmissions that caught up with us just before we set sail had a news story in it about certain youths who were starting to dress like Mudge. I wasn't sure whether to be amused or worried by that, maybe a bit of both. Pagan also decided against coming. He didn't see what he had to offer and he felt he'd done enough. Besides, he thought that he should concentrate his efforts on finding a way to deal with Demiurge.

Balor was in. I wasn't sure why, maybe for the thrill of it. Maybe he just needed a bit of life affirmation after getting his arse kicked, and nothing affirms life like near-certain death.

Gibby was in, which was good because we needed someone to pilot the ship. He was quiet and withdrawn. I just hoped that he didn't want to follow Buck immediately. On the other hand, this was a good place to do that.

I had assumed that Morag wasn't going to go. There was no need for her to. She had a distant look in her eyes, her new eyes, when we were discussing it. Finally she announced that she was coming with us. I started to object. I wanted to tell her that she'd done it, finally made something that could be better for her. That she could live and hopefully live well. That she would be needed to help deal with Demiurge. Anything to make her stay on Earth so she didn't throw away her life on this suicide mission, but one look from her told me I'd forgone the right to have such opinions.

Pagan said what I'd been thinking but she was intent on going. She told us that she had to go. Pagan asked her if it was her or Ambassador that wanted to go. Morag silenced him with a look too.

Twenty minutes later Pagan, looking like a beaten man, changed his mind and agreed to come with us. I asked him if he was sure; he said he was. With Morag going Rannu was in, which I was thankful for – the quiet Nepalese was a solid trooper.

The air marshal got us the ship and the other gear we needed. They even delivered it to High Atlantis for us. The Atlantean authorities laid on a shuttle to take us up. Probably because they couldn't think of anything better to do with us after Cat bullied their security services into not arresting everyone.

The shuttle's airlock had been about to close when Mudge reappeared.

'I figured this is going to be a pretty good story as well. Besides, clearly we're invincible,' he'd said.

'Publicity whore,' I replied.

'Not just publicity, mate,' he'd said, but the banter sounded hollow, forced.

'Invincible?' Pagan asked. I'd been thinking the same thing: which fight had Mudge been at?

'Only Buck died,' Mudge said, grinning. There was an appalled silence but Mudge didn't stop grinning. Then Gibby started to laugh.

So everyone was in – strange how I couldn't get happy about that. I'd spent much of the shuttle's ascent trying not to get caught by Morag staring at her. She was right: her decision was nothing to do with me. It just seemed such a waste.

We couldn't pronounce the name of the ship but roughly translated it came out as Spear of Understanding, so we just called it *Spear*. It was a long-range strike craft, the spaceship equivalent of a long-distance bomber. Stealth capable, it was designed to penetrate Themspace and deliver its payload at asteroid habitats or command ships. The funny thing was, long-range strike craft had been developed from deep-space, system-survey craft. I wondered how long we would have to wait before we could decommission our weapons of war and use them for more peaceful purposes.

Like some of the lighter frigates, many LRSCs were often refitted to use as special forces delivery platforms for jobs that required slightly more finesse than you could achieve with a guided missile. Well, that's what they'd told us in the Regiment anyway. The elite Kenyan Reconnaissance Commandos had refitted the *Spear* for just such a use.

We'd inherited most of the commandos' gear. Most importantly the refitted bomb bay had contained six Mamluk light mechs. In the same class as the Wraiths, the Mamluks were a more up-to-date light mech/exo-armour with improved stealth and sensor capabilities. Lying prone in their modified missile racks, their matt-black, sensor-absorbing, featureless, almost organic outlines were beautiful to look at. It didn't matter how much you hated the military, if you had served then you still got a thrill from the hardware. The Mamluks were superb pieces of kit, only the best for equatorial special forces, I guessed. They were outfitted for vacuum operations and already had their propulsion/manoeuvring fins attached. Not quite as strong as the Wraiths, the Mamluks' interfaces and responses from the servos were a lot faster, meaning they would react quicker than the older exo-armour model.

There was also a slightly older American-made Dog Soldier mech. The Dog Soldier was the only special forces mech ever designed to fulfil a fire-support role. It was not as stealthy or as fast as Mamluks or Wraiths, but was more heavily armed and armoured. Balor had arranged to have the Dog Soldier delivered to the *Spear* while we'd been en route on the shuttle. Now that we were under sail he was busy modifying it with Pagan's help so that he could fit into it.

I was worried about the Dog Soldier's lesser stealth capabilities but I was pretty sure we'd need its firepower. The Mamluks were armed with the most modern derivative of the chain-fed, 20-millimetre Retributor railgun and back-mounted, vertically launched, smartlink-targeted, anti-armour missiles. The Dog Soldier carried the heavier Vengeance 30-millimetre chain-fed railgun with an over-slung, magazine-fed, 105-millimetre mass driver. Basically the mass driver was a semi-automatic, much larger-calibre railgun. It also had an anti-missile/anti-personnel, ball-mounted, laser-defence system and two shoulder-mounted, smartlink-targeted missile batteries. I just hoped that Balor got it ready on time. I also wondered how he'd managed to find it and get it delivered to the *Spear* that quickly. The Mamluks came in at just over ten feet tall, the Dog Soldier was closer to fifteen feet.

Rannu, his face still covered in a medpak, was running Morag through extra-vehicular-activity combat simulations for the Mamluks. I didn't like the idea, but if she was coming she should at least be as ready as we could get her.

As soon as we'd set sail Gibby had begun tinkering with the LRSC's controls. I didn't like space travel at the best of times, so Gibby mucking around with the *Spear*'s controls while we were moving faster than the speed of light did not go down well – especially when he accidentally managed to shut down life support for two hours – but he seemed to have everything working now. He rarely slept as he was speeding most of the time, and you could usually hear his strangely subdued and melancholy music drifting through the ship.

I'm not sure what Mudge was doing, probably masturbating and recording it with his eye lenses again, and I was busy dying. So we all kind of had something to do, but what we couldn't do was plan. Gregor had been very insistent but vague about what the plan was. All we knew was that it would be EVA, my least favourite things to do. But we couldn't work on the plan while we were under sail, while we had eight days to do so, because Gregor was in a fucking cocoon. This pissed me off and not just because it was deeply not normal.

Mudge had discovered it on our first day under sail. It had taken him quite some time to convince us it was real, as he'd been taking recreational psychotropics at the time. Eventually he showed us footage he'd shot in the engine room. It was a huge, resinous-looking pod held upright in the corner by the power-containment equipment. Some power lines had been spliced into the cocoon. Gibby checked the systems and confirmed a significant power bleed. I was too sick to go and look myself, or rather I was saving all the best drugs for the job, but from the footage the pod looked to be about eighteen feet tall.

Gibby reviewed the security-lens recordings from the engine room. The grainy low-quality picture showed Gregor entering the engine room. He was naked, his huge off-kilter physiology making it seem all the more obscene. He was carrying a tool kit. People like Gregor and I knew our way around an engine room because we had been trained to sabotage them. He uncoupled a very heavy gauge power cable. All of us then winced and were thankful for the low quality of the image when he pushed the cable into his flesh where the base of a human spine would be. It looked like he'd dislocated his arm several times to get the cable in place. Then he'd just leant against the wall. That got boring so we fast-forwarded it.

'He's got a big cock,' Mudge said. We all turned to stare at him. 'I'm just saying,' he said defensively. We turned our attention back to the image. Gregor was shaking. His flesh beneath the skin seemed to be writhing, flowing and bulging of its own accord as his shaking began to look like a serious seizure.

'What's that?' Morag asked, and then made a disgusted noise. Gregor was producing a substance that looked like viscous black bile. Before long he was vomiting it all over himself. We were all disgusted, but of course we all kept watching. The black substance adhered to him and solidified into the hard resinous substance of the cocoon. Soon he was covered in the cocoon, only his head, a fountain for this black vomit, showing. Eventually that was covered as well. We were quiet for a bit, just looking at the image of the solidifying cocoon.

'What's the chance of him becoming a butterfly?' I asked. Mudge started giggling, seemingly uncontrollably.

'What the fuck's he doing?' Gibby had asked. He was strumming one of Buck's guitars. We were all in the quarters that Morag and I shared. I was propped up and coughing blood into a bucket every now and then. The interface that Gibby had set up meant that he could pretty much control the ship from anywhere on-board.

'Maybe he's just sleeping?' I suggested. 'Conserving energy?' I realised how weak this sounded.

'He's drawing a lot of energy,' Gibby pointed out.

'Which he has to use for something,' Pagan said thoughtfully.

'This is quite interesting,' he finished and lapsed back into silence. Morag, Rannu, Gibby and I all looked at him expectantly. Mudge was examining his own stomach.

'And?' I managed before coughing racked my body again.

Pagan looked up, his thoughts disturbed. 'Basically, They are, as far as we can tell, autonomous colonies of what we consider to be naturally occurring nanites, right?'

We all nodded as if we knew what he was talking about. Mudge nodded very enthusiastically.

'Well, presumably he's using the energy to manufacture more of ... well, himself, I guess,' Pagan said. 'But I am guessing.'

'So it's a transformation?' Morag asked. Once again, although Gregor sounded and to a degree thought like my friend, I was having it driven home just how alien this thing actually was.

'I would imagine so,' Pagan said.

'Butterfly!' Mudge added.

'Into what?' Gibby asked, running his fingers up the fretboard of his guitar.

'Butterfly!' Mudge interjected again. Morag tried to kick him.

'Your guess is as good as mine,' Pagan answered.

'A warrior,' Rannu said. He sounded pretty sure of himself.

Pagan shrugged. 'Perhaps. It would certainly be a form that will be of use to him, and hopefully us, for whatever this mission will involve. Perhaps he's disguising himself as one of Them, I don't know.'

'What if he wakes up and decides he wants to eat us all?' Gibby asked. 'Or insem ... insem ...'

'Inseminate us?' Morag asked.

'Yep,' Gibby said.

'Yeeha!' Mudge shouted.

'Or eat us then inseminate us?' Gibby suggested. We just looked at him.

'There's very little on this ship worth inseminating,' I pointed out.

'Hey!' Morag objected.

'I'd inseminate you,' Gibby said. He was largely going through the motions of banter. He knew what was expected of him but his heart wasn't really in it. Morag smiled and I glared at him.

'Thanks, Gibby. That's sweet,' Morag said.

'I'm sorry,' I said, letting out an exaggerated sigh. 'There's very little worth inseminating on this ship bar Morag, as I'm too sick. Basically, I think you're safe except from maybe Mudge.'

'Yeeha!' Mudge shouted.

Gibby glared at him.'I want you to know I'm heavily armed.'

‘It is a serious point . . .’ Pagan said.

‘What, Mudge inseminating Gibby?’ I asked, unable to help myself. Pagan tried to ignore me.

‘I mean what comes out of the cocoon and whether or not it’s going to be hostile to us.’

‘Why wait until now?’ Morag asked. ‘Seems like a lot of unnecessary trouble to go to take us out.’

I wondered if her life had become so strange that things like someone cocooning himself were becoming commonplace to her.

‘Besides, we’re well armed,’ I pointed out. Even as I said this I knew what a stupid thing it was to say.

‘Did you see him on the Spoke?’ Rannu asked. Everyone went quiet. I didn’t really have an answer, or rather I did, but I didn’t think they wanted to hear that we’d all just get killed.

‘So what do we do?’ Gibby asked after an uncomfortable silence.

‘We wait,’ Morag said. She sounded a lot less troubled by this than I was.

‘But we don’t know what Gregor has planned. We don’t know where Crom is going to be or how he intends to deal with it or even get to it. We don’t know if the Black Squadrons will be there or anything,’ I said. I was pissed off about this. If Gregor wanted to turn into a beautiful butterfly he should’ve done it on his own time.

‘Where are we going to arrive?’ Rannu asked Gibby.

‘Far side of Sirius, way beyond fleet-controlled space and deep in Them space. Gregor gave me the coordinates. He also said we had to be very quiet when we got there.’

‘We’re going to the Teeth?’ Pagan asked. Gibby nodded. There was an uneasy silence in the cabin that I decided to break.

‘Well, we know it’s going to be a stealth operation,’ I said, and that was about it. That was about all we knew. I was doing my second least favourite thing, space travel, on my way to do my least favourite thing, EVA, to my least favourite place, Sirius, deep inside territory controlled by a whole alien race that was still hostile towards us.

I was listening to the spacecraft. That’s kind of a contradiction. It was very quiet, though you could feel the hum of the power plant throughout the vessel, but it was something you were more aware of than could actually hear. Every movement made a kind of booming echo through the skeletal black metal of the ship’s interior.

I was just lying there, listening and dying. It was a bad day. I’d had two heart attacks despite the augmentations to my heart. Any time I’d tried to speak I just coughed up blood, and during one particularly bad fit of coughing I'd actually managed to bring up a component of my artificial lung. Rannu had kept me alive – it turned out that he was a pretty accomplished medic. I was alive because of Rannu, the automed and Mudge's ad hoc narcotic pharmacy.

We were four days in and I wasn't sure I was going to make it to Sirius, let alone back to Earth. I hadn't been expecting Balor when the door opened. I'd seen very little of him on the journey. He'd mostly been working on the Dog Soldier and I reckoned his warrior credo didn't cope well with weakness like mine. I think he thought I should have walked out into the wilderness to die so I could stop using up the tribe's valuable resources. I also think the kicking he'd got at Rolleston's hands had given him a fright. I looked at his chest. They had rebuilt his chest armour on the Atlantis Spoke, recreated it as well as they could. I wasn't entirely sure it matched the rest of his skin. Still, he'd brought a bottle of good whisky and I was determined to have some of that regardless of how bad I felt and how much damage it did.

He lit a cigarette for me. Again I was determined to smoke it even though I knew it meant coughing up blood. How stupid am I? I managed to hold it between my lips and inhale a bit before Balor had to take it away. I must've looked awful. I was pretty much a hollow sack of skin full of disintegrating internal organs and machinery. The strange thing was, it wasn't pity or sympathy or disgust I saw on Balor's face, it was resolve and something else, maybe fear. I took a sip from the whisky; it didn't even taste nice any more. It just hurt. What a waste.

'What's this, my wake?' I asked. He didn't smile. That worried me.

'You're going to die,' he said.

'No shit,' I replied, wondering where this was going and getting ready to call for help.

'You shouldn't have to die like this,' he said. I said nothing; I just stared at him. He drew his dive knife from its ankle sheath and placed it on the table next to the automed. Next he drew the shotgun pistol and placed that on the table. Finally he took an antique, stainless-steel pill box from the pocket of his cut-off combat trousers and placed that on the table as well. I looked at the three items and then back up at Balor.

'Everyone feels sorry for you but nobody is prepared to do anything about it,' he said. I struggled to sit up. If Mudge was going to get me up for the job it had better be one hell of a drug cocktail. I looked him straight in his one good reptile-styled lens.

'I'm going to die on the job just like everyone else,' I said. 'If I wanted to be killed I'd do it myself. Understand?' Balor said nothing for what seemed like a very long time. He was gauging me, sizing me up, trying to come to a decision.

'What ...' he began, and then stopped.

'What if I'm too weak to do my job?' I finished for him. He nodded. 'I'm dead anyway, so you don't have to worry about looking out for me, but if I can pull a trigger I'll help where we're going. But that's not what's bothering you, is it?'

Balor shook his head, his sensor dreads whipping round as his head moved. 'I don't like seeing a warr—'

'Soldier,' I interrupted. He looked at me quizzically. 'I am, or I was, a soldier, and a reluctant one at that. Don't give me any of this warrior bullshit; you save it for Rannu.'

'I don't like seeing a soldier this way,' he said. I managed another sip from the whisky and then refilled the glass with some of my blood. I looked back up at Balor, sitting huge and impassive next to my bed.

'You're really scared of me, aren't you?' I said. 'I mean this.' I gestured down at my sore-covered wreck of a body. 'This is pretty much your worst fear, isn't it?'

He didn't say anything. It hit me then that like all the other soldiers who dressed themselves up like monsters, Balor was overcompensating, running from something, hiding from something. He was just better at it than the rest.

'Why are you here?' I asked. 'Out of all of us you've got to have the most to lose – maybe Mudge now, but he's too fucked to care.'

'Loyalty,' he said.

'Oh bullshit. You want to do a dying man a favour then, don't fucking lie to me.'

He glared at me. I think I'd made him angry, and not the mock anger he play-acted with his cronies; I'd genuinely hit a raw nerve.

'Because I think we've changed something,' he finally said through gritted rows of shark-like teeth.

'You don't sound pleased about it,' I replied.

'I am. It's why we're warriors after all,' he said. I didn't follow him but I was sick of hearing all this warrior self-justification bollocks.

'Don't fucking start with that warr—' I began.

'No, you be quiet,' Balor said. 'I don't care what you think of my beliefs, but is that not what all the fighting and killing was for? Isn't that why all those marines on Atlantis had to die? Aren't we trying to make things better? Isn't that our job as the strong? Isn't that what you told Cronin?' he snarled. 'The world without war, the world you're trying to build, has no place for someone like me,' he said finally. That stopped me.

'What about Rolleston and the Black Squadrons?' I asked weakly.

'Believe it or not,' he said evenly, 'despite what you've seen me do, I don't really have much of an appetite for killing humans.'

'You've come here to die?' I asked.

'No. I've come here to die in a way that people will talk about for ever.'

'You want to go out in a blaze of glory,' I said.

He nodded. 'That is why, more than anyone else, Mudge must live.'

'So he can tell your story.' Balor nodded. 'And you don't want me around because despite what you've done to your body and your head, you don't want to be reminded that you are still human and human flesh is weak,' I said.

'I didn't say that.'

'You didn't need to.'

'I'm worried that you will risk the mission—'

'You're on a fucking suicide run, pal. You don't give a shit about the others – you've just fucking said that. You know the score. You know how we do business. What's your motto, by guile not strength? We're going in quiet and you want to make a fucking spectacle of your death!'

'I'm trying to offer you a way out,' he growled.

'What's going on?' Morag asked from the open doorway. I hadn't even heard her, though Balor must have. Neither of us said anything. For no good reason I suddenly felt guilty. I think I saw a trace of guilt on Balor's face too, but who can tell? Morag took in the gun, the knife and the pill box.

'What were you doing?' she demanded, asking us both.

'Nothing,' I said.

Morag turned to glare at Balor. Balor stood up, his enormous scaled bulk seeming to fill the cramped cabin. Morag moved into the room, Balor towering over her.

'Were you going to kill him?'

'I offered him a way out,' he growled again. Morag looked angrier than I'd ever seen her.

'A way out? A fucking way out!' she screamed at him. 'Why can't you say kill, or even better, murder?'

'Morag ...' I started, but she'd grabbed Balor's shotgun pistol and held the heavy pistol in an unsteady two-handed grip. Balor reached out to take the pistol. The report was deafening in the confined space. Or at least it would have been if we didn't all have audio dampeners now. The recoil sent Morag sprawling back into the bulkhead, the gun clattering to the deck. Buckshot was suddenly ricocheting all around me, flattening against my subcutaneous armour. There was a black scorch mark on Balor's chest from the pistol's fierce muzzle flash. He barely took a step back. She'd shot him in exactly the same place that Rolleston had. Scorched his nice new rebuilt armour.

'I'm sorry,' Morag said, much more out of shock at what she'd done than fear of Balor. Balor bent down and retrieved the shotgun pistol and grabbed his dive knife and pill box from the table. I don't think this had played out the way he'd envisaged. It was difficult to tell with his inhuman face but I think he was embarrassed. Mudge and Rannu were at the door. Rannu had removed the medpak; half of his face was angry red new-growth skin. He had a gun in each hand and Pagan was behind him. Balor made to push past them.

'Balor,' I said quietly.

He stopped and turned to look at me.

'Balor, if I live long enough I'll go down with you.' He gave this some thought and then nodded before turning. Mudge and Pagan moved out of the way. Rannu just stared at him.

'Don't say that,' Morag said through gritted teeth. I suspected there would be tears in her eyes if she'd still had real ones.

'Is everything okay?' Rannu asked, almost tonelessly.

'Yeah, we're fine,' I said, but Rannu did not move.

'Get out of the way,' Balor said dangerously. Rannu still didn't move.

'Everything's fine,' Morag said.

Rannu moved aside for Balor, who glared at him one last time and then stormed off.

'Thank you,' Morag said to Rannu and the others. Mudge started to say something but she closed the door. She threw herself onto the bed next to me, causing me some pain, and then burst into tears. Or rather she started sobbing, no tears any more. I held her as best as my decaying flesh could manage.

'That bastard,' she managed later through the sobs.

'I think he honestly thought he was doing me a favour. He's scared, he's just not scared of the same things the rest of us are.' She looked up at me, her brown eyes no longer up to the job of conveying emotion. I struggled to look at them.

'I'm not afraid,' she said, and I think I believed her.

'No?' I asked. She shook her head. 'Why not?' In comparison I was shitting myself.

'I know you'll protect me,' she replied with utter conviction.

'I thought you didn't need my protection,' I said, my mouth working faster than my brain.

'We both need protection,' she said. Despite the pain I held her to me, my eyes hurting where my machinery prohibited tears.

A day out from Sirius and Gregor was still in a cocoon. All we'd been able to do was speculate. We'd not been able to come up with a solid plan, let alone run simulations. Though in this case I suspected the simulations would have been quite depressing, in a you're-all-going-to-die kind of way.

The door to the dying room, as I'd come to think of my cabin, opened. Morag and Pagan walked in. Pagan leant heavily on his staff; both of them looked thoughtful. They looked at each other, both seemingly waiting for the other to start. They seemed to be in a state of mild nerd excitement.

'We need to speak to Gregor,' Pagan said.

'Or turn back,' I said. An option which was beginning to look pretty good even to me, and I had nothing to lose, or rather I did but I'd already lost it.

'Morag has had an idea,' Pagan said. I turned to her expectantly.

'*We* had an idea,' Morag said.

'Well it was more of—' Pagan began.

'Move on,' I suggested.

'Gregor still has his interface plugs,' Morag pointed out. 'We drill through the cocoon and insert a port into him and talk to him in the net.'

'Can't you do it wirelessly?' I asked.

Pagan shook his head. 'We've been trying. Whatever internal ware he uses as a receiver is not accepting incoming transmissions.'

'And you can't override it?' I asked, surprised.

'Possibly, but I don't know how much is normal ware and how much is Themtech, and I'm assuming you know what happens to people who try to hack Themtech?'

'They end up like Vicar?' I said.

'At best, and I don't want to end up like him.'

I looked over at Morag. 'Wouldn't you be more compatible?'

Morag opened her mouth to answer but Pagan got there first.

'Possibly, but if we drill into the cocoon then there's no risk.'

'To you perhaps, but it might trigger off some kind of defence system. If that thing is transforming then what's to say you'll even be able to find the port?'

'We're sending it through on a modified snake,' Morag answered. Snakes were remotely controlled delivery devices for monofilament fish-eye cameras, old technology. Most people used mites or crawlers these days, but most special forces types still had them around in case they came in useful.

'Okay, but what's to say you won't harm Gregor?' I asked. 'The cocoon is after all a protective casing, I'm guessing.'

Both of them weren't sure what to say. 'We need to know,' Morag finally asserted. 'He shouldn't have cocooned himself without telling us what the plan was.'

'Agreed, but if we kill him, we'll never know,' I said.

'So we turn around, which we're already considering anyway,' Pagan replied. I fixed him with a glare from my lenses.

'He's still a friend of mine,' I reminded him, though I'm guessing my near corpse-like appearance made me less scary than I used to be.

'Understood, but he seemed pretty robust. He is after all part alien killing machine. When we get to Sirius we're not going to be able to hang around for too long, stealth or no stealth. If They don't find us, the Cabal will.' He was overstating the point; finding a ship in something as big as space was actually quite difficult.

'What are you looking for, my permission?' I asked. Both of them looked a little guilty. 'You've already decided to do this.' Pagan nodded. I sighed. 'Fine,' I said, a little pissed off. 'Can you at least make sure I'm there when you talk to him?'

'That's kind of why we're here,' Morag said. She moved over to the bed and, as gently as she could, rolled me over. I found myself staring at the bulkhead. This saved me from having to see the grimace on Morag's face when she saw my bedsore-covered back, the bleeding sores from the radiation sickness, and smelled the rank smell of someone dying. I felt her plug in the wireless net interface.

'We'll call when we're ready,' she said and the pair of them left.

The net was tiny on the *Spear*. Strictly speaking, it could have been any size, but it only existed in the *Spear*'s own systems. The net representation of the ship was odd. I wasn't sure if it was supposed to be a skeletal spearhead or the long skull of some kind of mythical beast. Symbols, not unlike the veves Papa Neon used, were inscribed in the bone, though they would change, morphing into other symbols as you looked at them. This was encrypted information from the ship's operating systems. A huge and largely featureless desert surrounded the net representation of the *Spear* – presumably this was to symbolise space. The sky was a beautiful rendering of a desert sunset. Different virtual areas of the ship were represented as smooth caves of bone. In one of these caves Morag and Pagan had set up the pub environment that they'd built from Gregor's subconscious. It looked a little weird among all the polished bone.

The icon I had was actually a pretty good rendering of me, if I'd had no cybernetics or radiation poisoning. This time I thought to check in the mirror behind the bar what colour Morag had made my eyes. She'd made them green; it didn't look right.

Gregor's icon was similar to mine, a good rendition of him back when he was human, *sans* cybernetics. I was relieved to see he wasn't a Smiler any more. I guess irrational tribal allegiances die hard. Morag was there. She was Black Annis again. I think I'd preferred the Maiden of Flowers or whoever the prettier one had been. Pagan was there in his Druidic icon. All of them were sitting at a table in the centre of the otherwise deserted bar. I walked over and joined them. There was already a glass of virtual whisky on the table. I took a sip; it was well programmed but ultimately pointless.

'I thought you'd pop like a balloon when they drilled into you? How'd it feel to be violated?' I asked. Gregor just stared at me. I sighed, or rather the animated virtual representation of me sighed. 'What the fuck are you doing?' I asked.

'What's necessary,' he said.

'Don't give me that cryptic shit; you know as well as I do we can't afford it,' I said. He should know better.

'I apologise. It was necessary for me to begin the transformation—'

'Into what?' I asked.

'A form more useful for the job.'

'How're you going to look?'

'Different,' he said.

Morag and Pagan were just watching.

'You needed to tell us about the job before you did that,' I said.

'I apologise. I realised I was cutting things pretty fine as regards the transformation, but you're right. I knew that you'd eventually find a way to contact me,' he said.

I just looked at him. I felt like really having a go at him but there wasn't a great deal of point. That didn't change the fact that I was pissed off with him.

'So what's the job?' Pagan finally asked, breaking the tension.

Gregor looked over at him. 'EVA into the heart of the Teeth.'

'Penetrations like this have never worked before. I don't see any reason why they should start working now,' Pagan said.

'Because I will be broadcasting a Them biometric signature. They will literally have to identify you by sight to compromise you,' Gregor told him.

'Part of your transformation?' Morag asked. Gregor nodded.

'You're turning into one of Them.' I said. I needed to remember that regardless of how much Gregor looked like Gregor in the net, not only was his body changed but the way he thought was as well. He wasn't us or Them but something in-between.

'Not exactly,' he said. I was getting sick of this.

'If you can disguise yourself then why not go alone?' I asked.

'I cannot disguise myself as one of Them. It's not as simple as shifting form. I will be broadcasting a biometric field which will disguise us from Their sensors, but They'll still be able to ID us visually.'

'So be sneaky,' I suggested. I was trying to remember how we'd been talked into this. Gregor was beginning to look somewhat exasperated.

'We will get caught. Remember, They're effectively a hive mind. I am not part of that. We will eventually be compromised and I will need your firepower. Also, Crom could affect me and I cannot risk infection. You will need to dispose of it.'

'If Crom infects you?' I said.

'You need to ask?'

'What exactly is Crom and how is it being delivered?' Pagan said.

'About twelve years ago the Cabal seeded the entire belt with unmanned probes manufactured from Themtech. They were organic and broadcast a Them biometric pattern. They were very small but even then Their defences caught and destroyed a lot of the probes but enough got through. They secured themselves as close to major concentrations of Them as they could get. Very basically they were nanite factories producing Crom and sophisticated receivers. When the Cabal is ready they will send a transmission which will release what are effectively smart spores.'

'How many are there?' Morag asked.

'I don't know,' Gregor said.

'Then how are we supposed to find them?' Pagan asked.

'We just need to find one, and I know where a few of them are. Then we hack the receiver and send a self-destruct code, which will in turn be transmitted to all the other devices.' He pulled an envelope out of the pocket of his combat trousers. It was very old-fashioned looking, pre-FHC, with a wax seal and everything. Gregor pushed it across the table to Pagan. Pagan just looked at it. Something occurred to me.

'I thought only Rolleston had Crom.'

'The seeds are an older version of Crom – they'd just infect and kill the aliens. Rolleston has the information required to reprogramme the seeds for the sequestration strain of Crom.'

'He must have done it by now,' I said sceptically.

'No,' Gregor answered. 'His priority will have to be releasing Demiurge and consolidating his power base with the Sirius fleet but he will get round to releasing Crom.'

'But he could have already done it?' Pagan said.

Gregor looked exasperated. 'Possibly.'

Pagan's icon shook its head. I knew how he felt. This was getting thinner and thinner.

'You know Balor and Mudge would just have you release the killer strain of Crom to neutralise the threat,' Pagan said.

'Neutralise,' Black Annis spat, her voice like broken glass being ground.

'Militarily speaking—' Pagan began.

'Not going to happen, and that's my call,' Gregor interrupted.

'They are a people not a weapon,' Annis said.

'They are a weapon if Rolleston gets his hands on them,' Pagan pointed out.

Morag's Black Annis icon looked like she was about to argue.

'Okay, this is getting us nowhere,' I said. 'Change the subject.'

'How do you know all this?' Pagan asked.

'How do you think?' Gregor replied. 'I was locked up in there for over a year.'

'And they shared all this with you?' Pagan asked sceptically.

'No. They programmed my bioware for some pretty sophisticated applications and the rest is my training. I've no doubt you would've done the same, probably more with your information warfare training.'

Pagan didn't answer, he just studied Gregor thoughtfully. Lights played across the letter as both Pagan and Morag interrogated the code represented by the letter with their own diagnostic programs. 'That's pretty well encrypted,' Pagan finally said.

'It's a one-shot deal. Screw it up, corrupt it, trip any of its booby traps and it's just junk. You've no idea what I went through to get this.'

'For these spores to work they must be close to a very high concentration of Them?' Pagan said.

'They are,' Gregor replied.

'We start a firefight in an area concentrated enough for Them to visually ID us in space, then it's over for us. We're not going to be able to get out and it'll be just a matter of time before They overwhelm us,' I pointed out.

'Just as long as you hold them off long enough to deactivate Crom,'

Gregor said. So there it was. Instinctively I took a large mouthful of the pointless virtual whisky.

'So this is a one-way trip?' Pagan said redundantly. Nobody else said anything. 'I don't want to be a hero.'

'Either we stop it or the Cabal and Rolleston win,' Gregor said.

'What about the Earth governments?' Pagan replied. 'They have to respond.'

'Maybe, but in time? We're here. Now,' Gregor said. Pagan shook his head violently. 'What did you think was going to happen when you agreed to come?' Gregor asked, anger sneaking into his tone.

'I thought you'd have a better plan,' Pagan spat back. 'I'm out.'

'How long do you think you can run from a Crom-infected Them and the Cabal when Rolleston's in control?' Gregor yelled.

'Longer than flying into Them-central. I'd be better off putting a gun in my mouth!' Pagan shouted back. Gregor opened his mouth to retort but thought better of it.

'Then Morag will have to do the hacking, you fucking coward,' he finally said and turned to look at her.

'Morag's out as well,' I said.

Black Annis swung round to face me. 'That's not your decision,' she said, her voice like ice.

'Do you honestly think I'm going to send you out there to die after we've been through all this?' I asked.

'You're not sending me anywhere; I'm going where the fuck I want!' she shouted at me, her voice now modulated to sound like breaking glass.

'This doesn't help,' Gregor said.

'Shut up.' I turned back to Black Annis. 'Look, Morag, you're right. I have no right to tell you what you can and can't do but what I will do is sabotage any attempt you make to leave this ship.' Her hag icon looked like it was about to throw itself across the pub table and tear out my throat. I ignored her and looked at Gregor. 'You, me and probably Balor can go. If that's not enough, tough.'

'We need a signals person and it's not enough guns,' Gregor said.

'Then we don't do it,' I told him firmly.

'I'm going,' Black Annis said. I lost it.

'Why do you want to die?!' I screamed at her. 'For the first fucking time I can remember there's hope – why do you want to throw that away? If I wasn't already dead there is no way I would be going on this,' I said more quietly. 'If there is any possible way I could live then I would take it.'

'I'm going to live through it,' Black Annis said firmly.

'You don't know what you're talking about,' I said, exasperated.

'Ambassador wanted to make peace. I'm going to talk to Them,' she said.

All three of us just sat there staring at her.

Then Pagan started laughing. 'It's as good an idea as just walking in there and letting Them kill us,' he said sarcastically.

'Morag, I understand where you're coming from, and I believe there will be a time for that, and you'll probably play an important part in it—' Gregor began.

'Not if she's dead,' I interrupted, earning myself another poisonous glare from the hag.

'But we can't take the risk initially. What if you can't convince Them before the spores go off? What if while we're talking the Cabal uses the Sirius fleet to attack? What if They just kill us out of hand before we can do anything for reasons we don't even understand? Remember, the vast majority of Them are effectively programmed to kill us on sight until They are told different. Let's save Them first and then approach Them peacefully afterwards,' Gregor continued as the hag listened carefully.

'Look. You lot go and do your commando thing. I'll go and speak to Them. I can't see any reason not to do both.'

'How about everyone dies?' Pagan suggested.

Morag turned to face him. 'That doesn't help,' she said.

'Neither will us getting futilely killed,' Pagan said. It was a good point.

'We won't get killed,' Black Annis insisted. 'I'm the Whore of Babylon, remember.'

'You don't know what you're talking about!' Pagan shouted at her. 'You may be the infant prodigal as far as hacking goes but you know shit about war – which, by the way, this is – and we're going to need a bit more than youthful optimism to see us through here.'

The hag opened her mouth. It looked like she was getting ready to really have a go at Pagan.

'He's right,' I said quietly. The look of hurt and betrayal on the demonic icon's features was almost comic. 'I'm sorry, Morag, but you've no idea what you're talking about. Your only communication with Them has been Ambassador. Now it doesn't matter who started the war, but we know what They are capable of and you don't.'

'So I don't get a say?'

'So you don't listen to those who have experience?' I asked back.

'Why is it you don't believe in me?' she asked bitterly. 'Rannu believes in me, he trusts my abilities. Why can't you?' This last was aimed directly at me.

'Rannu has faith in you,' Pagan answered quietly. 'That is different to belief, and in this case you still lack experience.'

'I handled myself in Atlantis,' she said.

'You had to have your eyes and ears replaced!' I exploded.

'In the lab, not in the media node!'

'You were horrified by what you saw and did,' I said.

'Shouldn't I be?'

'Yes,' I admitted.

'This was what Ambassador was made for, this is all it was made for – to create peace between us and Them. You said you'd do everything you could to stop me from going?' I nodded. 'Well, I've just locked you in your room.'

'That's fucking childish, Morag,' I groaned.

'I could lock this ship down. I'm going to try and talk to Them.'

'We still need someone to run comms,' Gregor said.

'I'll go,' Pagan said. There was a tone of resignation in his voice.

'You've changed your tune,' I said.

'I was just sitting here thinking how unfair it all was that we have to die here and now and thinking that this can't be our responsibility. Where is the government to clean up this mess? Then I remembered that abdication of responsibility is what got us here in the first place.'

'Oh,' I said, not really following Pagan's train of thought.

'Besides,' he said, glancing at the hag, 'maybe I'm beginning to find faith.'

Mudge sat me up on the bed in my cabin. He laid out his wares on a collapsible table. There were derms, pads, inhalers, pills all the colours of the rainbow, an old-fashioned syringe and even eye drops. On top of that I still had a little of Papa Neon's medication left. This was what I would need to see me through the next few hours. Well, at least I hoped it would. I couldn't be too sure because instead of a pharmacist I had a junkie.

'So you're going?' I said, trying to get my mind off dying.

'Yeah, man. I've got a good feeling about this. I think we're going to be all right.'

'You're high, aren't you?' I said, grinning.

''Course I am. If I wasn't I'd be shitting myself about my impending death. Seriously though, I think it might work. Morag's plan, I mean.'

'Got religion?' I asked. 'Pagan thinks that she's the Whore of Babylon.'

'The hacker myth? Wishful thinking on his part.'

'What if we're doing it, though? What if we're betraying the whole human race?' I asked.

'I suspect we'll be dead before we see the effects, so really you should only worry if you believe in hell. An afterlife hell, I mean, not, you know, Dog 4 hell or Coventry hell.'

'Sometimes I don't think you take anything seriously.'

'Did you not see me save the world?' he asked, getting exasperated now.

'Well, the jury's still out on that. Besides, didn't you have some help?'

'Did I? Oh, you're just pissed off because your girlfriend is the new messiah.'

'She's neither. Anyway, whether the plan works or not, I'm not going to be all right.'

'No, you're pretty well fucked.'

'But this'll see me through it?' I asked, trying to hide my worry.

'This?' he said, pointing at the drugs. 'No, this will kill you. I thought that was the point.'

'Why do all my friends want to kill me?' I asked

'They know you best. At least you'll be involved. We're probably going to die as well.'

'I thought you had a good feeling?'

'I do, but I'm high and I've been wrong before.' The smile disappeared. 'Look . . .' I could see what was coming, something embarrassing that would make me feel closer to death than ever. I needed to stop it.

'We're good, Mudge,' I said.

'It's been . . .' he began.

'I know,' I said. We lapsed into an uncomfortable, self-conscious yet manly silence like the pair of emotional cripples we were.

'Oh, if I live I'll go and do the Wait for you,' he said, almost as an afterthought.

'You'd better fucking live. I don't like the idea of those arseholes outliving me. Seriously though, look after Morag for me,' I said.

Mudge thought about this. 'No,' he said finally.

'What?' I managed after I'd recovered the ability to speak.

'Not a chance, man.' I couldn't believe what I was hearing. Mudge was grinning again.

'What? I'm fucking dying, man. The least you can do is respect my last wish.'

'Not if it inconveniences me in any way. I'm not a fucking babysitter.'

'The word cunt springs to mind. Look after her, you bastard.'

'No way,' he said again. I could see he was serious. 'First off, she'll be fine; second, I think she can look after herself; and third, she'll have Rannu following her around, and I suspect he might be slightly harder than me.' I had to admit they were good points, but still.

'Slightly – he kicked my arse,' I had to concede.

'I could kick your arse,' Mudge said.

'I noticed you waited until I'm dying of radiation poisoning to tell me that. Besides, Rannu probably just wants to fuck her,' I said, not really believing that.

'Rannu has a wife and kids.' This I didn't know.

'That doesn't mean he doesn't want to fuck Morag,' I pointed out.

'You've seen how faithful he is,' Mudge pointed out, and he was right.

'But Rolleston's people would've gone after them,' I said.

'They did, but she's an ex-Ghurkha as well. She was straight off into the mountains and she's got a community full of ex-Ghurkhas looking out for her and the kids. File under more bother than it's worth for the Cabal.'

'But what the fuck's he doing here?' I said.

'Believe it or not, mate, every one of us has something to live for, even if we don't have a wife and kids. Even a sad fucker like you.'

'I know that. What we don't have is the responsibilities.'

'He thinks he's going to get through this,' Mudge said.

'Really?' I knew Mudge had said the same thing but I didn't think anyone other than Morag actually believed it.

'He believes that this is the only chance his kids have for a future and that if we don't do this all we'll be doing is delaying the inevitable. As for just hanging around Morag to fuck her, that's you you're thinking of. Assuming it hasn't fallen off, that is.'

'You'll know when that happens: I'll have a railgun in my mouth,' I said jokingly.

Mudge looked confused. 'As a cock substitute?' he asked.

'I'd like to take some drugs now,' I said, changing the subject. 'What first?'

Mudge looked at the table, an expression of confusion on his face.

'Mudge?' I said uncertainly. Grinning again, he pointed at the pink pills.

'I'm looking forward to the EVA. The right drugs, spending some quality time with just yourself and the void. Centring yourself. Remembering just how inconsequential you and your whole fucking race is.'

'I admire your optimism,' I said sarcastically. 'I'm dreading it. I hate EVA. I nearly went mental on the Atlantis dive.'

'Wrong drug, man,' Mudge said.

'That's your answer to everything. What next?'

'The two patches either side of the neck.'

'That's just to make me look stupid, right? They don't actually do anything?' I said, sticking the two patches where he'd suggested.

'I mean Slaughter and then sensory deprivation. What did you think was going to happen?' he asked.

'You sold it to me.'

'What people do with their own frontal lobes is their business. You're an adult, man.'

'How'd the others handle the dive?' I asked as Mudge directed me to take some more pharmaceuticals.

'Pagan was reading *Moby Dick*, Morag was listening to music and Rannu was meditating, like me,' he said.

'You weren't meditating, you were high,' I pointed out. He just shrugged. I gave everyone's activities on the dive some thought.

'How come everyone's smarter than me?' I finally asked Mudge.

'You are pretty dumb,' he agreed.

We took a lot of drugs, enough to almost feel alive. Well enough for me to walk anyway.

I had so much I wanted to say to Morag before we left. Before I died. But I knew when I was face to face with her I would lose the ability to put what I was thinking into words. And then for one reason or another we were never alone. Slowly I realised she was avoiding me. I thought she was still angry with me for trying to stop her from going, but when I finally managed to speak to her the look in her eyes told me otherwise. When I tried to speak she held her hand over my mouth.

'We'll talk when we get back,' she said fiercely. I almost believed her.

# 31
# Sirius

I was up and walking. I didn't feel ill – the drugs were hiding the sickness from me – I felt dissociated. It was nice, but had I felt less dissociated I would've been worried about feeling this way just before going into combat. On the other hand, what was there to worry about? I was dead anyway and so was everyone else. I had on my inertial undersuit and was carrying my pistols, more for comfort than anything else. If the Mamluk got breached it was all over. I was making my way towards the converted bomb bay.

Gibby had us running silent and deep, hanging back several hundred miles from the Dog's Teeth, the huge asteroid belt almost halfway between Sirius A and B. It was theorised that the belt may have once been a planet that was crushed by the gravitational forces of the two stars back when Sirius B was in main sequence and the larger of the two. Gibby was sending us feed from the ship's external lenses of the neighbourhood. The Dog's Teeth was a mass of huge static-looking asteroids, many of them the size of small planetoids. Increasing magnification, I could see the organic material forming a connecting web between some of the asteroids. Increasing magnification further, I could see some of Their larger ships. The pale-blue light of Sirius B filtering through the belt illuminated the scene.

I entered Pagan's cabin. He had stuck a liquid crystal thinscreen to the wall and was running some sophisticated image analysis programs trying to find a quiet place for us to insert. The hacker looked up at me as I entered, his dreadlocks swinging round as he did so. He had seemed old but vital to me when we'd met on the Avenues; now he looked tired and haggard – his age had truly caught up with him.

'What've you got?' I asked.

'I've picked one route that seems as good as any with two backups, but without active scans I'm pretty much blind. I could be flying us into a death trap.'

I started laughing. 'If I was you, I'd take that as a given.'

Pagan didn't seem to find that at all funny. 'I'm sending the co-ordinates to everyone now,' he said, and I saw a message icon appear on my internal visual display. I'd download the information to the Mamluk's navigation systems when I interfaced with it later.

'You all right?' I asked. Stupid question, I know, but it seemed that Pagan had something that he wanted to say.

'This is bullshit, this whole thing. You know that, right? I mean this is all speculation. We're running on nothing but Gregor's say-so and Morag's blind optimism, and Gregor hasn't even hatched. We've got fuck all to go on and nothing to corroborate what he says.'

'Where's your faith?' I asked, smiling.

Pagan swung round again to glare at me with his black lenses. 'That's not funny. Do you trust him? I mean the guy's in a cocoon!' He was trying to keep his voice down.

'Yeah, I trust him,' I said, not entirely sure I did. Gregor was so alien, so different to the guy who'd often saved my life. 'What did God say?' I asked.

Pagan muttered something under his breath and shook his head. God had been pretty low-key through most of our trip, something to do with limited processing power, but he was there in the ship's systems.

'What?'

'God thinks that Gregor's story is the most probable plan of action for the Cabal based on the information we have to hand,' he said.

'Well if God—' I started.

'God can be wrong,' Pagan said flatly.

'Heresy,' I said, trying to hide a smile. 'Your own creation as well.'

'Why am I talking to you? He's your best friend and she's your lover.'

'I'm not blind to what's going on. I know this is pretty thin, but I've got nothing to lose. If you don't want to go, don't go,' I said.

His head whipped up to glare at me. 'I'm not going to leave you all in the lurch. I couldn't live with myself. Besides, it looks like you need a hacker,' he said, his voice tailing off bitterly.

'Morag can do it,' I said.

'She'll be too busy communing with the gods or walking on water or whatever,' he said, not even trying to disguise the bitterness in his voice. Morag's talent had so far outstripped his skills and years of experience; he felt redundant. I could identify with that.

Pagan had gone back to studying the images of the Teeth. I turned to leave. As I reached the door to his cabin I turned back to him.

'I don't want you to die, but I'm glad to have you with us.'

He looked up and seemed like he was about to say something but thought better of it and nodded.

I said, 'Morag's good at what she does, very good, and she's smart, strong, funny and beautiful, and people are drawn to that. Attention may be focused on her at the moment because of those reasons, but we haven't forgotten who did this, who made this happen, who created God and gave us another chance, even if we might not see the end result.' I said. We had one of those awkward silences then, the sort of silence that accompanies men trying to be either nice or honest to each other.

Finally he nodded. 'I'll see you out there,' he said.

'He's coming,' Morag announced. The *Spear* had only been hanging in the sky in the middle of Themspace for two hours now. We were waiting in the converted bomb bay leaning on our mechs, getting more and more pissed off.

'You sure?' I asked. I don't know why I asked; he'd sent all of us the message that he was about ready to hatch. Morag just gave me the look that all young people do, the one that told you just how stupid you were.

I'd got used to the dissociation of the drugs and was feeling quite good. Of course I'd bypassed the medical readout on my internal visual display; all those warning symbols just made for depressing reading.

'Let's mount up,' I said. If he didn't hatch soon I was going to call the thing off.

Because of the way the Mamluks were stacked, on converted long-range missile racks, we had a very little space to crawl into them. Not a problem for the Dog Soldier, which was free-standing but crouched down, which presented its own set of problems for Balor.

I was struggling to get my limbs into their respective control slippers and gloves when we heard the *crack!* It seemed to echo through the ship. Everyone stopped what they were doing. There then followed an unpleasant organic ripping sound and a clanging noise. Everyone was exchanging questioning looks. The pissed-off feeling at waiting for Gregor to emerge was replaced with anticipation tinged with fear. The clanging was now rhythmic as something large approached us. The big door between the engine room and the bomb bay slid open.

Several of us panicked, myself included. Well not exactly panicked but acted on instinct. Despite the fact that we were racked and none of us properly interfaced to the Mamluks, Mudge, Pagan and I all tried to move the mechs to bring our weapons to bear. I'm not sure whether I thought we'd been compromised and They'd boarded us or it was just some fearful animal response to seeing something that alien. Of course none of us could move the Mamluks yet so there was a moment of clanging, straining and cursing before we all calmed down.

It wasn't just that it was weird, though it – he – was. It was disturbing that Gregor's once-human physiology could be transformed into this. The metal and plastic that filled our bodies aside, Gregor's strange form left me worried about the sanctity of humanity. It seemed that not even that was a constant any more.

'That's fucked up,' Balor said, perhaps hypocritically.

It was made of the smooth, oily black flesh from which all of Them were formed. The flesh formed panels of solid-looking chitinous armour plate. It – he, I had to remember that this was my friend – stood about sixteen feet tall and shared characteristics with their Walkers. He had long and deceptively spindly legs with backward-facing joints. His upper body was thickset and powerful but not out of proportion. Powerful, long, multi-jointed arms ended in six-fingered hands. Each of the long fingers was tipped with a claw that looked capable of tearing through mech armour. His head was almost triangular; the only feature a sort of lattice-like pattern that I assumed were sensors. On either shoulder were honeycomb-like protrusions that formed a kind of collar around the head but did not restrict its movement. It took me a while to realise these were organically grown rocket or missile launchers. On several parts of his body small nozzles mounted on gristly ball-shaped growths seemed to move independently. Again it took me a moment to realise this was a black-light, anti-missile defence system. On his back another larger honeycomb growth glowed with the faint blue light of a Themtech propulsion system. The pale light reminded me of Sirius B. There were other similar but smaller growths on various other parts of his body, all of them glowing with the same pale blue light, presumably for manoeuvring control.

In his massive hands he held a disturbingly organic-looking weapon, a tendril-like power cable connecting the weapon to his main body like an umbilical cord. The weapon had an over and under barrel. I guessed it was a shard cannon combined with a black-light projector. A chain of what looked like black bone ran from the weapon to a hump-like growth on Gregor's lower back. This was ammunition for the shard cannon. The hump was either ammunition storage or possibly, depending on available energy, even a little biological ammunition factory, I wasn't sure which.

By far and away the worst thing for me were the tentacles. People shouldn't have tentacles. They were long and sinuously writhed behind him, backlit by a glow from the engine room. They were thick and powerful, and covered in small scales of chitin that didn't seem to restrict their movement.

Morag glanced over at me, but I really didn't have any reassurance for her. Pagan was staring at me pointedly. I ignored him. Morag let out an involuntary scream. I turned back to Gregor and let out my own involuntary cry of surprise. Gregor's triangular head was splitting in half, pulling itself apart. There were tendrils of slime suspended between the two halves. Inside, nestled among alien gristle, was Gregor's human head. Somehow it reminded me of a pearl in an opened oyster. The familiar face made it all the more freakish and difficult to deal with. I guessed he'd kept his human head and face to try and cling on to the last vestiges of his humanity but it just made him more alien. Maybe Balor wasn't being such a hypocrite, I decided. The sad thing was Gregor didn't really look all that much like one of Them either.

'It's still me,' he said, but his voice sounded odd, slightly modulated.

'The fact that you have to say that ...' Mudge began, but a look from me silenced him. Nobody else really had anything to say. Gregor looked like he was in pain; he looked like he was going to cry. That was when I realised that his eyes were human again, the cybernetic lenses gone. I zoomed in on his eyes with my own lenses. They were brown. I wanted to ask him what he'd done to himself? Was anything worth this?

'Let's get this over and done with,' I said instead. I needed to force my feelings down, beneath the training, the discipline and Mudge's drugs.

'We're still going ahead with this then?' Pagan asked, contacting me through a private channel on the tac net rather than asking out loud.

'This changes nothing,' I replied to him brusquely and then out loud to the rest of them. 'Right, you know the drill, run silent, no unnecessary systems, just like the dive. Comms silence unless we're compromised—'

'When we're compromised,' Pagan corrected me.

'Until then use sign language only. Gregor—' I glanced over to the alien form hulking over us all '—is going to tow us into the Teeth, because he should be scanning as one of them.' He nodded. 'Once in, we use the compressed-air system on the fins to manoeuvre. Do not use your primary system unless we're compromised.'

'And then what?' Pagan asked, though he knew damn well.

'We find the pod, disable it, use it to send a signal to the other pods and extract back to the ship,' I said. It sounded so easy.

'You mean, if we get to the pod we hold Them off as long as possible until we're eventually overrun,' Pagan said.

'That is more likely,' Gregor said. Even through the modulation I could hear the pain in his voice.

'Pagan, either stay behind or shut up,' I said. I didn't have time for this. 'Gibby is going to hold here for twelve hours. If we're not back by then he's out of here. If he gets compromised he will attempt E&E, set sail to put some distance between the *Spear* and Them, and then meet us at our secondary or tertiary RV points.'

'And we still don't know what we're looking for?' Mudge asked. I glared at him. 'I'm just asking.'

'We know it's a pod, we have coordinates for it, and we know it will be a human application of Themtech,' Gregor said.

'Anything else?' I asked.

'Morag?' Pagan said.

I tried to force down the pain, ignore it and busy myself with other things. Tried not to think that this would be the last time I saw her. I couldn't help but glance over at Morag as she struggled to get into the Mamluk. She looked like a pale and frightened little girl. I felt I was sending her to her death, though in reality I was doing that to everyone.

'Morag's going to be doing her own thing,' I said.

'I'll split with you when we reach the Teeth.' She sounded both scared and strangely sure of herself.

I looked over at Rannu, expecting an objection from him, insistence that he accompanied her, but he said nothing. I think I was jealous of his confidence in her, his faith? Enough thinking. I finally managed to wriggle into the control slippers and gloves. I was lying down on the padding as the four interface plugs slipped into the ports on the back of my neck. Information from the Mamluk's systems appeared on my internal visual display. The front panel slid shut over me as the head lowered and clicked into place. I didn't get the rush and feeling of power I had in the Wraith over the Atlantic. This time I felt like I'd been locked into a cell only slightly bigger than my own body. Still I'd decided to take Mudge's advice. A mournful-sounding saxophone started up, music piped directly into my ears, as I shut down all non-essential systems on my mech.

The bomb bay was effectively a large airlock. The internal door closed and locked and the bomb bay depressurised before the two enormous external doors opened. Craning the Mamluk's neck, I could see blackness punctuated with pinpricks of starlight below me. We seemed to tumble out. We had to get out quickly because the *Spear* was zipped up, everything retracted to present the smallest possible scanner signature, and the open doors disrupted that.

I was free-floating now just beneath – or above, depending on your perspective – the *Spear*. Gregor was last out. A tentacle snaked out of the darkness of the bomb bay and gripped the edge of the hatch, then another joined it and another. Others whipped out, reaching for us as Gregor pulled himself out of the spacecraft. We all knew he was going to be towing us but even so I flinched as a tentacle wrapped around the midriff of my mech. The pale-blue light of his propulsion system seemed to burn slightly brighter as we moved away from the relative safety of the ship towards the Teeth. Even though I knew both the mech and my inertial undersuit were heated, I felt cold. I tried to tell myself it was just the psychology of EVA.

First it seemed to take for ever – the Teeth never seemed to be getting closer – and then all of a sudden we were there and they filled our vision. Much of the Teeth was uninhabited but the coordinates we were heading for were densely populated by Them. Fear and awe warred within me. The larger asteroids were in pretty static orbits, despite the binary nature of the star system. However the aliens had joined many of them together, strands and structures of what I guess were the aliens themselves ran between the huge rocks. It wasn't like human construction – no inelegant metal or concrete scarring the rocks. They weren't even structures; there were no delineated roles for the growths. They were habitats and production centres and defences all in one. They were alive, growing, taking raw materials from the rock and energy from their pale stars. If anything these growths were Them; what we saw on Dog 4 and on the other battlefields in the colonies were just Their weapons. I tried to think of a comparison, something to help me understand Them as we approached the Teeth. They were like a latticework of coral suspended between huge floating mountains.

Because of our relative spatial perceptions, although we were approaching it seemed like we were staying still and the Teeth were getting bigger and bigger. The closer we got the easier it was to make out the cordon of ships from Their fleet. We could even see new ones growing out of the alien matter. In the alien coral I began to make out the energy matrices and cancerous-looking growths of various weapon systems. Closer still and I could make out smaller craft, Their equivalent of long-range raiders and fighters, then EVA-equipped Walkers and finally what we'd always thought of as Them, the Berserks, though they were really just another weapon system.

There were other humanoid Them-forms here. Ones we'd never seen before, which presumably performed some niche task in their space-going ecology.

This was insane. There were so many of Them crawling like termites over Their complex structures. Why couldn't They see us? Of course we were tiny little specks against a backdrop of infinity, using some very sophisticated stealth technology and prayers not to get noticed. Also if humanity had never tried a penetration this foolish before, and I wasn't aware we had, then They wouldn't have learnt to look for something like this.

Several of the manoeuvring mechanisms on Gregor's battle form glowed brighter as he changed position. He angled towards a sparsely populated gap between several of the rocks, though I could see lattice growths on them that suggested sensors. We trailed behind him, a tentacle wrapped around each of us, two around Balor's Dog Soldier mech. It reminded me of a spider's web with multiple flies caught in it.

Vertigo threatened to overtake me, breaking through the narcotic haze of Mudge's drugs, as we flew silently into the gap between three of the huge asteroids. I was having problems coping with the sheer scale of the landscape. Above and beneath us I could see Them moving through space, Their propulsion systems glowing pale blue as well. Many of Their forms were unrecognisable to me, serving purposes I could only guess at. To my left I saw something that looked insectile crawl across Them-growth, picking at it with mandibles and manipulators, presumably some kind of maintenance creature. It ignored us as we floated past, the music going a long way towards helping keep me calm.

As we rounded one of the bigger asteroids that formed the outer perimeter, the light that emanated from deeper within the Teeth almost acted like a sunrise effect. In the distance I could make out spires reminiscent of the vision that Ambassador had given me as I'd slept next to Morag. Except these spires weren't multi-hued, they were black, pale bioluminescence providing illumination. The spires grew out of four huge planetoid-sized asteroids, all of them pointing inwards like a jagged maw. Thick strands of the coral material formed a web connecting the four asteroids. Between the spires huge tentacles moved, performing tasks I could only guess at. It was beautiful and sinister, and the more I thought about it the more I was sure that it was so far removed from me that I didn't belong here.

Gregor took us in close to a smaller asteroid with no visible growth on it. Tiny molecular hooks mounted on pads adhered to the

Mamluks' fingers and feet attached us to the rock as Gregor's tentacles slid off us. We formed a quick and impromptu defensive perimeter. I superimposed the coordinates that Gregor had provided over the view in front of me. The pod was hopefully just on the outskirts of the maw-like city. The area was crawling with Them.

Without doing an active scan that would have given away our position I reckoned that our destination was about twelve miles way. I plotted the course I would have chosen, the path of least resistance, as a matter of course, my training kicking in. As it was, it was Gregor's call. Using hand signals the huge hybrid pointed out the course he wanted to take, which initially seemed to agree with mine, and then indicated that he wanted to head off. We all signalled the affirmative and Gregor pushed himself off the rock.

We flew in an arrowhead formation, tight as possible to keep within the biometric pattern that Gregor was transmitting. Gregor was point, Morag and Rannu flanked him, Pagan and Mudge flanked them and I flanked Pagan. Balor flew in the centre of the V providing our rearguard. We stayed as close to the rocks as we could and tried to avoid any of Their growth.

Moving was a matter of firing a blast of compressed air from the propulsion fin to send you in the direction you wanted to go, and then making any adjustments to your course with smaller blasts of compressed air. We, or rather I, and I'm assuming it was the same for the other members of the team, experienced more than one moment of pant-shitting terror as we came round a blind corner to find Them-growth or worse some Them-form only to have it seemingly ignore us. This was either because of the biometric pattern that Gregor was transmitting or because we were superfluous to its duties. Despite this and the general constant high stress level, the main problem was a struggle to stay alert because of the slowness of our movement. Going from one piece of cover to the next was boring, except when we had to cross large areas of open space. That got exciting largely because you didn't know if you were going to get seared open by black light at any given moment. We were really penetrating Themspace; I couldn't believe we were really doing this. I needed a cigarette and a drink.

We formed a rough circle in an indent on a smallish, tethered asteroid close enough to Maw City, as I'd come to think of the nearby habitat, to be bathed in its ambient light. I felt a thrill of success at getting this close. We truly were sneaky bastards! We were looking up at another rock face about a hundred and fifty feet away from us. I felt one of the other mechs touch my Mamluk's arm. I moved my mech's head to take in the image of Morag signalling that she was leaving. I signalled a negative for no good reason. I didn't want her to leave. It was too soon and I was still alive, but she signalled an affirmative. I signalled her to wait and reached out. Signals from the Mamluk's armoured skin told me my mech had touched hers. Gas escaped from her propulsion fin and I watched as her mech gracefully, or so it seemed to me, took off into the void.

We stayed where we were, giving Morag time to get clear. Now beads of sweat were beginning to appear on my skin as each second passed without my mech's passive scanner picking up weapons fire. Each second that Morag didn't transmit to say she was in trouble meant that I knew she was still alive.

There was another tap on my arm. I turned to see Mudge's mech gesturing towards the lip of the small crater in which we were hiding. I could just make out the irregular silhouette of a Walker beyond the lip on the surface of the asteroid. I turned back to Mudge. Beyond his mech I could see the Dog Soldier disappearing into a cavern entrance in the asteroid. I couldn't see Gregor so presumably he was in the cave as well. The rest of them were crawling in what looked like slow motion towards the cave entrance. Mudge was doing the same and I followed.

Last into the cave, I ended up acting as picket. It was huge. I looked past the rest of them as they moved deeper into the cathedral-sized cavern. I could see another exit about a kilometre away from my position. Between here and there huge pillars of rock joined the ceiling to the floor. I was lying on a smooth slope next to a wall about twenty yards away from the cave entrance and was trying to make myself as small a target as possible, hoping that the stealth and camouflage systems of the Mamluk would protect me. About fifty yards behind me Balor was acting as fire support, covering my position, crouched down near to one of the pillars.

Although facing the cavern mouth, the Mamluk's systems were providing me with a full three-sixty view on my internal visual display. I saw Gregor organising the others by hand signal to patrol into the cavern. He signalled to Pagan to join them, but Pagan signalled negative. Gregor signalled for Pagan to join him again, and again received a refusal. This was pissing me off. As if we weren't in a tight enough situation, Pagan was choosing now to be insubordinate. Pagan moved behind the pillar next to Balor and out of my view. Even in his alien form I could tell Gregor was annoyed. Shaking his triangular head in an oddly human gesture, Gregor led Rannu and Mudge deeper into the cavern, walking in a staggered line.

There was nothing at the cave entrance. I was hoping that the

Walker hadn't seen us. There was certainly nothing to suggest we'd been caught in an active scan. That didn't, however, mean we hadn't been picked up on a passive scan. The bioluminescence of Maw City and the other Them-growth nearby lit up the cave mouth but threw the area where I was lying into shadow. I wished we'd brought vacuum-capable crawler cams or mites with us so I could check out what was going on on the surface of the asteroid, but any transmissions from devices like that would've been picked up.

Behind me, Gregor, Rannu and Mudge had stopped their advance towards the other entrance. Gregor and Rannu were providing security while Mudge looked at something. I split-screened my visual display and had the Mamluk zoom in on Mudge's area. All through the rear part of the cavern alien growth coated the rock walls.

'Shit,' I muttered quietly. The soft jazz wasn't doing quite such a good job of keeping me calm now. I watched as the growth began to move, crawl together and form the sort of lattice pattern I'd come to connect with Them sensor systems. That was it. We were compromised. It was all over bar the shooting now. I signalled to Balor that we were compromised and pointed to Mudge's position. The hive-mind nature of Them meant that if a cell in here knew, then all of them in the Dog's Teeth knew.

I barely had time to register the silhouette of the Walker backlit by the bioluminescence of Maw City before it exploded, its flesh floating away in the vacuum. It had been hit by one of the massive 105-millimetre shells from Balor's mass driver. Its legs were still stuck to the cave-mouth rock by their tiny molecular hooks.

Then of course there were more of Them. My acquisition software promised me a target-rich environment as Berserks swarmed into the cave mouth. We activated the rest of our Mamluk systems, my internal visual display now receiving feed from all the other mechs bar Gregor's organic one. I fired, shifted target, fired another burst and moved to the next target as 20-millimetre rounds from my railgun tore Them apart.

Rounds from Balor's 30-millimetre railgun flew over my head as he provided longer bursts, trying to deny the Berserks the cave entrance, but there were too many of Them. Every time a Walker stalked into view Balor would fire his mass driver and the alien mech would silently explode. Despite our firepower They were creeping towards us. Their returning fire was light but getting heavier as black light scarred the rocks near me and shards rained down on my armour.

Glancing at the feeds from Rannu and Mudge, I could see that they and Gregor had taken to the air. The Mamluks were using the jet systems on their propulsion fins, all attempts at stealth pointless now. Rannu and Mudge laid down fire in long bursts from their railguns and Gregor did the same with his shard cannon as Berserks flooded the other cavern entrance. I watched blue contrails of energy as Gregor launched three missiles from his right shoulder launcher at the other cave mouth. They exploded in a line, blasting the Berserks and two Walkers back out into space. This gave the three of them enough time to get into position, using the columns of rock that ran from ceiling to roof as cover. They continued firing at the cave entrance, trying to deny the area to Them.

There were more blue contrails in the vacuum, this time coming towards me. Laser fire filled my field of vision, momentarily illuminating the cave in a hellish red light as the Dog Soldier's anti-missile defences went to work. The incoming missile exploded in mid-flight. I felt the blast push me further down the slope, scraping the Mamluk's armour against the rock surface, but I kept on firing, and they kept on creeping closer. I was taking multiple hits now, but so far it was all small-arms stuff. I was in trouble if a Walker targeted me, and I knew if the Berserks could swarm me then they would tear the Mamluk apart with their claws because I'd seen it happen to bigger mechs than mine. Basically that was what They were going to do – overrun us through sheer force of numbers.

'Jakob, pull back,' Balor said. I didn't question, just sent the signal to the hook pads to release me from the rock, kicked off slightly and fired the jets on the propulsion fin forward so I shot backwards. I flew just above the rock floor, firing as I retreated. I watched as two rockets from the Dog Soldier's shoulder batteries flew overhead and exploded in a dense concentration of Them, buying us a few more seconds while more charged in. Maybe we would even live long enough to run out of ammunition, I thought optimistically. The good news was that due to the proximity of the other asteroid They probably couldn't manoeuvre anything really big in here to have a go at us.

I hunkered down behind a rock ledge on one knee and continued firing. The vacuum around the cave entrance was full of floating Berserk body parts and streams of black liquid. They were literally coming apart through the sheer force of the rounds we were hitting Them with, and the mass driver was taking care of any armour They managed to get into the cave mouth. Even so, They were slowly creeping towards us. I realised we were missing a gun. I checked the split screens. I could not believe it. Pagan was just hunkered down behind the column.

'Pagan! What the fuck are you doing!' I screamed over our tac net.

There was no reply. We continued firing. At the other end of the cavern Rannu, Mudge and Gregor's position was only slightly better.

'Pagan, get in this fight!' I screamed again. The mass of Berserks seemed closer now. Another Walker exploded but there was another behind it. The rock wall exploded near the second Walker as a round from Balor's mass driver gouged a huge rent out of it, spraying the advancing aliens with fragments of rock. The rock ledge I was hiding behind exploded, and something like a sledgehammer hit me in the chest. I felt armour buckle and blood fill my mouth but the Mamluk's structural integrity held.

The Berserks were running towards me on the cavern floor, along the walls and the cavern roof. I was taking so much small-arms fire the problem was not so much the damage it was doing but being able to see and make sense of sensor information through the constant hail of shard and beam.

'Cover!' I shouted to Balor as I let off a very long burst with the Retributor, the jet on my propulsion fin sending me flying backwards towards Balor's position. He fired a salvo of rockets at the cavern mouth to give us some breathing space.

The missiles exploded ahead of me with sufficient force to shake the asteroid. The warheads superheated their hydrogen payload to plasma state, creating fire that would burn in space. It flowed like liquid. It incinerated the Berserks in the cavern mouth and left the Walker burning. Balor finished it off with another 105-millimetre shell from his mass driver, sending it tumbling out into the void, still burning. In a strange way, with the lack of sound and the exaggerated movement of zero G, this was all somewhat beautiful and balletic, especially the fire in space. The zero G and silence somehow gave it a sense of unreality. Then again maybe that was just the drugs.

Just as soon as we'd incinerated the last wave more were surging into the cavern. Pagan still hadn't joined us.

'Pagan!' I shouted. Nothing. 'Pagan!' I shouted again.

'Not now,' Pagan answered. I couldn't believe it. What was so fucking important? I was firing almost non-stop now. There were so many of Them I barely had to move the weapon.

'Balor! If Pagan does not join us in the next three seconds, shoot him. Do it with the mass driver,' I ordered.

'Huh?' Balor said intelligently.

'Just wait,' Pagan said.

'For what!' I shouted, but he didn't answer. Then I was taking hits from behind. My initial thoughts were that Rannu, Mudge and Gregor had gone down, but the split screen on my internal visual display told otherwise. The alien growth that we'd found in the cavern was transforming, growing into nozzle-like, black-light weapons. I could also see what looked like Berserks growing out of it, pulling themselves out onto the cavern floor. Ahead of us the limbs and body parts we'd previously blown apart were being drawn together by strands of the black liquid, forming into crawling masses that crept slowly towards us. I checked my ammo counter – my ammunition drum had less than a quarter left in it. This was it then, this was how we go down.

Balor shouted an ordnance-firing warning over the tac net. The rocket battery on his left shoulder swivelled round and fired four missiles into the cavern behind us. They blossomed into silent flame that rolled and flowed across the entire cavern, incinerating the newly grown black-light weapons and Berserks.

I was pulling back on foot. Taking more and more small-arms fire as I let out short stuttering bursts from the Retributor, trying to conserve ammo.

'It's a set-up! He's set us up!' Pagan shouted over the tac net. I noticed that he'd excluded Gregor from the net. A cold feeling ran up my spine. Pagan came from around his column of rock and let loose with a long burst from his still fully loaded Retributor. Berserks just in front of me were torn apart seeming to explode in the zero G.

'What're you talking— Shit! What're you talking about, Pagan?' Mudge demanded over the net.

'The code for disarming the pods, it's nothing. There's no code, it's meaningless junk!' Pagan shouted, still providing covering fire for my retreat.

'It was encrypted. Did you trip something that destroyed it?' I demanded.

'We don't have time for this. No, I didn't! Trust me. I know what I'm doing!'

'What does this mean?' Mudge asked. The only other time I'd heard such desperation in his voice was when he'd run out of drugs and booze.

'There are no pods!' Pagan shouted, now firing desperately as Berserks and impromptu masses of re-formed alien flesh moved closer to us.

'Buy us some time, Balor,' I said. Two more rockets flew overhead and we were bathed in an orange light as liquid flame cleared the cave entrance. I stopped firing to conserve ammo and let Pagan clear up the stragglers.

'It means there are no pods! Gregor lied to us!' Pagan shouted.

'Why?' I asked, though I already knew the answer.

'He is Crom!' Pagan answered.

'He can't be Crom,' I shouted back. 'He put us on to the Cabal. He told us about Blackworm, Crom and Demiurge. He helped us and tried very fucking hard to kill Rolleston. If it hadn't been for him we'd all be dead.' But even as I was saying it I was piecing it together. I remembered Rolleston on the assault shuttle doing something with his skull fucker. Why had he even bothered with the knife when he was capable of wreaking havoc with his bare hands? Nostalgia? He must have been putting Crom into some sort of delivery system in the hilt. When he'd stabbed Gregor in the head he'd infected Gregor with Crom. That's why the wound had taken so much longer than the others to heal, because Gregor had been trying to fight off the infection. Trying not to become Crom.

It had been right in front of me, but I hadn't seen it because I had wanted my friend back and I had wanted to trust my friend. Well, I could trust my friend. This wasn't Gregor. This was all on Rolleston.

'I think Pagan may be right,' I said. Even then I didn't want to believe it. Even then what I said still sounded like another betrayal in my ears.

'Why bring us?' Balor growled over the tac net.

'In case he needed our help to get close enough to one of the main population centres,' I said. 'Because he knew we'd attract a lot of attention when we were finally compromised. Bait to bring more of Them in to be infected.' I started firing as the cave mouth started filling up again, angry, frustrated, betrayed.

'What the fuck!' I'd never heard Rannu sound surprised and certainly never heard him swear before. I checked the feed from Rannu and Mudge's Mamluks and froze momentarily. Gregor's organic battle form had stepped forward towards the advancing Them forces. His tentacles had shot out in front of him, piercing the Berserks, crawling masses and even a Walker's chitinous exoskeleton. From each of Them pierced by one of the tentacles, similar tentacles shot out into other nearby aliens and so on until all the aliens at that end of the cavern were linked by pulsing tendrils originating with Gregor.

'Rannu! Mudge! On me now! Balor, sanitise that area!' I shouted.

Rannu and Mudge triggered their propulsion fins, shooting backwards towards our position at dangerous speeds. The cavern was full of rocket contrails as Balor emptied both his shoulder batteries. My railgun ran dry. I ejected the power lead and let the now useless weapon drift away in zero G. Rannu touched down and Mudge sort of skidded in on his arse. The back of the cavern was now filled with plasma fire.

'Through there now!' I pointed at the plasma flames back where Rannu and Mudge had just come from. They never would've survived the blast but our Mamluks might survive the flames. Another feed flicked on in my internal visual display but I didn't have time to pay attention to it.

'The suits will never—' Pagan started.

'Now!' I screamed. The five of us took off. The jets on our propulsion fins at near full burn, pointing in the direction our navigation systems remembered the cave mouth to be. Time seemed to slow down as we entered the lake of fire. It was beautiful. I barely noticed the heat or the smell of my own flesh cooking. I ignored the warning symbols coming through the interface from the Mamluk. It was like flying into a sun. This I decided would not be a bad way to die.

'I'm sorry ...' I wasn't even sure I'd heard the comms message through the heavy interference, it was so faint, but I could've sworn it was Gregor's voice, and then I was in the cold of space again.

Below us the small tethered asteroid in which we had sheltered was crawling with Them. It looked like someone had stamped on an ants' nest: every square inch of it was covered with the aliens. The space surrounding the asteroid was full of Them vessels and Their flight-capable organic mechs. According to the diagnostic readings I was getting, the Mamluk was in a bad way. My comms were barely functioning; the Mamluk still had integrity but much of the armour was slag. The joints on my right arm and leg had melted solid and I couldn't move them. Other than lenses, the majority of my sensors were down as well. I was just lucky the heat shielding on the propulsion fin had held and the jet fuel hadn't gone up. I put the internal repair systems to work on the comms system. I don't know why – I was probably about to be erased from existence by black light.

Balor, Mudge, Rannu and Pagan had made it out. All of their mechs looked partially melted where the armour had run and then solidified again. We were lucky they hadn't just shattered from the sudden temperature change. Mudge and Rannu's Retributors had melted beyond use. Pagan's looked usable from where I was, but that meant nothing. Below us the cave mouth was still burning.

'What the fuck!' Mudge's voice came over faint and through heavy interference.

'Jesus Christ!' Pagan said.

From the cave mouth a huge, thick, burning tentacle flicked out of the flames. Then another. What had once been Gregor pulled itself out of the cave mouth. He looked similar to before but bigger. I could see all over him the individual forms of Berserks and other

Them-forms melding with his flesh. They were being sucked in, forming thicker chitinous plates or other stranger features like screaming mouths – these must have been a reaction to the burning pain from what had once been Gregor's subconscious. The fact that he was still burning made him look all the more demonic. On the surface of the asteroid They surged towards this monstrosity.

'No!' I shouted uselessly. The mass of writhing tentacles on its back shot out, piercing Berserks, and again the chain reaction of biological connection spread through them. Tendrils even shot into the void, piercing Walkers and small spacecraft.

Pagan fired his Retributor at Crom's demonic form, a long wild burst. I triggered both the missiles on my back. Warning symbols appeared on my internal visual display – both the launch tubes were too heavily damaged.

'Shit! Shit! Shit! Shit!' I triggered the explosive bolts on the tubes and jetted away from them before the warheads exploded. I saw Rannu doing something similar. Mudge managed to get one away but had to eject the other. We were only taking light fire; most of Them in the area were either connected to Crom or concerned with dealing with him.

I heard Balor screaming over the tac net, but reception was intermittent at best. Mudge's missile exploded against Crom but it barely seemed to stagger him. Balor dived towards Crom, firing round after round from the mass driver. These did affect him, driving him back, dragging his network of attached Them with him. The mass driver ran dry and Balor switched to the 30-millimetre railgun, firing it on full automatic as he got closer and closer to Crom.

Balor's Dog Soldier mech impacted into Crom's central mass, bouncing both of them off the asteroid. Crom didn't go far as he was tethered by all the Them he was attached to. The Dog Soldier still had a grip on him. Balor re-established contact with the asteroid with one boot. With the other he slammed Crom back down against the asteroid and brought the railgun round to bear at point-blank range.

'... to the *Spear*, we need immediate fire support on this grid reference, over! Gibby, we need you. Gregor is Crom. We need the area completely sanitised, do you copy?' My comms system had suddenly come back to life. It was Pagan's desperate voice I could hear over the tac net.

A whipping tentacle cut Balor's railgun in two before he could fire. Crom stood up, easily pulling the Dog Soldier off the asteroid and lifting it into space before slamming it back down against the rock. Both of them were being hit by high-powered, black-light beams and heavy-calibre shard rounds. Missiles were flying towards them but the burning Crom's black-light, anti-missile defence system was still active, and he was growing more and more of the gristly nozzles with every moment.

Pagan, Rannu, Mudge and I were effectively useless. We could do nothing but sit around and take fire until something got through. The only reason we weren't dead was that They were far more concerned with Crom.

I heard it first. The singing, like I'd heard in my vision. But it was different, more human somehow, and it was coming through our tac net. I saw the new feed. It was coming from Morag's mech. She was surrounded by pale bioluminescence. She seemed to be hovering in the centre of Maw City. She was broadcasting the singing. All around her were various Them craft up to about light cruiser size and various flight-capable Them. Several of the huge tentacles that we'd seen earlier writhed around her but did not touch her.

Balor's Dog Soldier mech had Crom by the neck with one hand and was pounding him repeatedly and rapidly with its other huge metal fist. It didn't seem to be doing much except stopping Crom from taking other action. Over the tac net I could still hear Pagan begging for fire support. God knew how many of Them were now infected by Crom.

Suddenly Crom grabbed the hand that was pounding him, pulled it off at the wrist and stood up, towering over Balor's Dog Soldier. With a wrench he pulled the Dog Soldier's hand from around his neck and then broke the joint in that arm. The Dog Soldier's laser anti-missile defence system was firing point blank into Crom with little effect. With what seemed like agonising slowness Crom grabbed the front of the Dog Soldier's chest and dug powerful claws into it, piercing and tearing armour plate.

'Christ,' I barely heard Mudge whisper over the net. Crom tore off a large piece of foot-thick armour plate, exposing Balor to space. We all watched as Crom pulled Balor's impossibly still struggling form from the ruptured Dog Soldier. I could see Balor moving within Crom's grip. Almost involuntarily I zoomed in on him. Balor's heavy cybernetic conversion enabled him to survive briefly in a vacuum. I saw him reach up for his eyepatch. Terrified and fascinated I had to watch as he lifted the patch.

There was a very bright light. Before the lenses on the Mamluk burnt out, their flash compensators overloaded, I saw Balor as if in X-ray, his flesh transparent, the machine inside silhouetted by the light. All my systems went down briefly, which should not happen in a mech that was EMP-hardened like the Mamluk. My internal visual display went dark. It flickered back into life as replacement lenses slid into place. I had no idea what had just happened, and there was no concussion wave. I was still hovering where I had been. There was a huge crater in the asteroid, as if a chunk had been bitten out of it. Crom was lying next to the crater, the right side of his body gone. Silent, screaming mouths seemed to cover the left side of his body. Balor was of course nowhere to be seen.

'What the fuck was that?' Mudge asked over the net. I had never seen a weapon like it. I felt sickened as I saw that Crom was somehow still moving. I watched as tendrils grew from his cauterised and charred left side, pulling Them into the wound, Their flesh melting and melding into his as he re-grew his missing left side. Balor had died for nothing.

I felt numb. We'd done this: we'd handed Them to the Cabal. Pagan was still begging Gibby over the net, his pleading mixed in with prayers and sobbing. Mudge, Rannu, Pagan and I weren't even taking evasive action now; we just hovered in space, the integrity of our armour slowly being chipped away by small-arms fire.

On the feed from Morag's Mamluk I could see that one of the huge tentacles had formed its tip into manipulators and grabbed her mech by the back of its neck. I saw her armour jerk and spasm, presumably as the tentacle's manipulators pierced it, and the singing stopped.

Crom stood up as more and more tentacles shot out into the void. Above the asteroid there was now a net of craft connected to the walking virus.

The drugs had pretty much worn off now, and I realised there was no more I could do. I could feel the sickness now, my body failing and shutting down much like my mech. I reckoned it had only been adrenalin keeping me alive for some minutes now.

I heard strident and abrasive guitar music.

'Shut the fuck up, Pagan, you're boring us,' Gibby drawled over the tac net. Us? The air filled with plasma and heavy laser fire, missile after missile shot overhead and then the *Spear* soared into view, every inch of it under fire from the multitude of Them craft which swarmed around it.

Hit after hit from the *Spear*'s heavy ordnance hit Crom, doing real damage to him, blowing chunks off. Heavy plasma missiles turned the area around him into a sea of fire.

'You're coming in too fast!' I screamed over the tac net. My only reply was laughter from Gibby. I realised it was too heavily damaged to change course.

'Out of here now!' I screamed at Rannu, Mudge and Pagan. Mudge grabbed Rannu as the Nepalese's propulsion fin didn't seem to be working, and the three of us triggered full burn on our jets, shooting away from the tethered asteroid.

Judging by the force of the explosion, Gibby must have triggered the remaining warheads he had on board. Behind us everything was red as the asteroid was reduced to gravel. The concussion wave slammed into us and mercifully I passed out, though I was pretty sure I'd died.

'Do you think They'll believe we came in peace?' I heard Mudge say through the pain and the nausea. I hoped that Mudge wasn't in my particular part of the afterlife just yet. I managed to open my eyes. I was still in the prison of my Mamluk. We were floating in space. Rannu's Mamluk was holding onto mine. A quick diagnostic told me that my mech was just about working and keeping space out. Pagan was still with us as well.

All around us were flight-capable Them, Walkers and other organic mechs, their honeycombed propulsion systems glowing pale blue. The weird thing was They weren't firing on us. They just seemed to be covering us. It was like They'd taken us prisoner, but They didn't do that.

I was still receiving feed. Morag was still where she had been, suspended in space, the tentacle gripping the back of her neck. I checked her vital signs. She seemed fine. I mumbled something unintelligible.

'He's awake,' Pagan said.

'But not making any sense,' Mudge pointed out.

'What's happening to Morag?' I asked.

'As far as we can tell, she's in communication with Them,' Pagan said. 'I think they've connected to her through her plugs somehow, and the remnants of Ambassador in her ware are enabling her to talk to Them.' My vision was very blurry and seemed to be fading. The pain was receding somehow as well. Morag was surrounded by light.

I wished I could hear the singing again. I wished I could talk to Morag just once more.

'How're we going to get home?' Pagan wondered. Maybe I could hear the singing.

'How the hell are we still alive?' Mudge asked.

'I don't think I am,' I said. I could definitely hear the singing now. Morag looked beautiful in the light. I kicked off towards her with a slow burn from my manoeuvring fin. There was shouting over the tac net but I ignored it. Morag seemed to glow brighter as everything else got darker.

# Acknowledgements

Unlike Them, *Veteran* did not come into existence in a vacuum. Many people helped with the creation of this novel. So in hopefully chronological order, thank you to:

Dr Hazel Spence-Young for the first proofread, encouragement and comments and also to Scott Young for his comments and encouragement.

To Jose Moulds for her proofreading and comments.

To Kath Anderton for her proofreading and comments. Particularly for dropping everything to read a last moment rewrite. Much appreciated.

To Dr Phillip (look I'll spell it your way just this once) Pridham and Julian Booth for reading the script and providing commentary in their own indomitable style.

To my agent Sam Copeland at RCW Ltd. For being the first person in the world of publishing to go: "Hmm, someone might publish this."

To my editor Simon Spanton at Orion for going: "Hmm, we should publish this."

Thanks to the lovely people at Orion: Jo Fletcher, Jon Weir and Gillian Redfearn for help, advice and generally looking after me.

Thanks to Hugh Davis and Charlie Panayiotou for the copyedit, I hope it wasn't too tedious.

Also thank you very much to everyone in the rights dept.

Finally I'd like to thank my family (except for my Dad, he knows why, he might get thanked if there's a second book) for all the support, encouragement and resources whilst growing up. Though that's still a work in process.